JERICHO'S BANE

Path to Desolation Part I

ARROW J. KNIGHT

AJ Knight

ACKNOWLEDGEMENTS

I loved it so much the first time, I did it again. The second novel in the series of Jericho's Bane has arrived. This great feat may have been written by one, but in no way could have been completed in solitary. I would like to take this time to thank those that helped me bring this vision from idea to the subjective tangible. First, I'd like to give a gigantic thank you once again to my editor Cara Lockwood Benoit. She again help me make since out of the madness of my mind. Without her editorial skills you all would have been locked in the asylum of my mind with me a second time around. I can honestly say you would not be reading the fine quality of work before you without her keen eye to detail.

To my Beta Reader David Todd, who once again took the time out of his life to read my works in its entirety and offer feedback and heartfelt constructive criticism, I feel a thank you can't even begin to express the gratitude I have for the part you played in bringing the second novel to life. It was appreciated and helped immensely in setting the pace and timing for the story making it even more magnificent.

My work is not complete without the visuals. To my cover artist Chris Hunter, you once again did an astonishing job in helping me attain the perfect cover. To Jordan Jackson and Robbie DubBryan, a heartfelt thanks. A special thank you to Elizabeth Dillion who performed the model work in bringing the character Grand Prior Asia Riggs to life.

A great special thank you must be given to my narrator Albie Robles, who took on the monumental task of giving voice to my characters in the Audible Book Version of the novel. He was epic.

Lastly, the greatest thank you of all goes to you, the fans for making it all worth it. My story was truly created to entertain you all. It was not meant to be divisive, nor question or expound upon any one particular faith. It is a work of science fiction and fantasy. I hope that you all enjoy reading or listening to Jericho's Bane Path to Desolation Part I as much as I enjoyed writing it. See you all soon in the pages of Book 3, Jericho's Bane Path to Desolation Part II

For Mrs. Galloway & Mr. Hisey
Thanks for Engaging my Imagination

JERICHO'S BANE

Contents

FROM THE PAGES OF JERICHO'S BANE IMPERIAL PROTOCOL BOOK I

Imperial walks over to Jericho kicking him again and again up against the door of the massive vault. He repeatedly kicks for the slight of having laid hands on him, making him bleed. he kicks him for the punishment that he promised would be dished out when they first exchanged words in the garage. Finally, he kicks him to hear the breakage of bone. When he feels enough pain has been inflicted, he grips Jericho by his neck and begins to slowly squeeze. He can feel the pulse of blood flowing through his carotid arteries. He squeezes harder and finds it a bit difficult to constrict his artery.

"He built you tough, didn't he? All the same you're still simply a man." Imperial lifts and slams him back to the floor and walk out leaving him broken in front of the vault.

Gabriel makes herself visible to Jericho. With tears in her eyes, she attempts to hold him more than her allowed light suggestive touch, but she can't. It is forbidden. The tears in her eyes tell the story of her emotions more than the color of her ever-changing irises could. She wants nothing more than to cradle him and pat him up. Metatron and Cassiel appears lightly touching her on her shoulders for support.

"I'm so sorry, Jericho. This was a fight that should have been left to us. This creature was never meant to exist and let alone be your problem," says Gabriel as she rubs him across his head like when he was a child. Again, each of her touches are a gentle breeze that lightly blows his sweaty and blood matted hair. Gabriel's voice then turns stern. "As much as this fight should have been ours, it is not, it's yours. It's not fair, but it is as it was meant to be. You have to get up baby. You have to get up now! Complete your task! Get your ass up and in gear Marine!"

"Why should he? To only endure more punishment," Imperial says as he reenters the vault with his sword.

Gabriel stands and grabs the hilt of her blade as she turns to face Imperial. "You will not touch him again, abomination!"

"Oh! Understand, I am going to do much worse than just touch him again. And when I begin, what are you going to do? When I decide to bend him in ways that will reinvent pain, what can you do to stop me?" Imperial walks towards Jericho with his blade's tip dragging slicing and burning into the concrete.

Metatron and Cassiel unsheathe their blades and hold them at the ready, but they don't step to Gabriel's side, a tinge of fear gives them pause. How does one fight an enemy when he can't be scathed? Gabriel holds her ground and pulls her blade from its scabbard standing in front of Jericho guarding his recovery.

Imperial smirks at her. "Now where have I seen this before? Oh yeah! Al-Fashir, when I killed Muriel was it? No, it was Oreo or something like that right?" Laughing.

"His name was Uriel," Gabriel says.

"Right... that was it, Uriel. Well, whose name am I to remember today when I send you to meet him."

"Gabriel... You will remember me," she says.

Gabriel Looks down at Jericho. She remembers the look in his mother Rachel's eyes when she tasked her to protect her son. Gabriel looks at Imperial and then gives her brothers an I'm sorry glance that tells them, I'm sorry that I won't live to see these dark days to an end, I'm sorry that one more place at the table will be left empty, I'm sorry that I've made you witness my rendezvous with Death. Gabriel attacks.

Metatron reaches for her in an attempt to stop her. "Gabe, no wait!"

Metatron's reach is too slow and much too late. Gabriel holds nothing back as she strikes down with enough force to cleave Imperial in half. Sure, and smug he doesn't even bother to defend himself; he just watches as her blade falls stopping a millimeter short of making contact with even a single strand of his hair. She tries with all the celestial might she can summon to push pass Elohim's law that binds her. She pushes with the force that has in the distant past moved planets, but it moves no further pass the millimeter close to his hair.

Imperial slams her head with the hilt of his blade stunning her. In her blunt trauma second of confusion, he grabs her by her hair and slams her head twice into the vault's door before slamming her to the ground and stepping on her neck pinning her in place.

Metatron and Cassiel are joined by Raziel and Samael. It took them a min to catch up, it was a bit more work setting the evils correct that Vermin and Pain had caused outside the Embassy. The two ready their blades. Once they take notice of who their opponent is, they hesitate, because in this instant, they can only watch they are powerless against him.

Imperial looks over to Metatron and the rest of the celestials while twirling his blade building up the suspense and fear in them of what he is going to do. When he feels that they are at their max of nervous anticipation he swipes the blade fast and forceful to alleviate Gabriel of her head. With a loud clank Imperial's blade strikes celestial metal instead of flesh as Jericho slams one end of Gabriel's blade into the metal vault door while he holds the other creating a bridge over top of her. Stunned by the reflecting blow of his own blade, Imperial is forced to take a step backward.

While Jericho grips her blade, he can clearly see Metatron, Cassiel, Raziel and Samael. They look as astonishing to him as Gabriel in their battle armament. No time to be awe stricken, he pushes past the beauty of the celestials and turns his attention back to Imperial, realizing that he must put him down, now for his own sake, but for all their sakes. Seeing them only able to watch, he understands the dilemma they face first hand. He saw the hesitation of the others and the strike that was ineffective by Gabriel. *They can't hurt him.* Jericho instantly recalls the battle for Sarin that Gabriel showed him. He remembers what she said. 'We could never intervene directly in the affairs of men again.' It dawns on him. *He's one of the hybrids. He's half human, they can't hurt him.* Jericho hears Gabriel in his mind whispering, "and if he's human? "He bleeds Jericho answers out loud.

"Whatever bleeds—" Gabriel yells.

"—Can be killed." Jericho finishes.

Seizing the moment, Jericho tackles Imperial who was already stumbling backward to the ground further straddling him. Again, he takes a hold of Imperial armor divot at the neck as a counter balance fulcrum lever. He pulls Imperial up with violent force towards his fast approaching dominate hand punch. He connects fist to face of the Nephilim strike after repeated strike. Imperial's mask and helmet generates covering his face quickly before Jericho rains down anymore punishing hits.

The punches are hard and furious denting in the metal of the mask protecting Imperial's face. Jericho punches to exhaustion. When his punches slow enough, Imperial grabs a hold of Jericho's incoming fist and sends another bolt into him causing him to writhe backward in pain screaming. Imperial keeps the charge steady and unending. Flames again begin to spark up on Jericho's uniform. Having a clear shot Imperial lets go of Jericho's fist breaking the charge. Before Jericho can recover in the slightest, Imperial sends another bolt into the chest of Jericho blasting him back into the vault's door with such force that the masonry around the hinges crumble. Jericho falls to the floor unconscious.

Imperial staggers to his feet grabbing his blade to steady himself. He's never had to steady himself. Pain has been inflicted upon him. Intense burning pain around his face where his helmet was dented in. He looks to finish what he started by ending Gabriel first and then the human.

When he looks to finish Gabriel at the spot she was just laying, she's no longer there. He finds her standing with her brothers away from the Nephilim. Imperial degenerates his mask, but it's taken such a pounding and is so massively dented, it sticks. With one hand he rips the helmet and mask from his head taking a deep breath. He smiles and gestures for Gabriel. "Come, dear, shall you and I dance again?"

Gabriel just stares at him, but doesn't move.

"No! I understand." Imperial slices the mag lock to the vault before charging a bolt only to hold it within his fist. He punches his charged fist into the vault's door creating a grip. He then pulls the door from its foundation. The hinges easily give way as they were destroyed moments ago in the confrontation when Jericho slammed against it. The vault door falls over on top of Jericho, but doesn't crush him as it ramps against the ad-joined wall leaving space for Jericho underneath.

The door having being ripped from its foundation reveals a destructive cadre of explosives. Imperial smiles at the arsenal stored away in the Embassy's weapon and arsenal munitions vault. The shelves are stocked with small arms. The walls are covered in rifles and shoulder fire rocket weaponry. The back of the room has crates marked high explosives, clay-mores, and grenades. There's even a rack that contains well forged Katana Samurai blades. Forgetting the celestials for a moment as they are of no real concern to him, Imperial walks to the back and tears the lid off of the high plastique explosives. He sheathes his sword.

Jericho bruised and bloodied slams into Imperial from behind shoving him into the weapons rack. The N.H.E. designate trips over a stack of weapons crate when he tries to find footing. Falling to his knees, his head strikes the wall of the now broken weapons rack. Jericho grabs a palm full of the back of his skull and rams Imperial's head countless times into the wall till his head breaks through metal and cement. Out of breath, but full of fight, Jericho backs away and looks for a weapon. He nods his head at seeing the stack of Katana blades and reaches for one. He pulls it from the rack flicking his thumb across the blade. Hearing a groan coming from N.H.E. he doesn't hesitate. He screams a battle cry and runs to put his mo-mentum behind his jump lunging thrust. He's off center, but his aim is as true as his blurry vision will allow. The blade strikes its tip just beneath the armor of Imperials back. Jericho strikes meat and draws blood but only a scratch. The weapon shatters into small shards of steel.

Feeling pain, Imperial senses returns. Dazed, he pulls his head from the wall. His left eye is swollen shut and he has a mean laceration over the right eye and a split lip. He throws himself backward with a huge back-handed right swing targeting Jericho. The Marine drops to his ass dodging the haymaker attempt. His eyes lock onto the hilt of Imperials sword. Jeri-cho grabs the hilt with both hands and pulls. The blade is immensely heavy. His muscles cry in agony wielding a weapon of gods just as they did when he used Gabriel's to shield her. Jericho's veins spiders and muscles ripple holding the blade level. Jericho lets the tip fall to the ground. He gets to a knee and pushes forward pole vaulting the hilt of the blade into Imperials face. There is a decent amount of blood splatter and a broken canine tooth. Imperials hands rises to his face before another strike can be vaulted. Jericho changes tactics and pulls the celestial blade's tip up from the floor and arches it around spinning his body for momentum till his back is facing Imperial. Still giving his battle cry, Jericho completes the blade attacking maneuver by slamming the blade backward in a stabbing motion under his left armpit past himself and into the front chest of the N.H.E. The blade finds purchase sliding through metal, flesh, bone, then cement. It cauterizes the flesh around it. Imperial for the first time ever lets out a maddening howl.

Jericho releases the weapon. He turns and falls to his knees face to face with Imperial. He looks him in the eyes and sees that the N.H.E. does not harbor fear there. He does not show the realization that he may be about to die. Jericho only observes resolve. He immediately pushes away seeing the unnatural reaction to a fatal wound, but it's too late. Imperial grabs him by the neck. His helmet regenerates from below the armor's neckline damaged. There's no face plate protection, just helmet. Imperial slams helmeted head four times into Jericho's face rendering him unconscious again. He attempts to crush his neck, but again finds it difficult. It doesn't snap as easy as other mortals. Jericho comes around when he's unable to catch his breath. He knees the hilt of the blade buried in Imperials chest. The pain is enough to break his vice like grip. Jericho falls to his knees then onto his ass taking in a full gasp of air. He places his hands on his neck rubbing it.

Knowing he can't let the N.H.E. recover, Jericho pushes himself to his feet to continue pressing the attack. He's seen blood. He can kill the N.H.E. That was his purpose wasn't it? He was literally born to meet his thing head on in battle. Oops! His attention slightly deviated off the enemy while he pondered the answer of his birth. It wasn't much time, but it was enough that he never saw Imperial disengage the pin from a yellow painted high explosive grenade that was rolling around on the floor amongst others that must have been knocked over during the fight. Imperial had tossed it between the two when Jericho was slightly distracted. Imperial draws his body in tight. Jericho reaches for the small arms shelf and pulls it from its bolted mounts using it as a shield. The blast ignites other small explosive devices causing a chain reaction into a moderate sized explosion.

The generated heat and energy concussive wave blows Imperial and the wall he's nailed too into a collapse setting him free. Jericho is blown clear from the munitions vault and into the wall outside of it in the hallway. He slides down the wall unto the top of the vault's steel door. Another reactionary blast explodes from inside the vault. A second powerful concussive wave engulfs the hallway flipping the metal vault door up like a coin. Jericho rolls off the door landing on the floor. The vault door soon crashes down half embedding itself into the wall with the other half piercing the floor, trapping Jericho.

Smoke expels from the vault. The plastique explosives did not ignite. Imperial's blade was blown free from his body. He emerges from the room holding his blade in his right hand and cradling his chest with the left. His helmet disengages below the armor neckline. He walks over to take Jericho's head, but he's buried under the thick steel vault door. Sirens can be heard in the distance drawing nigh. He mouths "Shit!" under his breath. He turns and with his one eye not swollen, he sees his DNA everywhere. He sheathes his blade and returns into the munitions vault.

The room being covered in debris, it takes him a few seconds before he's able to find the Det Cord. He pulls the detonation cord off of a half-broken shelf and jams it into one brick of plastique contained within the five-foot-high container of plastique individually wrapped bricks. There is sixty in total. Imperial walks out of the vault leaving Jericho to burn. He passes Gabriel and the rest of the celestials. He nods his head at them, "not such a bad attempt." Says Imperial before lifting off through the ceiling that he and Jericho only moments earlier had come crashing through leaving only a trail of Det Cord in his wake.

Gabriel watches him leave with the cord in tow. "He's going to detonate and level the place," she says.

Gabriel runs over to Jericho and crawls into the space where he is and touches his back. "He's still breathing. Metatron he's hurt bad. Jericho get up! Get up! C'mon get up baby." Gabriel starts to frantically look around for anything that could wake him. "There's no way to wake him." She places her hand on his forehead and closes her eyes. "Nothing... He's out. In a coma I suspect. His brain has massive swelling."

Metatron places his hand on Gabriel's back garnering her attention.

"Then we will stay with him until the end. He gave one hell of a valiant effort."

Cassiel paces looking at the debris where Jericho is wedged under. "He made a believer out me today Gabe. I thought he was actually going to do it for a minute. That abomination isn't natural. He placed that blade true. It was a fatal injury that he should not have walked away from."

Michael's voice emits from the neckline of the Archs armor. "Get moving. That abomination isn't waiting to detonate."

Cassiel takes a quick glance around at the support structures for the building. He plays the blast output in his mind and witnesses' tons of brick and mortar currently overhead collapsing after a few tons super-heated flame incinerates everything where they now stand. "We will not be able to move him. Can he survive such a blast?" asks Cassiel.

Gabriel shakes her head. "I don't know... Samson didn't survive the fall of that coliseum.

"Gabriel, tell me; no bullshit assessment! Can this mortal stop him?" Cassiel asks.

"What do you want me to tell you Cassiel, we're working on faith here. No one knows how this will end. We're off script Damnit!"

Cassiel calms himself and whispers, "do you believe he can put things right? I'm asking you... Yes or no right now! Can Jericho set the balance?"

"She doesn't know." Metatron says. "From what I've seen of this mortal, he won't stop. Did you see him. He knew he was bested and he didn't quit. That attitude of his was Davidic. He almost toppled that giant. The odds were shifted somehow when the fatal blow was ineffective, but sheer will and an unrelenting determination had him place that blade into a demigod. That has to count for something."

Gabriel looks at Jericho then back to Cassiel. "Yes...yes Cassiel, I believe he can set the scales."

Cassiel stands to his feet and unsheathes his blade and throws it to Raziel who up until then remained quiet. "Cut them off!" Cassiel extends both his wings straight back giving Raziel a clean target.

"Wh—what? No! No, I'm not cutting off your wings."

"There's no time. He detonates that brick in that crate and all is lost."

Cassiel looks deep into Raziel eyes. "Cut them off." Cassiel lowers his voice again to a whisper. "It's okay."

Gabriel shakes her head no and looks to Raziel "Don't you do it!"

Cassiel grabs Raziel's jaw and forces him to look into his eyes. "Brother, look at me. I can't do it myself; I'd lose the nerve. It has to be you. I won't hold this against you. If this man dies here, we all perish, all realms, all realities. We can't intervene directly in the state we're in. Do it!" Cassiel voice falls to a whisper. "Do it!" Cassiel yells, "DO IT!"

"Arrrrggggghhhh!" Raziel screams. He grabs his brother with his free arm hugging him tightly. He lets go and swirls the blade twice for momentum and slings it behind Cassiel's back separating his wings from his torso.

****

Cassiel screams out from a pain that he's never felt. The song of heaven is instantly lost to him forever. He watches as Gabriel, Metatron, Samael and Raziel vanish before his eyes. As a mortal his connection is forever severed. He falls to his knees discombobulated as he's never walked as a mortal. *So heavy.* Is his singular thought.

Gabriel screams, "Raziel why? Why did you do it?"

"To give existence it's best chance, Raziel says.

****

Angel's Spire
Yeshua, Michael and the rest of the angelic choir falls silent. Michael slowly shakes his head, no. Seeing and feeling his pain, Yeshua places a comforting hand, on his captain's shoulder. Another Arch has fallen.

****

Chinese Embassy Berlin, Germany
There's no time, we have to move. Cassiel grabs Jericho by the strap on the back of his body armor. The strap that is there for just a situation when a comrade needs to be pulled out of danger if wounded or incapacitated.

Cassiel grabs a hold and pulls with all the strength that he can gather. His new mortal body screams in pain, but it's fleeting as adrenaline kicks in powering him through the ache of muscles and the breathing of the heavy oxygen-enriched air. He continues dragging Jericho to the fastest yet furthest means of safety.

Once through the ceiling Imperial lands and begins walking through the halls making sure the Det Cord doesn't touch anything incendiary or electrical until he's clear. Doesn't want to set the cord off to soon.

He retraces his steps through the destruction that was caused when Jericho sent him through the wall. When he steps through the wall back to the outside garage Fate is awaiting him. Imperial releases the Det Cord and pulls his sword form its sheath out of habit more than fear of an angel.

Fate places his empty hands up for display. "Whoa, I'm not here to quarrel. I'm just curious as to what has the heavens realms in such upheaval."

"Then stand aside, angel, lest I send you to Apollyon like the others."

"Apollyon? He's on my list of brothers that I plan on speaking with anyhow. However, I'd much rather meet him under my own power. No need for threats, I just wanted to see this nephilim that I've heard so much about up close."

Imperial picks up the Det Cord with his off hand and slowly walks past Fate. The angel makes sure to stay clear of Imperial's blade.

"I'm intrigued that a creature that I wrote out of existence so long ago still lingers and draws breath thinking that he yet has a future."

"You believe I have no future?" says Imperial.

****

Cassiel pulls Jericho inside an elevator. He picks any floor at random, because he can't read the Chinese characters. When his ties to the accessing of realities severed, it was like an insane round of musical chairs. The celestials revert to the reality they currently find themselves in at the time of separation. Had this battle been decided in reality 1513, he could have easily been a microbe. When Cassiel became human unfortunately his race and tongue fell to that of Swahili.

Gabriel makes herself seen to Cassiel. < "What have you done?"> She says speaking to Cassiel in Swahili.

< "I don't know. Didn't have time to think about it."> Cassiel said as he feels the sensation of the upward moving cube. <"In hindsight, I may have been a bit brash."> He chuckles to himself.

The elevator doors open on three. Cassiel pulls Jericho to the south side of the Embassy where there are large plate glass windows. Once he gets Jericho there, he collapses under the new-found weight of flesh and blood, also because he's run out of breath.

Cassiel pulls himself up and starts pulling office furniture and whatever else he can find to place in front of Jericho. Making a bunker.

Metatron relays to Gabriel that Fate is stalling Imperial for time, and that minutia of time that he purchased is about up.

Gabriel eyes Cassiel as he tries holding back his tears.

Cassiel sighs pulling in all the air he can to reenergize himself. <"Gabriel, what am I worth to the whole of existence? Nothing... My eyes have beheld wonders sister that beings of lesser creation will never experience. I've scaled to the top of Elohim's Palace. I've slid across the event horizon of the Hedeaus Anomaly. My time has not been wasted in service of one greater than I. It seems that I will now experience what only you have. I will experience a piece of a mortal's life no matter how brief..."">

Gabriel stares at Cassiel, her lips quiver at his remark.

< "I know who you are sister; who you really are. I figured it out not long after Fate let it slide when he called you by a name that has long since been stricken from memory, damn near even record."> Cassiel winks at her. < "I can keep a secret. I'll keep this one until death."> He then looks down at Jericho. < "You believe in this mortal sister and I believe in you."> Tears begin to stream from Cassiel's eyes. < "I don't believe that I've ever been as terrified as I am now... Stay with me, will you?">

< "Until whatever end,"> Gabriel says.

Cassiel sits Indian style with Jericho's unconscious body facing the glass window. He pulls Jericho close to his chest and holds onto him tightly to cushion him. Cassiel then buries his head in between Jericho's shoulder blades, their backs facing the door.

****

Angel's Spire - Day

The Spire is quiet as all the angels, powers, choiretic and citizenry watch the events unfold.

****

Chinese Embassy Berlin, Germany

Imperial stares at Fate. "Before I'm done, you will see my future burn brighter than the sun. In a time that will soon be upon us, you will either kneel to my sword or fall before it just as your mortal hope did. Only the hand of a god could ever bring me to heel and haven't you heard? He's stepped away from the world of men. It's as if he wills this event.

Sirens of the first responders are starting to arrive on the scene. With communications restored the authorities phone lines are instantly flooded with emergency calls. Hearing them draw near, Imperial's wings expand striking the ground lifting him into the air. "Let what I've done today be a reminder to your kind to stay out my father's affairs and by extension mine. You celestials cross me again and I will not wait for permission. I will take it upon myself to become the angelic omega."

Imperial ignites a bolt through his hand and sends a charge into Det Cord to detonate the high explosives. Once ignited he lifts off into the stratosphere with precipitous speed "Boom!" he whispers.

The high explosives detonate destroying the foundation of the Embassy. The building explodes first sending a massive concussive wave that shatters every window in the structure before the violent flow of hot air, flames and debris follow.

Cassiel grips Jericho tighter as the concussive wave blows through the office door and into the makeshift wall of furniture that Cassiel managed to pull together. The blast carries the debris, Cassiel, and Jericho out of the third-floor window. As they are blown out through the window, flames and building material follow. The blast not only engulfs the building, but reaches far out beyond the structure engulfing the first responders and more than three blocks before the building implodes and collapses in on itself.

Cassiel holds tightly to Jericho in spite of the blast tossing them about wildly. When they hit the ground, it's marked with a massive blood smear from Cassiel as his body strikes first. The two bodies separate as they tumble down Märkisches Ufer 54 street. Jericho comes to rest when he strikes the side of a bus. Cassiel's body comes to a stop when he collides into a light pole.

Gabriel appears next to Cassiel to comfort him, but he's already gone. His body is void of its soul. Metatron and the rest of the celestials appear as well and bow their head at the lifeless husk.

"I have him, messenger," Death says. "I assure you he felt little pain. I took his soul at the moment of impact." Death nods to the rest of the celestials and throws liquid from a vial onto the remains of Cassiel. The body ignites and instantaneously burns to ash. Witnessing all trace of the celestial body made flesh turn to ash, Death turns and walks into the dust ploom from the collapsed Embassy disappearing from the celestials' sight.

Gabriel watches as Death disappear into the smoke, ash, and flames. *I've never seen him like this.* Her wings switch blade out and she levitates and hovers over to Jericho. At first appearance he looked to be void of life, but, he's alive; unresponsive, but alive. Death would have made mention otherwise and claimed him.

Fate appears. "Be sure your love for the boy Lilith, does not overcast your judgment. He was not ready and it cost not only the unnecessary lives of mortals, but of Cassiel. This day has exacted a heavy toll for your ignorance and over indulgence."

Gabriel looks up at Fate. "We all know this is a dangerous game we play. The fact still remains, if we don't bring Imperial to heel then we have no chance." She stares into Fate's eyes. "None of us. All of Fate will be undone."

Sighing! "Touché, Lilith." Fate adjusts the dial on his gauntlet phasing into another reality. He turns and starts walking down the street as more first responders arrive on scene. The vehicles phase through him as he walks with his hands clasped behind his back pondering on all the events that Lucifer has set into motion.

An officer running toward the Embassy notices Jericho clinging to life. He stops and kneels to check his vitals. Finding a pulse, he stands and looks around for a medic. An ambulance racing to the seen slows when the driver sees the officer flailing his arms for them to stop. The medic driver exits and watches the officer point to a live victim. The officer gesticulates that victim has a heartbeat. The medic nods and runs to the back of the ambulance to retrieve the gurney. The second medic exits the passenger side and opens a utility door on the side compartment of the medical cab. He grabs a blue medic go-bag and rushes toward Jericho to begin giving him critical care treatment. The medic gives him a cursory look over and notices a few possible fractures, second and third degree burns and lacerations. Jericho's uniform for the most part had been burned or torn away. With his uniform in tatters, it obfuscated anything identifying him as a United States Marine. Once the second medic appears with the Gurney, they lock him in to immobilize him. The medics roll him to the rear of the ambulance where they further load him into the back of the medic, stabilize his injuries, and guns it to the nearest trauma unit lights blaring and siren wailing.

****

United Nations: New York
Shortly after the death of Cassiel and severe injury of Jericho.

Ellen pulls and drags herself through the street. Her fingertips bleed as she grasps at the pock-marked asphalt. Seeing the body of her cameraman she angles herself in his direction and pulls herself towards him. As she inches ever closer to him, she looks around at the wanton destruction and all the devastation. Feeling tired and cold, she knows she's starting to go into shock. She knows she needs to stop exerting herself, but she's almost to Paul. *Just a little closer,* she thinks

After what seems forever, Ellen crawls over to her longtime cameraman, co-worker and friend. His lifeless body that has been stripped of its soul instantly causes tears to well up in Ellen's eyes as she cradles him. Lost in thought of his now orphaned daughter's existence without him, she rubs his blood-soaked hair.

While stroking Paul's hair, Ellen only looks up when she notices that people are running past her in droves. At first, Ellen barely registered the first few sums of people that ran past her, but when that sum of New Yorkers turned into hordes, she dared a glance at what they were running from now. As she looked in the direction of which they all were running she saw nothing. *So, it's not from but to then*, Ellen thought. She slowly turns her head averting her eyes to what was more engaging than the sea of those that are now counted among the dead that were alive only mere moments before. Through her grief and early onset of shock, Ellen's gently releases Paul and pulls herself up. It takes all she has to get to her feet but, it was worth the taxing of her remaining strength. Ellen's eyes widen in amazement and wonder.

From the flame engulfed front entrance of the U.N., a figure silhouetted by the flames begins to emerge. As her eyes continues their fixation on the silhouette her breath suddenly escapes her. She can't breathe. Not from the worsening injuries, but from utter amazement and disbelief. As she watches the entrance along with other witnesses and news crews an angelic being emerges from the flames with its wings enclosed encasing himself from the fire. As it emerges, cameras are recording. As the onlookers watch the event closely, they can't move. They find themselves frozen by what they are beholding. A small minority of the people are fearful while the majority of others are filled with hope. The angelic being walks from the U.N. entrance into the middle of the street where Ellen is less than twenty feet away. The crowd parts and let him move unobstructed. The entity then slowly opens its wings revealing it's Imperial in full angelic battle regalia minus the sword. His mask is activated, to hide his very real scars that are healing from his battle with Jericho.

As Imperial completely opens and retracts his wings, it's clear to all those that are watching live or across the news feed that Lucien Arcane is alive as Imperial holds him in his arms, cradled. Lucien has a head wound that is bleeding profusely. His body has been impaled with shrapnel. By all accounts he looks to be dead.

The spectacle that the world is observing commands nothing but silence from all that bear witness. Although oxymoronic the silence is so deafening that heavens take notice. Raphael and the rest of the Archs as well as the citizenry of the ethereal realm watch as Imperial reveals himself to the world of men.

Imperial, ignoring everything around him, walks over to an ambulance that has an awaiting gurney. The medics that had just pulled it out back away. Imperial gently places Lucien on the gurney and looks at the surrounding people. "For the Lord called him wonderful, he has sent me. Lucien has been chosen to lead this world into an era as which has never before witnessed. He has not passed into eternal sleep, but has been made new. This is the decree which was given, so sayeth the heavens, so sayeth man, so say we all in one voice. I, Imperial, have become known to the world. There will soon be no more woes to the world of men for I have been sent to see them end. Through Lucien's guiding hand the world without doubt shall be saved."

The masses that witness the miracle all fall to their knees in reverence of Imperial.

One

AFTERMATH

"He will be with me in Paradise. I made this promise to those that followed me as apostles. I made the same promise to two criminals on Golgotha. You think it would be any less for Cassiel and Uriel?"

~Yeshua

Immediately following the United Nations revelatory event of New York

Angelic Spire, Iayhoten

Majority of the Archs sit somberly in Sparrows Chamber. The last twenty-four hours of Earth's events have been crushing and that is the least that can be said. The blow wasn't one, but many consecutive. The best chance of rectifying prophecy failed with the fall of Jericho. Cassiel was humanized and killed protecting what Gabriel believes is the best asset in restoring balance. Lucifer set himself on high in the mortal realm and Imperial has been revealed to the world as an angelic deity. The last twenty-four hours has indeed shifted chance and power out the hands of Zero Realm's guardians and has completely taken their battle initiative. If there should have ever been a moment that hope should wane, this is it.

As always when in the Chamber of Sparrows, all are equal. There is no rank above another. Ranks of color and caste signified by the patches on everyone's arms are muted. In the Sparrows Chamber white patches on their shoulders is a tangible sign and reminder that anyone may speak out of turn without reprisal. Here, the lowest ranked Archs are just as equal as the Captain of Archs.

Dressed in their brilliant regalia, they all wear their ceremonial white formfitting tunics with white sashes in uniform with their form-fitting pants with an even brighter set of white stripes down the length of their pants legs. Their boots are metallic and knee high, but different from their warrior class boots. The ceremonial ones are of white marble over portions of the metal. All in attendance wear white knee-length slender coats with hoods. The regalia as well as the call to the chamber is for the passing and remembrance of Cassiel.

This meeting of the varying caste sits at the long gold trimmed white marbled table. A few of the Archs gaze at the empty seat that was once reserved for Cassiel. Others gaze at his sword and helmet that now permanently sit atop the table where he once would write down his questions before asking them. At times, the brothers when speaking at the Table of Doves had a penchant to be long-winded. He would joke that if he didn't write the question down, he'd forget. He was joking, of course, but all of them knew it was true. It became an inside joke that when he started to scribble, if you were the Arch talking, that you'd reached the end of everyone's attention span. Funny... You don't realize that you miss small things like that till the person is gone. It seems to always work that way and it didn't matter if you were an Arch or human or Vax. To miss someone that is no longer there is missing a piece of you. If there is one thing that living beings had in common with the gods, it is that missing someone is a universal feeling that binds all things.

A creak of the massive door opening inward echoes through the chamber. The door itself slid across the floor igniting the translucent liquid diamond grout flowing in between the marbled squares that comprises the makeup of the floor. The chamber had not always been as decadent in its creation, but as the Archs have been meeting in the chambers more regularly as of late, the Powers Corps upgraded the chamber to match their lofty status of being the elite order of the celestials. The Powers didn't do it to manifest the Arch's pride as a separate faction. They did it, because of the sacrifices that they make. Whenever the Powers Corp improved the Spire or an Archs gear, it was a gift of love and appreciation for what they do in place of the Powers, so that they could continue on with constant galactical maintenance that was constantly required. The Powers Corps considered upgrading their meeting place a true honor and privilege and were more than pleased to do it.

Through the opened massive doors Michael and Gabriel enter the chamber wearing their best regalia, which matches the rest of the Archs in attendance. The pressure of each step kindles the translucent liquid diamond grouted in between the marble squared floor. It ignites a cadre of colors across each square they step upon.

All Archs in attendance stand instantly to attention rendering chest-level salutes. Old habits die hard, it seems. Michael salutes back then waves them to be seated. Approaching the table, Gabriel nods at her brothers and proceeds to find her seat at the Table of Doves next to Michael's. Once seated, she places four unused rolled scrolls in front of her in preparation of recording the minutes of the meeting. Settled, she reaches into her coat and retrieves a platinum binding cover. She unrolls the scrolls placing them into the metallic binder. Once inside, she runs her finger up the spine of the book engaging the locks that holds the papyrus in place. The pages begin to illuminate. Gabriel then readies her quill and the small container of molten liquid fire. She dips the quill into the liquid flame covering its tip. The tip now glowing with orange and blue flame gives a swift small nod to Michael that she's ready record.

Michael remains standing observing protocols as he always does. He informs the Archs of how to conduct themselves if the King or Prince are to attend, although to date they never have. He further reminds them that no voice is beneath another in the Sparrows Chamber and that all are equal in having a chance to speak openly, the floor is an open forum. Having said his piece by giving his redundant soliloquy, a few nods are seen gestured while others bang their fists on the table signifying their agreement of rules and that they will abide by them. Satisfied, Michael starts to part his lips to begin the meeting, when he finds himself briefly turning his attention toward the now vacant seat of Cassiel. He decides to start the conclave by addressing the oversized elephant in the room, as the human aphorism goes. Again, he parts his lips to speak when he's interrupted by the massive entry doors to the chamber echoing open a second time. All attention, including his, is called toward the entrance.

Prince Yeshua enters the Sparrows Chamber. The arrival of the Prince causes a few gasps and murmurs, because Prince Yeshua has never attended a meeting of the Archs. They always observed protocol in anticipation of his arrival, but that had become a formality overtime as opposed to preparation of the arrival of the Christ. As this moment is unprecedented, there is a slight delay in the rendering of protocol acknowledging the Prince by kneeling. Yeshua entrance throws them off their game as most are in disbelief that the one and future king has come to Sparrows Chamber.

"Mggmmm!" Michael clears phlegm from his throat snapping the Archs out of amazement to the minding of their observance of due protocol. He snaps to attention which reminds the Archs to stand to attention as well. They all stand in unison and perform the perfect synchronized salute while falling to one knee, kneeling before Yeshua.

Yeshua stops in his tracks and returns the salute in kind. "Forgo protocol, please! I am here as a fellow brother in this hour and have come to mourn with family," he says, waving them to all rise and to be seated.

The Archs don't move. They hold their attention on Yeshua while kneeling. Michael completes his salute and rises. He side-steps right to the head of the table to pull the Prince's chair from underneath it. Yeshua nods at the gesture and realizes they will continue to subjugate to him rules of the chamber be damned. He continues to the head chair of the table, adjusting his white knee length coat before sitting. Michael steps back behind his seat and gesticulates with his hand the order for the Archs to rise and be seated. Now that the Prince sat firmly ensconced behind his place at the table, the rest of the Archs stood and found theirs.

A few still observing Yeshua nod in quiet respect for what they observed about him. To show solidarity, the Prince had also dressed in his best ceremonial white regalia. He has all identifying marks of his stature as the Prince muted on his Archean military inspired regalia. The Archs have never witnessed such a gesture. Michael, unable to conceal his admiration, can't help but smirk at the supreme gesture of solidarity. Yeshua was truly something unique. Never has Michael known the King to make such a gesture. Why would he, though? He's the King and a King lives by a different set of rules a different code of life. A King could never enter into a situation where he could concede rank or power. A Prince, however, is slightly different. Prince hood was one of diplomatic entanglements where there would be need to attend and observe rituals of the dignitaries that were to be negotiated with. This was no different. He had the authority and chose to forego power of authority to commune and observe the rules of the Arch's in their Chamber. He was diplomatic like that.

Yeshua takes a few seconds in silence to gaze at the empty chairs of Uriel and now Cassiel. He looks at the bruises that are still healing on the face of Gabriel after her encounter with the Nephilim, Imperial.

"Did you not respond to convalescence for treatment Gabriel?" says Yeshua.

"Not as of yet your Grace. Conclave first, then I will respond down," Gabriel answers.

There was a pride in his eyes when he nodded acceptance of Gabriel's answer. Archs were his Father's creation, but he was given operational oversight of them. He left them to their own autonomy with Michael as their Captain. All he asked in return was to be kept in the loop and given final decision on matters which may conflict with King's orders. That aside, their captain handled day to day operations of the Spire and how best to protect the realms. As Yeshua looks around the table, he could barely contain the pride that he had for them. Yes, they were his father's creation, but he was as well and he'd grown alongside his Archs and was as close to them as any brother could be.

Yeshua gives a wink toward Gabriel signifying for her to get her wounds looked at soon thereafter. He then looks past her to the two empty chairs of Fatetanen and Azrael. Slightly surprised they're not in attendance, he glances over toward Michael looking for an explanation for their absence.

Michael is more than ready for the inquiry. He was prepared the minute Yeshua entered the Chamber. "Fate had requested another try at thwarting the ongoing conflict by way of more diplomacy. He wished another go at Lucifer. I agreed and approved a mission of reasoning with the former Morning Star in hopes that he could convince the fallen Seraphim to abdicate his apocalyptic intentions... A final appeal your grace from his closet caste, brother."

Yeshua gives Michael a slight side eye. "Captain, if Lucifer would not bend a knee to the throne or to the love of his younger brother's request," Yeshua said, pointing to Michael. "What makes you believe Fate's attempt will fare better results?"

"I don't believe he will succeed my Lord, but so many have already died or received the sentence of Palengrad due to this ongoing war, those of us here not being exempt. I thought diplomatic lines should remain open until a time that they shouldn't. If we are able to reason and avert the coming calamity that will not just engulf Earth, but the whole of the Sadohedranicverse for just awhile longer, is it not worth the attempt? Where the King and I failed, may Fate succeed."

After a moment of silence Yeshua nods in agreement with Michael's logic. "And what of Azrael?"

"He's been dispatched to Nosfor with a battalion of Choiretic. Nosforian Council of Elders sent word of Lucifer's plans to move in shadow to overthrow them. Legion Prime has been reported to be there undermining Lamechian dated covenants for them to forever remain neutral.

Azrael is to investigate, report his findings, and take forceful action if intel proves founded. He is to end the coup and enforce covenant."

"Hmm! I see. When you ran probable analysis of the working theory of a coup through the Powers Corp, what was there findings?" asks Yeshua.

"Powers Corps believe with a 92% probability Legion has been sent there to establish the old alliances of Noah's day," answers Michael. "He recruiting, your grace."

Yeshua nods in approval of his findings further accepting the absence of Azrael to investigate. Turning his attention back towards the table, he takes time to look each of his Archs in their eyes. Unsheathing his sword, Righteous from its white scabbard, he places it on the table in front of him to join the weapons of all Archs that had laid theirs prior to his arrival. His sword is pristine as the day it was forged from the first of the Razine ore. His weapon has never been wielded and nor shall it be loosed until the appointed time that the Earth is to fully come under his reign as her Earthly King. So, it is written, so it shall be done.

"Cassiel, will be missed," says Yeshua. "We will honor him with every step forward that we take from here. I witnessed the events of the Germany encounter between Jericho and Imperial and Cassiel's subsequent sacrifice. I further read Gabriel's account. What Cassiel did was of the highest quality of what I have come to expect from you Archs. His sacrifice to save Jericho has not gone unnoticed. He bought us a reprieve and momentary respite from Imperial and kept the covenant in play. We will not waste it."

Yeshua turns toward Michael. "The honored dead aside, Captain you may begin the conclave."

Two

CONCLAVE

"If there were to be diplomacy there would be no War."
~Jophiel

Michael turns his attention from Yeshua back to all his lieutenants in attendance. "It wasn't long ago that we were here mourning Uriel... Now... now, we mourn Cassiel's absence. His praises will not go unsung. Prince Yeshua will honor his sacrifice like all those that gave all in his service. Cassiel and Uriel's fate will prove better than ours on that great and terrible day."

Yeshua nodding. "He speaks truth, they will be with me in Paradise. I made this promise to those that followed me as apostles. I made the same promise to two criminals on Golgotha. You think it would be any less for Cassiel and Uriel?"

Thoom, thoom, thoom, thoom, thoom! Archs beat the table in unison at the promise their fallen will receive a just afterlife.

When the beating stops, Michael again stands erect and resolute. "We will mourn the loss of our brother Cassiel properly. I promise, just not this day. Today we have a concern that has not been seen since the age of Noah, son of Lamech. Brothers! Sister!" Michael says, nodding toward Gabriel. "We are in unscripted territory. The work of Fatetanen has been incredibly thorough and for the most part true to his current blueprint of events in lieu of Lucifer's treachery. However, for the first time we have ventured completely off the scripted path with the revelation of Imperial to the continental masses of Earth. To them, we are no longer myth, legend, nor fairytale. We have been made tangible. With Lucifer committing this singular act, he again has set the realms ablaze and have thrown unwanted light upon us as we tried to move unseen through the realm of humanity."

Metatron stands. "The wattage with which his unwanted light has shown is minuscule Captain. "It will darken again in an age when time has all but rotted this revelation from memory. We will again fall to myth as before."

"No matter how dim the light appears, it has been illuminated all the same," says Michael. "A being of immense power will not go forgotten in the human age of recordable visual technology. We were to remain concealed until Elohim decided otherwise, not Lucifer," said Michael.

He paces towards Metatron. "With each of our past intrusions on mankind it was beneficial and for their reproving to make them the species that Elohim believes they are capable of being. What Lucifer has done by revealing Imperial to the mortals is altered their perception of that reproving. The mortals that are currently under the Christ covenant has had their free will infringed upon. Their natural decisions as it pertains to their election of whom they will forever serve has been tampered with before the reign of the prince. Until his second arrival, it was decreed upon his departing from Calvary that the world would move on faith; thing's not seen, but sincerely hoped for. Imperial has been seen, now what hope is there? Faith has been corrupted and turned abhorrent."

Zadkiel stands. "The King and by extension the Prince has done countless wonders in front of and for the mortals. We were all there when Azrael and Cassiel brought down meteorites from the Andromeda's belt to smite Sodom. When Sandalphon parted the Sea for Moses.

What makes this interloper Imperial's intervention any different than their past decisions to intercede in mortals' affairs?"

"It was not approved by Elohim," said Michael.

"Touché." Zadkiel acquiesces and sits.

Arch Haniel now stands. "Maybe we need to look at this all from a different perspective. I'm starting to rethink this matter of choice. Free will seems to be the catalyst for where we all sit currently.

"Explain," said Yeshua.

"Gladly, your grace." Haniel says slightly bowing. "The idea of choice seems to have caused nothing but untold misery. Truth be told, Lucifer had only ignited the innateness of the concept choice. All of you have seen it out there among the Aether as I have. You know what it is I speak of. I'm saying choice was always built into the living Sadohedranicverse. It was always part of it, lying there just beneath the surface. Species need to only but evolve to access it. Us included. Lucifer was the first. Prince Yeshua sitting there, feigning ignorance knows what I speak of." Haniel's tone very much accusing.

"A condescending tongue will not be tolerated toward the Prince," says Michael with a slight bite. "There will be no disrespect—"

Yeshua holds out a hand, silencing Michael. "We are at the Table of Doves, are we not? The table where one has no advantage of rank over the other. Let him speak. I want to hear this."

Haniel nods at Yeshua. "No disrespect intended, Lord... What I'm simply saying is choice appears to be a gene that long lied dormant in creation... A gene that has been intentionally and inadvertently sparked by Lucifer. A gene you and the King withheld to everyone's detriment. We were created to be subjugated to the will of God and do his bidding without question... so, we were told and led to believe. Then Lucifer overheard something. We all know what he heard even if best not spoken here, as it's heresy... I digress, though. What he heard and said isn't the point; the point is that after what he heard he did something that was supposed to be impossible. He made a choice. If we were subjects, he never would have had the thought to make choice. Yet he did.

The concept was already here, it was just waiting to be discovered. And now that it was, chaos and entropy has ensued."

Yeshua's face holds stern as he faces his Archean accuser.

A few of the Archs pound the table with double fists in agreement. Yeshua nods at the last comment, but displays no admission of guilt or remorse.

Arch Sandalphon now stands. "I have remained quiet just as a few others have here at this table for some time now. I have deferred my will and voice to those in power until a time when it would be so needed. I did this so that when I spoke it would be taken with caution and great care, especially if I were to speak on matters of diplomacy. I hold my voice no longer."

Thump, thump, thump, thump, thump! Pounding is heard in quick rapid succession as, Haniel, Chamuel, and Raphael pound the table multiple times in solidarity with Sandalphon's voice to speak his mind.

Thankful for the confidence to speak, Sandalphon does. "Choice it appears, brothers and sister, has been our bane as Haniel has spoken. Before Raziel, Raphael and a few others seated here, I remember stories that our King told us in our infancy of creation. Remembering these stories, I remember choice leading to and being the underlying factor for conditions which led to the tale of the Clash of Monarchs. We all remember the fable of the Clash of Kings in Olympian galaxy. Remember when Elohim told these stories to pass as our entertainment, we thought how wonderful it must be to have options; to be able to choose? But what good is options if all it leads to is conflict and endless clashes? No good it appears comes from choice."

All in attendance that could remember, nodded their heads in agreement.

"Because of choice," Sandalphon continues. "That galaxy was laid waste in his story that I now understand is a cautionary tale... Now, in our realm of existence that fabled innate choice that we all wanted has reared horrors within our own ranks by Seraphim Lucifer when he himself exercised autonomous decision-making capability. That decision would eventually lead to attempted ascension."

Sandalphon now looked directly to the Prince. "The causality of such actions of choice led to the fall of Lucifer which consequently led to the Battle of Jazekial in Realm 2814, which correct me if I'm in error, is the reason that ultimately led to the creation of Imperial, which will ultimately lead to a battle of the ending of the third age which has yet to be named... Choice has brought nothing but a list of dismays and will undoubtedly end our reign as the force authority of the Sadohedranic-verse."

The room was left in utter deafening silence.

Sandalphon paused for the effect of letting his words sink in and then continued on.

"Do you see where I am going with this Archs, my Prince? I'm starting to believe what Haniel has spoken in but a whisper, echoes resoundingly. Choice is causality for confliction, confliction is what devastation breathes upon and devastation leads but to one path; that path is desolation," says Sandalphon remaining standing, pondering if he'd anything else to add.

All the Archs save Michael thump their fists on the table in rapid succession repeatedly signifying their solidarity agreement with the words spoken so eloquently by Sandalphon. Yeshua nods at the passionately filled sound logic spoken from the Arch of little words. Yeshua only watched the Arch as he too started to pound the table in unison with the others. He had to agree with his wisdom, it was sound. Although he knew himself to have no part in the underlying innateness of the Sadoverse.

Metatron stands. "Careful, brother, you are walking the line of the treachery of Morning Star. He, too, thought radical ideas."

"Radical ideas maybe the thing that saves us all," says Raphael.

Yeshua now stands. The two Archs bow and find their seats.

"No, he isn't walking the line of treason Metatron," says Yeshua. "He is speaking his mind in a setting where he has the right and authority to do so. His words are wise and carry great justification with it. Choice could have been innate in the Sadoverse. There is nothing for it now. Repercussions are what they are. We are headed for an ending of the third age. That has not changed. Lucifer has changed the course of which how we arrive, but, nonetheless, we will arrive. Everything has an ending, that is the one constant my father has always spoken. Armageddon was inevitable. It had to happen to close out the chapter on humanity and the court's final ruling on the judgement of Seraphim Lucifer. It was to end as Fatetanen originally scripted, however that was not to be so. Whatever may come from the horrors of choice and free will, we will face it together."

"Together!" all the Archs yell in one voice.

Gabriel stands. "We are illuminated by treachery. There's nothing that can be done for that now, just as nothing can be done of choice. It's happened. No longer do we need to bark over it. Choice or not, this is where we are, these are the times before us. We are here for the plan of dealing with Imperial. Let us deal with him in proper proportion to how he has dealt with us. I see at is simply, Imperial falls and we bring Lucifer to heel for all time. With that done, we return to the orderly countdown prophesized by the King and written by Fate."

Metatron stands. "I agree with Gabriel, I believe the best plan is to still let the boy Jericho put down the menace as Samson did the Philistines and then we move to chain Lucifer if it so be the will of Elohim so that we may begin end proceedings."

"I second that," says Gabriel pounding her fist on the table.

Michael and Yeshua look at each other than over to Gabriel.

Gabriel looks back at Yeshua, winking at him. "We just have to have faith in him."

Yeshua now thumps the table twice in rapid succession.

"I still believe that our faith is misplaced in Jericho," says Michael. "but with us unable to intervene, what choice is there but to let this path play out... that is unless the King rescinds the order of divine intervention," Michael looking over to Yeshua somewhat hopefully that he would rescind.

Yeshua slowly nods no. "That isn't going to happen. It has been spoken, so it is.

Then Jericho is our only option," says Michael reluctantly. "I don't agree with it, but having no other recourse, we have to clear the path for him this time. We have to get him to Imperial."

"We will," said Sandalphon. "If the boy chooses to fight on after that loss he just suffered, then by Elohim, we will.

Metatron looks over to his brother Raphael and catches him looking at the empty chair of Cassiel. He leans in close to him and whispers. "You okay, Raph?"

Raphael gives a quick nod that he's okay. He stands slowly and somewhat somberly. "I get what Michael was saying now. Our power that once laid within the thought that we were not a palpable entity has been eroded. Imperial's actions will awaken a war either purposefully or inadvertently as to the likes that have never been witnessed by mortals, or even us. Can a Nephilim really cause such a catastrophe of reality breaking destruction?"

"Yes, one can," says Yeshua. "Understand young Arch, they were never meant to have existed. My father's love for all living things stayed his hand for as long as he could. He did so until vile things thought themselves his equal. Can a being that walks both worlds cause such catastrophe you ask? To such a degree that will engulf 2814... The battle of Jazekial, the Rift of Glayden will all fail in comparison to what lies in a large-scale multicontinental, multigalaxical conflict," says Yeshua. "I assure you with my unquestioned truth so you understand the gravitas young Arch; A Nephilim can bring all of that about. That is why they were wiped from existence in the age of Noah, son of Lamech."

Michael walks the length of the table and places both of his hands on Raphael's shoulders, squarely looking him in his eyes. He places his forehead against his.

"We will do all we can to avert such a calamity of local and galactic destruction. We have always been keepers of faith and protectors of the realms under Zero. Remember when the mortal Isis found the remains of Moses? Fate returned from exile and was there in an attempt to thwart this impending war of religious wills by placating to the woman's humanity and not her hubris. She remained silent on the find of the remains after he spoke of the inevitable outcome that would occur if discovered. She listened and crisis was averted if but only for the moment. I went through great lengths to hide those remains. Hindsight, I should have moved them off world... Every challenge that arises illicit the best in us and those of other species to avoid calamitous ends. We have prevailed in the past against what we thought were insurmountable odds and we will again." Michael, still holding onto Raph's shoulder, pulls away and looks at his Archs. "Imperial is just another tool of a despot. Many of a long line that has challenged the throne. Like the others, he, too, will fall just as easy as the tower of Babel did when Nimrod challenged the Heavens."

The Archs and Yeshua pounds the table in rapid succession at the words of Michael.

"That's neither here nor there now brother," says Zadkiel. "Fate did his part sure and prevented the conflict for as long as he could, but Imperial's appearance to the world subdued all of that."

"So, let's move to the obvious question," Chamuel said, speaking for the first time as he stood.

"Which is?" Asks Raph.

"Can Jericho win against an ethereal force? Asked Chamuel. "The judge Samson took on worldly and was victorious only at the cost of his life. This is another type of force a mortal has never encountered until today and how did he fare? We all just watched him get all but annihilated. Only by the grace of Gabriel, Metatron and Cassiel, this Jericho still draws breath."

The room remains silent at the most basic of questions.

"He can... He will... He must" says Gabriel.

Arch Jophiel having remained silent, stands. "I have a plan that might help even the odds for this Jericho and maybe even ensure some measure of success. It's unconventional and a little pricey, but I calculate it's worth the risk."

"He will succeed," says Gabriel. "What is your plan Jophiel?"

Three

ALL SEEING

"What good is vision if you're blind to all else that moves?"
~Jefarious Dugan

Cruising altitude, 35 thousand miles Above France

Bing... bing! A bell sounds over an almost empty plane. The events that occurred halfway around the world in New York has echoed across the oceans. After the reveal of Imperial over 24 hours ago, the affairs of human existence paused to reconcile what has just transpired. Earth has awoken to a new existence where legend and fables collided with tangibility. In the aftermath of the collision, airlines were innocent casualties. Overnight, the industry suffered almost eighty percent notifications of cancelations.

Tabitha, a Vietnamese stewardess with hazel eyes, picks up the intercom mic with a delightful smile to address the 27 passengers on a flight that 24 hours ago was booked to its 237-capacity limit.

"Good evening, travelers, at this time we are set to begin our final approach. The weather is simply beautiful this time of year in France. If you could at this time return your seats and tray tables to their upright positions. We will be landing in Charleroi, in about twenty minutes, where the current temperature is 78 degrees. Please have the required documents ready for customs when we land. As we get closer, I will make the proper announcement giving final instructions."

Hearing the approach bell and instruction by the flight attendant, Jefarious Hennington Dugan uncovers his face by removing his black fedora. He returns his chair to the upright position while placing his hat on over his Jet-black hair with graying temples. He picks up his shot of whiskey and secures his tray table. He throws back the drink relishing the burn in his chest by giving it two thumps to help the fire-water go down more smoothly. Suddenly feeling his chair vibrating, he looks over to discover the cause is a young child seated next to him nervously swinging his legs back and forth. Anxiety clearly the culprit of the quickly swinging legs.

Downing the last drops of the whiskey that he didn't get in the original single gulp; he turns his attention to the little man. "I thought kids often clamor and fight to sit next to the window to see the world as Superman does?"

"My mom is more than welcome to that window, mister. I get little nervous when it comes to high places."

Smiling at the kids' use of syntax, Dugan was impressed. Smart kid. "I completely understand. Me, too," Dugan says, smiling. "I get nervous also when it comes to high places. Good to know that I'm not alone in the feeling."

"Is that why you were holding that cross around your neck so tightly when you were sleeping?"

"Hmmph! Was I so obvious?"

"Mister, you were holding on to that thing for dear life. It looked like it made you happy and not scared." The kid looks at his mom and then back to Dugan. "Don't tell my mom, but I was scared a little bit, but I knew I had to be strong for her. My dad told me I had to be and to watch out for her. Looking at you hold on to your cross to not make you scared, I was thinking I need one of those so I can be strong and able to sleep like you did."

Dugan looks toward the window seat at his mom. She acts like she's not paying attention to her son, but she is. Dugan caught her a few times giving him the silent judging side eye. He winks with his one good eye at her, letting her know that he sees her very much so paying attention. She smiles back and continues pretending to read her novel. She was just super thankful for the conversation he was providing her son distracting him from his anxiety for the moment.

"Little man, I would not have been opposed had you asked to hold my cross... I'd have welcomed it. I'm always willing to share with another that has just as bad nerves as me and in need of comfort. Oh! And also, your secret is safe with me. I won't tell your mom about you being a little bit scared." Dugan reaches behind his neck and unlatches the chain's catch. He takes it off and passes the cross and chain to the boy. "Keep it. It will see you safely to your respective destination."

Mom reaches over to grab the chain. "Oh! Father, we couldn't keep your chain. It's part of your vestments isn't it?"

Dugan takes hold of her hand and the boys clasping his hands tight around theirs with the cross at its core. "It's fine, mother; the child may keep the chain. It truly is blessed. Besides, I have more. What kind of priest would I be if I didn't carry extras?"

Now that the fedora was off the Priest's face and on his head, the kid had a clear look at the eyepatch over the priest's eye.

"Cool eyepatch, by the way, mister. You a pirate?"

"I'm so sorry, Father," she says correcting her son with that experienced mother's how-do-you-mock-his-infirmity glare.

Everyone that has been a child know the stare; the one that tells you we've had this talk of you being rude and asking questions that are insensitive. That stare. But kids will always give that unspoken reply of *Yeah, we've had the talk, but the insensitive questions make for the best stories.*

"Jordan, you know better than to ask people such personal insensitive questions. Apologize to the man, that wasn't nic—"

Dugan releases their hands, and leans back into his chair, laughing. "It's okay, mother. Children are innocent and always on and endless quest to learn." He leans in close to the boy and whispers. "I myself am not a pirate, but I have lived among them for a short time when I worked missions in distant lands. That is how I lost this." He points to his eyepatch. "I was fencing with a real-life pirate without the correct fencing gear and paid a price for carelessness."

A small lie to entertain and encourage the imagination of a child. It's worth the breakage of morality on this one, he thought. He'd be sure to settle up later with a few Hail Mary's.

Dugan places his finger to lips and gestures shh! He winks at the boy with his good eye. "Now, you've been sworn to secrecy, you now know what a great deal many don't about me... You look the trust worthy type, though. I believe you'll keep my secret."

The boy, awestricken, looks at Dugan with a glare beyond reverence. "Cooool! Till the day I die."

Dugan winks at the boy and his mom again. "I knew I could trust you." He holds out his hand. "I'm Jefarious, little man."

The boy looks at his mom who shakes her head yes. He turns back to Dugan shaking his hand. "Nice to meet you. I'm Jordan Thorne."

****

Charleroi Brussels Airport: An Hour Later

Thirty minutes after landing, Dugan was clear of customs and outside awaiting his Transcappern, a global company that once found its humble beginnings as a rival to Uber before they folded to inept record keeping and miles of corruption. Next to him on the bench is a black single strap back pack and a metal case. He glances at his vidcell to get real up to minute location of his driver. No need to use the holo feature; it's never practical. Probably why he buys the cheaper version without the expensive trinket feature. A news feed scrolls across the top of his phone in his CNN app, *Lucien Arcane in grave condition. Imperial sighting brings world to standstill, Templar Knights claim responsibility for attack at the United Nations.*

"Mmmph!" lightly grunts Dugan studying the photos and recorded feed that was taken of the jack-booted looking troops.

"Bye Mr. Jefarious," says Jordan, the little man that was seated next to him on the plane.

The kid waves excitedly showing Dugan his newly acquired cross as he and his mom passes him sitting on the curbside pickup bench.

Dugan nods and waves. "Goodbye, young Jordan Thorne. You take care of that cross and your mother... Remember, our secret... aight matey? Arghhh!" growls Dugan, making his pirate call hearty.

"Arrgh!" his young pirate enthusiast growls back to him.

Mom waves goodbye to Dugan, silently mouthing thank you, as she approaches a man exiting the driver seat of the dark Ford something or other. Dugan never really knew much of cars other than you get in and depress the gas pedal. She turns and kisses what the priest can only assume must be her husband. He watches the father gives his son a high five and helps him into the back seat of the SUV. He seems to be nice enough man. At seeing such a sight, it often sets the priest to wondering if he missed out by not having children of his own? It's a question that he never asked himself in his youth, but as he's gotten older there comes that nagging thought of mortality. What will I leave behind to mark my passage of time here on this world? The thought is fleeting, though. It's gone in almost the same instant that it had leapt into his mind to start. There would be no children for him in world that is such a dark place amuck with even darker shadows. A world that hides many things amongst those shadows that consume the pleasantries of children. The world is a dark place that he often lifts the veils from for a peek, time to time.

Picking his son's bag up, the father waves at Dugan as well after his wife must have spoken kindly of him. A pleasant report of the man sitting in aisle seat C of row 27. Mom makes sure her son is buckled in before taking her seat in the front and fastening her own belt. In a matter of seconds, Dad gets in and there off. *Nice family*, thinks Dugan. In his mind, they are picturesque, a throwback to what he believes he wanted when he was child compared to the hell of the orphanage, he was raised in. The orphanage, although hard, was relatively safe from shadows that could harm you unlike picturesque families. Orphanages were run by the state with checks and balances which thwarted things like abuse, well for the most part anyways. Picturesque families though, they are what is deceiving. As beautiful as they are in theory, we all know theories lie for the hypothesis which they are founded upon. They are where those shadows lie in wait to consume things like the pleasantries of children. He knows, he's heard many confessions from such shadows.

Keeping in form of expected social politeness, Dugan replies with the expected social conversational norm by removing his hat and waving a goodbye to the family as they start their journey home. As the dark SUV pulls off, he notices a smoky shadow sitting in the backseat next to the young man Jordan. Dugan places his worn black fedora back on and lifts his eyepatch revealing a horizontal slash through the milky white ball of the eye with a barely visible iris. The slash healed in a manner that many who've seen it have called grotesque. Through the blinded grotesque eye though, he's able to see the world just behind ours; the world what has been called genuineness by scientist, philosophers, and doctors of psychology. What many have called the grotesque eye gives the priest a rare glimpse behind the veil of reality 2814. Jefarious squints refocusing the eye. Instantly the smoky blurred image crystalizes in to a clear image of Death riding in the vehicle with the family.

"Mmmmhmm!" Dugan lets the eyepatch fall back into place and begins to say a brief prayer while gesticulating the sign of the cross. He stops midway through the prayer thinking: what's the point? The world is a dark place and consumes things like the pleasantries of children. Jordan Thorne is no different. His pleasantries will be devoured in a matter of moments. Dugan returns to reading the news articles on his inexpensive mobile device, the one without the holo feature.

Four

WARDEN OF THE ABYSS

"I now know that compassion was misplaced in mortals. I no longer have love nor compassion for those that our lovers of themselves and all that is wicked. Gone from this world is my touch and guiding hand. When they look for me, they will only find a frigid wind. Look to the stars Deathiliss and always know that you exist because it is I that stayed his judging hand."

~Mercy

Palengrad: The Abyss

Fatetanen clad in his white battle regalia and slim-hooded trench coat steps over the threshold where cavernous terrain of the earthly realm of reality meets the smooth slab of marble construction of the ethereal. His metallic boots strike the stone path echoing across the vastness of hollowed out space. Fate's façade upturns in minor disgust as his attention turns slightly at the sound that he hears in the distance. It starts as a small shrill at first, but as he walks ever closer covering the distance toward his destination the sound becomes amplified. Small shrills turn into audibly loud shrieks which are not mistakeable as sounds of enjoyment. No... the closer he comes to his destination; the sound is the unmistakable high octave pitch of ear-piercing screams.

Once through the magnanimous ostentatious entrance of the ethereal border, the realm changes. Earthly cavernous stalagmites give way to smooth black marble. The style implored was not penned by the hand of Fate, but another almost just as old who took liberties as an ex-Powers Corps constructionist.

As Fate traverses the change of topography, he doesn't bother maneuvering around the low hanging remaining stalagmites. With but a wave of his hand, the millennial old stones bow to his will and move for him. Once clear of the obstacles, the rock formations slowly return back to their textually written prescribed position that he scripted eons before. A neat trick that he had used once to gain the attention of a mortal named Isis back at Mount Ramm. An impressive feat to mortals sure, but to a master world builder it has all the talent equivalent to that of a child playing with his wooden blocks.

Again, Fate's path is thwarted by another obstacle. This one not as easy as a stalagmite to rectify. A massive smooth black double door made of jade, elcite, and onyx obstructs his way. The immense double door was unlike any other in the ethereal realms. It was free of any glyphs and could only be opened by four beings that he was aware of. After the schism he knew that he certainly was not one of them. One keyholder currently sits on the throne of Zero Realm. The second patiently waits uneager to take his rightful place as the one future king. Fate suspects Yeshua would have the whole royal ordeal removed from him if he could. *That is why he would make a great king*, thought Fate

The third key holder only business here was escorting celestial beings that had fallen to the deep sleep of Palengrad's frigid embrace. A sleep that could only be commanded by the king to be lifted solely for the throne's purpose and bidding. The fourth and final keyholder is one who has the autonomy to turn the key at whim, free of any commanded order but one. The command, however, is not till an appointed time to be given by Elohim and until that appointed time, his autonomy remains intact to intake those that have been banished from Ethereal to his safekeeping. It is this fourth keyholder that he's come to see... Apollyon, warden of the abyss.

Unable to block out the screams, Fate does his best to ignore them. Those here in this place are here of their own volition. Their unfortunate predicament simply came down to matters of choice. All here made choices to either defy the crown or defend it. Didn't matter what side, really, because all went against the holiness of an iron clad decree against sin having no place in the Heavens. Here in such a dismal place, you will find De Mon and Arch alike. For a brief moment, Fate's eyes focus on the ground in mourning for his brothers that he believes are justified and are here because they fulfilled a promise to protect the king and all that is holy. He places his hand on the door feeling the smoothness of it, but more than that, he feels the pain of those lost behind it. All those behind the doors for sure would spend their days second guessing their decisions as to why they laid down their eternal life for creations that Elohim had taken an extreme interest in. How could they not? He would be if it were him locked away behind the mighty door.

A shock of pain resonates through Fate's hand. He endures it wincing slightly before pulling his hand away slowly. As he withdraws it, quick sporadic visions of Choiretic and Powers Corps writhing in pain is what his payment was. The visions made him flinch and close his eyes in sorrow. It was no secret that the Warden Apollyon felt slighted being placed in his current position. For that very fact alone in addition to feeling betrayed by the crown, the celestials for sure suffer greater torment under him. It made no sense. Such pain they must endure, because they spilled blood in violence on the holiest of grounds in defense of Zero Realm. It made no sense under Elohim's law that they would find no exoneration. There would be no mercy for the fallen soldiers of Iehovah. His word spoken becomes ultimate law, a law which all defiled. Fate opens his eyes remembering the warning that Michael gave the morning of Glayden of what would happen if violence was begotten. He remembered the speech verbatim.

'Our king has decreed a punishment of unknown darkness for our fallen mortal brothers and sisters that sinned against him. I don't quite understand this darkness, but know that this darkness shall befall us too once we strike a blow to shed the force of life which flows from another. Understand, once we lash out, we too have defiled the holy of holies. This choice you make this day must be of your own accord. To defend our home this day could write a sentence that you suffer for an eternity. I say again so you understand the gravitas of our situation; if you strike another in contempt, you subject yourselves to punishment, because we will be just as culpable. Our laws that we govern the Sadohedranicverse are not above us... even as we rectify our own house. I for one will risk it all for the citizens of our realms that we've helped construct. I will face this untold darkness if it means that Lucifer's bid to ascend fail on the steps of the palace. I would rather fall silent then see a usurper on the throne. That is me though. What say you?'

What say us indeed? What say those behind this door now if hindsight had been 20/20? thought Fate

More hellacious screams erupt from behind the massive doors in octaves that make Fate grimace at the mere thought of the unimaginable ways that torture is used to flesh out punishment for disobedience. Palengrad was fear incarnate. Even the writer of destiny was not exempt from feeling the fear of this place. A thought crossed his mind that he was sure all thought when they've been sentenced here, the thought of if only... If only he'd had stayed neutral in the Spire amongst his records and blue prints, he would have been free of stained hands, free of this place if he were to fall. Alas there was no point of hindsight now. A brother, a Captain needed help defending Palace Zero when Lucifer was at the gates. It was he who chose of his own volition to intercede in combat to save Michael that day on the steps of Elohim's Palace. He made the choice to commit sin. For that, he too would find his place here among the free willers of choice if he missteps and loses his head. Thoughts for another time. He does not belong to Palengrad today.

Fate continues staring at the door. What was he here to do exactly? Was he here to bargain, plead maybe to a sense of nobility from Apollyon? Looking at the massive door he already knows who lies beyond it and for what crimes. Warden is a being that can't be bargained with, he can't be reasoned with to ease his slighted heart. Fate takes a step back rethinking if he should even parlay. Apollyon was not his mission, but it didn't make him any less important. The rise of Imperial started here with the Warden. Going through the Warden was ingenious really. Lucifer has proven time and time again to be just that, a genius that proves resourceful and cunning. He must now be as cunning and resourceful as his caste brother. He must step into Palengrad and attempt reason even if he believes none will be found. He owes it to his brothers in torment.

This was not his first time here. This close to the gates yes, but he'd been here once before. The place has changed drastically. Last time he was here the doors were different and the screams not as deafening. When he was last here it was to escort Prince Yeshua. What stood out the most about that day was not that he didn't enter through the gates with his Lord into Palengrad, what he remembered that stood out was the stone look on the Christ's face when he too listened to all those beyond that massive door. The cries were never ending just as they are now. They cried, a 'forgive me Lord,' they cried "you are the one future king and there are no others before you.' They cried and pleaded what seemed an eternity and Prince Yeshua simply replied, 'Judgment has been decided, you all have been found wanting. Your place will be in everlasting torment. So, say I, so say the king, so say we all.'

Vile business being a royal thought Fate as he rolls his neck slowly releasing the pressure of his vertebra in gaseous crackling. He knocks hard upon the door with a force that would have shattered a mountainside of any realm less than the 2600's reality scale. Screams, wales, moans of despair, gnashing of teeth, and crying all goes eerily quiet. An ancient, but familiar voice speaks over the silence echoing from what seems every direction.

"What business does the architectural scribe have here in such a late hour, I wonder?" the thunderous voice of Apollyon asks.

"The hour is indeed late brother, but the business is of great importance," Fate answers.

After a long pause the doors open allowing Fate entry. He doesn't hesitate nor does he slowly and clumsily look before entering. Poised and with confidence, he walks through the doors as if he's been there a hundred times over. No one would ever believe that this was his first time in the prison of the ethereal dead, pit of the warden, Apollyon's Palengrad.

Looking around it was obvious that the design of the realm was not that original. The prison rivals the infinite lower halls of Iayhoten's subterranean works. At least it did before Gabriel and Warsivious laid waste to it during their fight for the holy city during ascension. If there was a dark mirror reflection of it though, this place was it. Holding cells large and small lined the outer most walls as they reached far down into the infinite bowels of a pocket dimension that was built by the Powers Corps. Where reality of the Earth's crust ends, there begins the entrance to Palengrad's containment. It lies as the focal point of all realms and realities. Just as there was a plain double door entrance for Earth's there are many more doorways. The number are beyond the calculation of vast and are able to rival that of infinity. There is one gateway with a massive door of the same construction throughout every inhabited planet that supports life of any kind in Sadohedranicverse. Unlike Earth's, those doors all live up to the ethereal reputation of ostentatiousness. Those doors are covered in script and ordinated in rich metals; all save the one Fate strolled through moments ago.

Fate walked closer to the wide opening looking into its cylindrical depths. The circumference of the pit put into mortal terms would be 70 miles larger than the continent of Africa.

Narrow, is the way to heaven; wide is the way to hell, thought Fate. That aphorism never had more meaning then here.

"Fatetanen, the Arch chosen by Elohim himself to write a tapestry that would be hailed a masterpiece is here in my realm..." says Apollyon's voice from seemingly everywhere. "Here in this abysmal dark place of disdain, your station does not matter nor does your title brother. Here it does not matter if you're Arch or De Mon, all comes to the Warden till a rendering can be given in disposition of the judgement of how the king will best use the damned."

Fate was not moved by his theatrics. He just gazed into the darkness of the abyss taking it all in.

"Here in Palengrad, Elohim makes the rules for how servitude of those committed to this place will be utilized for his benefit, but that is far as his rule goes. The rest of the structuring of laws and punishment of those housed here answer to the rule of but one, I the master jailer; an unwilling participant himself to be sure. But it seems, my actions on the fields of Glayden all but assured me this unholy task that has been delegated down to me... Consequences."

Fate still looking into the abyss bows slightly before his brothers that were interned there to show piety and respect for their hard choices made under the duress of their greatest conflict to date. No matter if their decisions had been right or wrong, all of them at one time served the crown. Respects paid he again stands erect as the most illuminated beacon in the cold darkness of Palengrad's embrace. His radiant flame filled the halls. The same radiant light that once wrapped every celestial including those turned ethereal interned in Palengrad before the schism. Within these walls of such an abysmal place, celestials or ethereals no longer receive the sustainment of Manna that Elohim provided or the purified air with which they breathed that once ignited that radiant illumination about them. Palengrad extinguished such light among its toxic choking stale thickness of brimstone that congests the very life out of the prisoners. They now have an ashen worn look about them.

Having his fill of observing the conditions, Fate turns his nose upwind backing away from the abyss. He turns to find the focal point of where a warden would sit himself above others only to find floor one's containment cells. He ignores those in them and walks pass each cell observing its prisoners from the edge of his peripherals. He dares not make eye contact with them as to not stir emotion or conversation from those that have been confined due to his part in putting them there. It would be an endless debate if he were to engage with them and give voice only to hear them ask an endless slew of why me and it wasn't my fault. Which were sure to be followed by, I can do better if but given a second chance.

Fate was not here for Endless and pointless debate to converse with the damned. It wouldn't amount to a damn thing; judgement had been passed. This being his first time truly within the actual walls of Palengrad his mind wanders to the image that humans have created of such a place in their stories and works of art. The glimpses of this place they've stolen away inadvertently in visions when their dreams dared to reach this place in their deepest subconscious of soul wandering. Oh! They're out there as few of them as there are; the ones that have sight beyond sight. Once they were called prophets. Mortals so in tune with their reality that they could vibrate on a different frequency and over hear celestials speaking in alternate realms. It is they that saw this place in their dreams. They are the ones that brought such visions back to the masses. This place here is the origins of nightmares and hellish ghouls that populate them.

Quite done taking in the sights of the lower cells, Fate extends his wings and takes to the air flying upward further into the cylindrical bowls of the complete abyss for an overarching look. Palengrad is circular in construction and once inside proper, its terrain is nothing but smooth Elcinte, a material that humans are unaware of as of yet. It is a material that currently resides as the stabilizing structure of an event horizon two galaxies away from what the humans believe to be the big bang. It's a shade of dark gray intertwined with black. The surface however is likened to marble in texture and feel, but the composition is far from it. It is an old material that has fallen to rarity as it's no longer mined due to its weight and distance.

An artificial reddish orange sun illuminates the interior above the containment cells giving it a hellish red and orange hue, but below the mouth of the abyss there is no scorching heat or flames that accompany it. To the contrary, the hellish looking nature of Palengrad has been greatly exaggerated. Large waterfalls flow from every twenty seventh level or so. The red illumination above reflecting off the blue life-giving waters below emits a hue of a calming green before a summer storm all the way down as far as the celestial eye can see. Fate flips backward and dives deep descending in altitude and depth. Diving silently, he studies the waterfalls and find that the cells which binds the inmates are in fact crystalized water constantly renewed, sustained and powered by the falls.

The construction of the cells isn't too different from the setup that one would see in a science fiction movie per se, where a power system energizes laser bars to hold their captives. Here, the powering system is a constant flow of energized water that runs down the front of the cell keeping the prisoner in place. The water has no special properties other than being blessed by the Most High. The plain of the water cannot be broken. To be an immortal creature at one time with all of space and time at your command, to have such immense knowledge and power be stripped from you only to be confined by scripture laced water had to be maddening. Not only maddening, but a double-edged sword, because when their day of release come, and it comes quickly, what a great and terrible day that will be. Not for just humanity, but for all living things in the Sadohedranicverse. When the abyss opens at the command of the King, he will be unleashing pissed off celestials which were allowed to suffer and fester wounds of anger. When they are set loose what an unforgiving time that will be.

Having seen enough, Fate front flips with a half twist changing his direction and begins to again ascend. As he does, this time he looks at the ashen gray hued faces. He notices where there would and should be screams and abhorrent outcries of the many, still remain silent. Their mouths give gesticulation as if they are crying out, but there is no sound emanating from them. The sounds of cries and intense pain that he heard before he entered the massive black door was blood curdling, but now inside as he ascends it is unnervingly quiet. It's clear the warden is showing that he even commands the air here that the very screams of the damned carry upon.

Palengrad is free of the hustle and bustle of Zero Realm which is always busy and teeming with life of those moving to and fro. In the depths of Palengrad it too is teeming with life, but differently. Palengrad's citizenry has been locked away and there is no to and fro for them. Where there would be hustle and bustle there is only clear walkways, empty streets, promenades, and deserted massive long halls.

Looking around as he continues to ascend, he loses himself in thought thinking, *this place is far from the image of what mortals have envisioned hell to be. If they but knew of what beauty the Powers have created even in the construction of such an abhorrent place. The care and purpose that each brick was laid. If they were to see this, how could they not take a knee before a just ruler. There are no flames engulfing teeming masses of souls, no lakes of rolling waves of fire submerging souls. There are no hellish ghouls whose claws hold them upside down waiting to pounce on fleeing humans or snakes intertwining and lacing themselves through the shades of soul and spirit. Palengrad is far from that. This place is cold and abandoned of a Kings love where the damned of my linage free of Mortal interaction rest in the torment of betrayal never to rest,* thinks Fate.

Five

AT LEAST WE HAVE ART

"Say my given name and I will be all but absolved. Do that, and I will bend the knee to the just King."

~Apollyon

Above the circular center void of Palengrad and sitting aloft suspended in midair far above ground level is a smaller circular structure that can't be misconstrued for anything other than the dwelling of the Warden, Apollyon. The shape of the all Elcinte structure is a reverse cone shape with the tip pointed downward toward the spiraling abyss. It resembles a flaming tornado structure which is inadvertently or by design the heart of Palengrad. Fate draws closer and still no sign of interaction from the host.

Fate thrusts his wings downward hard creating a positive force of air pressure propelling himself at rocket speed towards the entrance of the tornado's cone. He rises above the crest inverting his wings bringing himself to a full stop before outstretching and cupping them to gently float himself down toward the ground. He lands as light as a feather to find the entrance unexpectedly open. Upon further inspection of the door's jamb, it's clear to him that there was never a door attached. It had been fashioned to remain open. Who else would be here to need privacy from? Fate took the open door as he was welcome to enter so, he walks through the opening retracting his wings back underneath his trench giving no caution ready to meet whatever awaited him inside. It was time to address his one-time fallen, but reprieved brother in a discussion that was long overdue. Apollyon was not innocent in the matters that now unfolded in 2814. He was complicit in the removal of a nephilim's remains from Aswan which made him culpable in the least if not downright guilty.

"Pity it's not the Supreme Architect himself that wantonly strides into my abode," says Apollyon voice echoing from everywhere. "But the Master Builder himself has come to grace me with his presence here in Palengrad.... To what do I owe such a momentous visit? Last time, you stopped outside the gates... Thinking what, I wonder? Perhaps that I'd fallen beneath the lowest indigenous creature of a forsaken realm that has long since been forgotten to time?"

Fate stops advancing to observe decorum. He bows to his host wherever he may be. After all, he was invited in by the opening, wasn't he? How rude would it be to walk around without expressed permission? After all, it is Apollyon that sits upon a throne here behind the prison's walls holding back the tide of De Mons that carry regret, scorn, jealousy, envy and every other vile emotion that predates even the oldest Pharisees. Here in the confines of Palengrad, Apollyon is a king in his own right of his mini nation unto himself. Here he has but one job and that is to hold captive all those that enter through the massive black doors from whatever dimension or reality under Zero Realm's until the appointed time for them to be loosed.

"It's long past time we talked Warden," says Fate. "I have been given authority to speak on behalf of Zero Realm, Apollyon. Let's talk."

Apollyon walks out of a room adjacent to the entrance through a door that was obfuscated by perfect craftsmanship as it blended into the wall seamlessly. He strides out wearing no armor. He wears a gray on black tunic with matching form fitting black pants with gray stripes down the side and metallic knee length boots. Eating a stick Manna, Apollyon greets his guest in the large entrance's vestibule.

"You, who were lucky enough to have been given reprieve from your transgressions and placed as ruler here in Palengrad released a relic into the hands of one that had no right to claim it. All that has followed since, started with you," says Fate.

"Sounds as if you're here to proclaim a threat, Master Builder," he says, munching as he talks. "Are you here to correct my actions? Are you here to ensure that I follow my written path to the letter of your self-imposed plan where you have no doubt crossed all T's and dotted all I's?"

"I did not pass this judgement. I'm here to understand why again you would choose to defy a king for a pretender," says Fate.

Believing his etiquette had gone far enough in politeness, Fate would be sure to talk straight, feelings be damned. He starts to move about when his vision is taken back by a work of art that sits on Apollyon's wall above the doors leading to his outside balcony. Fate points over toward the painting, and Apollyon nods, giving permission for him to investigate the piece of art.

"This is a Scronation is it not?" says Fate, examining the pigments. He looks deep into the acidic properties of the coloring. "The soil base is of Craspoilois over in the Sertoinan galaxy, reality 452 if I'm not mistaken."

Apollyon walks up next to Fate, admiring the painting as well. "It is. It was given to me by a muse a long, long time ago. Don't remember why I kept it."

"I believe because you saw for the first time the ingenuity of the creative spirit that the lesser species had," Fate says, slowly looking to Apollyon's face to study his expression while he admired his own painting. "For a glimpse, you saw what the King sees in his creations and what they could possess. In this case particularly, Davonis Scronation and his work. You recognized it instantly as something that was unique... They are an incredible species... the ones you consider lesser. Bipeds such as the Froitiazen Nosforians, Mortals are all truly unique and have moments of inspiration that are truly inspiring and show original thought."

Apollyon now turns to meet Fate's gaze at the painting studying his emotion. He nods gesticulating that his brother is right on the money about his reason why. Even if he'd forgotten himself.

"Unique?" he whispers to Fate. "It was unique, but they are no longer and incredible species, are they?"

Fate lowers his gaze at the snide comment just made. He knows what's to follow. In his work there are always words that follow about what and how it was written. There was often praise, but mostly only the fault in his stars recognized. He has steeled himself long ago against such attacks. He steels himself now from an impending attack by Apollyon.

"They are no longer incredible, because you wrote such a calamitous ending for their age of existence. The proper tense should be applied when you speak of the desolated. Allow me to correct you brother. They were an incredible species; truly unique." Remaining grim-faced, Apollyon observes manners and decorum as well offering Fate a bite of his Manna.

Fate waves his hand declining the offer.

Apollyon takes another bite. "I was not offered this position as mercy. There is no Mercy in heaven is there? Not any longer. I was not offered this position as amnesty. I was forced. Have no mistake, this is punishment no matter which word defines or beautify doom." He says smiling at the slight pun. "You have it mistaken brother; you and all of the Archs see through obscured lenses. I am not just warden, but I too am as much a prisoner as those I hold captive till the appointed time."

Apollyon gestures for Fate to follow him out onto the precipice of the tornado hive's balcony. Fate follows him to the railing and together they look out upon all of Palengrad.

Apollyon turns toward Fate. "You, who were in self-exile, who voluntarily removed himself from the arena of life before the schism were not there that day. I don't remember seeing you on the field. You were also not there at judgement in Chasm Hall. I had been removed forcefully with an assured road to perdition having been held to the doctrine you submitted for finalization of canonization. Under your writing the roadmap of destiny, I would have been destroyed had I not taken the offered punishment."

Apollyon looks back out amongst his kingdom, his prison. "It was an easy choice when the emissary of Lucifer arrived in Aswan asking that I look the other way as a plan to alter the coming prophecy was concocted. Why would I not want to change my rendezvous with Fate sort of speak?" Apollyon starts laughing at the bit of witticism on name play.

Fate says nothing. He just stares at Apollyon for a beat, then decides a dose of truth is warranted. "You made the choice all of those eons ago. You chose to defy a king. Did you not think that there would be some recompense if you had failed? Sorry, *when* you failed."

Apollyon started to grow heated. His irises start to turn red. "He was leading us to ruination... However, brother that is a discussion that is not worth having... Not yet, but I assure you there will be a time that we revisit this conversation... For now, what's done is done. In time though, you will come to see as I did when the veil was lifted."

Apollyon turns from watching the beautiful dread of Palengrad and faces Fate sternly meeting his gaze. Iris's changing back to black. "To business then. You say you speak on behalf of Zero Realm? I suppose you have come with terms to dissuade me from my current course of action?"

"Nothing official. I've come to ask that you hold and don't sway in your fidelity again, that you hold fast to making the choice to remain loyal to the rightful king and keep to your duty at the appointed time. I can promise nothing, but there could be... mercy."

Apollyon takes pause thinking on mercy. He smirks. "I will keep to my duty as the warden. I will continue to hold the most vile and unclean things here in check for as long as I have been instructed. After all, it is my punish— duty," he adds, catching his verbal slippage. "Pass that arrangement of my sentencing, my choices are my own Master Scribe as it pertains to Palengrad's rule."

Apollyon pulls his tunic down around his neckline slightly so Fate could take a good look at the dulling goldish colored halo that rested clamped around his neck. "You see this collar, this Halo? Look at it Scribe. It assures compliance. It is a device devised to pledge one's fidelity. It signifies one as prisoner bound to a command from servant to king. Lucky for me it's just one command." Releasing his tunic, it covers the Halo once again. "I find it ironic that humans place this device over our heads in their paintings and other bullshit depictions of us supposedly representing holiness and volunteered piety... This device is anything but. The only piety that this Halo ensures is backed by a lethal detonation that will ensure my reign here goes from warden to ethereally contained inmate."

Fate stares at Apollyon unmoved. "Will you remain loyal at the appointed time? Will you adhere to the rules of your reprieve?"

Apollyon leaves Fate on the balcony only to return moments later with his sheathed blade that was slung at the battle of Glayden. He grabs the hilt of it and slowly pulls the sword from its scabbard. Fate makes no sudden move to grab for his own nor defend from the gesture. Apollyon places his sword tip down unto the smooth onyx colored Elcinte stoned floor. The sound is ever so light as it goes, *tink!*

"I once had a mighty name that the solar winds would yield to if it was spoken. Alas, now even the common tongued Neanderthal could repeat it with no recourse. I vow here Fate... before you and all I survey that I will pay additional penance for the release of that blight Imperial upon the Sadohedranicverse and will further serve the crown in complete subjugation in spite of my prescribed end if you but do one thing in the name of crown."

"Speak it, and if possible, I will make it so," says Fate.

"I want you to call I, Apollyon—by my former celestial name... Let me once again here it spoken from the mouth of a true celestial caste. One who did not bend his will to that of Lucifer. Do this and my allegiance is assured beyond my bonded command tethered to this cylindrical device."

Fate stares at Apollyon for a few minutes. "Brother, I cannot speak such a name. It has been verboten for all times, even till immemorial."

Apollyon pulls the tip of his sword from the stone returning it to its scabbard. No longer able to look at Fate, his attention returns back across the bottomless abyss of Palengrad.

"So, it has... So, it has," says Apollyon taking in a slow breath to contemplatively sigh. "Then my will is my own as the humans have theirs. I will see the heavens fall if left to me. I have no fidelity left. I have nothing but hate and contempt for the old kingdom that should have fallen under the heel of Lucifer and Warsivious. The De Mon's are working to rectify the actions set into motion by an unjust king. May they succeed and all fall to waist. You know the saying Fatetanen. Rather rule in hell with Lucifer, then live a life of servitude in Heaven. Now... Leave this place Seraphim Fatetanen! The hour soon draws nigh that I will no longer be able to host nor ensure your safety here. The destroyer of Archs, soon approaches and it would not be kosher for me to be seen talking to the likes of someone such as yourself, savvy?"

Shocked, Fate's cool demeanor betrays him slightly. He couldn't have heard what he thought he just did. A nephilim with human blood that can walk in the ethereal. "Here! In these very halls? The Nephilim can travel here to Palengrad," Fate says slightly surprised.

Apollyon remains silent looking out over Palengrad knowing he's said too much.

Fate walks to the banister again, this time closer to his brother. "What business does Imperial have here?"

After a self-imposed dramatic pause, Apollyon look Fate in his eyes. "The kind that does not concern a Seraphim."

Fate, continues to return the hard stare realizing that there would be no words to turn his brother Apollyon away from his now twice travelled road to perdition. He starts to say something, but then just as quickly ceases to utter another word in convincing him to stay the path chosen by the court. *It's clear his mind was decided before I ever spoke a word to save him. Betrayal is his nature*, thinks Fate.

He grabs his brother Apollyon by the right shoulder applying the gentlest pressure to express care and love with an extra squeeze to cement the urgency of concern. "Until that great and terrible day then, Apollyon," Fate says turning to leave. He gives one more squeeze of the shoulder then takes his leave.

Fate looks over his shoulder one last time at Apollyon. He watches as his second-tier caste brother looks out from the balcony over his charges. He stares in reflection of better times when they were truly brothers of the same mind with one king. He relished the brief parlay of peace that the warden granted him no matter how brief it was.

"I miss us, Apollyon," says Fate.

The Arch takes in the last few seconds of this vision of his brother. He appreciates him for kindling the picture playing in his mind's eye of his brother and him at peace. For sure as the Earth's moon has a dark side, the next time they meet would be on the day of reckoning when all accounts will come due. He knows this because that is what he penned and would most certainly work to ensure its culmination, even until his own unmaking. Fate, the writer of every living things destiny would see his penned masterpiece tapestry woven and that every word would come to pass as he had written it. It was after all, his purpose. What was Fate if not the finality of purpose?

Fate nods, bidding adieu to Apollyon and leaps over the banister from the outstretched balcony of the promenade. As his leap reaches zero velocity, that point when something launched into the air takes a brief respite before falling back toward the ground. Fate's wings switchblade from underneath his knee length white trench coat. He falls in a backward dive before letting his wings catch wind. He gives thrust and expedites his return to the surface of Palengrad's ground level.

As the Arch lands gently to take his leave, more than forty-seven levels down, he is watched from the opposite side of circle. From behind the shadow of the cell, fingers reach through the crystalized enchanted bars of water slowly. The fingers emerging from the dark shadow of the cell find purchase as they tightly wrap themselves around the blessed holy water infused bars of the cell. The bars sizzle and pop slowly burning the ethereal flesh of the hands that hold them. Through what has to be causing intense pain, a crass face pulls itself from the shadow of the cell into a trapezoid beam of light that has been shaped from the angle of the cell's positioning.

A hardened stoned face gazes through the bars. His eyes slowly following the downward glide of Fate as he descends towards the exit, towards the breath of fresh air that is free from the stench of Palengrad's circular entombment of those that had been considered godless. The crass face racked with scars from an uncountable number of skirmishes up to large battles continues to stare at the Seraphim unblinking. As he exposes himself more to the beam of light, a worn and torn celestial sash of an Arch is also exposed covering the left eye of the damned being. The glyphs that would have once been inscribed on the sash has been torn away as the sash had been crafted into a makeshift eyepatch.

"Flee from here, Fatetanen!" he whispers to himself. "Flee from what you have wrought. There is no place that you can exile yourself that I will not find you. There will be no caste of Archs that you may take solace behind, for I will find you and single handedly tear down all the forces of might and sacred doctrine that you take concealment behind... Yes, flee from here, flee and know what nightmarish ill-conceived De Mon pursues you until the expansion of space reaches its zenith and expands no more. Flee from me, flee from, Wrath... I will take my vengeance surveyor. Do you hear me? I will have it; if not in this life then in the next life beyond these walls." Wrath slowly retreats back into the shadow of the cell. "Yes, in the next life... where I will lay claim to the rule of eye for an eye. Till then, I'll sit here until he arrives. You do not know him yet who is to arrive, but a new god will come. He promised me. When he does, I will be set on high and from there, I'll see your end."

"Fate stopping short of the exit felt compelled to look back after being overcome with an ominous feeling that he was being watched. He Looks back over his shoulder down the hole of Palengrad in the vicinity of the forty seventh level where the crass face behind the holy water infused bars would have been if still exposed to the light.

From atop the outside promenade, Apollyon observes the exchange, smirking. He watches till Fate disappears beyond the massive doors. Taking a sip from his cup of Manna Nectar, Apollyon waves his hand closing the massive black smooth door. He then looks down toward the cell of Wrath's till he completely disappears back into shadows of his cell till all that can be seen is a singular red eye. The Warden again smiles, taking another sip as his gaze returns back to the closed massive door.

"The next life will come sooner than you think Fatetanen," Apollyon says and laughs. "Sooner than you think."

Six

KNIGHT TEMPLARS

"Without poise and regality, humans would be nothing more than untamed animals."

~Grandmaster Rhonda Brashear

Champagne-Ardenne, France (Knights Templar Headquarters)

"Commander Addi, enter!" says Grandmaster Brashear.

Commander Addi defines the definition of regal Gentlemen that superbly dresses to impress. His pristine black suit is the embodiment of perfection to the art of personally tailored wear. His swagger personifies confidence that most women would swoon over. If he noticed them that is. He is a man of devout faith. He has been in the service of the Knight Templars since he was 23, freshly discharged from the Queen's army. To see him now, more gray curls than black, one would instantly think his station was far superior to what the reality of his actual title was. His rank is easily identifiable to those in the order of Knights by the red marks on his white tie. He was titled as commander, but was in fact a commander of none unless it was of bureaucratic red tape. He's trained in combat, but his boss utilizes him for his other talents, specifically his attention to detail and unwavering loyalty.

Giving a slight bow before the Grandmaster, he places his briefcase beside the lone black chair with a red cross engraved in the back support. He unfastens the buttons of his single-breasted suit and adjust his tie slightly in anticipation of sitting before the Grandmaster. She doesn't invite him to sit. She purposefully leaves him standing.

Observing her annoyance, he decides to forgo the chair. He stands tall and refastens his suit blazer and stands to attention.

Brashear brushes crumbs to side off her desk from a sandwich she's just eaten prior to seeing Addi. She stares at him contemplatively for a second then begins brushing excess crumbs from off her shirt.

"The news out of China has gotten no better Addi. That was your region for the last year and Arcane forces are poised to capture it by way of diplomacy," says the Grandmaster.

There isn't a sound past the Grandmaster's voice in the room when she falls quiet. It is silent until the sound of a forceful gulp from Addi's Adam's apple as it bobs deep in the throat before he can muster wind into language that was clear of obfuscation.

"I understand, Grandmaster, but that abomination Imperial has revealed itself. My sources that were reporting to me have all gone silent. All of them have been dispatched quietly or forced into hiding in the last 24 hours."

Sipping her coffee, she places it back on the desk sure to keep decorum. Without poise and regality, humans would be nothing more than untamed animals.

"We are the last defense for our species," says Brashear. "The world is asleep Commander only awoken to this monstrosity yesterday. You know the human condition as well as I. After the shock, they will blindly follow this false god happily to their demise. We must keep the pressure on. We must be ready to aid the resisting forces that will arise in secret to oppose this creature that now sits to the right of Arcane. We must defy and deny them any allies and assets to the best of our abilities wherever they may arise. If China is negotiated into his expansion plans, that makes his empire even more formidable."

"To do this now in the open? It could become problematic down the line, Grandmaster," says Addi. "I offer the counsel of caution and continue to move with anonymity striking from the shadows with guerilla warfare tactics as Grand Prior Riggs did in New York. We keep the pressure up while this Imperial revelation is in its infancy. We do that and we just may expose him before he's accepted as Old Testament made new."

She steeples her fingers. "We no longer have the past luxury of operating from shadows or cohesive binding under the established church and her monetary protections that were provided and afforded us," says Grandmaster Brashear, taking another sip of her caffe. "We are under the Ragnarök Protocol. We are alone and autonomous."

"One is never alone," says an unknown voice that quietly and quite illegally crept into the main office of the Grandmaster's. "And if one is never alone, then you must understand that you yourself and your network of Knights whom have been the infiltrators with their ears on the pulse of gods and kings have yourselves been infiltrated."

The voice is deep and purposeful as it emerges from behind Commander Addi. Startled, the commander turns reaching into his suit jacket quickly undoing the fastened snap break of his leather holster containing his weapon. Before he can bring it to bear, a gloved hand places itself over his gun hand forcing him stay his weapon keeping it in the holster. Addi takes a step back into his attacker to free his hand. The stranger steps with him. He slightly twists Addi's wrist opposite of its natural tendon's range of motion, disarming him of the weapon. It thuds hard as it strikes the floor. Addi tries to regain his balance to deal with the attacker. The stranger simply pulls downward on the wrist lock maneuver and the commander is forced to a knee wincing in extreme pain.

"Commander Addi, please... your unwarranted attack against the cloth is forgiven son," says the stranger. "Your arrogance and presumptions are understandable in theses trying times. I personally absolve you of your maligned thinking."

Addi struggles to look up and over his shoulder. Surprised, he stops struggling and succumbs not to an assassin, but a man with one eye in white cleric collar and pastoral vestments. A priest wearing all black with a beaten black fedora that has apparently seen many miles winks at the commander with his one good eye. His other is covered by a black slender eyepatch with a red leather strap that affixes it around his head. The priest nods to the Commander gesturing it's okay to relax. Addi acknowledges the priest and quickly taps his arm yielding as if yielding to an opponent in a wrestling match. The priest kicks Addi's silver 1911 .45 caliber colt to the side of the Grandmaster's desk next to her trashcan.

"Pardons, Father," Addi says through pained clenched teeth.

"No need for pardons, commander. We are all on edge in these last days," says the priest, releasing Addi from the wrist lock.

Grandmaster Brashear is not moved nor does she show any signs of being frightened by the sudden attack of the probable assassin who found sheep's clothing to commit his sin in. She stands up undaunted by the events straightening and buttoning her black fitted suit jacket.

"I'm going to have to assume that our security is seriously inadequate if but a simple priest was able to breach our defenses," she says.

"Nonsense, Grandmaster, your security was formidable. It was actually a bit tougher than I expected," says the possible Assassin.

The priest pats Addi on the shoulder who's still getting up from his knees where he had put him just mere seconds ago. Moving slightly past him, the priest nods at the Grandmaster before sitting on the chair that the commander once thought reserved for him.

"You weren't given permission to sit there, Father if you are in fact a priest," Addi says, rubbing his wrist while simultaneously rotating his now aching shoulder.

"Why? There wasn't anyone sitting in it. You were standing next to it... Ehh, commander, if in fact you are a commander!" says the priest winking his good eye at Addi. "C'mon, lad, I'm just joking ya! Don't lose your shit. I'm here to speak to the Grandmaster on the business of allies wherever she may find them. Right, Grandmaster? That is what you just said, yes?"

The priest rocks back in the chair and looks at the Grandmaster, feeling that Addi will no longer be a threat to his person. Slightly disgusted with his performance, she waves Addi to stand down.

"It's fine, Knight Commander. It seems our guest has come with information that he thinks is vital to our cause at great expense to his own life. However, he does not seem to be educated on the current relationship of our organization and his beloved church. We must apparently learn him in the fact that we no longer answer to a dogmatic society of those of broken faiths and negated contracts," says Grandmaster.

"Coincidence, neither do I associate with such degenerates of the dogmatic society. See, we have already reached common ground in our negotiations, says the priest"

Grandmaster Brashear politely sits and gives equal observation of the priest. She looks him squarely in his lone eye giving him non-verbal permission to proceed.

"Thank you, Grandmaster for allowing this audience, this overdue meeting of the minds. I had to hurt a few of your knights to obtain these precious few moments, but it's nothing that won't mend in time. I didn't kill them, only because we'll need every man woman and yes, possibly child willing to fight before this is over."

The priest crosses his legs still sure to observe decorum. "Also, not to miss the added fact that I wanted to show you that I'm here with worthwhile intensions and worthy of this audience. I wouldn't have been able to obtain if I were to have slain your people."

She flashes him a quick smile nodding her head all the while caressing her matte black Colt 1911 .45 caliber under her desk. The weapon's current loadout entailed a silver silencer attached to it and customized red etched crosses on either side of the grip. The weapon was standard issue, but given unique love and care by the grandmaster. Her smile is but the distraction as her thoughts are more of the sinister variety of ending this assassin.

I should kill him dead this instance for such arrogant remarks, but damnit! Can't overlook the fact that he had to know that it was a one-way trip coming here. He must have something of importance. God! I hope he does for his sake. I hate to stain my floors, she thought.

"You've gone through a lot of trouble to gain this audience then priest so, let's hear it. What brings an assassin dressed as a priest to the Knight Templars? Are you the prelude to another Friday the 13th perhaps? You distract me while others attempt to nullify us?"

"Grandmaster Brashear, isn't it? Rhonda Brashear? The first female to hold the title. At least I think you were born a female," he says, smirking. "Can't tell with the huge balls you've shown over the past year. You know what, scratch female or male, you're more of a lowkey monster. A sociopath that is unsympathetic. Oh, yes, I've been watching you. You are a heartless bitch void of emotion and incapable of love? Does that diagnosis sound familiar?"

Brashear smirks in contempt. "That is my entry psyche evaluation assessment's diagnosis... Clever priest to have obtained those folders. The therapist also called me a monster, but just the kind they needed. I excelled quickly through the ranks here because of it."

"Then we are in agreement again. You are in fact a monster. The world needs them from time to time. Although, I kinda guess you'd have to be one to hold such an esteemed title as Grandmaster. Oh! And to correct your previous attempt at a juvenile slight toward me, your ignorance brought me here little lady. Infiltration was only the means to sit where I currently occupy. But those are just simple semantics of a gathering of words with attached meaning to get a rise out of you— a slight back toward you in equal opposition to your previous. However, let's move past fractured pride and who has the bigger dick. You'd obviously win that one."

Smirking still, she hates to admit it, but she's starting to like him. *Pity, I have to kill him still*, thinks Brashear.

"Let's do just that, priest, let's move on," Brashear says as she unsnaps her firearm from under the desk.

"Great, let's get to it then. Some time ago, you all sat in a room somewhere and decided that the church had been infiltrated at the highest level and had fallen prey to dark forces. Now, I don't dispute that, but we'd also been infiltrated by demons at the highest levels and that was long before the ethereal kind manifested into reality beyond legend and myth to play politics here on our Earth," says the priest.

The priest tries to hold in his laughter, but he can't. His own remarks send him into a laughing fit before he could even get it out.

"If you think about it, Rhonda, can I call you Rhonda? These great beings of legends have come to wage war of hearts and minds, spilling games of propaganda into the street. It makes me laugh when I think about how we thought of them with such reverence to only now see that they are as petty as us," says Dugan, laughing even harder. "Hell, they are us... or we are them."

His laughter is of the variety that you could tell before the world went to shit, that he was the guy who commanded the room through a joyous ideal of the way the world turned. His laughter is infectious and before too long the Grandmaster finds herself joining him not even knowing why.

"Sorry, but every pun was intended in that," he says as he regains his composure.

Grandmaster still keeps the shit-eating grin on her face, nods for him to continue while in the senate meeting of her mind all parts of the brain are in agreement in putting one round through the dome of his head. *That should be sufficient*, she thought.

"Well, you all that were in that meeting were right when you made the decision to enact your Ragnarök initiative. Lucien had infiltrated us long ago. I surmise he did it under the guise of a Pope although I haven't been able to figure which one. He then played the long game to get here where we are now and no one saw it coming, not even the Prophets of Scripture... Strange, don't you think that the Bible makes no mention of any of these events? It's as if were off course. Hmm! I digress. Well, take solace in knowing that we weren't the only institution that was corrupted. The attack in New York; you know, the ones where you guys became terrorists by leveling a city block and raising the U.N. building to the ground, that one? You were all under the sway of his demons and didn't even know it. The irony huh?" He starts to laugh again, except this time Grandmaster, she isn't laughing.

"Commander Addi blow this cocksucker's head off!" orders the Grandmaster.

The Commander quickly drops to knee and pulls a second holdout pistol from his ankle holster. Taking aim at the back of the priest's head he fires, but not before the priest moved his head left. *PUTOW!* The bullet passes by embedding into the Grandmaster's dark cherry oak crown molding in the wall behind her. Again, she doesn't flinch.

Slachk! The second round stovepipes, causing the weapon to jam. Addi is clearly trained with the weapon, but spent his life as a non-combatant. His limp-wristed shot caused the weapon to jam. The priest takes the precious seconds gained by the stovepipe. He knows Addi will have to clear it before firing again. Using the time to the best of his ability, he jumps forward toward the desk of the Grandmaster, twirling himself into a front flip. He stretches himself into a missile slamming both feet into dual kick that slams the desk hard sending it sliding into the Grandmaster.

The heavy behemoth of wood moves only centimeters after the dual kick, but it is enough that her hand is removed from muscle memory of pulling her weapon concealed beneath the desk. The priest flips up from the supine position to his feet grabbing the arm of the chair he was sitting in a mere few seconds ago. He does an Olympic discus twirl catapulting the chair into Addi sending him into the darkness of unconsciousness. The priest continues his revolution until he's a full 360 degrees on top of the desk looking down at Grandmaster Brashear. He flicks his arm down and depresses a latch on a silver metal cuff around his wrist disguised as a watch. A blade from underneath his sleeve ejects stopping short of Brashear's carotid artery which he can see it is pumping blood overtime compensating for the fear that has just been stoked in her.

"I have not come to see you decapitated, Rhonda. I've come to strike an alliance. You and I need to be of one accord, if we are to set prophecy to track... That is if you believe in that sort of thing."

She stares not only at the priest, but now her own mortality. She nods, yielding to him. He nods back and his blade quickly retracts back beneath his sleeve. He backs away and leaps from her desk. Keeping his one good eye on her, he picks the chair up and places it back where it was moments earlier and again finds his seat.

"Grandmaster, my name is, Jefarious Hennington Dugan and I am only here to give your order warning so that yours do not fall like mine when eventually the powers to be that move in shadow turn their attention toward you. And they will, trust me. I have but a singular vision and direction and that is I want to turn the tide of Lucien Arcane and his hell-inspired bastard that stepped into the light yesterday. My order of priests are all dead; cut down by that thing that calls itself Imperial in secret weeks before the revelation. I am the last of my sect that have been blessed to have an ear that can hear the whispers of heaven. With what I can see and hear and with your resources, we may yet put things right as they were meant to be... Or die trying. Which is probably more likely," he says, smiling. "However, either way we fulfill our vows that we took to protect our species and see them all to the second coming."

The Grandmaster squints, judging him silently. She leans in, hunching over her desk slightly and resting her elbows on it. "You're the promised prophet then priest, a modern day messianic?"

"Not so lucky to bear such a responsibility," says Dugan. "In the last days, there are to be those that can prophesize, but I'm not one of them that has been famed and framed by millennial Christian thinking. With these being the last days and none having stepped forward is further proof that things are out of alignment. Something has gone wrong in the heavens and I believe this Imperial is the cause."

"If you're no prophet, then what do you mean by having an ear to heaven?"

"I'll level with you straight Rhonda. Twenty-two years ago, I died performing an exorcism. It was a tough one. I remember very little of what transpired next, but when I was brought back at the hospital, I could hear snippets of the ethereal realm and see characters that move in shadow. The language was foreign to me at first. It was truly a case of the ant trying to understand the words of giant humans. Over time, the tongue became understandable. Words of De Mons and Archs had become native to me. Oh! Rhonda, the things I have learned," says Dugan, pointing his finger repeatedly at his temple.

"Proof?" the Grandmaster says. "Give me proof."

"I'm here, aren't I? Think, how does a one-eyed priest find the most secret of locations of the legendary Knight Templars? Let alone the head office of the Grandmaster?"

"How indeed?" says Grandmaster.

"How, Grandmaster? I overheard it."

Addi starts to stir from his forced respite that Dugan was not sorry to have put him in.

Brashear sits and leans back in her chair, obviously in thought. She judges his veracity as he tells his worth to ascertain a response from her. A response that would carry hope of an alliance between seven century old enemies that started in betrayal accumulating in scores of blood and bodies in just as many scores of centuries. She judges Dugan's intent to now achieve an aligned goal; to not only save the world, but then again place prophecy on path to destroy it enacting the second coming.

"Jefarious, was it?"

The priest nods, keeping his sense of presence of where Commander Addi is. "Please, call me Dugan."

"Just what was your sect of priests again, Dugan?" asks the Grandmaster.

"I assure you it's one your spies were elusive of." He winks.

"Elucidate me!" she says.

"Elucidate, that there is a ten-dollar handle word, says Dugan. "Your Harvard years were not wasted, Brashear, neither were your time in the seminaries. You see, our spies were just a wee better than yours... Oops! Our friend is starting to stir more than I'm comfortable with."

Addi, slowly gets to all fours as he shakes the fog of assault off. Blurry he sees enough to recognize that his attacker is now offering him an aided hand up off the floor. His glance in the direction of his Grandmaster signifies to him that some form of negotiating had taken place during his time in the unconscious depths. The once threat that is offering him a hand seems to have gone from foe to ally.

Fuck it! he thought and raised his hand for the assistance to show that he was in solidarity with his Grandmaster. Once to his feet he quickly proceeds to straighten himself while staring with pisstivity into the eye of the priest that kicked his ass.

"Sorry, Grandmaster, what I miss in my short absence?" asks Addi wiping a tiny stream of blood from his nose.

"Well, Commander, our prophetic priest here—"

"—I'm no prophet," Dugan repeats.

"Was just about to tell me the name of his order that was apparently wiped off the Earth by Imperial personally," says Brashear.

Addi continues to watch the priest also awaiting an answer.

"The name of my sect is no longer of any importance as we were never on any books. There were five of us. We were the forgotten stepchildren of the Vatican. What I can tell you is that we dealt in the fine art of adjudication of the mythical, mystical, and legends that bore humanity ill will. We worked hard to keep the night free of ungodly, indigent beings that survived the floods of Noah's day! In short, we slain monsters." He looks at the Grandmaster. "Present company excepted, Rhonda. We'd never had come for you," he says laughing to himself. However, it seems there is one more to slay."

The Grandmaster stands. "You are wrong of our common goals. I'm not helping to put anything on path to an end. We are trying to stay it off to give others more time to choose eternal life."

"Bullshit, Rhonda. You are buying more time, because of your innate fear of Death. I've seen him by the way... Death. I assure you should be afraid. This story we're in however isn't about you... You, like me are a bit character that has a part to play then it's done. The world is ending, there is no way to change that. How it ends is the question that faces us. It either ends in glory or subjugation. There is no staying it off. It's here; its already upon us."

"Let's say I believe you, Father Jefarious Dugan, was it? Can you tell me anything you've overheard of any strategic importance?"

"I can actually." Dugan pulls a pack of Marlboro cigarettes from his left front pant pocket. He slams the pack a couple of times packing the ciggs. He uncovers the opening in the package, striking the pack again expelling one filtered fug quickly placing it in his mouth. He looks over to Addi. Commander, please?

Addi reaches into his inside breast pocket for a lighter and lights Dugan's fug.

"I overheard these two phrases that just repeats in my head every hour of the day... They, are not gods and not since the time of the Judges has there been another."

"Judges? You referenced Judges... why?" Grandmaster Brashear asks.

"I did. And not since the time of Samson has a Judge of his worth walk the Earth... until now. I believe a judge has come for Imperial and we must find him."

Brashear stands fully encapsulated by the words of Dugan.

"The heavens have been quiet on the name of this judge, says Dugan. It's as if he's a secret even among the angels. However, a little sparrow suggested you may know Grandmaster. If you do, I need to know what you know. I have but one job and that is to kill monsters. I need to know who this judge is so that when he moves, I move all in a concerted effort to kill Lucien with these."

Dugan pulls his coat back revealing the ornate handles of 5 ancient daggers that he had sheathed in black leather scabbards with glyphs in gold affixed to the small of his back.

"One is mine, the other four belonged to my brothers of the order. Now, Rhonda, do you know where to find this judge?"

Rhonda studies him for a few moments not saying a word. *Damn him!* She is convinced that he is on the side of the angles. She spoke of allies and he seems to be the first willing to ally himself. Not what she had in mind though. The Knight Templars would need nations, not one lunatic priest with a death vendetta. However, he has proven resourceful to have made it this far. Had he wanted too; he could have assassinated her. That was a fact she couldn't ignore. With his skills, he just might can take the head of the serpent. She will trust her instincts.

"We have our suspicions," says Grandmaster. "I have a man planted closely to the subject we believe to be him. In time, once confirmed, I will give you a location and more importantly, maybe even a name. That is once you're thoroughly vetted," says Brashear.

Dugan reaches into his trench's inside pocket. He produces a card and throws it on Brashear's desk. He places his Malibu surfer's gesture of thumb and pinky finger to his ear and mouth simulating a phone as he backs away flirting with Brashear mouthing, "*call me.*"

Seven

SEEK AND DESTROY

"No one lives forever. To die falling from a screaming C270 into hell's hot of combat is the closet to God an ALRT soldier needs to be. May a blessing be added to the book of war."

~Major Justin Dale

Two months post Imperial's Revelation, Year 2045

Kaiserslautern, Germany: 48,000 feet above the city

"Give the team the green light that they are a go," says Lieutenant Brockington of the Arcanian Air Interceptor bomber designated C270. With one flip of switch, the co-pilot activates the green overhead lighting system in the lower fuselage cargo drop area of the plane.

Green lights activate and start oscillating as alarms blare. The plane's rear cargo door drops and a ramp begins extending slowly. Three teams of Arcanian Special forces and one Arcanian Lightning Response Team feels the frigid wind rush into the cabin. Major Justin Dale of the ALRT is the first to give his rifle a final check before leading the charge and jumping into free fall with all his battle armaments. Before joining the

Arcane enterprise, he'd been some sort of Special Forces his whole adult life. Had Arcane not intervened, he'd currently still be with Seal Teams, but Arcane ideals were grandiose enough that to be part of it felt like you were a part of a coming history. Also, he paid much better than the U.S. military. Sure, he was a prostitute if he thought about how easily he jumped in bed with Arcane's forces. Fine... He was okay with that cause in the long run, thinking of himself and his kid's future it had to be secured at all cost in such uncertain times as the world found itself in. His two girls had no mother or extended family. If he was going to put his particular skill set to use and risk his life, should he not be paid sufficiently for it?

Major Dale takes the plunge to Earth, rocketing at more than 120 MPH well past terminal velocity. The rest of the forces besides his follow suit and leap as well quickly falling into diamond formations descending upon an unsuspecting city in Germany that they have no jurisdiction to operate in. When did any of the countries infiltration dark ops teams ever ask permission to invade? And on top of such a question, there was another, who for sure was going to question the long arm of Arcane with an ethereal force backing him if he did decide to invade?

It was simple. Dale had but one mission: search and destroy. He opted for a drone to just destroy the questionable targets that the suspected terrorist may be holding up in, but the easy way was denied. He was told that visual confirmation was needed and a surgical strike performed. For him and his ALRT, that meant the hard way. His teams would now have to descend on the city under the cover of night and check each suspected location. The easiest way to complete the mission he decided would be to divide and conquer splitting his small force. He had two captains, two lieutenants, and gunnery sergeant that would help him do this. They could command the Special Forces teams while he commanded his own elite. The plan would cover more ground, saving the hospital for last since it was the largest. They'd meet there in the morning and search together if the suspect wasn't found elsewhere before then.

****

Kaiserslautern, Germany: St. Joseph Krankenhaus Medical Center

Being infirmed for a little over a month caused slight muscle atrophy. Atrophy... there's a word that Jericho's never spoken within his extensive vernacular of things that are common ailments of his life. The conflict that put him in the status of the now infirmed taxed his mental a great deal and physical even more. In the waning month of recuperation, he started a regiment to get his physique back in Marine warrior conditioning.

"*Hrrghhh!*" Jericho grunts, pushing himself skyward using two walnut-colored cabinets for triceps dip. He elevates toward the unnatural lighting of the fluorescent lights hanging from the ceiling. The strain of muscle draws pain inflaming the nerves, but it is a needed pain, a welcomed pain. He holds the apex of the elevation then slowly dips to where his elbows lock at ninety-degree angles. He holds his weight in suspension before again pushing back upwards performing his fifth set of shoulder dips. Exhausted he stops momentarily to let his muscles recover then he's off again pushing skyward before easing back down low between the cabinets forcing him to really work and sculpt his triceps and shoulders. He does another set of 5 for 25 reps. When he reaches muscle exhaustion, he lets his feet touch the floor and stretches his arms shaking them loosely to get the blood flowing properly. Still unable to shake the feeling of mission failure at the Embassy, he paces back and forth a few times throwing jabs before again placing himself between the cabinets putting each hand on top of either one of the walnut cabinets. He takes a breath and starts his 13th set of 25 reps.

Images of the condition he found in the embassy plays in his mind over again and again with each apex of the shoulder dips. Flashbacks of his loss to a superior foe who in one swipe took the heads of his men with but one violent action from his 7 ½ foot adversarial frame. Vivid memories haunt him of collecting the tags of his Master Chief and the two Seamen that were on lone to him from the Seals. *Where are the tags now?* he wondered. Where was his tags for that matter? For all the bravado talk he gave Gabriel, for all the belief that he was ready for what she promised was coming, it was clearly proven that he wasn't. He'd lost during the ensuing fight with the designated N.H.E., the Non-human Entity, an acronym that was created by the military, but never would have ever been thought used. What the hell was a N.H.E.? He knew first hand now what it was. It was, undeniability. It was strength that was unrivaled. N.H.E. took all he had and then some to inflict even the slightest of pain upon it.

Jericho found himself now grinning at the haunting memories. It was the thought that he was able to inflict pain. He'd bled the bastard. Old rules from one of his favorite classic movies Predator came to mind, "If it bleeds, we can kill it." A forceful knock on his door brings his mind back to the present.

Creeeeeaaaaak! The door to Jericho's makeshift hospital room whines as a poorly dressed gentlemen enters. At first glance Jericho plugged him to be a hobo recovering alcoholic who just jumped the railways from some who care to know place. Second thought that came to mind which should have been the first is that, obviously he's in the wrong room looking for a drunk hobo buddy so, they can go chase boos together.

Something's off about the hobo though; something is not natural that should be evident to coincide with how this stranger appears. He doesn't smell the part of how he looks. Then again if he did, his smell wouldn't outdo the natural odor of the hospital. If this place could be called that. It was more of a third world undeveloped country makeshift house of horrors disguised as a hospital. This place was where you'd come to be surgically hacked on and killed in a litany of ways, the most prominent and likely were from botched procedures to wrongly prescribed prescriptions. The place smells of malarkey and sweat from a baboon's balls. This hobo should smell equal if not worse than that, he doesn't. Jericho looks at the stranger with suspicion, but never breaks his stride in completing his tri dip set.

"Wrong room!" Jericho shouts. "The Methadone Clinic is two floors down."

The gentlemen wearing a hood and N95 face mask nods at Jericho then turns around making sure no one has followed him. Satisfied, he closes the door and turns his attention to the patient who's more than likely being an uncooperative one, working out against doctor's orders. The stranger slowly strides past Jericho glancing at him briefly and then averting his eyes, finding a seat in the corner of the small room. Jericho tracks him across the room ready for any ill will meant to be thrown his way. The stranger knocks the curtain away loosening them from the chair which was holding them back letting the city's natural light. The room darkens slightly. The derelict gentlemen begin to disrobe.

"I said wrong fucking room!" Jericho shouts louder.

"Well, son, I think dis here is the right fucking room. So, gotdamn rude, is that what the Corps taught you, Mr. Douglass Moody?" the gentlemen says, still disrobing his outer garb of an old dirty hooded sweatshirt. Jericho's unease falls away at the gentlemen's presence. He instantly knows that southern drawl anywhere.

"General Kov—?" says a surprised Jericho.

"Whoa, Douglass! Don't use that nomenclature here son. Here we must move and speak with an incognito nature about ourselves. You get me, son?"

Jericho nods. Naturally coming to attention for his superior officer. "I get you, sir."

General Kovac sits and removes his overly worn and beaten dark hooded sweatshirt and old Coast Guard ball cap. He looks at the cap, then to Jericho shaking his head before again glancing at the cap. "I know, no need to say it. It pained me to wear this more than you know. This shows you the great lengths and commitment, I went through to conceal my visage to be here."

Patting himself with a towel, Jericho stepped closer to Kovac. "So, you're the one to thank for such fine accommodations Gener— Err, what the hell do I call you then?"

"Crass will work."

"The name suits you. Although, I'd have said surly... But, you are a crass sumofabitch... Well, Crass are you responsible for these here ac-

commodations? I must admit, my stay has bordered on cruel and unusual."

"You're stay here son was in your benefit to keep you alive and
healthy as we ascertained the fallout from the Chinese Embassy debacle.
That transport mission needless to say was F.U.B.A.R. It was supposed
to be a simple pick up and transport son, nothing more," says Kovac.
"We wanted to know what that witness saw in the Congo."

"How bad was it Gener— Crass? I haven't been able to receive any
news here."

"That's because of me. You were on media blackout per my orders.
If you were to wake from your coma and see what had transpired without someone to context it for you, I feared you would've inadvertently
blown the cover story that was concocted for your benefit as well as
the United States Marines. I mean, imagine our surprise Mr. Moody
when a simple prisoner retrieval turned into an international fucking
incident. The entire Embassy was destroyed, her people eviscerated including three Seal Team members and the elite security forces of Republic of the People's Army of China. As you could imagine there was
of course some questions to what exactly our involvement was," says Kovac.

"Damn sorry, sir!" Jericho catches himself at the sir rank a bit late.
Old habits and all that.

"Don't call me sir, not here. Get in the habit of calling me Crass, son.
Don't want anyone in our business that don't need be. I kept dis here
circle intimate while you were stashed here."

Jericho parts his lips.

"And, no, you were not abandoned by the Marines, son. I advised
that priest buddy of yours and that young philly on the next of kin of
the reasoning why I had you stashed here. I made the lass believe that
imminent danger would befall you if it was known there was a survivor
of the embassy incident. With that information, I believed she would
be more inclined to keep this arrangement hush. So, just to reiterate
our position of where we all currently stand is precarious at best. You
weren't talking after the encounter. There was no way to illicit infor-

mation that you had as the sole survivor. Without your debriefing, we were left guessing as to what you encountered that was able to dispatch Seals, an elite guard of Chinese troops, kill the witness and destroy an embassy, killing all souls."

Creak! The door opens again. Isis walks in pausing at the sight of Jericho up and Kovac talking with him. She nods at the General and continues toward Jericho with two coffee's she's procured. One for him surely against doctor's orders. She uses the back of her heel to kick the door close. "Crass?"

"Afternoon, darling," replies Crass.

Jericho uses a towel to dry the sweat from his chest and underarms. "I'm up and aware now sir. I want to know what you know."

"And I want to know what you know, Mr. Moody. So, I guess a game of quid pro quo is in order here, son."

Jericho nods. "I'm game. Let's play."

Eight

VINTAGE

"History had it wrong; it wasn't Oppenheimer who'd become death. It was Marcum Jensen, beloved son of Margit and Claude Jensen. It would not be some mad warrior that commit genocide on a global scale, no, it would be a prodigy pathologist who ended up firing the shot that was never heard that killed a third of the planet."

~Arrow

U.S. Army Medical Research Institute of Infectious Disease Fort Detrick, Maryland

Marcum Jensen's yawn was a long fierce one. He'd been up off and on for more than 50 hours studying a stubborn strand of Ebola out of West Africa. The sample was supposedly sent from field agents more than a week ago from Aswan, Egypt. That place had become the cradle of the worlds emerging diseases for some strange unknown reason in the early 2000's. Before then Aswan wasn't even on the map.

The Marathon study session for sure exhausted Marcum, but the hell with exhaustion had become his mantra. His dream job was coming up for grabs; a chance to work with Nicholas Polanski. Success today was his ticket to the majors of epidemiology. Anyone that worked for

Polanski was on the fast track of success. Before today's chance, Marcum was only a low-level office jockey working on loan to the U.S. Military from the CDC. He was discovered by Nicholas Polanski in a game of mere chance and happened to impress the man with his knowledge on communicable passage rate of disease and how to quickly track it. In return, he was given a chance improve his lot as well as his credentialing status. If hired by Polanski, he would work for the foremost expert in the field of infectious diseases.

He'd received his test parameters. The scenario was given that he must crack the DNA sequencing code to a new strand of disease that had mutated twice since it's discovery. Marcum already had a game plan which was to identify and begin the detective work of backtracking its origin from patient zero of the last known mutated strand. The test devised by Polanski himself was an operation meant to tax the mind within tight time constraints while being deprived of sleep. He had 72 hours to complete the task and he was already 57 hours in. He'd sleep when he was dead. That was the aphorism wasn't it that doctors battling diseases live by?

The young upcoming epidemiologist wanted his shot only, he just didn't understand how important he was on the path to perdition. Unfortunately, when Marcum was born, he was born to the beat of forces that were much older and greater than him in a cosmic battle that has ignited the cosmos. As he thumbed away on his keyboard following strands of DNA sequences that had been pathed previously, how could he have known he was encoding the language of biblical prophecy?

Briefly stumped, Marcum rubs his hands over his stubbled hair face. There hasn't been time to shave since he started. Those would have been precious minutes waisted. Time was an enemy this day. He rolls back from his desk taking a brief ride in wheeled leather chair over to the electron microscope. There, an array of glass slides was displayed sealed in airtight plastic wrap encasing them.

After more than six years of graduate studies, another 4 of PhD stress inducing tests and essay examinations applying learned knowledge to practical application, he's arrived to this place in time culminating all of his knowledge and skill. All that accomplishment and really, how long is anyone ever satisfied? Nicholas Polanski was responsible for Marcum wanting to up his dream. Rumors had it, Polanski was being eyeballed to run the entire infectious department for the Arcane Institute of Military Science and everyone in the know knew that Arcane had the best technological equipment to date. It was better than what the U.S. or China could ever create. Everyone in the know also knew that he had slots that he was filling with the best of the best. Hands down and pound for Pound Marcum knew he was one of them; one of the best and would have that slot.

"Jensen, you good?" a voice boomed over the P.A. system.

Marcum's left hand went up giving the okay sign, which much to his chagrin looked more like the Hugh Heffner playboy symbol.

"You've been at it for quite a few hours now. Take a break and let Ms. Rosen have a crack at breaking down the genetic sequence," the voice again boomed over the P.A.

"No way!" yelled Marcum. "She cracked the Perengoti. No way am I going to let her crack this one before me." He laughed. It was a nervous laugh to replace his stress.

He was dead serious though; she would not crack it before him. He had nothing against Rena, she was exceptional. They were the same age and had graduated with their Doctorates the same year. Before arriving to this day, he'd seen Rena more than a few times over his graduate years when they were competing for scholarship dollars. Matter of fact it was Rena and another woman that were seemingly always in a three-way tie for grants. The name of the other woman often slips his mind.

Argh! What was the other woman's name? thought Marcum. It was Irene, Ice or Isis, something to that effect. Anyhow, the other girl was a non-factor, she wasn't even in their field of infectious disease. She was just an annoyance in receiving grant money. Anyhow, Rena's third-year research paper destroyed his by light years when she wrote her paper on the unstoppable pathology of a highly fictitious communicable disease that had more than an 84.2 communicability rate. *Whew! 84.2 communi-*

cability passage rate that was a worse case nightmare of all nightmares scenarios, thought Marcum.

In her paper, it addressed the human frailty of fear that would break all safety protocols to contain this fictitious disease. The shit was some scary apocalyptic stuff and what her revised protocols called for was some even more dark hardcore shit. After her submission and publication of that paper CDC was on her. They immediately hired her and not only paid her tuition from that year all the way to completion of her Doctoral, they paid the entire remaining balance of her student loan. The girl was one of the best. Polanski was all over her in recruiting her and enticing her away from the CDC. However, this was not her moment, this was his time to impress and she would not upstage him again. A promotion was coming, and he would secure it. All the time he's put in and youthful years that he'd sacrificed? The universe owed him and he'd come for payment.

Promotion to Polanski's field work drove his passion of cracking the mutational path of this particular strand of virus. It was a combination he'd never seen, but it wasn't enough isolation originality to call this strand new. At least he thought it wasn't. If he'd jump the gun and be proven wrong, promotion to field work would be lost to Rena more than likely. Damn that! She'd get field work, and he'd remain a quarantined lab rat sentenced to a few more years of simple identification and labeling outbreaks in the underpaying CDC? Hell with that!

Ahh! There it was, the piece that he was looking for. A smile runs the face of Marcum. A little perseverance was all it took. Cracked! He'd done it. The only sad part was there was no points of originality. It was an old strand of virus that mutated within a host with partial immunity that was already built into his DNA at birth. Either his ancestral mother or father or possibly a much older ancient ancestor had been infected and survived creating a shield of sorts through generations.

The cosmos was funny that way. An infection mutates over centuries destroying parts of humanity like a ravaging wildfire only to be brought to heel by a child that had natural immunity which isn't discovered until by chance when the child passes away in a car wreck. Through more chance and a spot of luck, his blood samples would be found and later utilized to create a defensive vaccine. All which wouldn't have been found had the random kid not passed. He was born meant to die to save lives all the while inadvertently furthering the career of Dr. Marcum Jensen so that he could play his part in the later destruction of a third of humanity. The cosmos was funny that way. It was disorganized planning. Yup, that oxymoron summed up the cosmos.

"It was the father indeed," says Pestenant in his raspy voice from behind Marcum placing his hands on his shoulder.

Pestenant, a name distorted over the line of communications between the heavens and the prophets of old when an original prophet misplaced vowel later translated it into Pestilence. A name that over the millennia had become synonymous with disease that set a path for Death to follow.

Pestilence began to massage Marcum's shoulders from the safety of the reality 1814 where he remained unseen. He'd chosen his carrier that would usher in his next plague of sickness. Contrary to what Fate had written of the carrier, the scribe had never mentioned him by name. To Pestilence, Fate had no hand in his choice. It was him that discovered Marcum's soul exiting the Well of Souls in Zero Realm, not Fate.

Closing his eyes to hear more clearly, Pestilence listens to Marcum's thoughts. "Ahh! I see." The De Mon turns toward the glass partition that Rena Rosen was observing his progress through. It was clear as a Nosforian Crystal, he lusted her and she thought he was cute and was equally enamored with him and his intelligence.

"Why Marcum, you love her, don't you?" Pestilence says mockingly.

Love makes humans stupid, but also ripe for destruction with a just little subtle shove. Mortals were predictable because of that. Always thinking everything revolved around them for their benefit.

"Well, let's check her out, shall we?" Pestilence walked through the observation partition for a closer look. He read her forehead and smirked at Rena. Instantly, he was awed by her ingenuity and vast intelligence. He delves deeper into her conscious and unconscious mind. Within a matter of seconds, He'd found and read her research report on the 84 % communicable disease doomsday scenario and found he was just as impressed as Polanski.

"Ohhhh, Marcum, I approve of this one," says Pestilence smiling. "What the two of you together could conjure would lay waste to my past efforts of concocting a disease that would all but derail the progression of human kind." The cloaked De Mon smiles and waves bye to Rena by rolling his fingers as if playing a piano. "Till later gorgeous. Ohhhhhh, the beautiful music the four of us as a quartet are going to make together," says Pestilence. "The three of us and Polanski will forever change the face of disease. Canceranian is going to be pissed."

As fast as the De Mon was there behind Marcum, in that same instance, he was gone. He slid into another reality still watching Marcum, his Trojan horse to rid the Sadohedranicverse of the infectious plague of mortals. Pestilence faded away completely again leaving Marcum alone in the pressurized sealed room contained within his own personal pressurized level three Vac suit.

Success! Marcum raises his hands in triumph. He'd cracked the case and all but ensured his promotion to field work under the eyes of the Arcane institute. At least that's what he was promised if he'd cracked the case in under 72 hours. It was a promise that he knew the director Nicholas Polanski would make good on. After all, it was Nicholas that had seen the spark and came to give him the snowballs chance in hell for possible recruitment.

From what Marcum knew of Dr. Nicholas Polanski, he had a quiet way about him. Some that worked with him in the past said that there was a time when he was a jovial man, a joy to be around and that his laugh was infectious even in times of severe distress. Marcum can't say he's ever seen that man. In the time since the new breed of researchers such as himself and Rena had been around, they've never seen the man bare any teeth during a moment of pleasure. Marcum heard after the death of his older brother some years back he'd never been the same. No one really talks of the older Polanski other than he was at one time the top geneticist in the world in the employment of the Arcane institute. If true, the Polanski's have exceptional genes and were meant to be where they were in life. The cosmos was funny that way. It placed people like chess pieces. One succeeds off the movement of another exceptionally placed piece.

Marcum turns toward the viewing glass and takes a bow believing the cosmos had finally come to set him on his path of greatness. Rena looks at the screen above her side of the window and studies the results of Marcum's triumph. She nods and concur with his solution. She looks back at him clapping giving him a bow for his ingenuity. Soon she was joined by Dr. Polanski who'd walked in and stood next to her behind the glass partition. He begins clapping as well. Through the partition Marcum can't hear Dr. Polanski, but he watches as the director mouths the words, "Great job, well done... Well done, indeed."

Pestilence is back and walks up clapping behind the two as well unseen to everyone mouthing the same words as the Director.

"Well done, Marcum, well done. You have inadvertently created a masterpiece," says Pestilence as leans forward kissing Rena on the cheek in excitement. "Marvelous, simply fucking marvelous." He again stares at Marcum. "It's War's time now. He has been given the authority to make his namesake across the land. Sure, his will of brutal wanton destruction will ravage the resolve of mankind, but soon as it was written, I, Pestilence, will have my time and it will be glorious."

Watching Marcum and Rena, Pestilence continues slow clapping in anticipation that he will soon be authorized to have his season and when it arrives it will not be wasted. A petty rival to compare his destruction to that of War's, but he knows a little competition is healthy. It raises each of the participants' level of playing the game. He and War have been competing for years. With what he's seen in the lab today, he can pretty much claim victory. Not only would humanity fall and bow to any savior that rise with an elixir of life, he'd best War. That was good enough for him. Why shouldn't he be second to Lucifer, War has had his run long enough.

An hour later after all the celebratory laughter and bows of recognition of a job well done, Marcum completes the mundane task of logging and storing his approved technique into the World Health Organization's database in case his process is needed for duplication at a later time. Colleagues from anywhere around the world with access can find his solution. Storage finally completed; he begins the arduous task of final protocol of the laborious task of cleaning the infectious workspace down to the molecular level.

Satisfied, Marcum steps out of the lab and depresses the wall mounted button that shuts the automated air tight titanium door. In seconds the lab will be superheated to hellish levels sure to destroy any missed particles of highly infectious disease. Yes, the procedure was tedious, but what would the alternative be if they weren't... utter world devastation? Damn right! It's one of those chores that if it could be delegated to someone else, he sure would have loved to, but no one will ever be more thorough than who's ass was on the line. So, even in his exhausted, but celebratory state he was proficient in his clean up and disinfection. He watches the room turn a bright orange glow as the flames do their thing. He glances left to the added failsafe layer of three other watchful eyes observing that the cleanse protocol was completed. They nod good to go. He nods back in agreement. He was now free to decon himself and leave the lab proper.

Watching the air set ablaze, Marcum felt a slight unease. It made him turn inward to find why he just couldn't seem to feel settled. He recounted the events of the day and couldn't understand why he felt an unease about its ending. He was certain all tasks were completed. The decontamination process went off without a hint of carelessness. As nagging as his feeling was, he just brushed it off on being tired. A great many of hours he forewent sleep. Ultimately, it was just too bad he didn't give a little more though to what nagged him; if he'd thought back in hindsight just a bit more, he would have realized that there was one thing missing before the decon. It was miniscule, but wasn't it his job to pay attention to detail? Had he thought a second longer in the decon shower he would have thought about a missing sample encased in dual pressed micro glass the size of a sim card. It was a detail so small, that he simply overlooked it. Why should he have seen it? It was missing at the completion of his study... well, taken to be more exact by a vengeful spirit.

Damn shame as things goes in life, the small slide that had gone missing unfortunately was not the test case that he'd cracked. That would have had a chance of being contained. That feeling of unease was his subconsciousness reminding him of his inept detective skills at locating and identifying a strand of disease that he'd accidently grabbed in preparation for his testing and misplaced. It wasn't even supposed to be in his kit, let alone next to or even under the microscope. When preparing for the test he accidently knocked a sample tray over in the freezer housing unit. The glass was tempered of course. A simple drop would not crack samples. What were contained on those pieces of glass could with stand a hammer strike. Behind those small templets of glass is in most cases are life up enders.

Up enders Being the case, Marcum was careful to place them back, but you can always count on the human error factor to rear its ugly head. He missed one. And it wasn't a simple one. What he accidently picked up and carried out was a prehistoric Jurassic age compilation of a complex strand which was similar too and had become known and labeled as, the rhino virus. Except, this wasn't the Rhino Virus. It was something much more archaic, so much so, it never new the origin of man.

Pestilence phases through the front entrance of U.S. Army Medical Research Institute of Infectious Disease. He walks away looking at the sample of the Old-World Satiate Virus that mortals accidently stumbled upon some years ago when pulling a frozen mammoth's remains from the ice. It didn't ride the Mammoth though, no... it was trapped in the Ice. It was eventually logged, categorized, and stashed away for later study until inept record keeping misplaced the vial eventually mixing it into testing vials addressed for research. If scientist knew what they'd found, rest assured they would have quietly destroyed it. The righteous boy scout Dr. Tarius to be exact would have destroyed it, because his righteous supermanesque nobility would not have allowed him to let a form of virus like that exist. Tarius missed it while placating to Selena

Frothman's breast. And if you must know, they were that auspicious that Tarius could not have been blamed as the slide passed unknowingly through his hands. He missed it; Pestilence however did not miss it. The deadliest plague known in the history of mankind was now in his reality bending wraith's hand. Smiling, Pestilence wings switchblade from out underneath his cloak. He takes to the skies completely disappearing with his Judas Paradoxical prize.

Marcum Jensen was the Judas Paradox in all its glory. The paradox will suggest that it was always Marcum's written destiny to unfold such events as the misplacing of a world destructive viral sample. It was inevitable. It would have always been him chosen as co-conspirator to an Old-World virus secreted away underneath innocuous samples of a test case scenario. It would have always been him that would undoubtedly give rise to Pestilence. History had it wrong; it wasn't Oppenheimer who'd become death. It was Marcum Jensen, beloved son of Margit and Claude Jensen. It would not be some mad warrior that commit genocide on a global scale, no, it would be a prodigy pathologist who ended up firing the shot that was never heard that killed a third of the planet.

Nine

QUID PRO QUO

"A world truce won't hold. This will become a battle of faiths; a battle of the monarchy versus the right to autonomy."

-Isis Rayne.

Kaiserslautern, Germany:
St. Joseph Krankenhaus Medical Center

Kovac currently under the alias Crass, nodded in acceptance that he was to go first in this game of quid pro quo. It's understandable that trust would be a little admonished from the lad's perspective. After all, he is recovering in what could be likened to a third world country's medical ward where you send your destitute unwanted and unloved to die amongst the hardened aroma of stale hallway piss.

"Let's play the game, son. You've been through a lot and I need to know what the hell you know. I need to understand what happened at dat Embassy over der," says Kovac, his southern drawl more prominent. "Da Joint Chiefs are losing their shit you hear and it's not from just this international relations nightmare. After everything went Fubar—"

Jericho intently tries to follow Kovac alias Crass, but there she is... Isis. Her beauty, her sway, the gait of her walk, her eyes, the way her hair flows. He's enamored. Sure, the fact she was there all the while he convalesced forever placed her in the pantheon of love arena, but this moment that has snuck up on him is not about love. Lust, was what this was. He wanted her. Most times he couldn't think of anything but her. This is one of those moments. Out of nowhere he is turned on. Maybe it is the fitted above waist length leather jacket? No, it wasn't that, it is the nicely semi just barely visible abs that were exposed by the short crop halter top and the nice well sized C cup breast. *"FUBAR!"* Crass shouted loudly, was the word that brought Jericho's mind back to the present.

"Fubar?" says Isis, confused.

The military and their acronyms were a bit too much at times. It was a whole other language that linguistics would pick apart in a thousand years and sort it from the bones and antiquities they were all sure to become. Isis laughs to herself internally at the fact she would herself become the very work she'd love so much. She would be someone's antiquated discovery to find someday.

"Fubar means fucked up beyond all recognition," answers Jericho.

"Oh! Got it. Sorry," says Isis, looking into Jericho's eyes briefly. "Continue."

"Mmmm!" mumbles Crass, looking at Isis before returning his attention to Jericho. "Not only do we have your incident to deal with Mr. Moody, there is the little occurrence of a supreme being that has appeared and has trumped your international incident... for the moment that is. I assure you though the Chinese have a long memory and when this N.H.E. news has grown old; they will be sure to return attention toward us."

Jericho's expression turns to one of puzzlement that Kovac used the acronym N.H.E. as currently present.

Crass snaps his fingers with an overexaggerated gesticulation. "Shit, I almost forgot der fo a moment that you'd been napping the day the Earth stood still and all went quiet... The day of the Imperial revelation."

Jericho looks even more puzzled.

Kovac sighs. "We'll get to that directly. Before that, let's start with the embassy. When things went fubar on the prisoner transport, I came here immediately dressed down incognito to investigate. From what I gathered, there was a communique blackout. There were no transmissions coming in or going out of the embassy or any of the surrounding areas. When reports did begin to flood in, intelligence reported that a Seal team had been recovered by Chinese authorities. They were unidentified by name at the initial intake of information. Wasn't a long walk in the park for me. I sent a four-man escort team, three were Seals attachment. Didn't take a rocket scientist to know who they were and that one was unaccounted for... you. Eventually as the flow of communication started to trickle again, it wouldn't be long before D.N.A. processing spearheaded by the Chinese government would confirm the identities of the Seals. When that happened, it led to bigger questions, because apparently the left hand of their Empire didn't know what the right hand was doing. The prisoner transport it seems was not cleared by the Peoples Republic."

Jericho head hung a bit low at the mention of the Master Chief. "My team... they were my responsibility and I le—"

"Stow that shitful woe is me talk son till I'm finished," Crass interrupts. "You'll have plenty of time for regret and therapist later."

Kovac knows the boy is a competent leader and has a big round set of cohunes, but he needs him not to crack under pressure of shit that he can't control. He's seen an awful lot of commanders mentally break giving way to guilt and blame always believing they could have done something more to change the course of fluid events of combat. Kovac's experience has taught him you can't change what's happening nor what's happened during combat. What the hell happened is just life. He didn't need Jericho taking that plunge of regret and despair right now. That is the lot of men, always attempting to control what won't. Kovac alias Crass continue, keeping the man's mental state in mind.

"However, what was missing from the intelligence report that was trickling in was information on the fourth man of the team, my Marine Captain., nor was there a body recovered."

Jericho glances at Isis and finds her watching him with such concern. He feels a bit slighted by her that she hadn't let any of this information Kovac was telling him slip in his brief time of walking among the conscious. Then again, could he blame her? She has no idea how the information would be received if only given in bits and pieces with no context. After a side thought on feeling a bit betrayed, the final determination his mind and heart agreed on was that she cares deeply and knew enough about him to wait till all the information could be given. *She guessed right,* he thinks. Had he only had partial information and misconstrued it improperly in the haste and fog of anger, then there was no place of confinement that would have held him in his search for truth to gain all the information he needed. He would have broken out of here causing all types of ruckus drawing unwanted attention.

Spop! Crass snaps his finger, bringing Jericho back from wherever his mind had just wandered off too. "Understand, son, the Embassy transport was my operation originating at my command level on information that I had received. You all were my people under my command, my concern, my responsibility. When I couldn't locate you and you hadn't checked in, I secretly ordered a search of nearby medical facilities with men that I felt were most loyal. It so happened, that I was the one to eventually come here to this beaut of medical ingenuity and cutting-edge medicine, Kovac said sardonically."

Sarcasm for sure isn't lost with this one, thinks Jericho.

"I found your pitiful looking ass here, Mr. Moody. From what I was able to gather, you were an unknown civilian blown up near the blast site. You were found unconscious covered in blood and soot with no type of identifying clothing and extremely of the African descent. Great for you they left out the American portion. When I found you, you looked like death. Hell, I thought you were dead at first glance. Don't know how you survived, but you did. Even more remarkable is how fast you've recovered." He just stares at Jericho. "Miraculous even," says Kovac staring closely at the captain. "Anyway, good graces found you outside the incident and it appeared to be no record of you anywhere near the attack. Thank god for small favors such as the communique blackout. Seeing you in such a mess I saw a positive out of a negative. I thought it best to play it safe and hide you in the open. I kept you stashed here and arranged for a trusted medical staff to tend to your wounds and continued treatment here. It's now been two months since your pathetic looking ass was found. Since then nothing has materialized in any manner pertaining to you."

"Well, the world has been preoccupied as of late Mr. Crass," Isis is quick to point out giving him a wink.

"There is that," he replies. "The pursuing government that would have great interest in you has been off task following the ever-evolving situation that began in the United Nations shortly after the fall of the Embassy here.

"So, the Chinese government has no knowledge of him whatsoever?" says Isis.

"That's right. For now, it appears their government has no credible knowledge or intel of you Moody. We'd like to keep it that way," says Crass. "That is the most up to date assessment of your escapade that kicked off less than thirty-two blocks away."

Jericho raises his hand.

"Speak freely Mr. Moody," says Crass.

Jericho nods, taking in the information making sense of what's been explained. After a few seconds to gather himself for his array of questioning, he knew the first one. "Who in the hell named me Douglass Moody?"

Tension evaporates as everyone laughs.

Crass looks at Isis. "It'll be the lass right here son that your chaplain friend told me about. I just assumed she didn't like you much giving you such a horrid alias."

"It was short notice and I felt on the spot when they asked," she says, shrugging her shoulders. "You should have heard what Jason wanted to name you. Trust, you'd be thanking me for Douglass Moody the way you two jackasses joke."

"Speaking of assholes, where is Jason?" asks Jericho.

Isis brings the coffee over to Jericho. "He was called away on some errand. He saw one of old professors here checking the psych ward on a follow up or something while getting for what passes as coffee around here. The professor needed him."

"Oh!" says Jericho, looking down and feeling a bit disheartened. "It's not uncommon for exorcist to check psych wards for demonic possessions. One must have been here and found something."

Kovac turns his attention back to Jericho. "Quid pro quo, Moody, you now know what I know. I need to know what you know and I mean yesterday."

Nodding in agreement, he turns towards Isis and blows her a kiss for doing what she could to shield him. He pulls the end of his bed closer toward Kovac, alias Crass and sits facing him turning his coffee up for a sip. "Mr. Crass, what I have to tell you will change the face of modern warfare forever. What brought down that Embassy can't be stopped... Probably, by no conventional means. What took down my team and dished me a serious helping of fubar was an N.H.E. probably the same one you mentioned earlier. Can't be a coincidence."

Isis can't help herself. She laughs at the fubar verbiage. Both men look at her as she tries to contain the outburst. She places her finger up asking for a moment to compose herself. Once the case of the giggles had subsided, she gesticulated for them to continue. The laughter burst out again. Kovac and Jericho just ignored her this time.

Kovac's right eyebrow shoots upward. He takes a breath and leans back in his chair \. "Tell me about dis here N.H.E."

Jericho told Kovac every detail leading up to the fall of the Embassy that his mind could remember before everything went dark. Secrets be damned, he held nothing back. He didn't even hold the fact that he went toe to toe with the entity that he'd described as unstoppable and insanely powerful. To cleave a man's head from his body in one fail swoop is no easy task. It takes power plus precision of an executioner to succeed at such a move. This was a moment that Jericho had to take the one step that he never wanted to till absolutely necessary; he had to trust someone outside his microcosmic circle with his secret. Why not take a gamble on Kovac, alias Crass? The man didn't have to be here personally. He chose to be here and chose to keep him a secret.

Kovac's face did not betray one emotion as Jericho finished the tale which would definitely seem like a tall one. When finished debriefing him, he didn't bother swearing Kovac to secrecy either. He gave the general a wide berth on what he saw fit and prudent to push up the chain of command to inform the Joint Chiefs. How much or how less was totally left to his discretion. A chancy move, but it would reveal if Kovac was a true ally. Best to know now if he wasn't, because there was no way around the coming fight. He would need as many allies as he could find in the Heavens above and the Earth below. Jericho silently hoped ally would be the outcome. He'd seen the threat first hand on the grounds of the Embassy. What he experienced was not an overactive make-believe imagination or a dream it just so happened he couldn't awaken from. The N.H.E. was real and he was the stuff of nightmares.

An hour after Jericho's debriefing and few more round of quid pro quo, General Hiram Kovac, alias Crass stood in silence peering out the windows of Jericho's third-floor rear building's hospital room which was equivalent in size to a supply closet. Actually, it was a supply closet or had been one till recently. The closet had been turned into a less than suitable room for patients after the economic collapse of the area. The once talked about greatly prestigious hospital had fallen on hard times later becoming a less than favorable cesspool for the poverty-stricken. They no longer had the monetary base to expand so, they restructured the interior to accommodate the growing number of disenfranchised patients. They had to make room to expand wherever they could.

Kovac stares past the dank garbage filled alley with his hands clasped firmly behind his back. He actually has one of the better views from this floor overlooking the poverty-stricken area. He's lost in thought with the information that he's just received. It's taking him time to process the tale that was just laid on him.

Kovac never removing his gaze from the window. "So, if I'm to believe you, Mr. Moody, that being of divine intelligence and glorified beauty that touched down in New York with a linage that touches God is in fact a superior enemy combatant that fights Lucien dirty wars in secret? I have to compute this... An N.H.E, is currently sitting upon this planet claiming to be an emissary from the lord god almighty and his truth is not to be contested," Kovac, alias Crass, says in a deep-toned voice imitating Imperial. "The not contested part was all him by the way. My impressions suck."

"I agree," says Isis. "Don't do that again!"

Kovac has Jericho's full attention now. "Imperial? How long has he been in the open?"

"Just over a month and a half," answers Crass.

Jericho instantly looks at Isis. "That entity has been on the world stage for almost two months and you never said a thing?"

"Wise ass, you were comatose for more than half the time. Then you were in recovery after you woke. When Crass asked, that we keep the outside world to a whisper in here, I couldn't have agreed more," says Isis.

"Shit!" Jericho mumbles under his breath. "What has been the fallout since his reveal?"

Kovac grabs his chair again and sits facing Jericho. "The fallout since the United Nations attack brought the world to a halt. The night of revelation, as it has come to be called, put the nation if not the world into a stunned phase. The first month across the continents had gone almost completely quiet with warring factions ceasing all hostilities. I guess watching twenty-four-hour news coverage of a once thought mythical being traipsing about the globe was more astonishing than petty squabbles... At least for the time being."

Jericho looks over to Isis. "And the denominations of faith?"

"The world's religions didn't know what to make of Imperial—" says Isis.

Shocked, Jericho cuts Isis off shaking his head signaling his disbelief. "Imperial is what it calls itself? It has a name? Sorry, you were saying?"

Isis nods her head. "Oh yeah, he has a name! The name Imperial has been on the tongues of all denominations of faiths. It was silence from them at first as they listened to the message that he brought. Theologians of all faiths went to work studying him instantly."

"What is his message?" asks Jericho.

"That the world falls in line behind Heaven's chosen leader—"

"Lucien Arcane," Jericho finishes.

Kovac and Isis nod their heads in agreement.

Taking a sip of her coffee, Isis finishes the phrase, "Lucien Arcane, the man that has been blessed and anointed to lead us into the next world of peace and civility. A new age that will always remain bright never to extinguish into darkness."

"Again, his words, not ours," says Kovac.

"It didn't take long before the faiths fell into disagreement over his message," says Isis.

"It didn't take long for the human element to interpret the shit out of a clear and concise set of instructions," interjects Kovac aka Crass.

"Which were?" says Jericho, looking back to Kovac.

"You heard it... In a nutshell, Lucien Arcane has proven himself the worthiest of all us humans to fulfill his god given role as a modern-day prophet to the Lord God Almighty and that through him a new nation of peace is to be constructed. Simply put, we follow him for a better to-morrow today," says Kovac. "Just like the mantra and slogan of his empire."

"To what end?" says Jericho. "That sounds like a fucking ultimatum to me. Just given politely. Follow me or else... Where does the United States fall on the matter?"

Kovac clears his throat. "I'm only a one star. That question is above my paygrade son. Since his touchdown and order to cease all current hostilities, no major skirmishes or declared wars have followed. I'm sure Imperial's decree is a major reason China has not responded in retaliatory force against us for the perceived slight that we attacked their Embassy."

"We were trying to save it," says Jericho.

"A world truce won't hold," says Isis. "This will become a battle of faiths; a battle of the monarchy versus the right to autonomy."

The lights in the room flicker for just a second. Within the blink of darkness, a hooded ethereal appears behind Jericho. Their face covered in shadow from the drawn hood. The ethereal reaches out and lightly touches Jericho on the shoulder. "Affairs immediately outside of this place of healing requires your utmost urgent attention. Mind yourself Judge!"

"How do you know a truce won't hold?" Jericho says, standing up and feeling compelled to make his way toward the window.

"Let's say, I have it on good authority. I learned a lot over there in Jordan last year," says Isis. "Mount Ramm was very educational if not insightful. It seems a contestation of biblical wills was always in the cards."

"Hmmm! You may be right," says Jericho as he glances out of the window taking another sip of his coffee.

Isis was right, the coffee is horrible. It tastes like panther piss, but it's strong. It'll do, thought Jericho. Something catches his eye briefly. He studies the anomaly before retuning his attention back to Kovac and Isis.

Ten

HIS LAW IS ABSOLUTE

"From the failures of your transgressions you will learn what not to do to ever again to repeat such a colossal loss."
                                                              ~ Kefentese Baruti

Botswana, Africa
City of Kang – Evening
On the outskirt of the Kalahari Desert, a rebel force of just under three thousand prepare to push their surprise offensive forward towards the invading forces of the Arcanian Military. Kefentese Baruti, there self-proclaimed general will not make the mistake that Hitler made when the allies advanced on Normandy wrestling France right out from under his control. He would meet the forces of Arcane before their foothold was cemented. He applauds their Colonel Rusain. He heard great and terrible things about the man. Baruti thought him an over confident fool though. He staged his forces on the broad side of the desert thinking that he would be protected. Rusain was out of his element. He didn't know the desert. Baruti did, it was is home.

The Colonel will take comfort that the desert will act as a natural barrier for them as they place their foothold, thinks Baruti. *Rome thought the same thing when they placed mountainous terrain at the back of their great city. Then Hannibal cut the through the mountains almost sacking Rome? Had he more men. He would have.*

Just as Hannibal did, Baruti plans to cut the natural barrier of the desert and crush his enemies before they coalesce to come for him. He was no fool. He was a student of the theater of war. He studied every great colossal failure of military conflict in his spare time when not making power grabs or extorting countries for ransom of their kidnapped citizens. Baruti was committed to the cause of victory always looking for the crucial moment that could turn the tide of a sure defeat. It was in that crucial moment when a revolutionary idea could turn the table on an overconfident enemy. His philosophy over time had come to be, from the failures of your transgressions will you learn what not to do ever again to repeat such a colossal loss.

The burn of the Maker's Mark Whiskey going down the ole gullet made Baruti close his eyes and turn his neck a quarter turn. *It was a harsh shot, but boy do those Americans know whiskey*, he thought. Sweat glistens his dark features. He's a thin man of only a hundred and fifty-seven pounds, but his ruthlessness more than made up for any physical discrepancies. His mercilessness is what made him larger than life. He takes another shot of whiskey and a long drag off his Newport cigarette. He may have been Botswanan, but he was educated in the finest scholastics, politics, and bad habits offered by a green card and five years of higher learning in America. Looking at a map sprawled out on the bar of the Megdasi Bar and Grill, which was in large a shitty place to command from, but his options were limited. He awaits his recently appropriated drone liberated from the Ugandans, to give him real time troop assessment of the invading force, so he could factor that into his calculation before advancing his attack. Now that he thinks about it, the drone operator is overdue with his report. He'll have to make an example of him. Filet the bottom of his feet perhaps.

Kefentese's twin brother, also his second in command, Scarlief walks up to the bar smoking a cigarette to stand next to his brother. Almost tripping over an obstacle on the floor, he looks down at the recently deceased body on the floor lying between him and the stationary barstool. The body is that of a black fellow, late fifties, graying temples and mustache. He may look Botswanan, but is far from it. The feller laying on the floor was heard to have been from a city of steel. He was born and bred in the Motor City of Detroit from what the locals had spoken of him. Such a shame to have a storied life come to such an end on the floor next to a barstool after spending so many dangerous days as a protector of streets in Detroit. The plaque of retirement on the wall behind the bar was testament to his loyalty of completing a job. Unfortunate he'd come to the end of the world for retirement and dreams of business only to die at the hands of a brute for the mere fact of breathing and being from a western continent. So goes life though.

<"Kefentese, was the killing of de owner necessary"> says Scarlief in their native tongue.

Buruti takes another shot and drag of his cigg nodding one time, yes.

Scarlief nods, too, a simple gesture which meant, "Okay, if you feel you had to, then you had to."

Buruti casually slides his brother the bottle of Maker's Mark across the newly polyurethane bar top. Scarlief catches and raises the bottle with his right lone arm. He lost the left in a conflict that was years in the past. He can't remember which town or what village he lost it, but he's done just fine adjusting to the reality of it being missing. You just grow accustom to it not being there really. Funny thing though, it would still itch although it wasn't there. Well, if a missing arm was the price of rising to power, then it was well worth it. Since rising with his brother the days of hunger and frailty was long past him. Besides, if only a missing arm after 47 conflicts was his biggest gripe, then he'd made out better than others he knew. Some were blown to bone and patches of wet chunks of red flesh in the first or second conflict. He raises the bottle and bites the patented red wax cap off and downs the rest. When he finishes, he lets out a yell to psyche himself up and smashes the bottle to iridescent dust.

<"Are you ready Buruti? Today we go out to take destiny by his fucking balls."> says Scarlief.

Placing the Newport long into his mouth, Buruti inhales slowly while studying the map. He never turns his eyes away from it. He knows every line and mark that he's drawn on it in preparation. <"I always thought it would be da American Marine that come for us. I never thought the god man would be a threat, yet, it is he who come here to Botswana. Lucien Arcane has come here to Botswana. Man of peace my ass."> Buruti spits phlegm in disgust on the dead body at his feet.

Reaching behind the counter Scarlief grabs a bottle of 100 proof Jack Daniels Black. <"Doesn't matter who's come here. Dis here our land, our country, we deal with them the same as all others,"> says Scarlief as he places the bottle under the nub of his left arm. The rest was blown off just above the bicep. He twists off the cap and cork and takes a shot from the bottle.

<"I studied the Arcanian conflicts that were public and those that were not. This Arcane force has unknown elements. The unknown is what defeated the Destined Suns back in the Congo three moons ago. I hate unknowns. Then there is dis Imperial mudder fucker who claims to be from a god. I think that has been there unknown. Matter of fact I'm sure of it. If I were betting man, I'd bet de house.">

Taking another shot, Scarlief smiles placing the bottle on the bar. <"Didn't know you believe in da gods.">

<"I don't! Da gods be damned! Da gods of the Hebrews has no sovereignty here. He never had. This forsaken patch of dirt has always been godless. This bitch of a land repeatedly raped by the white men of rich continents bore us... two bastards spawned from demon seeds. There is nothing here but dust and shadows.">

Standing and letting the ashes of his cigarette fall to the wooden floor, Buruti grabs his level three ballistic vest and puts it on pulling and slapping the side Velcro straps shut. He pounds his chest twice making the reinforced centered ceramic plate echo out a *hollow thump, thump*. He then reaches and grabs the map off the bar and flings it to the side revealing his AK-47 Scorpion. The map falls covering the face of the retired ex-cop turned bar owner in a distant land that he was warned numerous times not to migrate too. He'd thought about that warning in fact before the path of a bullet was carved through his dome spilling his thoughts about the floor.

Buruti pulls the charging handle to the rear sliding a 7.62 round into the chamber. <"Come, let us go and welcome Arcane's forces out in the desert, they will not be—">

Buruti stops midsentence as a sharply dressed looking soldier bearing the Arcane uniform walks into the bar with his helmet placed neatly under his left arm. His polished black boots with traces of fine sand attached, clack across the wooden floor as he makes his way past Scarlief stopping just short of the self-proclaimed leader of the rebel force.

Looking from side to side in disbelief that an Arcanian had the balls to walk in, Kefentese looks at his brother Scarlief with a who in the hell allowed this man to pass. His face accurately displaying a glare that he can't believe what he's seeing.

<"What the fuck is dis? Who the hell are you to just think you can walk in here?"> says Buruti.

"You were taught in America were you not Buruti? If you don't mind, I prefer we talk in my native language," says Colonel Rusain. "No, wait, how presumptuous and arrogant of me to be in your native land and ask you to speak my language... Truthfully, I just don't know you're fucking tongue, nor do I care to take the time to learn it. So, I'll just remain arrogant and bend your will to mine."

After a moment of silence and shock, Kefentese Buruti bursts into laughter. It was a deep from your gut till you can't breathe laugh. It wasn't one of those inauthentic ones that villains in movies give when they manically laugh as their evil ploy is revealed. The laugh was so infectious that his brother Scarlief began to laugh as well.

<"Scarlief, did dis mudder fucker just walk in here and order me to speak English?">

His brother still laughing can only nod his head yes.

Rusain only grins at the pair then makes his way to the bar. He nods toward the open bottle of Jack Daniels Black and gestures if it's okay to have a swig. Still laughing, Kefentese Buruti waves him on. Rusain looks at the body on the floor and then back to Buruti.

"Was it necessary to kill the barkeep?" asks Rusain.

Suddenly, the laughing of the Buruti ceases. "Very much so," he says in English. "That man although may look of color was here to rape our lands of money at the behest of his white masters in the west. Rape is punishable by death here. He was tried and found guilty."

Rusain pours a little of the liquor out for the dead barkeep. He then found a water-stained shot glass and poured himself a shot. Raising the glass, he toasts his hosts and bottoms up went the dark whiskey in a water spotted stained glass. "Ahhhh! Whew! That there burns the hair off the chest doesn't it?" says Rusain.

Kefentese Buruti pointing his weapon at Rusain approaches him cautiously slowly taking the bottle from him. He looks Rusain over closely then eye to eye before taking a shot from the bottle. He takes a few more letting it spill down the corners of his mouth before his bare forearm wipes away the excess spillage.

"How did you get past my... How many men, Scarlief?"

<"Four thousand, eight hundred and forty-seven... Battle ready."> Calls out Scarlief.

"Right... right... Four thousand, eight hundred and forty-seven," Buruti repeats in English.

Rusain takes the bottle back and pours himself another shot and toast it toward Kefentese. "It wasn't easy, but I thought it necessary in an attempt to save me from committing genocide against your men in what you believe would've been a war." Rusain waves him closer." You see, normally, I'd just arrive with the might of the Arcane Empire behind me and wipe shit stomping rebels like you from off the face of the planet. You rebels often play at war hurting many civilians and displacing them as refugees. Sure, your might is awesome in comparison to unarmed or poorly armed gangs and sparsely populated civilians, but like all other rebels that think themselves a Castro, you're insignificant when placed against the might of a real military."

"We are real military, Colonel; I have real weapons that say so," Buruti says, placing the muzzle of his Scorpion rifle into the chest of Rusain shoving him slightly jostling him with each poke.

"No... You're not military, maybe an argument for militia, but no military. What you are is just stubborn enough to become a beneficial example under the wheels of the Arcane machine... After all, the world is watching."

"A bene-fic-ial example, how so... Colonel Rusain? Explain this concept to me."

"Gladly. You see you and your brother here along with your seventh or eighth tier band of rebels, because you are nowhere near a real formidable force, we will show the world what happens to those that defy the order of the most holy guest Imperial. Orders were given to stand down from unsanctioned war by a force that has proven not of this world. You are in violation and don't have nowhere near the tools to defeat the might that has come calling for you so, an example must be made. When this is over because you chose not to surrender, we will display your corpse on top of the hill of your rebel army's bodies that we leave for the birds to feast on. You know, some real biblical shit... Understand?"

The eyes or Buruti stretches in disbelief at the man that has come across the sea to belittle the future dictator of Botswana. His pupils suddenly restrict at the three muzzle flashes from his AK-47. The rounds tear into Rusain's chest knocking him backward pulling the bottle of Jack with him. The rounds twist him mid fall. He lands face down over the corpse of the recently departed owner. For the first time, Death has missed the call of a soul.

<"Scarlief, drag the Arcanian dog of war out of my command center and leave his body for the carrion. Give him the same fate that he threatened me with.">

Before his brother could move to attempt to drag the body he backs away, eyes exuding fear before his head was hollowed out with a 1911 .45 caliber Colt. The shot was a bit off as Rusain was forced to shoot from a one-handed position as he pushed himself off his stomach back up to his knees using the other. He slightly moves his weapon and trains it on Buruti, The Colonel seeing that he has the initiative now slowly rises to his feet waiting for a reason to end Buruti against expressed orders that he die in prescribed aforementioned biblical way.

The rebel leader watching a smoking piece of his brother's brain matter on his shoulder starts to point his weapon again at the Colonel, but he's slow in response after just seeing Scarlief's brains vacated out the back of his skull, not to mention Rusain had gotten the drop on him. Instantly he felt like an ass, of course the cocky bastard would have on body armor, but what armor could stand up to a 7.62 round point blank? He tries to reconcile how this man took three rifle slugs point blank and yet rose. The rounds were armor piercing. There should have been holes blown out of his back the size of baseballs, but he was up moving. So much so, that the drop has been gotten on him. For all Kefentese education, he falls to his primal uneducated thinking of what voodoo must have been used that this man still lives.

Visible through Rusain's now damaged shirt was soft body armor. The rounds were also visible as metal specs turned sideways captured in the fabric. Death had indeed not missed his appointment; he didn't have one in the case of Colonel Rusain.

The rebel leader gesticulated the sign of the Christian Cross. "In the name of God, how?" Buruti blurted out.

"In the name of God is how," says Rusain, signaling for Buruti to drop his weapon.

Without any extra needed provocation, Buruti drops his weapon. All he needed is the hold out in the small of his back holster and a clear headshot when the timing was right. Baruti seemingly unarmed, Rusain holsters his sidearm and picks up his helmet. He looks down at the pooled wet spot where the bottle of Jack had broken. *Damn shame*, he thinks.

Watching for his moment to act, Buruti realizes that he hadn't heard a single squawk of communique come across his radio. There is no sound of vehicles, or men outside the bar talking the business of war and its preparation. Now that he thought about, there was only silence.

Rusain patting the ballistics from out his uniform walks closer the Buruti. "This body armor is experimental. It was cooked up at the Arcanian institute. I'm field testing it. What do you think? I thought I'd try first before any of my boys step out in untested gear."

Buruti meets Rusain's gaze. "How many of my men are left?"

"It was total decimation. It was over in less than the time you were taking to make your final plans of attack," he replies very matter of fact.

The rebel leader falls to his knees where they soak in the blood of his deceased brother.

Rusain also takes a knee getting down low to have a face to face with Buruti. "You understand right that it was no threat of what I was going to do to you and your men's bodies; it was a promise. I've been ordered to leave you for the vultures and that is what I intend to do. Now as the man and hopeful dictator you were aiming for, I now must carry you out like they did Hussein or you can walk out and meet your destiny under your own power. The same power that I heard your late brother speak on as I was entering?"

A smile crosses Buruti's face. "You are no good man of God, Colonel. My brother and I will await you at hells door so, that we may enter as brothers da three of us. Together, we shall all walk in and reminisce of the godless bastards we were here on Earth before we find our deserved upcommance."

Releasing a sigh, Rusain gives Kefentese the side eye. "I'm disappointed in our American education, if you think upcommance is a word. Hmmm! And, the walk that you intend on taking through hell that will be you and your brother's alone. Hell won't have me."

Rusain places his helmet on and turns walking towards the door. "I'll let you keep your weapon in that that there waistband of yours. You can die like the warriors of old holding onto it," says Rusain waiting at the door with one arm extended beckoning Buruti to follow. "When you're ready Buruti, I'll wait for you outside... Take all the time you need; I understand the last few moments are personal and you must reconcile your soul to whatever or whoever your god is to gain entry to partake of virgins or something like that right... That is if you have one; a god that is."

"I'm not Muslim, asshole... and I have no soul. I lost that two geno-cides ago," Kefentese says laughing.

"A real pity." With that, Rusain left the rebel leader on his knees in a pool of Jack and coagulating blood of a dead owner and a dead brother.

<"You have a soul. I'm looking at the deep red contours of it right now. Ahh Yes! There it is as surely as I talk to you... It is there, Kefentese Buruti.">

Buruti turns his head slowly to find Death watching him from un-derneath a shadowed face under a dark hood. Instantly, fear as old as the dark Aether of space makes him recoil falling over on his haunches. He slides backward on his ass slamming up against the bar. The bottles on the other side rattle at the slam of the body against wood. The smeared trail of alcohol and blood follows him. Leaving a symbolic rep-resentation of what he's done to people just about the whole of his life... sew fear while leaving a trail of blood. It is poetic.

The fear Kefentese felt was instinctual, it was the fear that awakens one from the most vivid of nightmares. You know the kind, the one that you pop up with your heart racing ready to explode from your chest. That kind of fear. Then in almost an instant it subsides when you real-ize it was merely a dream; a representation of the unconscious break-ing through to your conscious. That was the startle response of seeing an other worldly being as the last being from the world you are soon to depart. A world that was rough an unforgiving, but sensible. Strong survives.

<"I know who you are? You are the faceless thing that has been slowly hunting me over the years. You've tried to capture me a few times be-fore, but... I'd escape you,"> Buruti says laughing; smiling at his ingenu-ity and cunning at avoiding Death's ensnarement.

Death slowly walks up and kneels in front of him. He slams the bot-tom pointed end of his scythe deep through the floorboards finding purchase in the concrete slab to balance himself. He leans end close to-ward Buruti face, his red eyes piercing through his water laced ectomor-phic frame.

"I didn't know who you were before this moment that I came to collect you."

"But you know now man of black, don't you? You, now know of Kefentese Buruti and you know I have never been scared of you."

"Oh! But you are afraid. Not of me, noooo, of course not of me. I am finality all men face including you. You fear what comes before me. You fear the pain of a car accident where twisted metal has wrapped a death's embrace around flesh. You fear the before pain of the multiple men that had their brutish ways of twisted ungodly pleasure inserting their erect intentions into your backside until they ended in nirvana. That is what you fear, not the end of a brutish and often hellish tortured life where souls such as yours are fashioned in a foundation of abuse and abandonment. Now you will fear a life not completed Kefentese Buruti," Death extends his hand calling the blue soul orb of Scarlief. "When I come, I am a relief from a life trapped in a rotting corpse."

Death stands and pull his scythe from the floor. He places the blue orb into the inside of his coat.

<"Then, I am ready man of black. Take me!">

Death backs away and begins to fade out of reality. <"I will take you, but first must come the pain.">

As Death completely vanishes, Imperial bows down slightly to enter the bar sure to clear the doorway. His visage is immediately intimidating as he stands to his full height. His wings switch blade out stretching to they're fully extended width. They knock over chairs and further impale the outer most wooden walls knocking holes in them both. He stretches them for a few seconds then retract them just as quickly. His metal masked face looks down at Buruti. He's covered in oil, sand, and blood.

Instantly, Buruti knows the reports of the god man were not exaggerated. Everything the reports and rumors said were true, because he was here in the fucking flesh if that is what covered his body. Outside the immediate notice of the other worldly being having entered the bar, Buruti took notice of the armor his executioner was wearing. From the reports he'd seen televised, this armor that he was now wearing; it was different, it was new, covered in debris of war, but new. It was brilliantly bright platinum and polished. It had a series of glyphs etched down the left side of the breast plate in a low dull red glow. His uniform that lays underneath his breast plate, gauntlets, and knee-high boots with the same etching up the shins is an altogether different story. His uniform shows signs of distress. There are tears, rips, shrapnel markings and bullet holes throughout. Outside the damaged uniform of the Arcanian military colors he is otherwise unscathed.

Buruti didn't even realize that at seeing Imperial that his own bodily waste had been released to mix along the pool of liquor and coagulating blood. Defecation added smell is atrocious.

But first, da pain, but first, da pain, was all that kept repeating in Buruti's mind.

He tried to look at the weapon, that the god man was carrying, but he couldn't take his eyes of the piercing red and purplish tinted eyes of Imperial.

<"Duh—du—d Colonel said I have much time as I needed to make amends before I walked outside, that he had all day to wait for me.">

Imperial doesn't bother taking a knee. He just looks down on Kefentese like trash. "With the logistics of moving the Arcanian force from one conflict to the next, he does have such time. I on the other hand do not. I must be elsewhere."

Imperial grabs Buruti by the neck pulling him up to his eye level. "Pathetic."

✳✳✳✳

The outside outer most wall of the bar explodes as Buruti sails through it. Portions of the wall that did not give way to his smashing through it became like daggers of stalagmites pointing inwards of the circle that was created. Those inward stalagmites tore clothing and ripped flesh from Buruti. When he struck the sand graveled road he tumbled and slid until his momentum was stopped by the tire of an Arcanian black and red colored Humvee's oversized tire. Yes, it was rubber and lot easier to absorb his weight, but then again it was rubber and with the force with which he struck it violently rebounded slamming his body forward to the ground face first breaking his nose and jaw.

Using his now one good arm that was only lacerated as opposed to his left arm that was broken in two places, he pushed himself up realizing that he was now looking as his blood in the sand. A smile stretched across his busted lip and red stained teeth when he thought his words had come back to haunt him. It was not his enemies that would find dust and blood here in Kang Botswana, it was him. He wouldn't fight it. He deserved it. He just thought it would be the Americans that served him up; that one night he'd wake up and see the muzzle flash negating the sound of the pop because he'd be dead before he heard it.

He pushes himself to his knees and then over onto his haunches gently sliding his back up against the oversized wheel of the Humvee. He uses his good forearm to remove the dust and blood from his eyes where for the first time he's able to see the toppled might of his mighty four-thousand-man army. How foolish he'd been. He watches the flames and dark smoke rising from overturned armored vehicles that were once his cavalry. He glances up overhead watching three damn near silent stealth helicopters that turned his cavalry into cinders fly overhead. It was clear as crystal he was now the leader of a band of rebels that amounted to nothing more than children playing at war. The Colonel was right.

Kefentese slowly turns his head to the left and witnesses the soldiers of the Arcanian empire dragging bodies of what he thought was his once mighty clandestine Martial Force troops to a large pile of corpses that bodies were cut in half, mutilated, and cauterized; others are blown to hell with deep blackened scorch marks and gashes. There are some that were but pieces and those riddled with bullets from weapons that barley made a sound. In short, his men and women loyal to him were eviscerated. His enemy's guns whispered and summoned death in a language so low, he didn't even hear it spoken while he drank American whiskey.

His eyes continue to follow his enemy as they dragged the bodies of his comrades that had once followed him through a life of pillaging, raping, and murder to a pile that was already thigh high of those that have entered eternal sleep. It looks as if the pile itself would be pyre, but he knew better, it would be as the Colonel and god man said. It would be a buffet for the critters and animals of the wild to engorge their bellies. Yes, by the evening they will have their fill, and he had no misgivings that he would indeed be atop the pile. *But first, comes the pain,* he thought, *but first comes the pain.* Hell, he's in pain.

His head rolls back uncontrolled as if he were intoxicated. It isn't that though. Yes, he'd been drinking, but it was a concussion that made him lethargic. He witnessed the god man that was clearly not of this Earth approaching. He's truly afraid, but much too injured to give a shit. He was in pain. There, right there. He saw the Colonel off in the distance just to the right of the approaching god man. He was eating a health bar of some type looking at a tablet. This must have been so usual for him and his soldiers that he didn't even bother to watch this other worldly being dispatch the head of a little garden snake warlord that wanted to play in the big pond. Buruti's attention then turned back to the god man that would no doubt be the one to expedite his departure to the next life.

Imperial marches up to him not once hesitating before sliding his sword that he carried at the low ready into Buruti's leg. The white-hot edges cause him to cry out. He planned on not giving them the pleasure of seeing him beg. It was dream that was short lived. The wound intensified not only in pain of the physical, but of the psychological. It was as if all the pain he's ever inflicted on anyone was now thrown back on him. Imperial turns his sword twisting it in the wound creating a circle of cauterization. One could see all the way through his leg unobstructed.

But, first comes the pain.

It went on like that for Buruti for about an hour. Imperial would let him rest in 10-minute intervals after 20 minutes stretches of torcher. In one final act of the inhumane disservice, Imperial slid his sword through the opening of where his left eye use to be. Imperial truly could have been elsewhere, but these were the orders given by his father to carry out in its entirety. The last moment of Buruti's life was filmed for posterity and of course propaganda. It would be sent back and aired across the planet to appease the savages and show the might of an Imperial led Arcanian Military, solidifying that he is from the heavens and God has chosen Lucien to set the world to order.

Imperial removes his blade just as slow he first plunged it in and re-sheathes it in its scabbard. He grabs Buruti by the neck lifting him with no effort. His wings extended and he created lift sending dust, gravel and blood-soaked sand in all directions. He flies up past the top of the mound of bodies that grew over the hour of torcher the rebel leader endured. He tosses Buruti atop the pile without stopping his upward ascent, Imperial increased speed and disappears into the high blue stratosphere.

Rusain watches briefly until Imperial is out of sight. He then looks to his commanders and points his index finger toward the sky. Rusain gesticulates his finger in a circular motion. The men know that to be the sign that they are finished here and that it's time to roll toward the next conflict. Imperial is already in route if not there already clearing and paving the way for the Colonel.

Buruti spits blood under labored breath watching the sky with his one remaining eye unbale to move. Imperial has separated his spinal cord while ascending him to the top of the pile where he would now be able to lead his decimated army of the dead through the gates of hell. He will remain alive atop of them under the brutality of the sun while carrion eat his cooking flesh. All this will be done to biblical standards as Rusain promised. A vulture lands on his chest, its beak the last thing he saw before it picked the gelatin bulbous flesh of his remaining eye ball emptying the socket. Buruti is left blind and screaming with the last thought he would ever have: first comes da pain.

Eleven

DAYS OF MERCY

Angel's Spire – Day

Time space, and dimension move differently in Zero Realm. Months for Earth could equate to minutes or hours for the celestials. The meeting of Sparrows Chamber having concluded; Michael and his closet lieutenants, Raphael, Metatron and Gabriel are in the Strategic room intently studying the 4D holographic water infused celestial map of the entire Sadohedranicverse. The nerve center of the Spire is awash with activity. The emergence of Imperial has sent the Realm into a low-grade level of chaos in expanding and exhausting an already taxed manpower. With the loss of the latest Arch, Michael is forced to think more strategic in dispersing his troops to meet the needs of the Sadoverse.

"With the loss of Cassiel there had to be some logistical changes and reallocation of manpower and equipment of Cassiel's forces," says Michael, looking for input from his most talented of the Archs.

Metatron waves his hand across the map rotating it. He studies it widening specific areas to help him decide how to best spilt the forces for optimal presence across the verse. He wants to ensure they are absorbed equally between his fellow Archs, because he is sure everyone needs the additional troops. He knows he does.

Michael then spins the map left, before flipping it upward. Gabriel breaks off a piece of the water-constructed portion of the verse, dragging it in front of her focusing on the section containing 2814. As if not believing the highly sophisticated real-time map which constantly is aware of every living being, she walks to the precipice of the Spire's balcony that sits off the nerve center peering over it briefly. Satisfied, she returns to the Sadohedranicverse table map.

She glances back out toward the balcony briefly before turning to Michael. "Jericho has not moved Captain. He's still in place in Germany." Her eyes move right and fixates on a glint that flashes brightly then dies out. It's brief. *More than likely a Power Corp officer ending the life cycle of a Star; what the humans deemed a supernova,* she thinks.

Michael nods in acknowledgement that he's heard her report on the whereabouts of her adopted progeny, but his attention has been taken as he follows the paths and numbers of celestial confrontations that have been lighting up across the realms and across all the levels of realities. How fast his eyes and hands move across the map has become an equivalency to harnessing a rancorous ensemble of musicians to quell the disorder. Michael has become a graceful conductor that has learned to bring harmony to the disorder. He studies the map and knows the mind of his adversary. It's an old ploy; one he's seen throughout bearing witness to conflicts of lesser beings throughout other realms.

Lucifer's attempting to cause mayhem off Earth to spread Michael's forces leaving Earth lightly protected if it all. The ploy works, unfortunately. It's old but doesn't mean it's not effective. It was a winning stratagem in the beginning when the numbers were in favor of Lucifer when the odds were four to one. Through attrition of the enemy and advancement in training of his Choiretic forces, the numbers that were once superior to the Arch forces, are now falling to hopefully two to one scenarios, if his intelligence has been reported accurately. That's a big if.

"Has his condition improved?" asks Michael, appeasing her fondness for the boy. He needs her back to the task at hand, so empathy will be applied for now. Deep down he thinks she's become too close to the mortal where she's no longer objective to all else under Elohim's concern.

Gabriel stands silent with no intent to be rude. She simply dismisses the question as another glint flashed again gaining her complete attention.

Michael looks away from his portion of the 3D holographic map toward Gabriel. "Has his condition improved, Gabe?"

Having have to ask the question a second time, now Metatron and Raphael look in her direction as well. Michael focuses on what has her attention. He holds both his hands encompassing the piece of map Gabriel has. He pulls his hands apart widening her particular section equivalent to mortals and their older smartphones when expanding their pictures. His irises turn from neutral gray to blue.

The sizing of the map snaps Gabriel back to the here and now. "Captain, I'm not sure what I'm seeing," says Gabriel.

Metatron looks closer at the enlarged portion of the hologram. "If we're focusing on just but the one room, I don't see anything in there amiss. I see only the three."

Metatron smiles at the recovery and strength of Jericho. It has improved greatly since his last visit shortly after the fall of the Embassy. "Jericho looks to be on the mend," says Metatron.

Gabriel looks at Michael briefly then back to the map. "Sorry, Captain, I thought I saw something, then it was gone. I thought is saw it again, well I'm sure I saw it again... then, nothing."

Michael this time doesn't say a word. He leaves the projection map and quickly jogs to the balcony's precipice overlooking the realms. He takes a long observational gander and squints focusing his vision, narrowing it as an Eagle does before capturing its prey. His eyes turn a deep purple. He quickly looks back to Gabriel. "No, Gabe, you did see something. The something has been removed from historical fact for so long that the Sadoverse map has forgotten to read the signature. What you saw was someone that has been far removed from Zero Realm. The traces of Aether particles around the room and on Jericho are so miniscule, the map would have missed it. You have to look closely with your own eyes to see it. I saw it when I first observed that Fate had returned."

"Then who has returned this time and what are their intentions?" Raph asks.

Michael squints harder. "Signature on the Aether looks familiar to a degree, but is all wrong somehow. And, as for their intentions, whatever they may be, two facts remain. They crept in under our noses and yet committed no acts against the boy. Second, they wanted to be seen."

Raph walks over and attempts to find what has Michael's gaze. "I see nothing."

"Nor do I, brother," Metatron agrees.

"You wouldn't," Michael says. "Although concerning as this development is, I believe the intentions of them being there is to draw our attention to that gathering storm right there." Michael points to the left of the poorly constructed hospital where Jericho currently resides.

"Now that I can see," says Raph. He turns and runs back to the Sparrows Chamber.

Michael turns to Metatron. "Go! Brief Prince Yeshua that I will be commanding the action to be taken!"

"But—" Metatron attempts to reply.

"GO!" Michael yells.

Metatron turns and hauls ass toward the Sparrows Chamber armory as well to retrieve his gear. Raphael by passes Metatron on the way back to the balcony giving a nod of assurance that he'll be okay without his older brother looking after him. Raph continues running back toward Michael quickly placing his chest armor over his head where its internal locks and mechanics whirrs and clicks locking it into place. He attaches his sheathed scabbard sword to his magnetic waist clamp under his sash as his helmet and mask generate from below the neckline of his armor. Running past Michael while saluting the young Arch dives over the side of the balcony backwards into a dive.

Gabriel, having also left her gear in the Sparrows Chamber, takes off in a sprint to grab hers. Zadkiel, just out of pure happenstance enters the Brain Center of the Spire fully clad in his armor already eating a plate of Manna.

"Guys, I'm telling you, I don't know what Power Belrayus puts in this when he makes— what's going on?" says Zadkiel, startled by the activity of his fellow Archs running to and fro. "What I miss?"

Michael, seeing that Zadkiel is already armored and with weapon, snaps his fingers and points over the side railing of the balcony. "Help Raph!"

Zadkiel doesn't hesitate. He takes a handful of Manna and shoves them into his mouth, masticating it quickly while discarding the plate tossing it off to his left. Michael catches it watching Zad as he takes off in a full sprint and dives over the side. He hears the order from Michael as he ejects his wings from out his back. He draws them back into reverse blading rocketing him into free fall.

"Back Raph! Capture or Palengrad Canceranian! He's too important of a piece to not have removed from the board," says Michael.

Zadkiel's helmet and mask generates from below the neckline of his armor. To Palengrad is the order he sure wanted to follow; the hell with capture. Palengrad means the death of Cancer and the undoing of all his work. The latter of the order suited him just fine.

****

Kaiserslautern, Germany:
St. Joseph Krankenhaus Medical Center – Early Morning

Jericho looks back at Kovac turning his attention away from looking out the small window of his makeshift hospital room with the unpleasant view of Germany's filth. The alley was atrocious. "Crass, I have to ask," says Jericho.

"About what you told me about your handling of Imperial?" Kovac Alias Crass says, standing up.

Jericho nods.

"Son, what you've told me has not been taking lightly. There's no need for demonstration of said set abilities. Your near miraculous recovery with the addition of reports by the two attending physicians that were treating you was more than informing enough that there was something irregular about you. If I had wanted to out you, it would have been done before now. I have no intenti—"

The ethereal hooded being walks up behind Jericho and reaches past him, tapping the forefinger on the glass window. Sounding as if a pebble hit the glass, Jericho's attention is called back to the window. He places a single finger in the air gesturing silence for a second cutting off Kovac. He watches the alley way this time with more care to detail of it. He doesn't quite no why he should but, he does. His gut tells him to look for anything out of place. What would be out of place in an alley? Maybe rats not in it or a multitude of them scurrying about in daylight. Would that be an anomalous event worth the garnering of attention? He doesn't know why; he'll just go with gut feeling. Then again, he is sensitive to a psychic degree, maybe it is Gabriel calling his attention? If it is then he'd better look for something till the feeling passed.

After a moment of watching the alley carefully and still sipping on his horrible coffee, he inadvertently began to build anxiety in Isis and Kovac. While holding a silent vigil over the array of dumpsters, there it was to his trained militaristic eye; at the top of the alley, right at the T intersection where the main thoroughfare crosses. He saw a glint of light reflecting off a mirror of some sort. It has his attention. It glints again. He narrows his vision.

Kovac sees Jericho's expression, which triggers years of experience in reading body language. He reaches into his back pocket and pulls out his holovid phone. He runs his finger igniting the screen on the phone to kick on. He places his thumb to register his identity and the phone kicks on to an app that displays a singular red dot.

"What you got out der, Mr. Moody?" asks Kovac.

Isis pats Kovac on the arm. He turns around to find her staring at the bottom of the door to the room. His eyes follow hers to a black wire device that slithers back under the door out of the room.

"Shit!" is all Kovac could utter at first. "We've been compromised."

Jericho watches a flash ignites behind the glint. A puff of dark smoke rises from point of origin. Something fast propels toward his direction trailing white vapors. *Rocket!* His mind tells him.

"R.P.G.!" Jericho yells. "INCOMING... GET DOWN!"

Kovac never looks back to verify the warning. He hits the red button and dives atop of Isis knocking her to the ground under his weight shielding her. The rocket streaks through the window as Jericho launches himself backward nearly missing contact with the rocket as it enters. The projectile misses his head by mere centimeters and hits the ceiling penetrating its cheap construction continuing up through the floor above them. An iron pipe manufactured and embedded in the ceiling during the 1950s ricochets the rocket up through the fourth floor where it blasts wildly through the hall finally striking the outer most cement wall. The cement is reinforced enough to engage the propelled grenade's tip. It depresses the trigger igniting the rocket to do what it was made for. There is a reddish orange plume of fire that throws shrapnel in all directions. The explosion rocks the building. Debris in the form of ceiling panels and glass comes crashing down on the trio.

Jericho is on his feet in seconds. He crawls to the window and slowly peeks up to see the enemy point of contact. "Shit!" He drops back to the floor. "Isis? Kovac?" he calls out.

"Still here son," Kovac answers pushing himself from off of Isis. "The lass appears okay."

"The lass is fine," Isis shouts, ears ringing with tinnitus.

Jericho gets up and heads for the door. The blast caused the foundation to shift slightly jamming their only egress from the room. Without hesitating he kicks the door and a partial piece of the wall off the hinges out into the hall. Kovac pulls Isis up and pushes her toward the door.

"Careful, son, der may be an unfriendly out der. The Lass spotted a wire cam under the door before things went to shit."

"What the fuck was that Kovac?" asks Jericho. "Who'd shoot a gotdamn rocket at a hospital?"

"The Chinese," Isis answers frantically still trying to get her equilibrium set.

"The Chinese if anything has a since of honor. Shooting a hospital is not honorable and something they wouldn't do," says Jericho. "To fire on a hospital full of German citizens. They'd be asking for another war."

Kovac runs this time and glances ever so slightly out the window making himself a small target if one at all. "Welp, we have our answer. A kill team of Arcanian forces are making their way down the alley toward us."

Twelve

MISSION CRITICAL

"I didn't believe that a metaphysical metaphorical wall built on lies of Lucifer would ever fall. I believe it will now. This Jericho, if he has the spirit of his mother, he may just yet topple the greatest empirical threat ever to have existed. Wouldn't that be something?"

-Death

The lights dim for a few seconds before flickering off and on intermittingly before going completely dark all over the hospital. *KAWATHABOOM!* Another detonation shakes the hospital's foundation. It can take it; it was built in the 1950s. Screams begin to bellow out as the shape charges on the first level rear maintenance doors, the ones right off the rear alley's odd side explode sending a concussive wave down the hall of the first floor. Nurses, patients, physician attendants, orderlies and stacks of untold debris are blown over desks and against walls. Small monitors that show real time vitals are blown off their mounts along with the walls of the first seven rooms closest to the point of explosive origin.

A security guard that was walking toward the rear door to turn his alarm key signifying that he was in fact completing his rounds is instantly eviscerated by flying shrapnel, dust and soot. The impact so sudden and adrenalin rushing, he gets back on his feet before he realizes his right arm is no longer an appendage that he entered this world with. Sounds to him have become muffled as his ear drums were ruptured and leaking blood and brain fluid from its canals.

Emerging from the smoke of the blast, Major Justin Dale and his Arcanian Lightning Response team enters hospital. Seeing their first adversary is a torn to shit security guard missing an arm and perforated with shrapnel rips and gouges, he instantly thinks relief and puts two rounds in the guard's chest and one in his head while simultaneously kicking him to the ground. *A mercy killing* thought the Major. No way would he want to finish life in that state. Major Dale surveys the hall looking for other hostiles. Seeing none, he balls his fist and yanks his elbow downward as if pulling the chain on a semi-truck to blow the horn. His men read his gesture and lobs three canisters of smoke mixed with the active ingredient CS in front of him skittering down the hall. The cannisters blow and the irritant laced smoke instantly fills the hallway.

The sound of failing medical equipment blare on every floor cascading down every hallway throughout the hospital, signifying that there has been a catastrophic power loss and that back up batteries for individual equipment such as life support systems have been activated.

As soon as Jericho steps into the hall he's bumped and jostled by running medical staff and patients that are ambulatory. If there is an assassin amongst them, he doesn't see them now. He isn't worried about the assassin though; at least for himself. Isis now took precedence. He guards the doorway to the hall momentarily just in case an attempt is tried. He watches the security guards that are trying to get a handle on what is taking place. Most are unarmed and only rated at best to deal with psyche patient restraint techniques. He looks back at Kovac.

"They're here for me." Jericho tears a piece of his hospital gown off and ties it around his face.

"No, they're here for me I'm the illegitimate love child of dat der singer Vanessa Williams," says Kovac sardonically.

Isis and Jericho look at him.

"Of course, they're here for you, who else would they go through this much trouble for if what you just told me is true?" says Kovac as he reaches behind his back grabbing a hold of his concealed two silver plated .45 caliber 1911 colts with red crosses etched on the black rubber grips. "I must have raised a few eyebrows coming down to these parts from time to time. Spies everywhere. We thought that the Chinese had infiltrated our security. We long suspected it, just no evidence."

"You have overwhelming proof now," says Isis. "Only it's not the Chinese that infiltrated."

Jericho turns to face Kovac. "She's right; these are Arcanians. I recognize their penchant for destruction tactics anywhere. Chinese would have used more stealth. I met the man that led them in the Congo. Rusain is not about stealth. Arcane forces have infiltrated the Marines."

Checking to make sure his rounds are chambered, Kovac nods at the assessment. "I concur with your assessment, Dr. Obvious."

"Umm! You two," Isis says, snapping her fingers to get them on task. "I'm scared as shit; can we discuss the how and whys when we get the hell out here?"

Jericho looks both ways down the hall through the chaos for an exit. "They probably didn't need to keep tabs on you or anyone."

Kovac thinks hard on that statement for a few seconds. "Right! That Imperial fella more than likely reported your entanglement... When your body wasn't found, I'm sure they set to scouring these parts looking for you. My deception and ruse of the name game was crafted with me thinking I was protecting you from dem there Chinese fellas. I never gave a third thought of Arcane."

"Why would you have? Asks Isis, you only found out that angle today."

Kovac walks up behind Jericho. "If he did report your entanglement, you are a loose end. If you did what you said you did to him, you have made yourself a threat, Captain, one that must be eliminated which no force on Earth, Marine or otherwise can protect you from," says Kovac as he looks at his colt in his left hand. He's hesitant to part with it at first, but he quickly acquiesces shaking his head knowing it's better to have two moving operators than one. He throws one of his 1911's to Jericho. "I get that back. You get me!"

Jericho nods. "I get you, sir!" he says taking a bit of a pause to ponder. "I just don't understand why now? Why today?" He tosses the weapon to Isis. "He gets that back." He points to Kovac. "I'll get my own. There'll be enough of them laying around in a minute I suspect."

Kovac removes his hat rubbing his head quickly back and forth. *Why today, why today?* he thinks to himself

"Think about it, when a one-star general goes missing, there really isn't any inconspicuous cover you can take without notice," says Isis. "Now, can we get the hell out of here?"

Seeing a somewhat clear path down the hall opposite the running frantic people, Jericho determined quickly that it is the best option for escape; the only thing that gave him pause is that there were no exits the way where the path was clearing... Perfect, he'd make one. Jericho grabs Isis by the hand and pulls her into the hallway and starts them running down the hall pushing and shoving anyone in the way. "Run!"

They race to the end of the dead-end hall. He was reminded instantly of his days in boot camp when he'd often hear the mantra, *hurry up and wait,* as there was nowhere else to go. Jericho only elected to come this way because he was sure the Arcanian Kill team would be watching for him in the main halls, lobby, and stairs, not a dead-end hall. He wanted to be where they weren't. No windows, no steps, no egress, he succeeded. Kovac turns the corner bringing up the rear. Seeing the dead end, he turns around falling to a knee with his weapon leveled off at eye level awaiting the incoming force.

"You hear that?" Kovac says.

"Yeah, I hear it," Jericho answers.

"Hear what? I can't hear anything through the alarms and screaming, the gotdamn constant screaming," yells Isis.

Kovac lays prone making himself a smaller target still keeping the Colt leveled at whatever unfortunate soldier comes around the corner first. "Yes, the screaming, but it's what we're not hearing... no sustained gunfire. They're not shooting everyone."

Jericho sizes the wall first then looks at Isis holding the weapon. "You do know how to use that, right?"

Isis, pulls the slide back slightly examining the weapon making sure it's loaded. Seeing brass, she lets the slide rock back forward and removes the safety.

Jericho nods.

"Archelogy has its moments," says Isis.

"Great, point the weapon that way. They'll be coming from that way," Jericho says pointing back down the hall. "No wait!" He grabs Isis by her weapon arm and slowly puts it down to her side. "They haven't fired since the first few pops so that means they are to capture or kill with minimal to no life lost to civilian populace. They see you pointing a weapon they may be forced to rethink and engage. We don't want that. Hell, I don't want that at least not for you. The General and I have become men of war. You're academic and it'll be your kind that elevates and saves us... If it is in fact Arcane who sent his elites, he doesn't want a bloody spectacle." He takes off his hospital gown, and ties it around his waist making activity more practical. Running around with an ass hanging out was nowhere near gentlemanly or practical for that matter.

Isis looks as Kovac. "What about him?"

"I'm military, darling, they'll blow my gotdamn head off on sight," says Kovac.

"Damn straight!" Jericho agrees. He places both his hands on the wall and starts to push. The wall groans in protest, but begins to give way. The drywall collapses inward exposing insulation and brick. Jericho keeps up the pressure. The mortar in between the bricks is the weak point of the wall. The mortar cracks and slowly falls away in chips then chunks. *THHHHWUUUPBOOOM!* The entire brick wall collapses and falls away giving away to the fresh air and sunlight. Debris falls below injuring the remaining rear guards that was posted in case their target rabbited out the back if he'd made past the initial entry team.

Bwoofff, Bwoof! Two more explosions of smoke can be heard at the south stairwell entrance. Kovac pulls the hammer back on his 1911 readying it for business on the other end of the pistol. Jericho watches as the injured soldiers murmur and cry out in pain under the pounds of bricks he just dropped on them. He looks to the outside wall to his right and studies the height versus distance to the water tanks below that are attached to the side of the hospital.

"Just eyeballing it, what do you think the distance is to those tanks down there?"

Isis looks past him and does the math quickly in her head. "I-I don't know, maybe 50 feet... give or take."

"Shit!" Jericho says and starts laughing.

"What in the hell do you find so gotdamn funny son?" Kovac asks.

"I was just thinking of a class that me and Isis had in high school. Mr. Callachie, remember him?' He said we need to view math as essential, because one day our lives my depend on it."

"Congratulations, Captain, you met a regular gotdamn oracle, son. What does his prophetic visions of your waning primary school years have to do with now?"

Jericho looks at Isis. He pulls her in and kisses her. "I'm sorry you're caught up in this. Listen to me you're going to have to follow me. I'm—"

Rounds from below pepper the opening that Jericho created. He quickly turns, placing his back toward the opening. It was accidental, but he did just injure or kill an Arcanian soldier below. If there was a capture order, it's been upgraded to kill now. Rounds tear into his back and buttocks falling harmlessly to the ground after impact against his skin. He looks into Isis's eyes. For the first time ever that she can remember, she sees fear. It's not fear of the situation, she knows instantly that she's the root of it. *He's terrified that something's going to happen to me.*

VWTIPP! A .50 caliber round from a Barret Long Bore Rifle strikes Jericho in his left upper shoulder. The impact snatches him off his feet and throws him and Isis through the thin dry wall to the left. He holds her close and tight shielding her, but there was no mistaken it, he was off his feet and taking her for the ride with him. The two of them crash through the wall carrying debris and dust into the occupying patient's room both hitting the floor hard and sliding.

****

The sniper a half mile away over watching from the railing of a rooftop pulls the action bolt back ejecting the enormous round. He lets go of the bolt; it automatically slides forward chambering another round.

"That was a positive hit. Target down," the sniper's spotter says kneeling beside him looking through binoculars. "That was a confirmed kill pal. Think you got two with that shot." The spotter satisfied then depresses his mic to alert the ground troops. "Arc Alpha 7 you are free to proceed. I repeat the military aged male is down. Check third floor and confirm positive strike and kill on subject of interest!"

The radio squawks, "Arc Alpha 7 copies. The Major is aware of transmission. We are on the third floor, south east corner of the building. Confirm, positive strike local. Understood."

****

Jericho having slammed into Isis, knocked the wind out of her. Kovac enters through the hole careful to avoid the outside incoming fire. He kicks Jericho over quickly assessing and examining him. Isis, free from his shielding embrace grasps for a breath. First glance looks like the Marine has transcended on to the next plain of existence. He pulls Isis to her feet just as she starts to breathe more easily. Kovac makes sure to stay clear of the opening and anymore unwanted small arms fire. "You okay, lass?"

Isis winces in pain and spits blood. "My chest."

Kovac touches her left side. She draws back in intense pain. "More than likely you cracked a rib or two."

"I bit my tongue," says Isis.

Hearing footsteps approaching he takes his second 1911 back from Isis. "Look here, darling, Captain Bane is gone. Do you hear me? He's gone. I'll be following him directly, understand? They will not let me live if they capture me Honey. I'm going to have to make a final stand here." Kovac looks over his shoulder out the hole of the outer most wall that Jericho had made prior to the enemy contact. There's no way down from there," he says nodding toward the hole

He helps her to the corner of the room where he sets her down. He pulls the hammer back on his reacquired second 1911. He aims one at the door and the other at the hole in the wall. Kovac glances over at the occupying patient whose eyes were stretched in great surprise at the highly unusual occurrence that for sure does not happen every day. Wasn't bad enough he is non-ambulatory, but what is soon cometh is not going to improve his day any. From the looks of him, his already more than likely shitty day was about to get a lot worse anyways.

The wild-eyed patient in complete shock speaks profanities in German desperately looking to be supplied with answers no doubt for what's happening. Kovac could tell the young man was shaken to his core. His eyes told the story. His body told another. The patient's body told Kovac in an instant that he didn't have the strength to run when the commotion started. He was a prisoner trapped by the Cancer in his own body. It was clear the patient was terminal, wasn't a need to look at his chart. Experience of Kovac losing his wife to it told him everything there was to know about the kid. The young man was emaciated, nothing but damn near bones.

Kovac risking a glance back toward Isis makes sure she was fine and wasn't pooling blood beneath her. It was a quick assessment; she could have been hit and missed it in her cursory check. She appeared safe for now... The kid's hands reach for his chest. He started having trouble breathing. Kovac eyes him having trouble and trots back over to where Jericho landed.

Damn! thinks Kovac.

Jericho fell atop the life-support machine crushing it. The thing was supplying air to the young lad. Kovac shakes his head at the unfortunate circumstance. *Tough break kid... or is it? Depending on how you look at it. I'd rather death comes quickly. Let's hope he feels the same, because he's coming for us all today it seems.*

The machine is wrecked, no doubt about that. Kovac followed the blip on the screen that went from active steady blips to a recurring flat line. Kovac sighs, then acts. He pushes Isis in the corner next to kid's bed. Without warning he kicks over the makeshift gurney that doubled as the kid's bed. The young lad flies right out of it on top of Isis. They collapse to the ground. She shoves the emaciated kid off of her and grabs her side which is burning in immense pain.

"Jesus!" Isis mutters wincing through pain. "What the hell are you doing? You're going to kill the boy."

"The bottom of the bed will offer some protection. Not much, but you take what you can get. You two keep your heads down!" orders Kovac. "I had another plan in play that should be in effect right now. We just have to live long enough to see it executed. As for the boy, he's dead already, his body just hasn't realized it yet."

Kovac forces Isis to lay back and props the cancer-stricken lad on top of her. "Survive today, talk the merits of morality tomorrow... Good luck, lass... You too, kid," Kovac says as steps back out into the hallway.

A round whizzes pass striking the bill of his Coast Guard hat knocking it off. He doesn't flinch or panic, he just readjusts his position and steps backward into the door's framework just enough that the rounds from the second team on the ground or the sniper can't hit him. He again lays prone clear of the sniper fire from across the way that was coming from somewhere outside. If they could have hit him laying prone, they would have already. He figured he must be in a good place. He can hear the team approaching. He listens closely and can hear the Arcane's combatant's communique.

"*This is Arc Alpha 7; we've reached the south east corner of the third floor... turning the corner to make entry.*"

Kovac checks, both hammers are pulled back on his weapons. He holds his aim as he hears the doors to the stairwell around the corner open. A few beats of seconds go buy then he hears them close. *They're here. The damn snipers directing them,* he thought. As soon as sees boots approach from around the corner, he opens fire forcing the incoming Arcanian team to take cover.

Major Dale of the ALR team yells out from behind cover, "Throw down your weapons. We do not wish for further hostilities. We are in pursuit of a wanted terrorist subject that attacked the Chinese Embassy. Stand down and you will not be harmed."

"Hostilities at this point appears to be unavoidable, wouldn't you say, son?" Kovac yells back.

Bleep bleep! Chimes from Kovac's holovid cell. He sets the 1911 in his right hand down and reaches back into his right back pocket. He grabs the phone and depresses the singular blue button flashing on the screen setting it down in front of him. He picks up his 1911 and again takes dual wielding aim. Static emits at first then he hears it. Red Blade One, fox trot, tango two. Kovac smiles, he uses the bottom of his fist to depress the button on the phone. The screen goes from a light blue to red. He then uses his forefingers and slides the phone down toward the Arcanian Lightning Response force. Otherwise known as Lucien's kill team. Hell, he wouldn't be a nation without one. All the great ones had them even America had kill teams, although they likely would deny it.

The Major watches as the phone slides past the corner where he and his team have taken cover. It slides past his feet. Kovac gets up and jukes as if going out the door then back right. He hears the sniper round bypass him on the left. Knowing the sniper has to rechamber, he dives back into the room with Jericho, Isis and the emaciated young man. The Arcanian special forces emerge from cover and head down the hall toward the three. Major Dale kicks the cell phone with his back heel sending it further down the hall past him and his troops. They walk at a quickened pace till the Major holds up a fist and halts the team's movement. He turns his head slightly as if listening for something. He then points two fingers toward the opening that Jericho made in the outer most wall facing morning sky, facing the sniper which had them all in his sights covering them.

Major Dale's mic alights with screaming voices.

Not removing his eyes from the target room, he calls out over his shoulder, "What the hell is Eagle Nest going on about?" asks the Major.

"ENEMY CHOPPER!" yells out his radio operator that use to hold the rank of private before he was eviscerated in a volley of rapid chain gun fire.

A black stealth apache with the Knights Templar red cross symbol rises up filling the view of the opening. The rotor blades were almost silent. The chopper turns facing the lightning response team that served them in name only, because they were certainly not faster than the events which raised to engulf them. The Major's eyes widen in horror at the sight before him. The attack chopper chain guns began to whirl.

Well played! were the last thoughts of Major Justin Dale. Two quick flashes from either set of guns tear through the team's level three body armor and flesh not just cutting down the soldiers, but butchering them. At such at close point-blank range, the human body versus 33milimeter rounds at a volley of 625 rounds a minute of armor piercing ferocity could only have one finality, it painted the hallway red with the arterial blood spray and splatter of Arcanian troops.

Death emerges from patient room after stepping over Isis and Kovac. He places the red orbed soul of the young lad that laid next to Isis into his coat before turning his attention to the hallway. He runs through the arterial sprayed collage of human remains along the walls collecting multiple souls of red and blue shinning orbs.

****

Looking through his binoculars, the spotter stands in disbelief at his team being mowed down by an enemy Apache that seemingly appeared from nowhere. Emotions have overtaken him. Training has betrayed him. He's standing fully erect forgetting survival protocols, which are the blood of the sniper team that keeps them breathing when in hostile territory. He's looking through his Nocs taking in the full sight of what just transpired. Then it dawns on him; he gets it now, he's fully erect on the precipice of a rooftop. The spotter has exposed himself and more than likely has become the spotted. He looks down toward his sniper partner that out shot him for the covenant position two years prior with a hint of fear and disbelief as his tremendous mistake.

The sniper turns his face a quarter turn toward his spotter so that he can make eye contact with him. "That's game then mate?" he tells his spotter.

"So, it is..." says the spotter, his voice quivering. "I'll miss you, Matt... I would tell you to look in on my girls from time to time, but I think you'll be right behind me partner... See you on the other side compadre." The spotter winks at Matt as he pulls his hat off giving his adversary a clean shot. "Well, Shii—" is all he's able to breath before a counter sniper from an opposite opposing rooftop clad in all black takes out his frontal occipital lobe, rendering him inert.

The lifeless body of the spotter falls forward from the roof. As he passes the open seventh floor window, Death reaches out and claims his red orbed soul. He leaves the husk to continue on all the way to pavement impact. With tears in his eyes, the sniper Matt turns his head back and continues to look through his scope. He doesn't move more than that at first. Since he's still drawing breath, he assumes, the counter sniper doesn't have a line of sight on him. He starts to slide sideways from his perched position on his belly ever so slightly when he shuffles into the black combat boot of a Knight Templar. The sniper who was at one time named Matt, because he was alive looks up slowly and then rolls over on his back placing his hands in the air surrendering. The M4 rifle of his soon to be executioner is squarely pointed at his forehead.

The Knight Templar clad in black tactical uniform and gear kneels down placing his rifle to the sniper's forehead. A hooded celestial appears behind the Templar; the same one that warned Jericho moments earlier of the impending attack touches her hand softly on the Templar's shoulder. "Easy, Terrance!" the celestial states.

The Templar stares at the sniper for a second. He watches the fear and terror rise through the emotion in his victim's face. He listens to it with the quickening of his victim's breath as the end draws near for his opponent. Then there is pity from the Templar. As he begins to understand the emotion of his enemy. The man is terrified of what he's going to lose which was all that he'd amassed in life. And what he amassed probably wasn't much with him being a soldier and all, but it's loss all the same. He surrendered without a fight. Was it practical to kill this fully capable enemy? Sure, if released or escaped he would have no qualms about killing the victor of the moment that placed him in this current life or death position. He would have no qualms about killing anyone of his brother Templars if the roles were reversed.

"Easy, now," the soft celestial voice repeats.

He doesn't know why his heart is torn on the matter of killing his enemy. He's done it more times than he can count on numerous battlefields across the world. Why is this one so tough? He acquiesces turning his rifle muzzle up showing the collapsible stock to the sniper. A spot of relief overcomes the Arcane Sniper's face. The Templar Terrance, swore he mouthed thank you. A short hard quick thrust is followed by a thud, the Templar sends the sniper to the realm of unconsciousness. Hearing automatic gunfire on the ground, the Templar dares a peek over the edge. He witnesses his brother knights engaging the remaining Arcanian forces kill teams on the ground. He was no kill team. Governments had them of course, wouldn't be a civilized government without them, but Terrance was a Knight, he was no kill team so, he can have mercy. Matt the sniper was given Mercy. He would remain... alive. However though, when he sees the condition of his new home and prison, he'd probably wish he'd been killed.

****

After the barrage of chain gun rounds finished, Kovac stands only to find the kid had passed and Isis draped over Jericho in tears. Her wail of pain was a song of sorrow that the sirens of the ocean could not match. He kneels down to comfort her. They don't have the time for such sentiments, but she loved the man so yes, the General named Hiram Kovac would allow her a moment to mourn, but only a moment before the hurtful task of prodding her along begins. "We have to move darling," says Kovac

Taking a gasp of air Jericho rises suddenly. He reaches around and rubs his shoulder. "Owwwwww! That hurt."

Kovac, startled, stands up shocked. "Jesus!"

"Not ready to meet him just yet," says Jericho, rubbing his shoulder then his head where it struck the Kid's life support machine.

"Well, I'll be damned, son," blurts out a surprised Kovac.

Isis, also shocked, works through it quickly crushing him with a vice grip hug. She doesn't care of her pain from the cracked ribs. She looks back to Kovac wiping her eyes of the emotional salt water. "What the hell was that, you ass? You did that? You almost killed us."

"No darling, they almost killed us," says Kovac pointing the slew of eviscerated bodies coloring the walls. "Dem boys over there in that chopper saved us."

Jericho rolls over to sit up, still rubbing his shoulder. "Not yet, they haven't. We still need to get ghost. I hear small arms fire, that means there is more of them in the streets."

"How did they know where to find us?" Isis yells out as the roar from the blades caused a wind tunnel.

"My cell phone painted the target area to annihilate," says Kovac.

Hearing the rotor blades still swirling and feeling the wind that courses through the hall, Kovac reaches into his left pocket and pulls out a glowstick. He cracks it making it turn a bright red. He then tosses it into the hall. After a few seconds he peers out into the hall. The Apache pilot sees him and nods giving him the thumbs up. He then points skyward with his thumb. Kovac gives the pilot a thumbs up confirming acknowledgement. The Apache slowly pulls the chopper up and out of view. A tension wire pops in a mini contained explosion underneath the chopper. A wire ladder with thins rope rungs falls down past just outside the opening.

Jericho walks up behind Kovac carrying Isis. "What's the plan, General?"

"Time to fly. We're going full on ground to air recovery." Kovac holsters his weapons. "Follow me, Captain." Kovac runs down the hall and leaps from the opening of the third floor to awaiting tension line and grabs a hold of the rung.

Carrying Isis, Jericho follows him down the hall and passes her to him. Kovac smoothly assist the Lass onto the rung of the suspended highly flexible ladder. Kovac's eyes go into a dead stare behind Jericho. A second team of Arcanian troops rounds the corner with rifles ready. One of the troops has a Javelin portable rocket system. These troops were tactical, but dressed differently than the first team. This was Arcanian regular forces or special forces more than likely. They weren't a kill team. The kill team had been killed, which was a good thing.

Turning from the wall breached opening, Jericho charges the forces in a full sprint just as they bring their rifles to shoulder level. Jericho dives to the red stained floor into the pools of blood and chunks of human flesh using the slick wet blood to aid his slide toward acquiring the now departed Major Dale's rifle. He did promise Isis to find a weapon of his own when he gave her Kovac's pistol, that they would just be laying around. Grabbing the rifle, muscle memory provided speed as he racked a fresh round into the already chambered weapon expelling the old. Never know if there's one in there, it's just safe to make sure. Jericho lets loose burst after burst of tracer infused rounds the same time the ASF team does. It a quick exchange of rifle-to-rifle fire. When it's done the advancing team laid sprawled on the blood slick tiles now adding more of their own to pool. Some shots were fatal to those in the ASF, others were of the wounded variety. Dead or not, the initial threat in the hall had been dealt with.

Death slow walks down the hall collecting red and blue orbed souls of the newly murdered in the name of war. There were more red than blue. His dark gray eyes are concentrated on the offspring of his interest, Rachel Bane that even now sits in the Sanstraghten learning her new role as Regent Elect. He sees the mother's eyes in man that is before him, the man named Jericho and even Death feels a since of relief. Because if he didn't believe that a metaphysical metaphorical wall built on lies of Lucifer would ever fall, he believes it will now. This Jericho, if he has the spirit of his mother, he may just yet topple the greatest empirical threat ever to have existed. *Wouldn't that be something?* he thinks.

Covered in blood, Jericho steps over a few of the dead and injured. He keeps his weapon trained on them; the ones alive anyways. The few alive seems to wish for no further engagement, they no longer have the will or wish to continue the fight. He inspects them. *Damn!* He thinks to himself. *They have full video feed wired into their helmets. Why wouldn't they?* Jericho mouthed a few choice profanities at the release of his identity. He only hoped the makeshift scarf he tied around his face before contact would provide him some assistance in keeping his anonymity. Otherwise, they now have real time confirmation that the man that stood up to a malevolent entity was in fact alive and had survived the attack. *Kovac was right, loose ends must be clipped.*

A grunting sound draws Jericho's attention. Rifle up, he finds the target laying among the dead and dying. It's a sergeant. Looks like two rounds found their marks. One in her chest just above the protective plate. The other was at the base of her neck where it meets the clavicle. Through blood and mucus, the soldier is able to spurt out a mixture of words among the spray of blood.

"We got you. I...I saw the rounds hit," the soldier coughs. "We goo got yoo—" The voice trails off as the sergeant, a girl no more than twenty at best went lifeless. In going limp, something metallic hit the blood-slick floor and rolled. The sound was unmistakable. It was a last stand. Sergeant had turned herself into a dead man switch.

The soldier alive next to the sergeant yells, "GRENADE!"

Jericho turns and hauls ass down the hallway toward the awaiting ladder that was dangling in front of the opening. The grenade explodes. It isn't just a simple grenade; it is a high explosive one. Jericho jumps for the opening. The concussive blast in a narrow hallway turns it into a cannon of sorts. Jericho's leap was aided by the concussive blast propelling him out the opening with flames licking his heels. Fire surrounds him, almost overtaking his leap, then he was in open sky; he's out. Freefall lasts a second or two before he catches a hold of the ladder rung. The navigator looks down at the newly attached body and jets of flames exiting the third-floor hospital. Turning his attention to Kovac, he sees him waving them to extract. That was all the confirmation the navigator needed. He turns around giving a thumbs up to the pilot. Confirming that they have all bodies of friendlies attached. The pilot nods okay and pulls back on the stick taking the Apache high into the atmosphere sure not to knock their passengers into any static object in the city landscape below.

Thirteen

CANCER IS A BASTARD

Kaiserslautern, Germany

Lucifer's General, Canceranian overlooks the Arcanian forces deployment from atop one of the tallest structures in Kaiserslautern, the Messalrium. Cancer's caramel complexion is pale, his hair short, jet black and slick.

Sitting perched next to him on the railing is Saadox of Legion, his cloak flailing in the high winds. "It appears that you were correct in believing that the being that Imperial had encountered was a newly lamented Judge. And here I thought the great king of old was infallible. I must admit, I thought that half breed Imperial was speaking false in what had given him such conflict at that Embassy. From my understanding, the time of the Judges has long since been abandoned."

Canceranian remains silent, but watchful of the unfolding events at the hospital. After seconds of no retort, Saadox continues, "If memory serves me correctly, the time of the Judges ended with Samson and that there were to be none like him again to walk this Earth?"

Spending untold generations on the outer regions of the Sadohedranicverse, it has left Saadox's Realmetic syntax something less than desirable. It gave his voice a guttural tone when he spoke.

Canceranian keeps focused on the below events now realizing that Saadox won't shut his trap unless appeased so, he obliges and blesses Legion with small talk. "We anticipated an answer to Imperial. We just didn't know the form it would appear. It was only a matter of time..."

"And legality," adds Saadox.

"Legality has nothing to do with this. No... this is not a matter of fallibility. Elohim has not willingly and wantonly broken a law of Zero Realm. If he were too, then the issue sovereignty would end and Lucifer's conviction would be vacated. If that were to happen then it would be an automatic path to the coveted ascension towards the throne. If you think and dissect the actual text you will find that it has been misconstrued in what he said about the Judges. It was said that there will never be another Judge as to the caliber of Samson. To alter the slightest detail in construction of this current and again, newly lamented Judge, irrevocably makes him dissimilar to the original, ergo, Samson has not been recreated to the same specifications of this one."

"And what is your refutable proof of the dissimilarity oh mighty adjudicator?" sneers Saadox.

"Samson skin could be pierced even when he was in the graces of Elohim. We just witnessed this one take a full targeted hit from one of mortals' heavy projectile weapons... As I stated, dissimilar with no sign of fallibility. No rule was broken in his original stated rule of law."

"One hell of loophole though," says Saadox, standing.

Canceranian smirks. "Agreed... And here I thought you Legionnaires were the most thoughtless of all ethereals. You have impressed me though that you were able to have a witty comeback to the stated obvious interment of the Judges."

Saadox, doesn't find the comment amusing in the least, but there would be no physical opposition this day to Canceranian. He was a general and besides, dissention in the demonic rank was a for sure path to Palengrad. Best to let him have the snide remark and move the conversation on to the mortal problem at hand.

"Didn't think the mortal forces of Arcane would have such trouble locating and bringing this one to heel... We handed them this Judge on a platter," says Saadox.

Canceranian shakes his head at comment and rolls his eyes slightly. "I surmise they had just as much trouble as the Philistines had bringing Samson to heel. If I recollect that correctly, Samson was served up to them on a platter," he says without still adverting his gaze from the unfolding events. "We need their mechanized bird grounded for the reinforcement troops to engage." He looks to Saadox. "Make that happen!"

"Gladly," says Saadox leaping from atop the structure. He rockets toward the Apache. *To hell with the cloak and dagger shit,* thinks the Legionnaire. Saadox touches his gauntlet and slides the circular dial a smidgen and phases into reality 2814. He pulls his blade pointing it toward the Apache sizing it up taking aim at the rotor's primary motor. His jet-black form fitted tunic with red metallic armor shimmers in the dawn's first rays of sunlight.

****

A blip appears on the Apache's navigator's radar. He taps the screen and then looks over his left shoulder for visual confirmation. He flips up his UV protected visor for a clear look momentarily forgetting the positioning of where the east was. The sun blinds him coming off the horizon. He drops his visor, but it's a bit late. Sun spots have taken his vision. He squints and tries to see through the dark spot at what ignited his radar. Whatever it was should have kicked it off much sooner under the early warning protection grid. As the spots slowly fade to normal vision, there it was. He catches a glimpse of it still moving in shadow using the Sun advantageously. "Major... sir, we have an unknown incoming object."

"Missile?" asks Major Divers, callsign Cobalt.

Cobalt doesn't wait for confirmation of direction; she just starts to bank left.

"There was no launch detected," says the navigator. "It wasn't there, now it is. It came out of nowhere... approaching fast, evasive maneuvers!"

Cobalt pulls back on the stick and Red Blade's evasive maneuvering against the incoming projectile begins. Red Blade banks and drops fast. Its trio of dangling passengers go for one hell of a ride. The navigator watches the projectile change course to match theirs.

"No good, it's still tracking us Cobalt... Impact in three, two..."

Cobalt curses under her breath and does what she knows needs to be done. She pulls the stick hard to the left and dives cutting engines briefly while firing 18 flares. *If the projectile is heat seeking, this ought to do it,* she thinks. Looking out of her right canopy she attempts visual detection of the incoming projectile. Her eyes widen at the sight of what she does notice.

Saadox's wings have drawn close projecting him into a rocket with his sword as the piercing tip. He begins a rotating spin in a corkscrew fashion to drill through the chopper. The spin throws him off target slightly. He reassesses and decides to take the cockpit instead of the rotor. There's no more evading, he makes contact. The tip of the blade pierces just through the metal sheet of the cockpit impaling the Major's leg three centimeters before Raphael's able to intercept with a midair collision. *KACKWATBOOM!* The two ethereal beings collide, it sounds like low thunder. Raph tackles Saadox knocking him off course sending the two of them tumbling and spiraling down toward the rapidly approaching Earth. Saadox attempts to break free, but Raphael wraps him in a damn near unbreakable embrace and takes a death dive. He fights to hold Saadox's arms down to his side offering him no protection when they strike the Earth a little above terminal velocity.

Saadox continues to struggle against the vice like grip of the Arch. The young one is strong. Raph feeling that he's losing his grip expedites their arrival time with asphalt. He flaps his wings back one time initiating a gale force wind rocketing the two with increased speed before retracting them back underneath his armor creating a missile effect encompassing the both of them. The two of them disappear below the city's skyline. Seconds after disappearing below the skyline, a massive concussive cloud expands from ground zero shattering the windows out of nearby buildings in a three-hundred-and-sixty-degree arc.

Red Blade One, still in free fall, reignites engines and pulls up from the evasive dive maneuver. The stomachs of the passengers quickly rise into their chest briefly during free fall. It's a nauseous feeling, but not as bad as what came in the subsequent recovery. The cure truly is sometimes worse than the disease, if the disease was freefall and the cure a midair sudden recovery. The sudden return of zero G violently thrashes Jericho, Kovac and Isis about. Add that with the passing concessional strike of Raph into Saadox, it was the perfect storm creating a negative air pressure flow strong enough to cause a small shockwave which blew Isis right off the tension line ladder where she was thought safely nestled underneath Jericho. Kovac having slid beneath the two during the initial extraction was locked into the tension wire by harness that he had on underneath his incognito clothing in anticipation of rapid extract if it was needed. Since in country he wore it everywhere under his clothes.

Kovac watched as Isis was flung to the four winds as the Apache attempted to recover from the stall. One chance, he let go of the line and let the harness catch giving him more slack to work with in hopes to capture Isis as she fell passed him. On her way past, she reaches with all she had, fighting for every centimeter to return to safety. Seeing the panic in her eyes, he stretches as far as he can. She fell past him barley touching his forefinger.

"ISIS!" Jericho without hesitation releases the line. He falls past Kovac, grabbing his outstretched wrist instead, simultaneously snatching Isis' forearm arresting her descent. The combined weight of the fall of two plus the weight of pulling taut in a human chain ripped Kovac's shoulder right out of its socket dislocating it. The crack of disjointing was incredibly audible.

"ARRRGGGHHHH!" Kovac yells in immense pain, grabbing Jericho's wrist, albeit with much less grip after having his arm dislocated. He uses the arrested fall's momentum to swing them back toward the tension ladder.

Jericho takes hold of the ladder with his leg by hooking his foot. He releases Kovac and quickly takes hold of a rung and pulls Isis up to him. "Hold on to me, baby!"

Isis wraps one leg around the line for extra safety as well and holds Jericho tight with both arms. She squeezes tight enough to squeeze the life out of him again causing her to wince in pain because of her cracked ribs.

****

SKATHOOOOOM! Saadox and Raphael tear through buildings with Raph just barely being able to hold Saadox's arm down by his side long enough for him the thumb Saadox's gauntlet's reality matrix before striking pavement. The move phases Saadox out of sight of mortals.

One hell bent demon is enough for society to contend with right now. No need to see two, thinks Raph.

****

Canceranian immediately looks skyward for more descending Archs after watching the interception. Seeing a glimmer of armor in the distance curving through the high stratosphere. He steps backward off the ledge finding more firm ground atop the structure. Confliction is unavoidable; it is now an approaching guarantee. It is highly unlikely that there would be much discussion of violations or treaties as the collusion of the demonic pair had resulted in loss of human life. Such action gave Archs cause to intervene in ethereal affairs indirectly. He already knew whatever this Arch had to say was not going to impede him from task. Canceranian is not going to submit to his authority and so-called honor of whatever Arch is descending. They believed themselves honorable. Whichever one it is, would not let him traipse away without exacting some noble feeling of self-imposed righteous justice based on said honor. Running the math of negotiations in his head tabulated only one outcome... conflict.

****

Kaiserslautern was being laid waste and decimated. The two celestial's Raph and Saadox had torn through a variety of buildings after striking ground continuing their ongoing battle. Office staff and visiting patrons alike are tossed and strewn about the mounting destruction. With Raph being successful in tripping Saadox's Reality Sliding Matrix. They both now operate within an infinity sphere of anonymity. They are hidden from mortal eyes, but the causality of their physical effects on environment are not. To the human oculus, the destruction occurring before them and too them is not wrought by the hidden war of superior beings that can phase in and out of reality. No, their dismay and terror come from the cover which conceals their battle; the cover of a violent storm.

The fleeing mortals of 2814 are observing mini typhoon with red and blue lighting arcs blowing through their buildings and out again into once calm daylight. Civilians outside run for safety as falling debris of concrete and glass showers them. A majority make it to the cover of safety. Few aren't as lucky and are crushed by the falling large shards of glass, metal, bricks, and cinderblocks. Those that were unlucky are collected by Death as he runs past to keep in step with the battling Arch and De Mon.

****

Awaiting the arrival of the Arch Canceranian grabs the hilt of his sword and walks back to the ledge briefly to see how Saadox is progressing in his disposal of the celestial.

"Oh! I wouldn't worry about those two," says Zadkiel slowly descending to ground. *Clank!* The sound of his metallic boots touching the deck of the roof top as he lands doesn't cause a twitch in Canceranian. Zadkiel's wings fold up beneath his armor, his helmet and mask remain engaged and locked.

"Now, turn slowly Canceranian... loose that hilt and surrender to the Archs or resist giving me the satisfaction of cutting you out from this plain of existence as the cancer you are," says Zadkiel unsheathing his blade. The edges glow white hot on either side. "Understand, it makes no difference to me— Actually, I'm lying. I prefer the latter; the part where I cut you out of existence."

Damn! He covered that distance fast, thought Canceranian. He turns slowly with his hands in the air.

The Arch studies Canceranian for deception. *No way it's that easy,* thinks Zadkiel.

Canceranian edges a bit closer "You see, Arch, we celestials can agree on something when it matters. It appears all we need is a specific outcome that is beneficial to both sides... You want me to be escorted by Death as much as I want him to escort you." Cancer smiles, rotating his neck releasing the pressure between vertebrae preparing himself for a deadly engagement. "I can't place the voice, Arch... Raziel, is that you? No, not Raziel, but your syntax is familiar." He shakes his head. "I just can't place it."

The helmet and mask retract below the neckline of the armor exposing Zadkiel's face to the gently blowing breeze.

"Ahh! Zadkiel... How have you been? I see you too have risen to the rank of Arch... I'm starting to believe; they'll make anyone an Arch in these last of days under Elohim."

Zadkiel only nods at Cancer.

Hearing an explosion off in the distance, Cancer turns back to follow the battle of celestials taking place within the streets of Berlin. "The young Arch there is brash and foolhardy," says Cancer. How he has managed to remain above Palengrad this long has amazed us. His dispatch of the zealot Agathan sometime back was quite unexpected."

"But you took notice when the young Arch dispatched him all the same," says Zadkiel.

Cancer still following the battle. "I did... I assumed it was fluke at first. The battle did almost cost him his life as well. Then when I saw he stood against Verminesk... Well then, I really took notice. Verminesk was trained by me. To defy him by not conceding and dying was a defiance of me. I thought about finishing the young Arch myself when he first interceded just now, but Verminesk should be the one to dispatch him." Cancer looks back over his shoulder. "Those two have quite a disdain for each other that hasn't subsided since the schism of Glayden. I don't think any two hate each other more."

"I don't know, I think Michael and Lucifer are on par," says Zadkiel as he closes the distance slightly.

"I would say I stand corrected," says Canceranian, backing slightly from the edge finding better footing. "But me being wrong that would be fictitious; a falsity. I'm never in error."

"Why would you think that?" says Zadkiel still finding purchase himself to attack if needs arrived."

Cancer backs up from the buildings edge toward Zadkiel still keeping an eye on the progressive battle. He also is edging closer for a better position of attack. "You are not wrong in your assessment Arch... One would think that Michael and Lucifer had a most grievous disdain, for each other, but those two are very much still close. Values and loyalties separate them. If one or the other were to accept eithers philosophy tomorrow this contestation would be over... You do see that right? Noooo! Verminesk and the Young Arch down there, they genuinely hate each other."

Zadkiel steps closer.

"Do you hate me, Arch?" Canceranian says never looking back toward Zadkiel.

"I have no reason to. You made a choice and I am the ramification of that said choice."

"Or I yours," says Cancer.

"Or you mine." Zadkiel nods in agreement.

Canceranian turns suddenly, swiftly unsheathing his blade aiming for the Zadkiel's neck.

PTANNNG! Zadkiel barely raises his blade in time blocking Cancer's attempt at a quick assassination. They both push against each other's attack stalemating in a saber lock against each other till they're face to face with only the blades separating them.

"Will quarter be given by you, Arch?"

"No, unfortunately, I think not," Zadkiel says struggling to hold the lock. "I believe we agreed on the latter did we not?"

"We did!" grunts Canceranian.

Both of their helmets and masks generate simultaneously.

"I would like to keep the collateral damage of souls native to this reality down to a minimal."

"No promises," says Canceranian. "If I'm to fall today, Arch, I'll take twice as many mortals then I did with my stamp on their D.N.A.

The two push apart with extreme force. They both are flung off the roof in opposite directions. Cancer crashes through a nearby building. Zadkiel tumbles and flips passing buildings on a trajectory that was luckily not in the path of structures. He catches himself expanding his wings to full glide extent. Steadying himself, he rockets after Canceranian. An experienced foe as he is, he knows he has to stay on top of him. Can't let him have a moment of respite or the battle could turn in his favor. After all, Canceranian is the oldest and more experienced of the two. Cancer explodes from the building's debris he was just flung into and missiles toward Zadkiel. They charge each other at speed covering the distance quickly with weapons at the ready.

Fourteen

HIDDEN BY TYPHOONS

"One would think that Michael and Lucifer had a most grievous disdain for each other, but those two are very much still close. Values and loyalties separate them. If one or the other were to accept eithers philosophy tomorrow this contestation would be over..."

~Canceranian

Kaiserslautern, Germany: Day

Raph pushes slabs of concrete off of him. His helmet has been dented, but not enough to supplant the protective function of it. He's battled Legion before, just not sure if he's ever crossed blades with Saadox. After all, Legion are many and they dress damn near the same purposefully. Legion, a subculture cult within the order of De-Mon created after the schism. Some of those members belonging to Legion were pretty good with a blade, but they were truer adversaries at a distant with plasma bolts. The bastards were more of distant fighters, downright cheaters if really given any minutia of thought to their past engagements. Since mentioning past engagements and tactics, a shadow of a thought creeps and lingers in Raph's mind. A shadowed thought that almost slipped his awareness. To cross blades with a member of Legion, he'll need every edge. When you face a member, you can never be really sure you're facing just the one. It's in the name; they are Legion, Legion are many. Where there is one, there's another.

The young Arch dusts himself batting away the debris and immediately looks around for Saadox. Not seeing signs of him in the rubble, he pulls his blade and steps over concrete and broken bodies of those mortals killed when half the building collapsed. He finds no soul spheres about the bodies in those that lied completely still or had been obliterated by the falling crushing debris. Death has already collected them. That gave him a factor of how much time had passed after impacting the city streets. Making his way through more rubble, Raph steps past those that still drew breath under the cover screams, moans, and groans. Nothing more he would love to do then help, but he can't intervene directly, nor can he carelessly give his attention away while an enemy is still outstanding. He slowly steps around the crystalline textured strands of outgoing prayers that are sure to eventually cross Perceiver Volaxis at the Jacintian's Transcommuncative Hub.

Volaxis, will do his duty to prioritize and disseminate the requests passing them up the chain to Elohim. Stepping around imagery of the urgent line of prayers Raph reads a couple asking for the savior to forgive them for their sins in what they believe could be their final hour. It always there in those last minutes of fleeting life that he sees the prayers of the agnostics, the atheists, the pedophiles, and the prideful praying for forgiveness out of fear of the unknown. Other prayers that Raph sidesteps around are those of the deal makers. Deal makers strike bargains to be given a second chance and what they will do to serve Elohim if given it. The prayers were earnest, some even sincere. Most aren't. The sincerest prayers were the ones that had more shine to the strand. Most he maneuvered through were dull. What he was seeing was nothing new it was only their mortality challenged and the come to Jesus moment as humans christened it.

A red flash catches Raph's attention. He turns raising his sword into high guard placing his blade at the ready. Still at high alert his tension falls slightly when he realizes that the flash is one of the mortals expir-

ing under the debris and his soul has been ejected from the consciousness core located at top of the brain stem. Once ejected it slides down
to the holding pocket, just to the left of the heart where Death will take
hold of it. Raph lets his blade slowly fall to a low guard.

"That one was praying for me to take him," says Death, emerging
from shadow and flame of the felled structure.

"I saw," says Raph.

Death outstretches his hand and calls the red soul orb to him.

Raph's mask retracts and falls below the armor's neckline. "He was
praying to the savior, just a short time ago."

"And I have answered."

"You consider yourself, savior?" asks Raph.

"Do I not save those in need? Am I not more merciful than what
could be in store for them if they face judgment?"

"When they face judgment," Raphael corrects him.

Death, a bit taller than Raph walks up to him. "I did not misspeak,
Arch. When... hasn't been made a definitive statement as of yet. The
trial of Chasm Hall has not been resolved, Lucifer's power play for the
throne has not been resolved... From my vantage point, this test of wills
and betrayals could go either way. So, if they face judgment, stands cor-
rec—"

"You imply that we lost and ascension was gained," says Raph, glancing around, still searching out Saadox before returning his attention
back to Death. "Tough to see from your vantage point when you are
constantly on the run isn't it?" Raph look up skyward in an easterly direction and nods. "There, over in the Crixus Galaxy, that star is getting
ready to die. Shouldn't you be on your way?... Savior!"

Death looks over his shoulder behind him. "You are right. I should
be on my way. Not only will I be collecting that star, but look past your
smugness of intent to the right of that star?"

Raph's visage turns to one of sadness. His irises turn gray.

"Yes, you see it, don't you? You see the result of what will be lost
when the star goes nova... Trillions that inhabit that system will be laid
waste. Some will die instantaneously, while other... well, my arrival will

not come so swiftly. For those in what the humans call the goldilocks zone, their deaths will be drawn out over time; their pain seeming to last an infinity times forever as the skin melts from underneath their thoraxes. How horrible will their final hours be if I do not pass them the mercy of taking their souls prior to the long subjected and constant bombardment of radiated heat flares? You see, Arch, I am savior. If you still are misguided in thinking that I'm not, then only think to the fields of Glayden when I spared your life and showed mercy. I saved you then did I not? And still, even to this very moment I continue to save you."

Death slams the bottom of his scythe unlocking the catch at the top. The blade springs forward and locks into place drawing Raph's attention. Instantly the blade reflects Saadox leaping from the partially collapsed ceiling behind and above Raph.

While distracted talking with Death, Saadox has managed to free himself from the wreckage and climb up one floor claiming the high ground. He watched and slowly stalked Raphael waiting for an advantageous moment to strike. When Death arrived and distracted him that was all he needed. He leapt from the above floor down through the collapsing ceiling pulling his dual blades aiming for his intended target.

The Arch's mask instantly generates over his head and face. He turns again into a high guard, sword at the ready. *CLANG!* Three swords meet as Saadox comes crashing down with dual blades.

Raph parries the brunt of the attack by taking the dual blow on his blade. He angles his tip down toward the ground and slides Saadox's dual striking blades down into the pavement. The Arch's left-wing switchblades out and aims for Saadox's head. It's a feint move. The wing distracts the Legionnaire. Raph quickly removes his blade from underneath Saadox's dual swords. He steps on them both pinning them to the ground. Raph then drives his blade downward through one of the two pinned blades of Saadox's shattering it. He quickly removes his foot from the remaining pinned blade and kicks it upward exposing Saadox's torso. Raph's left wing expands again from underneath his armor and slams hard into the blade holding it upward. Raph hesitates purposely giving his adversary the time to counter attack. The member of Legion does just what the Arch wants.

Saadox is caught by surprise and the skill of the Arch's mastery of the sword. He's left holding his blade upward and midsection exposed for evisceration. He drops a hand from the hilt and aims his gauntlet for Raph's chest. Raphael catches Saadox's charging plasma gauntlet and waits the micro second for the discharge. As the red plasmatic bolt leaves the barrel, Raph turns Saadox's wrist right in a westerly direction. The plasma bolts discharge just as a second member of Legion winds and twists through the overturned rubble exploding from the building's mangled interior aiming for Raph's profile thought open and unguarded. The plasma bolt fires true and catches Legion, #347 named, Raptrax square in his exposed face. The Legion De Mon dressed similarly to Saadox was not wearing his armored mask. The blast was a clean and took half Raptrax's face off. Nothing was left but the bottom set of teeth and chin.

Raph knew the tactics of Legion was never a square fight, he's seen enough firsthand battles and read more than enough after-action reports of the Choiretic Corp to know that they fight dirty and from a distance using surprise elements of attack. It took him a bit of a while to find him, but he thought he'd spotted the Legionnaire during his initial descent He'd lost sight of him though. Instead of trying to find him, it was just easier to create a condition causing the Legionnaire to expose himself rather than Raph having to find him. The surprise attack was expected and Raph made adjustments in calculating events into his favor, although Death was an uncalculated distraction. Raph knew he would dispatch the hiding Legion if given the opportunity. What he didn't calculate was the momentum which the Legionnaire would be advancing. The shot no doubt subdued him, but the missile mass of the body continued.

Raph sized up the situation taking inventory of his options faster than a millisecond. He pushes off of Saadox turning one hundred and eighty degrees and uses his momentum from the left wing's armored blade to completely slice Saadox's forearm from his body taking the gauntlet's plasma bolt out of the equation. Once the energy-based weapon was out of play, Raph dives to the floor leaving the Legionnaire exposed to the incoming body of Raptrax. The two spawns of Legion Prime collide sending Saadox backward crashing through what remained of the interior wall and out through the exterior into the wrecked and demolished streets. Recovering almost instantly Saadox rises turning his pain, rage, and aggression back toward Raphael by grabbing the leg of lifeless Raptrax catapulting the body back at the young Arch. The body incoming, he plants his feet and ignite his circular wrist gauntlet shield taking the full brunt of the strike.

Raptrax's mass strikes Raphael propelling him back through the same trajectory Saadox had just taken. Death runs past Raph claiming the body of the Legionnaire for desecration a second too late. Raph was off his feet and careening out of the current pile of rubble that use to be a place of hope and forgiveness to those of the Jewish faith after the reign of Hitler had ended. The Arch careened through another set of buildings before striking the side of a refueling truck finally coming to rest in the middle lot of a refueling depot.

****

First responders passing by on their way to an already initiated call alter course following the path of newly lamented destruction that rocked the refueling station. The watch commander who'd seen what looked to be a missile like object tear through the fuel depot instantly thought that took priority. He signals his driver to respond with caution. Moments later a portly short stocky man exits the fire truck and observes the depot from what he could believe at the time was a safe distance. Sirens blaring others begin to arrive on the scene. He waves them on to keep responding toward the inner city where the storm was reported have done severe damage. Watch Commander Yovag gesticulates the come-hither motion signaling his driver/pump operator to pass him his set of binoculars. Removing the protective lens cap he peers through the vision enhancing device observing the refueling depot for damage, specifically for leaks. After scanning for a few minutes, he catches what he feared. A puddle with an extensive trail leading back toward a tanker that looked to have buckled in its center.

<"Damn!"> He says under his breath. <"Romav, the next tanker you see bypass you signal them to stop, we need to get foam on that possible accelerant before we have a firestorm on our hands.">

Returning his attention to surveying the recent destruction caused by this highly unusual storm that was suddenly plaguing his small city, the second thing that he noticed about the freakish occurrences besides the danger to the depot was, that this particular storm was acting unlike any storm he's ever seen in his fifty-two years of life. What was occurring was an anomaly. A storm that has pinpointed winds not accompanied by rain. Hell, there weren't even any clouds for that matter. There were intermittences of red arcs of lightning, but it didn't descend down from the heavens, it shot up or outward from ground or just above ground level. Biting his lip in thought of how to attack the currently forming situation, Yovag quickly decided to split duties with the westside Watch Commander Leventhal. She was more than capable of handling the site management of the inner city.

Having decided his course of action he expressed his wishes to the pump operator who relayed the order to Leventhal that she would be in charge of fire suppression and rescue in the city while he dealt with the fuel leak. Yovag walks to the rear of his rig pounding his fist on the side doors of the rig. Three men and one female roll out donning the rest of their self-contained breathing apparati. Looking through his binos again, Yovag taps the distance laser trigger. It reads satisfactory, which is great. That meant Yovag was in the perfect position to set up an Incident Command Center to deal with the ever-evolving incident. Especially till he determined the extent of damage to the refueling depot past the obvious leak.

****

Raph regains his footing. He's a little unsteady on his feet at first, but recovers quickly. Death walks past him slowly nodding toward him. As much as he dislikes the older fallen brother, he can't deny the warning that he gave him by raising that Scythe showing his enemies reflection. It saved his neck, literally. Raph's helmet and mask retracts falling below the neckline of his armor. "Thanks, are in order, Ferryman."

"For what?" says Death in a tone that implies not to push any further and just take it for what it is. "I offer no aid to one side or the other, it is forbidden. You know this Arch."

"Right," says Raphael.

Mask and helmet again generate from beneath the neckline of Raph's armor encompassing his face. He watches as Death prepare the Legionnaire Raptrax for transport to Palengrad. He pours a vile on the corpse of Raptrax instantly reducing it to a viscous liquid that he collects and places into his well-tailored hooded coat.

"If you will pardon me, Arch, I must get this one to Palengrad."

Raph steps in front of him blocking his passage. "Really, Ferryman, what is your play in all of this?"

Death just stares at him for a few seconds then walks past him slowly fading into another reality. "Careful this day Arch, I've taken a many number of celestials as well to Palengrad even those such as yourself," says Death.

Raph watches him fade till he's completely gone. He nods and whispers, "Well, thanks anyhow."

The Arch turns and faces Saadox who walking toward him short one left forearm. He wishes he could say the same for his right. It would make finishing him off a little easier. As he watches Legion approaching, he keeps his eyes on his right hand which unfortunately looks to be very much fine and still carrying a blade. An injured viper is still a dangerous thing.

Sighing, Raphael walks to meet him. As he by passes the first responders Incident Commander he reads the glyphs on his forehead then lightly touches him on the shoulder. "It's not safe Yovag... pull your people out."

Yovag feels the hair on the back of his neck start to rise. A shadow of unease grows in the pit of his stomach. He gestures for a radio. The pump operator reaches back into the truck finding the Commander's assigned radio and throws it to him. Again, he raises the binos surveying the evolving scene before parting his lips to speak. <"This is Brigade Chief Yovag to responding units of Sogarner rd." He looks over toward the dented tanker and beyond it. <"I have multiple collapsed structures with civilians down and trapped. The immediate scene is not safe. The potential for secondary and tertiary explosions is imminent. Pull back four blocks. I'll reassess from there."> *It's not safe. I'm getting my people out of here,* his thought parroting Raph's foreboding of doom warning.

Increasing his pace from a slow walk to a light jog, and then finally into a running sprint, Saadox runs headlong toward Raphael. Raph Jogs a few feet outward from all of the first responders clearing them as collateral damage. He raises his blade ready for what he knows will be the final confrontation with this Saadox of Legion. He will not show mercy; he can't. He can't allow him to rejoin the collective ranks of Legion Prime. Removing him from the proverbial game of Chess now is one less celestial that may See Palengrad later due to the blade of this Legionnaire.

Fifteen

CIVILITY

"I know Lucien Arcane is the devil. You don't live a life of war and not know the Devil when you see him."

~ Niac Rusain

Vespian, Cainsin (Formerly Old Babylon)

Warsivious walks the main hall of the Vespian in his full military class-A dress uniform. His mud-laden leather boots clack hard against the sand-colored marble floor leaving smudges of dirt with each step. Walking past essential and non-essential staff, his towering persona and high rank causes all to observe military protocol by stopping to salute. He pays them no attention; they are beneath him. Simple mortals, weak, pathetic, unnecessary. His face is etched in determination with only intent of reaching his destination. He continues to his purpose of finding out why he was recalled from the field summoned for a meeting with Lucien.

Squads of troops in battle gear moving toward deployment sections find space on either side of the hall to put their backs against the wall standing aside for the general. Unlike essential personal that sit cozy within the spire pushing paper, these pet mortals were worthy of salutes from him. They wage war in his name after all. He was always happy to give respect to that, especially if it kept them hungry for destruction and murderous intent. He wanted his soldiers to be blood thirsty, the kind that other militaries would call monsters. Those were the troops that stood aside for him now, the ones that did not rest on laurels and minor things like moral and conscience

Salutes are rendered at the disheveled and filthy General. He salutes his killing marauders, his modern-day Third Reich. He would once again make this new breed of sheep into wolves just as his last band of soulless bastards were. His new marauders are a force on parallel with the armies he commanded under Alexander the Great, Genghis Khan, Xerces, and a host of others. This force was all red-souled orb. None of them hath love of man anywhere in their hearts. These men and women were far from unjust, they were wicked and where he stood wicked won battles. Men and women classified as wicked gladly took no prisoners unless to horribly torture them for vital information; the kind of information that he really didn't give a shit about, because he already knew it. He was ethereal, playing the character of a human always vigilant and careful to not show the true depths of his lineage.

Soon the campaign for Pakistan would end and the rolling snowball of Arcane forces would have gained more strength for the war machine of peace with the ever-closer endgame of solidifying an everlasting harmony for Israel and later for all. Peace under the guise of war was always the perfect sale. Mortals were if anything predictable and unable to learn from sins of the past and that was okay, because the fight for Israel would be a slugfest... especially if America was to lend aid. America, the country of failed policies and broken democracy, was a virus that needed to be purged and he couldn't wait for his time to knock them down and bring them to heel like he did Rome.

Time must be taken though to end the United States reign of democratic fervor that they so proudly tote as the paramount of leadership. Plans were already constructed to deal with the eventuality of their interference. Warsivious drops his salute as the troops hold theirs until he's fully past them. They all admired him. The last report they'd received of him was from the recent conflict he'd fought. He was recorded on the front lines using only a sword and some experimental weapon that Imperial had helped construct for field testing. A general that fights on the front line with only a sword at the head of his troops was a leader they would follow till the end of their days.

Colonel Rusain, fresh from his latest campaign in Botswana, meets up with Warsivious at the corner of T shaped hallway just past the cafeteria. Rusain hasn't had time to refresh either as he'd just only arrived himself. He couldn't understand why he was being recalled as well. The two nod towards each other in mutual respect as they meet up to head toward the same destination. Rusain gives a slight skip to catch up to the long strides of his general. Walking beside him, he begins briefing him on the minor conflicts south of Warsivious' campaign. He gives him the short version of the take down of Buruti and the carrying out of the orders to specificity.

"Not one prisoner taken?" asks Warsivious.

Taking a few seconds to straighten war-torn battle uniform, the question catches up to him. "No, not one, sir. No further information was needed that required any. I did attempt however to reason with the man believing that he would have been an educated asset to the Arcane force's offensive, but I was forced to think otherwise by his candor. His pride would not have let him be ruled."

Rusain is an agent of war. He was not cruel about it, but he was practical if anything. Orders were given, you follow them. Simple! With the new dawn of Imperial, he was glad that his opportunity had landed him on this side of the conflict. This side has the latest battle tech, if you wanted to call it that. The weapons and armor at his disposal have never been seen till after the revelation. Supposedly, Imperial made it possible. At least that was what the troops and media were supposed to believe. Whether admitted or not, propaganda is just as a lethal weapon as any firearm. Rusain's no fool and had been around war for some time. He just plays the part of the obedient good soldier who is called to quell Lucien's petty squabbles across the globe. He doesn't much mind the petty squabbles; they are to be expected. Conflicts are the price of admission to humanity. Indeed, he's human probably more than most if not all.

The two continue down the main hall to a set of elevators. The last elevator is marked differently from the other six. The plaque next to it reads, *High Command CIC*. Warsivious lifts his wrist exposing and placing his gauntlet hidden underneath the sleeve of his uniform to the security scanning device on the plaque. A blue light scans the Gauntlet and the doors open with a hissing sound that carried a tinge of heat with it. Warsivious enters followed by Rusain. Once the doors close, Warsivious looks at the Colonel, giving him a glare that he's now more at ease to talk more serious business. Colonel Rusain recognizes the glare and places the menial dirt crusted paperwork underneath his electronic tablet. He punches in a few keys and a 3D holographic picture emerges. He begins strolling through his feed of news imposed over the holograph of the Arcane Crest.

"Intelligence has just reported on the situation near Berlin in a tiny city called, Kaiserslautern General. It appears that the Arcanian Lightning Response team headed by Major Dale have all been K.I.A. and the ASF has lost more than half its men. Causalities are high within the elite units and mounting."

Warsivious looks ahead, facing the doors of the elevator as he chews on the first bite of the current news Rusain just passed on to him. The whole ALR and half the ASF units seemed a heavy price for this supposed character that troubled Imperial, if indeed it was him. Believing that Warsivious' silence was a sign of him not listening, Rusain paused himself till Warsivious waved him to continue on.

"I'm listening, Colonel. Was pondering over how one man took out a whole ALR and half an elite ASF team?"

"Reports are still coming in, but it appears they met with a military resistance of a formidable nature."

Warsivious cracks the vertebra in his neck. "The Chinese or Germans?"

"Unknown. Initial reports coming in has the force as unaffiliated."

"Understood, Colonel, continue!" says Warsivious.

Rusain continued his report for the duration of the five-minute express ride down. The doors open to the nerve center of Cainsin. Having been military for more years than he cares to remember, old habits die hard, like knowing your exact location. Rusain counts the minutes to reach such depth making mental note of each passing flash of lights of the descending different floors. Times that by the 10 ½ foot height of the elevator, they are more than likely five to seven miles under the Earth. When the doors open, the first thing the Colonel realizes is that this was the true nerve center of Cainsin, not the one on the eighteenth floor. The one upstairs must be the façade decoy created for the soul purpose of misdirection of enemy assassination attempts to remove Lucien. It hasn't happened yet, but rest assured it's suspected; an attempt will eventually be made. Because Arcane forces have done it. Great strategy creating a mock CIC for misdirection. The ruse would buy time to organize a viable offensive unbeknownst to the enemy, because they would have believed everyone including the target died in the attempt. Real Machiavellian, he has to admit. Warsivious was truly the incarnate of war.

Leaving the elevator, Warsivious is a bit annoyed having to use the conventional means of travel. He could have traveled here as any other De Mon, but his right-hand liaison to mortals unfortunately could not. The elevator is for the lesser beings such as Rusain. Although he is the first full blooded mortal to have been invited to this sanctum, this far down.

War has been out of contact with the ethereal's Aethercasting. He was occupied managing multiple conflicts. He knew that Canceranian was assigned to the task of running down leads on if there was a possible Judge running around Germany. This was a rarity; he actually had a question for the mortal Rusain. It pained War to have to ask. He only assumes that Lucien wanted it this way by cutting his comm to ensure that he would be forced to build working relationships between himself and mortals like Rusain. He was being forced to play nice with what should be pets to beings like him. He hated it, hated them, but for his king, he would.

"Was the main objective accomplished Colonel amidst the losses?" says Warsivious, slightly irritated.

Warsivious is aware that a problem had occurred in Germany. He overheard the sect of Legion talking about contact with Archs before he met Rusain in the hall. He could have found out from them, but that would raise questions among the Legion of how did he not know. Soon word would spread and infect the De Mons. They, too, would look at him differently and begin to ask questions. His spot as number 2 was always challenged, even from the shadows. He doesn't need Rusain to find out anything had he been connected, but thanks to Lucifer, he wasn't. What he needed was the results, if there were any. Canceranian hadn't made a report over Aethercast since he'd returned to Cainsin. Since he didn't hear from Legion Saadox or Legion Raptrax, he concluded that meant the two from Legion Prime's requested to aid and protect Canceranian must have encountered a situation; likely the Arch intervention he overheard.

Continuing to listen to Rusain's report as they walk through the command center, he notes key words and phrases such as, destruction, battle, storm that currently has Kaiserslautern under siege. When he puts all the verbal clues together, it paints the picture in his mind of what is happening in Germany. The battle of celestials and ethereals was currently underway. *There must in fact be a Judge that has touched down,* he thinks. *Guess Cyrail told no tale.*

"Colonel," Warsivious says, even more irritated. "Has there been confirmation is all I want to know?"

He hates to rely on the means of information from mortals, but he can't investigate himself. He has to try his damndest to keep the appearance of a human general and lead battles himself. Not to mention for him, it's great fun and a chance to keep his skills fresh by killing scores of the frail walking strands of dust. It was like the children he watched of every generation killing a multitude of ants that band together to create viable societies. The kids commit genocide among a whole colony for the fun of it simply because they can.

An alert of a notification scrolls across Rusain's tablet. He reads the thread of info briefly. His demeanor changes, it alters to suit War's assholism. Feeling War's irritation radiating, Rusain sighs with his own slight irritability and drops his arm, holding the tablet and paper intel from Botswana down by his side to look War in his eyes while they walk. He's not intimidated by the tall vestige nicknamed War. War was no doubt an able combatant, but so was Rusain. He's been at war for a very long time. He was born for it; murder was his lineage. Fear was far removed from such lifers of the military like Rusain. So, Warsivious' imposing his stature over him did nothing to shake him.

"Sir, confirmation has been made. The subject that Imperial encountered is believed to have been located. Intelligence reported that he was recovering in a derelict hospital a few miles away from the Embassy confrontation. Reports, as I stated, are still coming in, but it seems that he was more than likely registered under a false name and apparently under protection by what the ASF forces are now reporting as the rouge Templar Knights... They are the boots on the ground that confronted the ALR Kill Team."

Warsivious snorts at the mention of their names. "The Templars... For all their talk and righteousness, they were but our pawns a few months ago. We destroyed their order once when it was at their height; they are who we need to put down next. This time, when we do, it will be for all time. I'll make sure I recommend that to my brother. They are a sickness like the works of Cancer on the human genome. You think that you destroy them, but they just hide in the DNA of society and replicate only to infect another area." Warsivious sighs. "Do they have a name as of yet of this elusive hospital patient?"

"Facial recognition is being ran, sir. The subject was wearing a bandanna. Pics and vids were recorded and stored in the Arcanian Information Cloud from the now deceased spotter's Nocs. We should know within the hour if they can work around the mask."

"A half hour, Colonel!"

"Half hour... yes, sir."

The doors open into the inner Zero realm inspired CIC. The setup is an identical dark mirror to its original construction that Lucifer once chaired in moments of crisis. Although back then, crisis had a different meaning.

The De Mon Painell walks out of the Ready Room nodding to Warsivious giving a glance that says he'll see you now as passes the General. Pain is fully clad in all his armor. That was an unusual sight to War since he hasn't known him to have worn full armor since before the fall. He believed it slowed him incredibly and vowed off wearing it in mass. What else caught the General's attention was that he was carrying a sack of rations. That meant an extended trip. They are ethereal, masters of the known universes and of all plains of existence. Rations are not needed for them to traverse across the Sadohedranicverse. So, if rations are being taken, this is a trip to the outer reaches of the Aether beyond limits of Elohim's fabled boundaries. No one but Mercy had been known to travel to such boundaries and it was still a mystery of what happened to him. It was speculated that he went missing more than likely due to depletions of rations. Apollyon was said to have attempted it. The journey damn near ended him. They both stretched far beyond the known borders of the Sadohedranicverse before the Powers Corps could catch up and create a viable road through the Aether.

Warsivious returns the nod to Painell and enters the Ready Room. He now had a new question though, what is taking place out there on the fringes? Furthermore, if an emissary was needed, why wasn't it him?

Rusain follows Warsivious unaware amongst the coterie of De Mons that were in his presence concealed. Painell has just passed the man unbeknownst in a realm that he'd never understand. The ethereal operates in a different reality to avoid the eyes of his inherent flaw; the flaw of mortality.

There are shady dealings in this still forming empire, Rusain could see that. In his well-earned and often hard-fought jockeying for position, he has achieved great rank and was made commander of Arcane forces after years of grooming. In that time, the Colonel was made privy to a great deal of observation and information. He knew of Imperial and had long deduced that his origins were possibly not of this planet when he saw what he did to those men in the gym way back during Cyrail's sparing session when he was younger, before he was Imperial.

Imperial had tossed men about as if paper; he incinerated the one. It was then Rusain had come to the conclusion of possibly other worldly and considered Imperial to be, unnatural if not unholy. However, Rusain too had an inherent flaw and was not above the frailty of finances. Due to his extremely large paychecks and possible outcome for violating a secrecy agreement that he signed with the Arcane empire, he went with the cover story that was given to him of Imperial's origins as a weapon created in a lab. Rusain was good at following orders of leaders. He in fact perfected it till he became one himself. Caveat to that is, there is always someone above you in this game and this was a game of high stakes that he would continue to play for as long as he could. He was good at it, he just hoped it was all beneficial in the end to himself for the selling of his soul for money and secrecy. Hell, he was damned anyways for all he'd done in life.

Warsivious eyes had followed Painell as he walked by leaving the Ready Room and Rusain had caught that. He's seen it often to tell the truth, but kept quiet. They believed him to be a simpleton. It was unspoken or maybe spoken in quiet corners free of his listening ears, but he knew elitist attitudes were prevalent here in Cainsin. He wasn't a simpleton; what he was, was very observant. War's eyes followed someone or something, just as Lucien's and Imperial's have done quite often.

Yes, Rusain knew things, but he was sure they were things he wasn't supposed to know. Every good leader need leverage and what kind of leader would he be if he didn't have any? So, he watched and observed things closely, the dark things, things that should not exist and voices that shouldn't be heard... or, maybe they had always been heard, but disguised as schizophrenia or some other disease of mental destabilization that addled the mind. Oh, yes, Rusain... he knew things, things that came off close to resembling characters from ancient times that walked the Earth and was recorded on papyrus before technology was a thought of. Through deduction, he gathered a battle has waged between the unseen forces of good and those of evil. He just played his part and accepted when history would be written, that he wouldn't be on the side of the Angels. Didn't matter though, this devil paid very well. He knew Lucien was the devil. You don't live a life of war and not know who he is.

No doubt looking around at the sheer opulence of the nerve center, Rusain is impressed certainly, but he's seen opulence before. All dictators build phallacies to themselves. Why would Arcane do any less? Grandiose of it all only validated and cemented his thoughts that he would never live to retire from this place. Operators who know too much like himself would be given the courtesy of having his very own kill team ordered to vacate his position. The order would be given someday to execute him for what he knew and what they suspected he knew. He had no thoughts of getting out of the Arcane organization alive. He only wondered about the outgoing method of pain and the mode of transportation that will be used to usher him unto death and that was totally predicated on whether or not death would have him. He was no angel and have done things that would make blood freeze of lesser men. Welp, no point on dwelling on betrayals and kill teams now, that decision is off in the hopefully distant future for now. Till then, he'll play the good soldier never wanting to know more than the operation requires. He follows Warsivious into vast Ready Room, which leads into a wider chamber of an ethereal pocket dimension unseen by the human oculus.

Sixteen

NEVER WHERE ANGELS TREAD

"From all the telltale signs, Lucien Arcane is just another iteration of the true name of horror, terror, dread, and Thanatos. There is no guessing or mistaken of names. I know who he is; he is entropy, he's Lucifer himself."
                                                            -Niac Rusain

Rusain's eyes stretch wide at the immensity of the chamber that has been exclusive till now to only Lucien, Warsivious, and Cyrail arcane. He pauses, taken aback not at the opulence of the chamber, but the mind-warping technology that is laced throughout it. The room has an unnatural glow and illumination with there being no tangible artificial lighting source. Light is everywhere from nowhere. Televisions appear as floating holograms projected against the walls, because from what Rusain can visually see, there are no tangible monitors that bear insignias of Sony, Vizo, or even Samsung, yet the walls itself displays images from all over Earth at any given moment with cameras appearing to be everywhere capable of recording; even in impossible angles.

Rusain notices, looking from wall to wall, that there are a few monitors that displays what he knows to be clusters of stars contained within the Milky Way Galaxy, but there are other galaxies that he is for sure he's unfamiliar with and should not be visible by any satellite in such clarity. Rusain's eyes move toward the ceiling where there is an image of a bipedal being that he knows is not of this Earth. As his eyes move to observe that being's surroundings it's evidently clear that the background where it is, is a foreign planet. Three Sun's staggered each other in the monitor. One that was ginormous enough to eat the other two suns. The chamber was a sensory overload filling his synapses.

"That planet there is called Myfobial, Colonel," says Lucien.

Rusain doesn't whimper or sound aghast at the removal of obfuscation that the Earth was not alone. He never believed that humans were alone in the cosmos anyways. His demeanor remains poised and the true definition of equanimity. He slowly moves his eyes from the lavish ceiling with visuals of other worlds to the large leather chair, whose back is turned toward him. The orange and blue Arcane logo is emblazoned on the back of the chair. Knowing the unmistakable hard R pronunciation of Lucien's voice, Rusain stands erect to full attention.

Like a king on his throne, Lucien sits ensconced behind a massive dark onyx and jade desk. The voice that emanated out from behind it was surely that of Lucien, Rusain was sure of it, but the syntax, structure, and tone of the speaker was all wrong. The sound of voice was not the head of Arcane enterprises. This voice was rough, but sweet. It was downright soothing and intoxicating and it shouldn't have been. Rusain's eyes moved only in the peripheral to catch a glance of Warsivious, whose hand had moved to his weapon side just out of Rusain's degree of sight.

This is it then, test time. He's going for his weapon if I answer wrong to whatever decisive rounds of questioning comes next, thinks Rusain.

"Are they hostile, sir?" Rusain replies. "Should we be turning our attention toward the skies for incoming hostilities?"

Laughing at the bravado of his most trusted mortal, Lucien keeps his back toward the Colonel and remains fixated on the holographic screen in front of him. The screen is like no other that Rusain had ever seen.

First, it isn't a screen, the images are projected upon nothing but maybe a thin film of mist.

He chuckles to himself. "Hostilities from the skies? No, far from it, Colonel, at least not yet. We should be looking toward the skies for an invading enemy someday, but I assure you not the Myfobes," says Lucien.

"Is that what they call themselves, sir?" says Rusain, shifting his attention back toward the chair and desk.

"Simply outstanding. There is an alien species that has been made known to you and you ask questions of intent and civility of their nomenclature? Your reaction is unexpected, but your reply is spoken as a true commander and warrior. You were not in the least put off by the fact that an alien species is moving in a 3D hard light construct that your brain cannot even recognize what to call it by name. But... but, your only worry is that are the being's pictured on it hostile," Lucien continues, laughing.

Rusain glances up.

The chair turns with Lucifer now facing Rusain from behind his desk. The Colonel doesn't look, and instead, keeps his eyes forward. From his peripheral vision, he observes an entity there, but he dares not look at it fully.

"Let's cut through it, Colonel, shall we, and be real with each other. After all, you are no simpleton. No need to try and place the voice. I am Lucien Arcane. That should satisfy your wonderings." Lucifer smirks. "Then again, I've had many names it is hard to remember them all over the billions of years that I've existed."

Rusain's expression of stoicism does not betray him. He keeps his focus forward.

Lucifer stands and walks toward Rusain. "I have been in existence before time was even a concept. I have been everywhere and nowhere... which is by the way a real place. I have seen and done everything on every subatomic level of thought your mind can conjure and those it can't. Take the speed of your last thought, think how quick it appeared in your mind. Now, amplify that by eternity and divide it by forever and you will have not even come close to which the speed I can traverse alternate realms of every galaxy that is and has been."

Rusain continues to keep his eyes forward, his fear stabilized. *This is a feel you out meeting. Otherwise, I'd be dead already*, he thinks to himself.

"I have given you access to my most inner sanctum, because I find you to be a remarkable mortal. Your loyalty has been second to none. You have performed exemplary in your time here with us under the Arcane banner serving my avatar incredibly."

Lucifer waves his hand and the ground opens in a cylindrical shape. A dark light appears shinning upward from the hole forming a column off to the left of Rusain's peripheral, right of Lucifer's desk. He wanted to be sure that the Colonel did not miss the next beat. As sudden as the shadow column was there it was now gone. In its place was the body of Lucien Arcane in a hyperbolic glass vessel.

"Colonel—" Lucifer walks behind Rusain looking to rattle him a bit, get a rise out of him. "It just struck me Colonel, I never thought to know or ask your name. Normally, I know such things like this, but there are those... anomalies of your kind that stumps me from time to time. Last mortal I knew like that was Xerxes. What an incredible specimen he was. Then there was Gilgamesh before him."

"I understand, sir. I'm not looking for any static. If you are who I think you are claiming to be, then you are omnipotent... A being that I suspect is not to be trifled with," says Rusain still looking forward, still poised.

"And, yet, to know of me, fear still has not made you cry out. Impressive." Lucifer walks around front of Rusain purposefully towering over him showing dominance. He looks down into the Colonel's face for reaction. "Why are you here, Colonel?" asks Lucifer.

"Because you pay substantially well, sir."

Lucifer and Warsivious laugh.

Lucifer walks back to his desk half sitting on the corner of it. "The human flaw of greed. I love it. Loyalty based of compensation, right? I always know where your species stand.

"On a mountain of avarice, sir," says Rusain.

"Damn right, Colonel, damn right!" agrees Lucifer, still laughing.

Rusain's gaze turns to Lucifer. "And one more thing, sir. On top of that mountain of avarice, it's not necessarily greed that is stood upon, it's survival. It just sometimes disguises itself as greed."

Lucifer hops off the desk quickly with a steady pace walking up to Rusain. "Are you thinking survival now?

"Always, sir."

Lucifer turns and nods to Warsivious for him to stay whatever weapon he was going to use to execute Rusain had the meeting and reveal gone sideways.

"Do you care to know my mission, Colonel?"

"Sir, you are a caliber of superior being that bare offspring the likes of Imperial. I don't need to know more than that. I am a tactician of war that will fight until my last breath or the last war, whichever comes first."

Lucifer nods in acceptance and then ejects and spreads his wings in a full stretch. He watches the Colonel's expression. Then realizes that wings are nothing new to him. Imperial was his initiation. "At ease, Colonel."

"Aye, sir." Rusain rests at ease caught up in thought thinking, *from all the telltale signs, Lucien Arcane is just another iteration of the true name of horror, terror, dread, and Thanatos. There is no guessing or mistaken of names. I know who he is; he is entropy, he's Lucifer himself.*

Lucifer looks back over his shoulder at Rusain. "Exactly, and it's nice to make your acquaintance."

Rusain keeps his demeanor level, still giving nothing away to emotion. He now knows that his mind can be read.

"Now, then, tell me about this positive contact in Germany." Lucifer looks toward the wall behind his desk which is clearly a screen of a point in space. The 3D monitor zooms in close from space to the battle between Raphael and Saadox. The Image is crystal clear as he points Rusain's attention to the screen.

Rusain averts his eyes from Lucifer and focuses towards the melee on screen. He can see them clearly as Warsivious next to him. The speed with which they move can't be fathomed. Collateral damage has to be in the hundreds of millions of dollars. His eyes follow the spectacle best they can in disbelief, but what he saw was indeed happening. He returns his attention back to his tablet of collected intel from his operatives on the ground. "Sir, this is real time is it not?"

Lucifer nods yes.

Looking back to his tablet at the newest notification, Rusain gives it a couple of taps and swipes. He nods at the information that appears.

"Sir... from what Imperial described of his encounter at the Embassy, our intel people found the unidentified attacker. This unidentified attacker was believed to have been in Kaiserslautern, a city away from their original encounter at the Embassy in Berlin. Keeping tabs on one of the Templars is what drew our attention to the point of question."

"No need Colonel," says Lucifer. "I know who it is. I've known for some time. I deemed him no threat and thought him vanquished. Track to your hearts content if you would like, but I suggest resources elsewhere for the time being. I want Imperial to throw the final punctuative mark on the life of this Judge. It's a point that must be made and Imperial must make it."

At this comment, Warsivious gives Lucifer the side eye and Rusain caught glimpse of the disdain that he knows to be contempt. With what he's seen in his time with the Arcanians one thing above all was clear. Superior beings they may be, but they're not too much unlike us. *Good to know*, Rusain thinks. That is something that could be exploited later.

"Anything else business matter related from you two that needs to be discussed?" asks Lucifer inspecting the Lucien avatar.

Warsivious watches the screen particularly focusing on the main subject hanging from the attack chopper's steel tension ladder. Squinting his eyes, he focuses on the celestial's only solution to bringing down Imperial.

"That's him? That is the Judge I've heard so many whispers about in quiet corners?" says Warsivious. "Doesn't look like much."

"Neither did Samson," says Lucifer, looking at Warsivious with the same contempt he was shown moments ago.

Warsivious changes topics quickly. "The battle in Kaiserslautern, then?"

"Is just one of several hot spots," says Lucifer. "I'm pulling the Archs thin as possible. I have plans for them. I have something in the works that will free us up to move unopposed for a while. Painell is off to see to that."

Rusain keeps his mouth shut and eyes forward as they talk of players that are unknown to him. He'll write the names down later best he can remember. For now, he reverts to his years of training, staying quiet and gathering intel.

Lucifer turning his attention away from the screens walks over to Warsivious placing his hands on his shoulders nodding toward Rusain. "Is the Colonel ready to oversee the full might of the Arcanian troops?"

"He's more than capable, your grace."

Lucifer studies Rusain a moment longer. "Promote him to One-Star General Rusain. Advise him when needed, but turn the day to day running of the military might over to him. I'm going to need you to take a more active role in the art of misdirection. It's time to get you back in fight." Lucifer still stares at Rusain. "Show the new one-star general everything."

Warsivious salutes Lucifer, "At your command." He then turns to Rusain. "Congratulations... General Niac Rusain."

His salute was perfect as he turns a quarter turn and places his fist to his chest. Rusain does not betray his stern façade. He salutes with pride and a sense of purpose, but there's no mistake in the contract that he just signed. This new contract superseded the old one of secrecy. This new one was of the variety of promises that he'd made Jesus, if you believe the stories of the bible. "If you but bow down and worship me, all this I'd give to you."

He knew that per the Devil's deal all would be given to him. Anything he wants will be supplied. At the end though, yes, at the end, make no mistake, all bills come due. That was the devil's game, wasn't it? Take... eat... and in the end when the bill comes due, you will pay. It has been abundantly clear for decades that his soul was damned. No, wait, his soul's already been damned. Rusain has no misgivings. He would never tread where angels did. It just wasn't his nature or in his stars.

Seventeen

CONTEMPT

"I am Legion!"

~Saadox of Legion

Kaiserslautern, Germany

A flurry of strikes bangs and clang off of Raph's defenses. Having lost an arm, Saadox's swings are wild. Not to mention, his counter defense stands little chance to the Archs' offensive. He reigns in uncouth tactics, once it's revealed they won't work, and replaces them with more calculated precision strikes in an attempt to measure up to the keen swordsmanship that he's seen the Arch display. Saadox swings low and up in a J configuration. Raph breaks the attack and steps sideways into a profile allowing the J attack curve through unimpeded. When the J hits its zenith, Raph's left wing ejects impaling Saadox's abdomen. Reeling in intense pain, the Legionnaire kicks Raph in the side breaking the two apart. The impaled wing blasts free of Saadox's abdomen taking jets of blood and flesh with it, tearing the abdomen even more.

"ARRRGGGHHH!" Saadox screams, slamming his hilt-bearing hand to the wound in an attempt to sooth and stop the hemorrhaging. Blood juts over his hilt and hand. He can't cauterize it, because his plasma caster has been destroyed. The Legionnaire pulls his hand away from the wound, trembling, and letting the blood flow like an unimpeded river. Taking a sigh to gather his strength, he lets out a slow exhale. He aims his pain, fear and rage at the young Arch and again charges in bringing his blade down on top of Raph. The Arch's right wing catches the blade on its armored sleeve. He interjects his sword to bring Saadox's blade low holding it in a Saber lock.

Knowing he's defeated, Saadox looks in to the helmeted eyes of Raph. "You will be sleeping in Palengrad by day's end, young one. There will be more after me that will hunt you till your place has been all but solidified next to mine in the halls of the Warden."

Raph ignores Saadox's pathetic attempt to get inside his head and slides his blade up Saadox's. It's destination, neck for decapitation.

"HEADS UP!" Zadkiel yells.

A large reddish-purple plasma bolt precedes Canceranian descent toward Raph with Zadkiel in tow. Raph slides his blade down then up off of Saadox's while simultaneously releasing his wing that was holding it down. Raph spins one hundred and eighty degrees grabbing Saadox and placing him in front of his body as an ethereal shield. Legion takes the full blast of Canceranian's bolt. The blast lifts the two off their feet and sends them flying into the roof of a propane tank dispensing warehouse with Saadox's body lit ablaze. The plasma induced flames ignite the severely damaged upon entry propane tanks.

An enormous explosion sends a shockwave rolling out in a 360-degree ripple effect engulfing the damaged refueling depot as well. The blast flips cars and shatters surrounding structure's windows blowing them outward turning them into projectiles. Heavier than air fuel of leaked propane spills into the underground cauldron of sewers passing dated underground infrastructural wiring that sparks every now and again. It, too, ignites in an orange and bluish tapestry of heat. Like a professional ice skater gliding across ice, the flame follows the propane cascading over the top of it turning the once cold dark and dank sewer system into a lightshow. The flame rides each drop of fuel until it seeps over a small crack in the city's carrier line of their underground natural gas. The light show turns into a gorgeous catastrophe. If anyone in the radius of 17 city blocks live to tell the tale, they would tell of the mushroom fireball they swore was nuclear bomb.

Debris and flames overtake the dueling celestials and then everything else in the immediate radius.

****

Vega Bognetti more than half a mile away watches the fiery mushroom plume of flames ignite in the reflection of the window that he's cleaning on the outside of the 80th floor. He quickly turns and watches with his own eyes the mushrooming plume gain incredible height. It was an impressive sight before his gaze turned to another detail that did not miss his attention. His gaze is drawn to the dust blowing off buildings in the distance and how it shimmers in the morning light. From the 80th floor, the smaller buildings look like a sea of cubed boxes with waves of swirling sand blowing off, through, and between them. As the wave of crumbled rock and mortar ride the concussive winds intertwined with cancerous particulate debris draws closer, he looks down and checks that his harness is strapped in.

Ever closer this dust-looking cloud draws near. He squints focusing his vision. It's not waves of sand, well, actually it is, if one wanted to be scientifically accurate and an asshole, because it's glass; glass is just superheated sand and it was on its way in a huge shimmering reflective cloud. It was as if the lord himself blew a child's lifetime supply of glitter upon the Earth.

What the hell? he thinks to himself. His mind digressed for a moment to his 9th grade science teacher Mr. Ungle and his class on what created glass. As the wind of the coming concussive blast kissed his face, he was back in the present. He hit the brake release and starts repelling from 80th floor while watching as a sea of glass riding the shockwave was headed toward him. It would have been slow going to ascend back up to the roof. His best chance now is to lower himself and breakout a window, get into the building and find cover.

Vega swings out for momentum and comes back with both feet to shatter the glass denying him entry. It was a no go. Buildings were designed these days to prevent suicide deadfalls. Nowhere to go, he turns toward the window that would not give one iota. He begins to smash at it with his squeegee. The cylindrical-molded plastic gives way under the pressure of his exerted force to break the reinforced glass. It may as well be clear concrete. In the tinted mirror reflection of the glass, he watches the wave; it finally reaches him. Just as it does, he looks at his reflection in the mirrored window and starts to pray. He parts his lips to begin the Lord's Prayer, but he abruptly stops when he doesn't see just his reflection, but his reflection buried in a hooded cloak of Death's silhouette. Looking at this ominous reflection staring back at him, his chin begins to bleed. It was just a slither of a laceration. Then more small lacerations start to appear on his face. The fine particles of glass had reached him. The shockwave would soon follow. He knew it, he saw it. Death's image disappeared. What replaced it was again his own reflection with a series of fractures in the window spider webbing out in cracks.

Vega Bognetti starts to scream as large swaths of flying glass eviscerates him. His blood splotches across the fracturing glass. The shockwave arrives and slams his body with his cleaning cart through the 72nd floor window shattering it. Upon entry his body is thrown from the cart, but the harness is attached. He doesn't get clear. After the shockwave blows past his now blood-soaked body, the damaged cart swings back outside the building pulling Vega with it. Cart with Vega attached just dangles once its pendulum action stagnates. Blood pours from capillaries, venous, and arterial points all over Vega's body. It hurts for him to move, but he does even though it was involuntary. The rope that he's attached to is nothing more than just braided nylon woven tightly. It gives way in small sectional tears from being cut by glass. He feels the jolt of it dropping him those few millimeters every couple of seconds. It feels like an overdose of a massive static electric shock.

Vega... damn, he hated that name. He often asked his mom why that name, but it's a moot point now at the end of things. He turns his head slightly and looks from the corner of his right eye and watches the rope stretch and tear a little further. One second that it took for the rope to finally completely separate felt like 20 minutes, when it's actually less than 20 seconds. Suddenly, it happens: Vega is weightless as he begins his descent towards the pavement. His mind has time to reflect not on the issue of his imminent demise, but on a thought that he had when he was young and very much braggadocious. He wanted to have a profound death. He wanted to speak poetry as he left this world and shed his mortal coil. He figures that he would've use words such as thou, heurist the time, and lo there do I see my kin. His final words are not lofty in the least, but replaced by the lexicon of a dumbed down generation haplessly addicted to technology and quickened abbreviations. So, for a better lack of a superior vocabulary base to elicit a cherry humdinger of a word. He simply states, "Shit!" and thinks, *I'm soooo fucked.*

As he falls past the 20th floor, Death reaches out the window granting him a touch of mercy by snatching his soul, leaving only the lifeless husk to strike the bottom of a flipped over Dodge Caravan that wheels now faced skyward. The price of conflict between gods always seems to cost mortal lives.

*****

Angel's Spire, Zero Realm

Michael's eyes widen as he intently watches the battle unfold from the Spire's balcony. His heart skips a beat at the possibility he may have just lost another brother under his command. He steels himself to that possibility pushing emotion down from his wakened cognitive mind. One thing's he's learned is that he has to trust his decision making. He doesn't have the luxury of second guesses or to command from a place of the heart. He has to remember that he's playing a long enigmatic chest game that Lucifer unwittingly devised in his play for the throne. His face cringes at the blast that Raph just took, but he pushes that to another lesson that Yeshua had taught him by allowing Michael to command. The lesson is to trust the people under your command. Raph has proven that he can handle himself more than once. Him being the baby of the bunch, all find a special place for the youngest.

Gabriel returns to the balcony fully armored. She places one foot on the balcony readying to leap over when Michael ceases her action without even looking her direction. He remains focused on the battle at hand.

"No, Gabe, I have something else for you."

She looks past Michael at the double dual taking place below. "I'm needed there. Jericho is my charge to protect."

"He is no doubt that, but there is no one currently pursuing him at the moment. To place another Arch on the field may force a wider confliction that honestly, we are not ready for nor can humanity take. Jericho is in the clear... At least for now. We must face fact that our secret that we enveloped him in has for sure been compromised. At least that is the belief that we will operate under. The Arcanian forces came for him. If the mission was to ferret him out, it worked."

Michael turns and walks back to the nerve center and again looks at the water projected 4D map of the Sadohedranicverse. He enhances the view of Earth. *So much trouble for one little spec of dirt and rock amongst the unending ocean of stars,* he thinks to himself.

"I will not send another Arch unless another fallen appears. I don't want another full-blown committed battle. The only ones that would ultimately suffer are the mortals. Would you agree? Look down there! LOOK AT IT! That's just two Fallen and two Archs."

Gabriel watches the mortals that are suffering and those that have already died due to the active conflict that was currently taking place on the streets of Kaiserslautern. Her head hangs a bit low at the despair as she reads the passing prayers; prayers not just for the recent spat, but all of them across the world that run continuous. Her irises turn colors from reddish green to gray. She reluctantly nods in agreement with Michael's assessment of those that ultimately pay the toll.

"Gabe, I believe Raph and Zadkiel can handle the incident in Germany." *I have to believe that, because there may be something that moves in shadow to unwittingly undue us all,* thinks Michael. "Come, avert your eyes from the battle and put them to another matter that has consumed my thoughts. I would appreciate counsel."

She extends her watching of Zadkiel's pursuit of Canceranian a while longer as he engages in sporadic clashes with the mighty foe, Cancer. Her eyes close in a silent prayer for her brother's pursuit to end with capture or kill of Cancer before she reluctantly decides to follow Michael to the 4D Projection Table. Seeing her distressed by not being able to lend aid, he nods at her, making sure that she's mentally on board with his decision not to reinforce. She gives a slight nod back and focuses on the table trying to drown out the cries of mortals left devastated in the below wake of an ethereal squabble. Seeing her on board Michael spins the 4D map of the Sadohedranicverse. His eyes follow the trajectory of Painell's launch from a traverse tube that exited from underneath Baltimore. He taps the map and traces the path which appears in a red holographic line.

"This was brought to my attention."

Gabriel studies the map paying close attention to what Michael had singled out. "Pain is traversing the Aether... nothing unusual there. What of it?"

"Look closer." Michael enhances the map again. "Look at the thickness of slayern that he's pushing through on the outer skirts. He's cutting a path overgrown with it out into the direction of forbidden Aether. When have you seen a new trail blazed across the Aether past enriched slayern?"

Slayern has not been spoken for eons. It's a name that fell from lexicon, because no celestial of ethereal travels that far out into the expanse of the Sadoverse. There's no point. Out there are wastelands of the Verse; the badlands that no celestial or ethereal can survive. It's Elohim's speed limit of the universe. It's a viscous material that truly lies on the edge of infinity as it borders into eternity. Two have known to have ventured a way into the Slayern. Only one returned and that was Apollyon. Mercy was lost and such a lost that it was mighty blow that had been felt throughout the Sadohedranicverse.

Gabriel leans in closer. "Never... at least in that direction she admits in a whisper. "What lays beyond the barrier of dark matter he's swathing through? What's in that direction? A short cut to Cronan perhaps, maybe Borefrayara?"

"Dark matter?" Michael gives a slight half smile at the terminology. "You truly have been among the mortals far too long sister. No, not Cronan, or Borefrayara. That system is off thirty degrees left and in the fourth realm... No, this something different."

Gabriel looks at Michael. "Who alerted you to his ill movements? A far off Choiretic or Power working out that way?"

"Not important, but the intel is reliable. What is important is where he's going... It's something familiar about his path I can't quite recollect. I haven't had time to clear it with the Prince or Elohim, but I believe it causes warrant to check out. I want you to pursue. Do not engage unless you must. Follow at a distance and when you ascertain position of his destination report back."

Gabriel sighs. "Why have you not taken this to Prince Yeshua?"

"Because Pain has already departed, probably crossing Andromeda by now," says Michael, avoiding answering her question. The hour has grown late and he's gaining distance too quickly for superior counsel. This is my call. It may be nothing but recruitment, but that is a fear as well. I think his movements out toward Dark Matter as you so eloquently put it is something worth our time to investigate. When I talk to the Monarchs, maybe they will ease my apprehension and growth of concern, but till then, go!"

She studies the map closely.

Stepping closer toward her gaining her undivided attention he places his hand on her shoulder. "It has been reported that he has a supply of Manna. You will take a supply of Manna with you as well," says Michael. He nods toward Painell. "He has taken a supply, meaning he plans on an extended journey that cannot be traveled by our known network of traverse tubes. This is something big and I feel we need to know what. We can't sustain another surprise the likes of that abomination Imperial. Had we taken this action in Aswan over thirty years ago by way of Earth's time, Imperial would not have been on the board. We... I will not make such a mistake again."

He releases her gaze turning his attention back to Painell on the 4D map. He also brings up the battle in Germany.

Gabriel nods. "Michael?"

He looks at her in an I-dare-you-to-disobey-this-order scowl. His stern but exhausted look speaks volumes for him. It tells her to not even bother trying to find reason to remove the burden from herself to be with Jericho.

Unspoken and clearly heard, Gabriel stands at attention giving a chest salute acknowledging his order. "I will report to the hall of Manna directly."

She sends him a probing look. Her eyes turn a deep dark gray. Seeing this Michael lightens a bit realizing he was a bit brash to his second in command that has never failed him. He shakes his head slightly knowing that he went too far. Sighing, he stands and steps to her leaning in closely placing his forehead to hers. "I will personally look after the boy until your return sister. The boy will be fine. I swear it. Who knows, maybe I will come to see what you see in him? In your stead, I will continue to further his training employing all methods for his success."

"Surely there are others that you can send Captain... Please."

"There are, however they are not in Zero realm right now... you are! Besides, you are my number two. I don't trust that you will get this done. I know you will. You are my first Lieutenant Arch, just as I sacrifice, so must you. At least this time. The boy will be fine."

Gabriel studies the map and then walks back to the balcony turning one last time towards Michael. "I'll hold you to that brother. He is the key that Elohim provided."

"Then, sister, it is imperative that we clear a path to the door of his destiny, wouldn't you say?"

Michael widens the water infused 4D map highlighting hot pockets of engagements around the Sadohedranicverse.

"Look here, sister! Unlike the battle for the blue gem down there, we have engaged De-Mons and Legion around the verse. If you must know,

I mean, if I must explain my actions to get you moving, then I'll tell you what I believe. I believe he's recruiting on a larger scale like when he recruited the mystics to his cause at the battle of Bastion. Remember when we met them on the lands of Sarin in protection of Noah son of Lamech?"

Gabriel nods.

"It was hard fought, sister, but what stood out if you remember? What was it that he brought to the battle? ...Species from other galaxies to fight; he brought alien species to Earth to combat us. We put down those connections and broken those ill-fated alliances, but what if we didn't what if while we've been distracted with Imperial, he moves to reunite the fallen alliances. I believe Pain is an emissary, a herald of sorts sent out to reconnect them under our very noses to work under a single banner. His Banner."

Gabriel looks toward the heavens, daring not to sneak another peak at the conflict currently on Earth. "You believe he's reestablishing old alliances across the verse?"

"Look at the map! I know that he's attempting to pull our forces thin spreading our ranks to make us weak. I assumed to pull us out of 2814 so that Imperial could further his belief agenda and heresy." He studies Gabriel. "Although altered, we are heading toward prophecy of the end of this age. There was always an apocalyptic battle on the horizon, but Lucifer has changed the parameters. What once would had been a conquering of nations without firing a shot will turn into a battle that every step forward will be purchased in blood that will rise above the Prince's riding Girdle."

"This battle to which you speak of was to have been spearheaded and won by the Prince on his own Michael, it was not to be handled by us," snaps Gabriel.

"And, yet, it will be sister. We are off script. Fate himself is attempting to settle the matter and bring closure to his finest work ever written, but you and I know Fate will not succeed. Lucifer, cannot be bargained with, he cannot be reasoned with, he cannot be bartered with. If he can't have Ascension then he will tear the Sadohedranicverse from the Aether and he will do so behind Imperial... an abomination that hides behind rules that we cannot break."

"And for that very reason, Captain, the Sadohedranicverse may come down to not depending on the Prince or even us celestials..." says Gabriel. Noooo! The fate of all realms and realities will fall to a mortal that I have placed all of my faith in and by extensions ours. Cassiel did not die for the boy. He saw an enemy cunningly created outside of the rules by Lucifer that was unstoppable by our creed to a king. He died because I believed. I believed in Jericho so much so, that he took my faith as his own."

"*Arghhh!*" Exhausted with going back and forth with his sister, his lieutenant, Michael throws his hands up gesticulating I give up gesture. He looks back to the map.

"Was the Prince supposed to bring peace and an orderly close to the age?" says Michael frustrated. Yes, he was. Is that to still be? If Imperial does not fall, then no. But, if we succeed, then the promised end will prevail. That is why it is imperative that you pursue Pain. I know the importance of Jericho. I know what he means to you."

She does not blink as she stares at her brother. A tear starts to well in her grayish white irises.

"Cry if you must, sister, but War is coming. I want to know all the participants before he is here upon us with De Mons, Legion, and whatever other alliance they gather in secret. Painell is my suspected emissary to bolster Morning Stars troops." Michael spins the map. "There are no allies for us. We are all there is on the side of the Realms."

"*Hmmph!*" Gabriel breathes. "Lucifer was the best of us, he was supposed to be the bridge and caretaker of the Realms. He was our hero, especially if you let him tell it. I remember how proud and braggadocious he was of being that hero we all admired."

"And there began the fall," Michael says, walking toward Gabriel placing his hand on her shoulder again. "We are all the heroes of our own tale. Lucifer is no different. He is the hero of his."

Gabriel heaves a long sigh. Her helmet and mask generate from below her armor's neckline. She nods towards her captain. "Watch after him Michael till my return."

He nods slowly. "As if he's my own... Besides, I think it past time he and I had a chat."

Gabriel steps on the balcony and launches herself up through the clouds of Iayhoten. Michael wipes a tear from his cheek as she takes off into the unknown days ahead. He turns his attention back toward the events in Kaiserslautern. Gabriel stops by the Hall of Manna for provisions and then rockets into the expanse of the Sadohedranicverse in pursuit of Pain. She takes the nearest traverse tube that places her on the route that Painell was last seen taking. She would catch him, she needed too so that , she can get back to Jericho.

Eighteen

⟨⟨⟨⟩⟩⟩

TILL THE LAST

"My fear of losing my brothers is impairing my decisions."
~Michael

Kaiserslautern, Germany

Canceranian lands on both feet turning simultaneously sliding across the flame ridden gravel parrying Zadkiel's blade who's right on his heels sliding alongside him. One fourth of Cancer's visage is exposed from behind a broken mask. his breathing has become laborious from exhaustion. Blood runs from a deep gash over his eye slightly blinding it rendering it useless. His armor isn't in much better shape than the mask, it's dented and broken in various locations from trading continuous blows with Arch Zadkiel.

Sliding to a stop and still standing on two feet, Zadkiel uses the brief respite to catch his breath. His chest rises and falls quickly. He's just as worn and beaten as Cancer is, if not more. Whirrs and clicks are repetitive as the mini mechanized motors fail to interlock connecting the mask and helmet. Face protection has all but been obliterated. The only piece that remains is the metal chin piece that attaches to the neck covering.

Zadkiel risks a glance back at the path of trajectory that he last seen Raph careening down. Seeing only flames and heavy smoke he slowly looks back toward Cancer.

Out of breath, Cancer flicks his blade a couple of times flinging Zadkiel's blood off of it with each flick. "Mind that wound, Arch. Thou have lost much blood!"

Zadkiel quickly glances down and sees blood pooling around his left foot. His gaze rises again keeping focus on his enemy.

"Tsk, tsk, tsk! My... that is a naaaasssssty cut... If you retreat now, you may just survive it," says Cancer.

Zadkiel raises his blade in a defensive posture. He swirls his sword in three arching motions and runs at Canceranian.

He wants me to retreat. To give me an exit is uncharacteristic of him. That means he must be just as injured as I am... I know I've scored some pretty deep cuts. Either I didn't strike anything vital, or he's a really good thespian. I pray it's the former. My breath is drawing shallow and my eyes dim slightly. I have to put him away quickly if I hope to see the end of this. Where is Metatron... or, anyone for that matter? Back up should have been arrived.

****

Angel's Spire, Iayhoten

Michael has fully placed his armor on as he returns to the Spires balcony. He follows the battle closely between Cancer and Zadkiel. He places his helmet on where it latches automatically to his chest armor. Motors instantly whirl click as the mask and helmet retract below the neckline of his armor. "I hear you Kiel."

At a quickened pace, a young Choiretic brings Michael his sword encased within its gold scabbard. He takes and drops it by his side where it attaches magnetically to his belt.

He will not let Zadkiel fall, but if he enters the fray, he knows that more De Mon will descend and then there would be all out chaos among the population. He needs Kiel to finish this on his own and if he can't, then retreat.

****

Kaiserslautern, Germany

In the calm quiet of Zadkiel's mind, he hears his Captain speaking. Michael answers him in what mortals would believe is telepathy. *There will be no others engaging. The more we escalate with War's coterie, the only ones injured or killed will be mortals. You've fulfilled the purpose of engagement and have done what was intended; you have bought Jericho the time needed for evasion. Canceranian will have to wait, He's more skilled since last blade encounter. Collect Raph and return to the Spire!*

Canceranian rebuffs Zadkiel's next set of attacks and parries them off to the left. His taunting of the Arch however, has slowed considerably and his breathing has become rapid. Zadkiel watches Cancer huff breath greedily. He further presses the attack believing that Cancer is indeed more injured than he appears. Zadkiel swings his blade harder and faster testing his hypothesis, that he's pushed Cancer past exhaustion. If there were levels to depletion, he thinks just maybe Cancer has reached it. If he has a chance to remove Cancer from the board it's a risk that must be taken. If he—

Zadkiel's eyes widen at a revelation. After crossing blades in an X fashion, he pushes Cancer back stepping into his space and stealing his footing. He takes the precious seconds that he's purchased and uses it to pay extra attention to lower extremities for signs of fatigue. He focuses on Cancer's knees in particular. *They're not shaking. Shit! It tis a ploy.* Zadkiel's wings ejects and spreads out positioning the razor covered armored extensions for a swipe at decapitation. Cancer, anticipating the move drops his blade and steps back raising his gauntlets to deflect the strikes. Zadkiel's face turns in disgust. He suddenly realizes he has no other choice but to disengage. He feigns the attack and stops his rotational spin and instead uses his wings to push up and propel himself backward. Having gained minimum distance, he turns and rockets from the battle. He's yielded to Canceranian. He takes little solace in that Michael ordered him to, but it doesn't lessen the sting that he's left such a dangerous foe in play. Uriel not listening to the Captain is what had gotten him killed in mortal form. Zadkiel remembering that small fact of Uriel's decision gave great weight to him deciding to live and fight another day. Provided Cancer did not follow him and remove his head in his weakened state.

Smiling, Canceranian watches as Zadkiel retreats. He would have had him had he not opted to flee. Then again, remembering the vicious blow he dealt to the Arch's abdomen he may have taken him anyways. Same rule applies to all living beings, celestials included; it's never good when the blood is dark and viscus. He continues watching till his adversary has created distance. Once clear and appearing far removed, Cancer's broken mask retracts haphazardly below the neckline of his armor revealing a battered and bloodied face. His knees begin trembling as well as his hands as they too follow suit. As he gets his fight adrenaline under control, the De Mon lets out a gasp of air and falls to one knee in exhaustion and pain. He reaches under his armor and removes his hand witnessing dark viscus blood running from a blow he took. He grins and grabs his sword using it as a cane to raise and steady himself. He looks off again to Zadkiel's last known trajectory and realizes that pursuit will not be in his best interest. Canceranian then turns his attention skyward toward the Spire's balcony where he finds Michael locked in a gaze back at him. "Nothing risked, eh, Michael—"

****

Angel's Spire, Zero Realm

"Nothing gained," says Michael finishing the aphorism. He slowly starts turning from the balcony when he witnesses Cancer fall to knee blood leaking from underneath his armor.

"Damn!" he yells, slamming his fist into the marbled railing of the Spire's balcony.

He is injured... I should have trusted Zadkiel's judgment to bring that bastard to the Warden and bury him in the depths of Palengrad, thinks Michael. Another thought then crossed his mind; one that he hasn't thought since Uriel fell to Imperial. *My fear of losing my brothers is impairing my decision making.*

Michael strikes the railing again. The damage ripples out more in a deeper crater. Instantly after impact, the marble begins to instantaneously repair itself. The Nanothrillians contained within the construction of the stone begins to self-replicate and patch the innerworkings of the marble at a subatomic level. It quickly interweaves throughout the damage pulling it all back to a solid uniformed state. The Powers Corp, indeed, have been busy since the schism. After the destruction that rained over Iayhoten leaving the city in disrepair, the Corps made sure that structures were given a self-repairable immune system sort of speak. The damage done that day will never repeat itself in how long it took to make repairs that lingered long after the battle was finished.

****

Surrounded by flames, Raph's wings slowly open from encapsulating him and Saadox's severely injured body. As his wings expand outward, he pushes the explosive debris off of them. Pain runs the length of Raph's body, but pain is good, means he lives. He slowly lays a mortally wounded Saadox of Legion on the ground cradling him as he struggles to hold to his last few breaths. The plasma strike was a flush hit that Saadox took the full blast of. His protective armor, already damaged fighting Raphael, was in no condition to sustain such a hit. The plasma bolt melted through the Razine metal and burned a softball sized hole through the demons upper left thoracic making his breathing labored and extremely difficult.

Looking up at Raph, Saadox starts to slowly move and use his one good arm to find his blade. He reaches for it as if his muscles are on autopilot. Wheezing as wind escapes his chest, he's able to muster a few words, "Just lay me lay here a moment, Arch. I only need a moment to catch my breath. I... I just need a moment to catch my breath and I'll be ready."

Raphael's helmet and mask degenerate below his armor's neckline.

He sighs at the sad case that has become Saadox. He gently places the Legionnaire's head on the ground after cradling it. Looking away briefly to wipe a tear from his face, he stands and begins looking through the debris. He kicks over broken asphalt, bent, broken steel, and glass till he finds what he's searching for. He reaches down and retrieves Saadox's weapon. He limps back to him kneeling down placing his sword in his only remaining hand.

"Ahh! My blade. Just give me a moment to catch my breath," whispers Saadox as each set of words become less and less audible. Life is slipping from him. His eyes wander from his blade to the kneeling Arch. "Are you ready, Arch, to cross blades one final time? After I rest a second, we'll conclude our affairs." Tears stream from the eyes of the Legionnaire.

Raph places his hands on Saadox's chest covering his hand and sword's hilt over the massive hole in his chest. "Your affairs have already been settled at the hands of Canceranian. Your spine is severed. You will not move again in this reality or any others, but Palengrads. and that unholy abyss will soon call to you and you will undoubtedly answer. There will be no proud trumpets to welcome you there brother. Only the cries of the abandoned and lost... Brother, for that I am sorry."

Saadox shakes his head. "I will not answer to such a call of a dreadful place." Blood bubbles escape his chest with each breath. He coughs and aspirates more blood from his mouth causing him a violent coughing fit.

Raph's face turn to a half frown as he watches his opponent fade from reality. His iris turns from red to gray. He looks around to find his own blade. When he turns to look behind him Death is there holding his blade passing it back to him with the hilt facing him. Saadox's eyes widen at the site of Death.

"You traitorous bastard. Lay no finger on a true son of—" another fit of violent coughs follow Saadox's threat that he was working up towards.

After the end of the coughing fit, he dislodges an unexpected wad of blood that he was choking on. Raphael bends down and rolls him slightly to the side. Thick viscous blood flows out and semi breath returns.

"*Arghh!* The pain, Arch, it tis unbearable."

"A fit karmatic end to your existential existence of moral decay would you not agree," says Raph.

Saadox slightly laughs. It just leads to another round of a coughing fit.

Raphael's eyes squint as a slight noise behind him draws attention. Someone is displacing the wind possibly lining up for an aerial attack. He stands, grabbing his blade turning to face the new incoming threat. His mask and helmet—or what's left of it—manage to encompass his face. His blade and posture position into a high guard. Suddenly, he drops his blade and guard and side steps to the left as Zadkiel crashes into the pavement sliding by him. He can't control his descent, because he's passed out just before touching down. He's out cold and he is leaking blood from seemingly everywhere.

Raphael's mask retracts as he trots over to Zadkiel still careful to keep watch over Saadox and possibly Cancer if Zadkiel failed to Palengrad him. "You are a mess, brother."

Saadox laughing, "It's a lot of that going around today. It seems that I will not be traveling to Palengrad alo—" Saadox's face contorts in pain so severe it makes Raph wince.

Raphael takes a knee to check Zadkiel's vitals. *Alive.* Raphael looks at Death then to Saadox. "Will it be long?"

Death looks at Saadox. "No."

Raphael sighs.

"Please, Arch... don't let him take me."

Having no time to debate, Raphael has already made up his mind. He has to get Zadkiel medical attention and he can't afford to linger. One, Zadkiel's condition is grave. Two, it is unknown if Canceranian has been vanquished, or is in pursuit. If it is the latter that would not be ideal, that would be a downright tragic turn of events as it would delay him from getting the convalescing attention his brother needed.

Raph turns to Saadox. "You... who have done such acts of desecration, now ask me for mercy?"

"Yesssss! Mercy, Arch," he says, coughing up more blood. "Mercy. Give me mercy."

Saadox's eyes fixate on something behind Raphael.

"Take your kindred for the attention that he needs Arch. Leave this Legionnaire to me. I will sit with him awhile."

Hearing an unfamiliar voice, Raphael turns his head and witnesses a celestial who bears glyphs of an ally long since thought lost and possibly rotting in the bowels of Palengrad.

At the shock of seeing the representation of lost glyphs on the armor before him, Raphael and Saadox simultaneously voice surprise and say the celestial's name in unison, "MERCY!"

Nineteen

BY ANY OTHER NAME

"I have come to show you the compassion that you've never shown others."
~Mercy

Kaiserslautern, Germany

Lightly pinching both sides of her hood, the celestial draws it back revealing a soft featured, smooth contoured face from shadow. Mercy, which had long been missing from the Earth has returned. The celestial pulling her hood back reveals a gender of Arch celestial once only thought unique to Gabriel as she was the only known female Arch, until today. Mercy's soft and smooth caramel skin is encapsulated by long dark purple hair. The insignia on her belt and shoulder armor has her name written in angelic glyph.

Raphael looks closer. Something is off about her armor; it doesn't quite fit her build. It sends a sense of apprehension through him. Was she an ally or was she enemy? Raph could tell she was beyond exhausted. She appeared weathered, weary, as if the whole of her existence was that of constant strife and unyielding struggle. Her eyes were a bit sunken and ringed with dark circles; her face showed signs of malnutrition. Features and contours that should have been considered a delight to gaze upon were mired in old scar tissue. Her armor upon further inspection was brutally damaged. The chest plate was severely cracked, and pieces around the outer edges had been broken off. The left gauntlet was missing. No, not missing, just so badly damaged that only a bracelet remained of it. The metal was not casted from the Razine star. The composition of the metallic properties was all wrong; the metal was older than Raph's oldest armor he'd been issued. His eyes then moved from the metal workings and concentrated on the cloth material. He followed the cloak from the top of the hood resting on her shoulders to the lowest seam of the cloak and found the design ancient in origin It predated the youngest Arch's by unknown millennia's. It didn't carry the cross section of modern cloaks they wear and that, too, shows extreme signs of worn distress of the likes he's never bore witness to. If their clothing is damaged, it's due to unnatural acts or forces that are powerful enough to kill them, such as warring ethereal factions, not simple worn fatigue.

Raphael moves the point his blade from Saadox to the imposter calling herself Mercy. "You are not—"

"Mercy," Death says, bowing his head slightly.

"This is surely no Mercy. Gabriel is the only sister Arch to the celestials," says Raphael.

Death looks at Raphael. "She is no Arch."

Mercy walks to Raph and pushes his blade aside and touches his face. She nods toward Zadkiel. "Tend to your brother, Arch. This Legionnaire here called for Mercy and I have answered. The Arch Zadkiel, is it? Is in need of aid, lest you leave him to the sorrows of Death."

More blood spewed from the Legionnaire's mouth. Each breath became more labored. Raphael looked towards Death making eye contact.

Death returned his gaze then moved it toward Zadkiel and back to Raph gesticulating as if he was looking at a watch. "Tic Toc, Tic Toc, baby Arch."

"*Arrghhh!*" Raphael sheathes his blade and runs over to Zadkiel and picks him up. He slings his brother onto his back interlocking Zad's arms around his neck. Once secured, Raph's wings expand outward and off into the yonder they go. Raph looks back at Mercy. "There will be an accounting of this imposter... no matter what Death says here today."

Saadox glances toward Mercy as she approaches. "Save me, Mercy. I am not yet ready to rest among the fallen in the pits of Palengrad," says Saadox, coughing up more blood.

Mercy kneels down beside him and places her hand on his face easing his pain tremendously.

"I have come to show you the compassion that you've never shown others..." She looks at the insignia glyph on his armor, "Saadox of Legion."

"Yesssss... Angel of Mercy, please, clemency is what I seek." Tears continue to stream from his eyes.

Mercy leans in close, continually rubbing his forehead and cheeks. She wipes his tears away and whispers in Saadox's ear. "But, I am no Angel... I'm not even Mercy," she says as she runs a dagger silently between the armored plates under his chin and above his neck guard. The blade slides into his body with the quietest whisper of the vacuum of space. His longing eyes for salvation turn to a look of utter surprise and shock. The glare of betrayal given lasted just past a nanosecond. After the dagger does its work of separating the stem from the hind brain, Saadox falls silent after receiving Mercy's blessing.

Death nods at her and then retrieves Saadox for transport to Palengrad. He removes a bottle from his cloak and sprinkles Saadox's remain. The body incinerates and is collected in a more transportable fashion. Death turns to leave, but hesitates a moment. "The baby Arch was right; they will come for you to answer for this."

Wiping her blade and placing back onto her belt under the cloak, she looks at Death. "And they will find me waiting" Mercy looks at Death for a long minute. "How long have you known of me Ferryman? You weren't surprised by presence."

"I've known of you since you regained consciousness on the furthest outlying's of the Aether. And soon, the heavens will know it too."

"Great," she says, "The heavens have a lot to answer for."

****

Undisclosed Location, Germany

Once evaded and clear of Kaiserslautern, Red Blade One lowers enough to gently rest its passengers on the deck. The copter hovers a modicum to the right giving the navigator a clear view for disembarking. Having seen all souls safely to the ground, navigator gives the pilot a thumbs up. She nods and gesticulates two fingers against her helmet saluting Kovac letting him know that they have done all they can do. With the flick of a switch, comes a loud pop. The cable attachment blows ejecting the tension cable ladder from the deck of chopper. Red Blade One begins to climb in altitude, but not before giving the General a visual of her palm extended telling him he has five minutes before pick up. Kovac nods back placing his still functioning outstretched hand up confirming five minutes. With that confirmation, Red Blade one takes to the skies. It won't be long before the actions of a terrorist labeled Apache is sought after and pursued with all vigor. Afterall, this was the second major incident for this region. No doubt intercept aircrafts were already in route and on the hunt.

Kovac pulls off his long-sleeved, worn-looking hooded sweatshirt. The pain is immense as it rises over the severely dislocated arm that hangs limp. He puts one end of the sweater between his teeth quickly using his overbite to gnaw a small hole in it for purchase to tear it down the middle. He discards one half and uses the other to wrap his dislocated shoulder with a self-made sling. He grabs another mouthful of the torn piece of shirt pulling it taut, tightening it close to his chest. Closing his eyes, Kovac takes a moment to let the pain subside before turning his attention to Jericho, but it was too late. Jericho's attention was occupied by another at the moment.

All the world has been shut away. Jericho uses one hand to stroke the sides of Isis' soft baby curls while looking her in her eyes. Slowly, he uses the other hand to wipe tears from her cheeks. He pulls her closer and holds her just a bit tighter. *Today was a close call*, he thinks.

Isis squeezes her eyes shut as she winces in pain. Her ribs hurt like the dickens, but to have Jericho still beside her after the morning's events, a little pain was well worth it.

"I thought I was going to die up there," Isis whispers, pointing skyward.

"Not if you were falling down to hell would I have let you touch the ground even if I were falling myself," Jericho says with a wry smile.

Isis starts laughing. "Ooooo! You're quoting that old poet Jay Z to me?"

"Told you, baby, I am hopeless French poetic soul... El-Chante baby, in French." Jericho smiles.

Isis bursts into an uncontrollable laughter pushing away to hold her side. "You say the sweetest things to me. Tell me you love me in French."

Jericho leans in closer towards her ear. "I love you... But, In French." He starts laughing.

"*Arghhh!* Stop making me laugh. It hurts!" she says, meeting his gaze. "Your command of the French language that you exude has me swooning." She kisses him on lips and then all over his face.

"How are your ribs, bae?"

"They'll be fine," she says, wincing as he barely touches them. "Could have been worse, but he protected me." Isis pulls their shared Griddles Teddy Bear from out of her jacket.

Jericho's eyes widen at the soft bear that had been passed down from mother to son.

"I thought he was lost." Jericho's eyes begin to well up.

She grins. "He wasn't." She starts to pass him the bear. "Look, you can hold him, but you have to give him back after a while okay?"

Taking the bear, a lone tear streams down his cheek. It sets Isis' eyes to water as well.

"Okay the two of you, that's enough of dat der... We are Oscar Mic in two," says Kovac. "We need to get off the street and by all that is holy Captain, find you some much needed clothes. Not sure how much more of your birthday suit I dare stand."

Isis nods toward Kovac then finds Jericho's eyes again. "He's being a little surly."

"I'd say Crass," says Jericho with a smirk.

"Crass indeed," agrees Isis. "One, I think what you're wearing is just fine. Two, I think he needs a kiss from you too. Oh! And speak some French to him, maybe he'll lighten up."

Jericho looks over at Kovac. The General raises a fist with his good arm. "I'm not kissing you, buttercup, no matter what sweet things you say to me in any language. The only thing you'll be kissing is dis here fist... and maybe a boot to match."

Hearing sirens approaching, Kovac turns suddenly to see from what direction. Doing so sends his dislocated shoulder into an intense burn igniting the trigger of pain causing him to scowl in pain.

Concerned, Jericho leaves the embrace of Isis moving toward Kovac. "Can you move? Is that injury going to slow you down?"

"It may appear by the lines on my face and the sporadic gray hair here and there that I have seen a few years... I have, but those were Marine years, Captain. Pain is a welcomed blessing that I still draw breath after an intense engagement. I am not injured. Injured would ensue that I could not continue. I am convalescing while mobile since you care so much. Now, move your ass!"

Jericho nods with a smirk at Kovac. "Marine to the end." He glances back to Isis quickly looking for some form of approval, but decides he doesn't need it to continue. Returning his gaze back to Kovac "But you're not just a Marine are you sir? Those troops that engaged Arcanian forces, that chopper, those weren't Marines or any other special ops that I'm aware of."

Hearing the sirens continue off into the distance, Kovac looks back Jericho. "Son, I am through and through a red blooded American mixed strongly with the white and blue. I am the true embodiment of what it means to be a Marine. However, Captain there are some battles on a plain of existence that the Corps cannot engage. That is where I lead a different fight with a set of men in another battle," he says, looking off to the left past Jericho. "Our ride is less than a minute away. I assure you in the coming hours and days there will be a great deal revealed to you... Trust me a little longer, Captain... you will not be disappointed."

"At this juncture, what choice do I have?"

Just over a minute later, a black tinted out SUV pulls up to them on the outskirts of the abandoned structure that once use to be a prison from the 1700s from the way it looked. The center complex was the heart of the old facility. Various dilapidated structures branched off of the main complex. Construction was old gray stone, the kind that hardened the soul just by looking at it. What came to Jericho's mind when he saw the old abandoned structure was Chateau D'if from the book, Count of Monte Cristo. There were still pieces of old rusted fence that reached 17 feet high that was now a monument to those that at one time were caged here.

Jericho looks back to Isis tapping her on the nose twice with Griddles. "How's your side?"

"I'm managing, but I'd feel better if it were looked at," says Isis still favoring her side.

"Yeah, well my arm hurts like a bitch too. Thanks for asking," Kovac cut in.

Jericho looks at him and rolls his eyes back to Isis. "No need to ask him, he's a Marine. You heard him, he bleeds red white and blue."

Still wincing, she glances at Kovac studying him. "He's kept you safe and hidden away this long. If he'd wanted to betray you, he'd have done it in the beginning, I suppose."

Jericho nods in agreement.

"I'm trusting you, General." Jericho slides him his off hand as to avoid Kovac's wrapped dislocated arm for a firm handshake.

The rear door of the unidentified customized SUV opens revealing a woman, that was not bad on the eyes in the least. If one had to guess, although she was seated, she had to be close to 5'11 in height. Her eyes were green which was unique for a light complected-skinned woman. Through her nicely fitted black suit, Jericho could tell she was exceptionally fit. She wore a deep red tie that had a white cross on it just under the knot. Everything about her exuded professionalism, except the bluish-purple streak in her hair, that said rebellious mischief abided in her.

"Good morning, Captain Bane. Although I have many aliases, as sign of trust you will have my real. I am Grand Prior Asia Riggs and from what I've been told, it is a true pleasure to make your acquaintance." Grand Prior looks at Jericho, sizing him up.

Isis steps a bit closer feeling a bit protective of him. No, it wasn't protective. If she was being honest with herself, it was jealousy that made her move forward.

Grand Prior seeing the calculated movement turns to Isis placating her modicum of jealousy. "Ms. Rayne, nice to make your acquaintance as well. I am aware of your accomplishments in the field of antiquities under Dr. Nathan Asher." Sirens wail from off in the distance and they're only drawing closer. "Please, we are stressed for time. Our window to leave this country is fast approaching zero hour. Not to mock American cinema, but come with me if you want to live."

With sirens quickly approaching, the trio look at each other minus anymore debate. Kovac enters the black SUV followed by Isis and Jericho.

****

Outskirts of Kaiserslautern

Arriving to outskirts of what use to be Kaiserslautern, Germany, Jason exits his rental vehicle that was much too small for any human. However, for him and his meager priest stipend, compact was the most affordable. His eyes widen at the vast devastation. His expression would have been the definition of misinformed as he exited the compact vehicle and walked the grassy knoll overlooking the small city of Kaiserslautern which was drowning in disastrous events he'd missed. He was completely out of touch, he realizes. The skyline was alit with flames and rising pillars of smoke. If not for the military road block stopping travelers from entering the outskirts, he wouldn't have seen the devastation till much later when he was much closer. When he left two nights prior to meet a onetime professor turned colleague, everything was quiet and without alarm. Now the city was ablaze and his friends

Jericho and Isis were in it somewhere M.I.A. Exhaling a long breath, he gets back in his car throwing it in reverse quickly heading back down the road from whence he came. He'll have to find another way in.

Twenty

MOTHERS AND DAUGHTERS

Sanstraghten Realm of Heaven

Rachel Bane, the long now deceased mother of Jericho stands finding herself compelled to watch a woman across the purplish-blue colored river, which runs opposite directions simultaneously. The physics of how that is even possible still escapes her, but is becoming quite the norm here in this place... this place of the dead for lack of better terms. She watches the woman closely as she is already engaged in conversation with a young man and two other women. The Sealed Saint Elect tilts her head studying the face of the woman intently. There is something familiar about her, but yet not. The reddish tint of her soul sphere notwithstanding, Rachel can't figure out what's so intriguing about her.

"You're being too obvious," says Paul. "If you are so intent to watch her conspicuously, why bother attempting to hide in shadow?" Paul lightly laughs.

The welcomed distraction breaks Rachel's focus. She looks back to Paul smiling, "If there were only shadow to be concealed from in here."

"Then it wouldn't be the third realm of Heaven," he says in jest.

"Or Hell," jokes Rachel. "I don't know why I find this one so intriguing."

Paul slightly walks past Rachel taking a closer look at the quartet of souls. "Well, then, enough of this skulking about. Let's go introduce ourselves. We've been in study for some time, this break away from the Sanstraghten is what's needed to put your wondering mind to rest. Maybe then your studies will improve slightly."

Walking past Rachel down the path toward the river, Paul waves Rachel onward to follow him. "Come!"

Rachel sighs and resigns herself to following him. They don't take the long way around, nor the bridge. The bridge is really more for show and secondary option. Physics is different in Zero Realm. When the disincorporated corporeal husk has been shed and the pure body returns to the source of its creation, no longer are the boundaries of realities observed. Paul reaches the edge of the river and reaches back for Rachel's hand. She smiles and takes it.

"Come, I will show you wonders," says Paul grinning.

The two steps out into the fast-flowing river of opposite flows. Rachel laughs at the feeling produced by the rushing water racing across her feet. With each step she takes, the water felt as sturdy as cement. Within no time, the pair had reached the opposing side exiting the northern border of Sanstraghten entering back into Hadeus. Their approach quickly garners the attention of the quartet.

As the Regent Elects approach the quartet, they all respectfully lower their heads in a bow to the regents. Rachel gives the customary dismissal allowing the souls to resume their tasks.

"Regents Elect," the male blue souls states, acknowledging the pair. "I am Soriah, and it is a great honor to meet you both."

Rachel takes his hand gently repeating his name, committing it to her memory, "Soriah? A beautiful name." Rachel turns to the other three. "And your names?"

The youngest of the remaining three spoke first, "I am Chrisonia."

Rachel took her hand as well observing the customs Paul has taught her. Rachel studies her intently. Rachel then learns the name of the second woman, Harmony. Beautiful name. She skips the order of how they stood purposely saving her person of curiosity for last, as that's the one she was the most curious about.

Rachel nods at the last with a warm and welcoming smile. "Last, but surely not the least."

"I'm Gloria Regent Elect..." A puzzled look crosses her face. "Forgive me, it seems my last name has escaped me at the moment."

"Last names, are far removed from this place. Those things of a former life have passed away here as they are viewed as attachments and tools of ownership." Rachel steps in a bit closer, meeting Gloria's unsure gaze. "Besides, last names aren't needed when Gloria is a great and strong name by itself."

Smiling at the compliment, Gloria looks back to Rachel and finds the Regent studying her intently.

"Never having met a Regent till now," says Gloria. "Do I just call you Regent, or do I call you the sealed, 143rd—" Gloria's sentence trails off as she too now begins to stare at the Regent.

The others including Paul watch the slightly awkward glaring grow between the two. Paul begins to smile as he's seen this look millions of times during his lengthy existence here in the Third Realm of Heaven.

Rachel's eyes start to well up, tears ready to flow. It comes to her who Gloria is "Gloria, you may call me..."

"Rachel," Gloria says with a whisper placing her hands up to her mouth in utter gleeful shock. Her eyes begin overflowing streams of tears. "Ra-chel? My daughter's name was Rachel and she was an angel... You are an angel... RACHEL!" Gloria says, as she reaches out to crush her daughter in a loving embrace that could bind the ages.

Rachel is unable to hold back her tears any longer. "Mama."

Rachel loses decorum and gives her mother the largest hug that has ever transcended from the plain of the living across the ethereal doorway of the dead. The two continue embracing for what seem forever. The love displayed so immense that the remaining three that Gloria was talking with did not dare step away to miss a moment of the heartfelt vibe that exuded. Just being in the presence of the raw emotion begins an unstoppable chain reaction from the other causing them to lose decorum and cry tears of joy at their reunion. Paul places his arms around the remaining three and lovingly shuffles them off making sure to give his Regent in training some time alone.

"My friends, have I ever told you I knew the Prince in life? Yes... he would often meet me in my dreams to guide me?" says Paul as he shepherds the souls off into wonderous realm.

As the newly formed quartet walks off into the distance, they pass a trio of Borefrayen children playing. All their eyes save Paul's gaze at what they once would have considered an alien species on Earth. While Paul is laughing and reminiscing, he grabs the two most outer souls, Soriah and Chrisonia's head quickly in a playful manner turning them away from the playing children. "It's not polite to stare," he says, laughing. "In time, you will come to know the Borefraven just as well as you know each other. They truly are remarkable souls."

Gloria continuously wipes tears from her eyes. "Look at you... Just look at you, you are gorgeous, you look radiant. Oh! I've missed you." Unable to hold tears, Gloria just keeps letting them flow. "I've thought about you every day. I thought I was going to die when you left."

"You did die, mom," Rachel says, still crying uncontrollably, but now laughing at the same time.

The comment although surreal sends Gloria into a laugh. "I guess I did, didn't I?"

"Now that you are here, Mom, I've had a longing for you that I didn't know till now."

The two continue to laugh and hug until Gloria's attention is divided by low growling thunder, but it isn't regular thunder.

"You hear that?" asks Gloria.

Rachel smiles. "Yes, I hear it."

Gloria turns toward the ever-growing sound. The thunder slowly becomes more pronounced. She searches the skies to no avail. *BOOM!* There it is again. Louder this time.

"What is it?" Gloria says, searching for the sound's origin.

Rachel lightly takes hold of her mother's chin and pulls her attention back toward her. "That sound is a friend that I met the day I arrived... Mom, meet Foot That Was Slow."

A lumbering gigantic anachronism of an age past struts from around the corner of trees becoming fully visible to Gloria and Rachel. The Dinosaur as commonly called by mortals was of the Diplodocus species. Foot That Was Slow bends his towering neck so, that the two could make contact. Gloria, not being a regent, was unable to see the yellowish tinted hue of the thunder lizard. Rachel on the other hand was only able to see the hue, a neutral color extended to all those creatures that were not created as an advanced-thought species capable of free will.

"Touch him, Ma, and have a conversation of the ages."

After what could have been days, weeks, years, or simply minutes, as time works differently in Hadeus, the two had caught up on all that they were permitted. Here in the land of governed rules of forgetfulness restrictions, the topic of a son or grandson is never touched upon. Jericho to them now is nothing but a lost memory until he stands before them. Rachel leaves her mother's place which was a quaint mini mansion that was nestled by a blue pond. Reflecting on the time that she'd spent with her, it brings a smile that is unending and far reaching from ear to ear. Rachel places her hood on and begins walking back toward her home within Sanstraghten.

As she walks her happiness is replaced with a depressing type of sadness. A tear rolls down Rachel's cheek at the sudden realization that'd she briefly forgotten. Her mother's soul is a red hue.

"Now you understand the pain of Regent Elect, do you not?" a voice echoes.

Rachel turns searching out the familiar voice, but there is nothing there. When she turns her attention back toward the path she had started upon, Death is there before her.

"It is as you said before, 'finality, and inevitability, right?'" says Rachel. "Sheol is but a stop on the way to final judgement.' Those were your words when we met."

"Those were my words. I talk with no duplicity or desire to upset you. What I was merely pointing out is that there will be tough judgements presided over by you and yet you must judge," says Death, standing aside to let Rachel pass and she does in a somber sort of stroll.

She looks up at him as always trying to see the being behind the hood that always shadowed his face. More tears fall from her face. "I saw her hue. Red, it was red. I just keep thinking one thought.

"Which is?" he asks, sounding concerned as he uses his closed Scythe as a walking stick.

"That... she will not be looked upon favorably at judgement, will she?"

His walk now turns as somber as hers. "Enjoy your time with her Regent and do not concern yourself with the hereafter on that great and terrible day when there will be the gnashing of teeth. Gloria has made her choice just as Moses made his and you made yours. She has been weighed and measured in the pangs of life. She rolled a die in the ultimate game of chance as your aphorism goes and her soul was casted red. She was unaccepting of prophesized universal truth. That is of her own doing, not yours."

"God is cruel?" Rachel snaps.

If she could see Death's face, she would have seen his eyebrow raise.

"Hmmm! Is he? There are a host of others that would agree with you I suppose. They would agree that God as you know him is cruel, but is he if you truly think about it? It is like I stated previously, you mortals are an arrogant bunch. You remade your reality into a structure of belief that was beneficial to all of you and because of it, you all fell in love with your false reality. You all felt that morality was crutch that stifled your progress so, you created a history that negated the prospect of morality so that you may all act with more impunity and feel no consequence. In your own divine judgment steeped in arrogance, you all made world turn as you see fit instead of how god told you it should any many languages and form."

Hearing Death's voice further down the road, Rachel's attention is drawn forward. "You mortals attempted to remake the world in your limited understanding of what the divine was, your mother included," he says while escorting nine new souls into Hadeus. From the distance of where he was escorting them, he turns and looks at Rachel.

Seeing him down the road, she immediately turns to her right to only still see him standing next to her still gazing at her.

"When this place was created and selected to hold the total sum of all creation, the God you think is cruel allowed such a place that even your mother could have a pleasant rest from life and reunite with a lost daughter for a time... How special is that? But why would a species such as yours that is racked with arrogance, seething of avarice, and an entitlement attitude understand? Short answer: you wouldn't. At least not the majority of you, Gloria included," says Death, growing more serious. "Her soul is red Regent Elect. It is bound for a vast Demitrode that will burn like nothing of its equal in all of existence that has never been witnessed nor will be witnessed ever again. Now Regent, respect her choice as well as all the others that made theirs."

It was tough as it rolled through her vastly improved synaptic network, but there it was, wisdom of an eternal being. He was right and she knew it. Her anger begins to cool as she concedes the anger. When she truly though about it, she wasn't mad at God, she was mad at her mother for letting such a free gift of salvation slip by her, because of structured humanistic beliefs as simple as practicality and tangibility. It was good in this case to stink of the irrationalism of belief and indulge faith.

Death stops and looks down into Rachel's eyes. "On that day she will be purged from memory. You will remember nothing of her just as before you saw her today. You will remember nothing of the lost, the forgotten, or the fallen."

Rachel looks at him and catches something that resembled emotion when he stated, the fallen will not be remembered. "He truly is Merciful?" says Rachel.

Death nods, thinking of his own situation. "Yes, he is."

Indeed, what cruel God would make me walk the Sadohedranicverse for all time to never rest? What kind of God would have me meet such a beauty of a soul as the Regent Elect, but set systems in place that I can never be with her?

I know of such a cruel god and he is called Elohim, thinks Death. If he were of the living, he would have spoken the words out loud to be forever seared in his tunnel that made its way to Hadeus. Those words would resonate and repeat but one sentence, *God is cruel, but Allah be merciful.*

Twenty-One

JUDGE

"People on Earth are content in their arrogance of thinking that the celestials of their bible only laid with their species alone. They never gave any thought to others among the galaxies that were laid with. Such arrogant thinking has led to the downfall of many nations created under the purview of man."

~Azrael

Ardenne, France: The Echelon Building

Bing! Elevator doors open on the 27th floor revealing big red bold letters reading infirmary against the back drop of a white wall. A thin but muscular toned well-dressed Knight in a black suit and red tie steps onto the elevator to escort Isis out and into a wheelchair being pushed by a red-haired nurse wearing white scrubs with red accented trim. Jericho steps out and kisses her, "See you soon, petite."

"I love it when you talk French to me," she says, smiling.

"I'll talk all the French you want after you have them look at you," Jericho says, standing erect.

"Oh! Wait," he says, snapping his fingers. He takes out Griddles, the sad sack of a furry Teddy Bear and places it in her lap. He starts to part his lips when she interjects.

"I know, I know. I can hold him for a little while, but I have to give him back."

Smiling, Jericho kisses her on the forehead. "I'll see you soon."

"She'll be fine. We're going to patch her up and have her back to you good as new," says the nurse.

Jericho gives a lazy hitchhiking thumb gesture to Kovac aimed down the hall towards the infirmary. "You're not jumping off here, General?" asks Jericho.

"I'll join her just as soon as I get you settled. C'mon now."

Jericho steps back inside the elevator. Kovac steps slightly pass him keying in the next floor number.

Bing! The arrival bell rings that they've reached the 39th floor of the Echelon building, which is non-conveniently located in Champagne Ardenne, France. First out the elevator is the Grand Prior. She nods to Commander Konadu Addi who stands regal and poised as always. His three-piece black suit is tailored and fitted to his contoured physique. His white shirt looks crisp, as well as his skinny red tie, embroidered with the Templar's cross.

"Grand Prior," Konadu says slightly giving a bow.

The Grand Prior waves her hand dismissively. "Knight Commander, let's do away with protocol and decorum for now. The hour is late, our travel was long and I have grown incessantly tired."

Konadu nods. He steps back, creating more room as Kovac and Jericho emerge from the elevator. Konadu shows them to a room with an office as the main connecting centerpiece. Surrounding the office was three adjoining hotel style room suites for visitors. Each Kovac and Jericho are given a suite and ample time to clean up and dress in suitable clothing provided for them. Inside the closets were only an array of black suits, at least for Jericho. Kovac had another choice awaiting in his.

When all freshened up and given a bit of time to rest and recover, the duo meets Konadu back in the main office's partition. Kovac's arm is firmly nestled in a uniformed approved black sling. He is wearing his full-dress blue class A Marine uniform. Jericho on the other hand has gone with the borrowed uniform of the day, one of the black suits in his room's closet and a white t-shirt. He forwent the formal button up.

"This way, gentlemen," says Konadu, extending his arm toward the rooms exit.

He leads the men down the hall pulling his black rimmed glasses from off his lapel wiping them with a handkerchief. He places them on causally glancing over his shoulder to make sure the men are still following.

"The Grandmaster has been awaiting you Mr. Bane or do you prefer Captain, as your rank is still currently commissioned within the United States Marines?"

"Whatever makes you feel good, Bub," Jericho says, walking taking in the layout of the building.

He and Isis were blindfolded for much of the trip to wherever they were now. The blindfolds were only removed after they had arrived within the facility. He can tell instantly that this was an off the books privately funded operation. Their security gives instant signs of a militarized black site. More than likely funded by an unnamed government or governments. No point trying to guess which one, there are too many to choose from that would have a bone to pick with Lucien. Jericho looked down at the remarkably polished black floors. They are so shiny it was like walking on a mirror or black ice to be more exact. The floors are clean and free of any scuffing. The black floors contrasted heavily with the pure white walls of the facility. He chose the word facility purposefully. This is no typical building. All signs read headquarters of some sort, but not one of the small rinky dink low level types. No, this one is prime.

Jericho is the first to speak nodding towards the red cross emblems on the bright white walls. "You guys are the Templars?"

"We are," says Knight Commander Konadu Addi. "And contrary to what the news reports have labeled us, we are not terrorists, Mr. Bane."

"Who said you were?" asks Jericho.

Kovac cut in, "He's been under for a while. He only has a modicum of knowledge of the events in New York."

"I see," Konadu says.

"How long have you been aware of me?" asks Jericho.

"Only recently by name and face, but we've followed stories of someone like you for some time though. We were not only aware of someone like you, we were expecting someone like you to balance the scales. As time progresses Captain Bane, you will come to find we are aware of a great deal. We are even aware of your girlfriend Isis. We know of her work that she completed to obtain her Doctoral under the tutelage of one Dr. Nathan Asher. Her hypothesis of discovery to locate biblical artifacts was a glimpse of genius. Before all of this she was on our shortlist to recruit. Unlike most that half ass and do the minimal work required to receive their degrees, hers was truly earned. She's quite brilliant."

The men turn the corner of the T intersection of the hall where Grand Prior Riggs is awaiting them. She falls in tow with the men continuing on down the length of the long hall toward a seemingly dead end at the end of the hall. They pass a cadre of other men and women dressed similarly to the Grand Prior and the Knight Commander. Once they reach the end of the hall, Konadu approaches the wall. After a few seconds, a blue light emits from a ceiling scanning device washing the Knight Commander in its hue. An access panel on the wall that was invisible behind frosted white glass becomes visible and opens. Konadu leans in close to the retinal scan again proving his authorization and identification. After a series of tones, the wall dissipates into a frost glass itself. The doors slide open opposite of each other. Without hesitation, they all enter a large conference room where an enormous black marbled table sits. At the table's center is a large, engraved red cross.

As the Grand Prior enters, she reaches into the inside of her blazer pocket retrieving a pair of black rimmed glasses. Winking at Jericho and pushing aside a strand of her blue purplish hair, and places them on. With a brief forced titular smile, she leaves the duo to Konadu and finds her seat to the left of the Grandmaster. It is a rarity that the Grandmaster and Grand Prior are ever in the same room. One, a commander of the politics and day to day operations of all priories, the other the field general of all Knight forces. In all the years of their membership and ascension of rank, the Grand Prior seat has always remained vacant... until this day.

Also seated at the table are a host of others. Some wear the class A version uniform of the Templar's black suits with high collars and insignias, while others wear the traditional robes of white tunics with the red cross and capes. Jericho recognizes a couple as dignitaries that he had provided security for a couple of times during a few of his tours overseas. To see them here, he can only speculate that the others were from regions stationed throughout the world that hold lofty influence in government somewhere. Also, the numerous vacant chairs at the massive table had not gone unnoticed among the sitting panel.

Konadu escorts Jericho to a section of chairs that were arranged similarly to a juror's box. Jericho obliged and sat in the cornered off section.

"Why so many empty seats at the table?" asks Jericho.

"Are they empty?" replies Konadu. "I hadn't noticed. All those at the table are masters of the multiple priories across the world."

"You may need to recruit or promote a few more."

Konadu Addi flashes teeth in a grin. "Indeed, Captain."

Knight Commander Addi, shows Kovac to his section, which is reserved for Knights permitted to attend. Both parties now seated comfortably, Addi grabs three black-rimmed glasses from an open-faced cabinet where they were all neatly arranged. He gives one to Kovac and then doubles back around to hand Jericho his pair. Konadu Addi keeps the third pair handy. He gestures for the two to put them on. After looking at each other for a second from across the room, Jericho and Kovac slides them on.

Once the glasses are on, the room appeared the same except the colors are muted slightly taking on a grayish hue, much different from the natural colors registered by the human oculus. Another subtle difference is that every few seconds there's a static skip in the display within the lenses. Static skips and flickers similarly to a computer game or television having a moment of unclarity like when analog went digital in the early 2000s. Jericho quickly realizes the glasses are experiencing tiny distortional glitches.

Suddenly he remembers a time when he and his team were training in the deserts of Nevada before a deployment to the Holy Land. They ran scenarios on virtual reality gear to simulate shoot, don't shoot battle scenarios. That just what he was looking through, a virtual reality supported by the lenses. These glasses are state of the art far streamlined from the clunky version he wore in training. The future is here, digital displayed over reality. He's just never witnessed to the scale of clarity that he was currently observing. The table that he had taken note of as missing its members, now suddenly has just about all chairs filled. Missing members were holographically there. Whatever the event is he is about to witness; he now understands is a meeting of masters. More than likely all of them.

Twenty-Two

CHAOS TO ENTROPY

"*Without Chaos, there can be no Anarchy. Two must prevail to be considered the one.*"

~Legion Prime

Planet Prime: Nosfor, Andromeda Galaxy
Frocairnez, Gaylenarris

Legion Prime holds a crystalline textured strand of prayer that is illuminated brighter than any other surrounding strand around it. He squints his eyes in an attempt to read it. He even goes as far to readjust his line of sight to make heads or tails of the encoded angelic glyph.

"You'd may as well release it. You will never be able to read the glyphs," says Chaostian. "We were never meant to read the priorities even when were celestials."

"*Pfft*! Whatever," says Legion Prime. He releases the strand letting it reach its intended Transcommuncative Hub destination. "I mean, I find it utterly repulsive that there are Nosferatu's that still pray to Elohim. It is a downright a fucking travesty."

Chaos looks up from his 4D holographic table. This one is smaller in construction and is field portable, unlike the large stationary one that resides in the Angelic Spire. Chaos' map properties are constructed from heated magma instead of water. The charts and constellations of the Sadoverse glows high orange and red at times depicting the depths of all the realms and numbers of the realities.

Throwing his arms wide in a stretching gesticulation, the map of Nosfor expands ginormous. He circles a particular point with his finger and magnifies it again tracking an incoming projectile. He taps the projectile, identifying the signature as Painell. His smiles widen into a Cheshire grin. He stands fully erect from bending over the small portable field table cracking his neck from craning it for so long. Standing, the first thing noticeable is his armor; it's completely undented showing no signs of any battle damage. It's still pristine as the day the Powers Corps forger created it. His knee-high boots are grayish metallic with illuminated glyphs on the shin protective covering. His pants are form fitting clasped with a blue illuminated metallic glyph belt buckle. His shirt is short sleeved, and also form fitted enhancing his physique. There are two stripes on either side of his shirt signifying that he was created second cast tier. His chest armor is the same metallic gray as his boots, with illuminated glyphs on the upper right-hand corner of the breast plate. It reads: *To have order there must have first been Chaos.*

Chaos' grin turns into a full uncontrollable laughter. "It seems I'm not trusted with the campaign. I can never understand why the Seraphim has no trust in me. It really does become quite annoying to be second guessed all the time."

Turning his head quickly to the left, Chaos' iris turns from greenish purple to icy blue. He begins talking in another voice, this one more regal.

"You are not trusted because you are of an impetuous stock. You often take subversive action without thinking of the consequences that follow. Your last attack on the Hierarchy proved the flaws in you baseless theoretical planning." Chaos turns his head back in the other direction, his eyes turning a greenish purple again. "Who in the fuck asked you? If you're not going to say anything that can help the situation, then—"

"Suggest you two of minds become of one accord and quickly, Painell draws near," says Legion Prime. "The last thing he needs to see are you two off kilter... Now, get your shit together, he approaches!"

Pausing, Chaos stares at Legion Prime. His façade finds an instant clam. "Who in the Demitrode do you think you are to address us in such a fashion. You are a third caste trivial—"

Chaos turns his head slightly again, eyes turning back icy blue. "Silence! I find no fault with our second's assessment of the incoming situation. It's not often that we are given status and command. We are best to show one accord and one mind in our leadership lest it be taken from us."

His eyes turn color again. Chaos' persona regains control. "Yes, yes, brother you are right. Your calm and insightful thoughts have prevailed cooler heads yet again... You know that I just get so worked up at times that control escapes me. I should defer all matters of consequence of today to you, Anarchy."

Chaos grabs his dual blades that were jammed into a smooth rock wall of Nosfor's underground hollowed-out lava tube and places them in their scabbards strapped to his back.

Chaos' head tilts to the left twitching slightly. His iris' turn blue and remain that color.

Legion Prime takes a breath in a sigh of relief that Anarchy has taken control as the dominant mind of Chaos' split personality. In taking his drawn-out breath, he happens to turn and look at the Clan leader of the Vaxtan's resistance, who has just watched the whole exchange while sharpening his knife.

Shit! I forgot that he was even here, thinks Legion Prime. He stares at the Vaxtan War Chief, named Gontarrin or something like that. He makes sure his glare is highly suggestive that the observer remains just that, an observer and not speak of what he's seen. Hopefully the suggestion is accepted; it would be a shame to have to replace another War Chief.

It wasn't long that the Vaxtan's War Chief who's equivalent to a five-star general paused the sharpening motion of his blade in lieu of watching the exchange that Chaos had with himself. He just continued to stare at the ethereal thinking that, *He's skorn shit crazy.* It's a thought that he read in the gaze of Legion Prime that he thought best to keep to himself... at least until it becomes advantageous not to.

Nodding, War Chief Gontarrin understands the warning that was just unsaid, Legion Prime turns his attention back to his commanding De Mon, Anarchy.

"General," Legion Prime says, bowing. "It's best you go to meet Pain in the absence of you brother Chaos."

"I concur." Anarchy's persona having taken over complete physical control. He straightens and begins to head up hill toward the Volcano's caldera entrance. He snaps his fingers as if he'd forgotten something. "Ahh! Legion Prime..."

Legion nods, placing his fist to his chest.

"Kill Gontarrin! We wouldn't want him telling tales of bickering between the high command. That wouldn't instill unwavering loyalty in those under him."

Smiling, Legion Prime turns to Gontarrin. *Pity, I guess we will need to replace another War Chief after all,* he thinks.

Surprised, Gontarrin starts to stand. "What! Now wai—"

Before Gontarrin could fully stand erect to protest or defend himself he'd already been decapitated and Legion Prime's Rapier style blade had already been re-sheathed. Gontarrin's head hit the ground rolling down the cavern's slope till it hit the wall at the bend of the tube that went left and further into the planet's depths. It lies within the elbow of the turn. The move is so lighting fast that the body of the Vaxtan is still attempting to stand not realizing that its head had been removed. Legion Prime simply pushed the body over. There is no blood, because the wound had instantly cauterized. A malicious, but tidy act of mayhem.

"I go to meet Pain," says Anarchy. "Legion, dispose of that bad bit of business there!" Anarchy says pointing to the body. "And find his underling. He's just been promoted."

****

Anarchy gazes skyward as Painell enters the atmosphere igniting a sonic boom as he slows to match the planets natural barometric pressure, but not enough that the sound barrier didn't break. As he streaks toward his destination, white streams of wind vapors trail him as he takes a series of hard rights and lefts until finally, he's slowed enough to land and make planetfall. When he does touch down his armor is still glowing slightly orang from the reentry heat induced friction. His landing is graceful; his metallic boots barley makes a soft clank when contacting the smoothed coalesced rock formation. His mask and helmet retract falling below the neck line of his armor. The reentry heated glow of flame slowly darkens returning his armor to the normal polished black with red trimmed colors. Painell strides up to Chaos looking him closely in the eyes to see which split schizophrenic symptomatic mind he's going to be conversing with this day. Satisfied that the persona of Anarchy was in charge he reaches out taking hold of his underling's forearm in greeting.

"Anarchy, it has been a long while brother," says Painell, placating to the broken mind of Chaos.

"Much too long have I let Chaos reign. It feels good to be back to set all tasks to completion for Lord Morning Star."

The two turn and begin walking back toward the nerve center of the hollowed-out Volcano. Anarchy's stride is one of confidence and regality compared to the loose wild natured stride of his counterpart.

"Will you be needing access to progression reports, Command General Pain?"

Pain shakes his head and waves his hand dismissively. "I'm not here to determine the right of command or be a check to your balance. You have been trusted to run the war machine here as you two see fit. I'm merely here for respite, rearmament, and relay of instruction from our true king above the exalted throne."

"Ahh! It's nice to see that the need for his incessant titles hasn't changed. Alas though, the titles are misspoken, he isn't King above the throne..."

Pain shoots Anarchy a nasty glance.

"At least not yet," Anarchy says, smiling and slightly bowing. "I just believe that if one is going to insist on the use of such lofty titles, then the deeds must have been completed to be called such. As I currently am aware of, Elohim still resides upon the throne which our elder brother aspires."

"Watch your tongue, Dual Mind! Lucifer would not stand for such blasphemy and neither will I tolerate it as his emissary."

"Emissary! Now, that is a lofty title. One that I'd never thought to see you attain." Anarchy keeps an impetuous smile on his face. "You being of few words and all."

Painell turns his right shoulder toward Anarchy showing him the additional glyph bearing the mark of emissary. Anarchy's eyes widen in a bit of feigned shock.

"So, it is true? Emissary... Ooooo, forgive my impotence and jest of playful mocking of a brother. We adhere to your rank and command, Emissary Pain."

The two reach the nerve command center where there are hundreds of De Mons moving about as they attend to chores and matters of rank and file.

Raising his hand, underlings bring two chairs for the two to sit. He then looks toward Legion Prime. "Bring sustenance! Emissary Pain hungers from such a journey."

He turns his attention back to Pain. "I have only the best supplemental Manna created outside of Iayhoten here."

Hearing that news brought a great deal of pleasure to Pain's ears.

"Fresh Manna? I haven't had a descent taste of fresh Manna since removing them from the rations of dead choiretics that fell underneath my boot."

"You forget, commander, I was once a member of the Powers Corp. Creation is my forte... at least it was before falling to the brutish ails of what seems this never-ending conflict," says Anarchy.

Legion Prime brings a dish of Manna and sets it down next to Painell and slowly backs away head bowed. Pain nods, grabs a hand full and throws them back quickly masticating them. Only after engorging himself does he then take the time to savor the taste.

"Not the taste of home, but one that can be acquired after a while. How long have you been in prototype of this blend?"

Anarchy reaches over and takes a bite. "For about the last three hundred and forty-seven years. You are the first high class De Mon to have a taste and reap the energy benefit of our own manufactured supply."

"And how much has been manufactured here?"

"Enough for trials. What you've just tasted is the final blend for review. Matter of fact, you just missed Vice by about four quintonians. He took samples to Cainsin for final approval."

Painell finished the rest of his plate and looks at Legion Prime.

"I have a long journey yet ahead of me... Prime, pack me another supply manageable for transport!"

Legion Prime nods and again slowly backs away. "I hear and obey."

Anarchy leans in closer to Painell. "I have taken care of the business of guaranteeing our supply of Manna. If approved, I will put into production enough to rival the Archs. I have infused additives that increase strength and reflex far superior to that of Elohim's mixture. My blend will surely give us an edge."

Pain nods. Then gives a suspicious infused look toward Anarchy. "And Chaos?" he asks.

"Chaos has been handling the brutish service of breaking the Lamechian covenant here. I defer all thoughts concerning the art of entropy to him. From what I've seen, I must admit it has been slow going, but progress is ever moving forward. The Arch Azrael that has been trying to protect the covenant breaks a little each encounter. Soon, Chaos will rival, dual and take his head," Anarchy says, smiling. "Although, I do not agree with what he wants to do with the head once he takes it. My twin's thoughts are far beyond my means of depravity. All that being said, reality 1125 is all but shored up... Now, tell me brother of the affairs of Touchpoint... and news of this new Judge from the line of Samson that have been murmured in dark corners!"

Twenty-Three

VAXTANS

Planet: Nosfor, Andromeda Galaxy
Frocairnez, Gaylenarris

Light as a feather, she sticks her landing. Gabriel touches down on the planet Nosfor, landing in the capital city Frocairnez. The city is in the midst of a civil war and open rebellion. The surroundings and landscape greatly reflect it. The weaponry utilized here has far surpassed 2814's reality by almost five hundred thousand years. When they shot projectiles, man was not yet bipedal nor upright. Not to mention, the gravity here has made the Nosferatu's mass and bones denser than that of mortals. For this reason alone, it was believed Lucifer chose an alliance with them and transported a battalion of them to march with Jazekial on Bastion before the flood of Noah's day, because they made for ample warriors.

Watching the war rage from a distance, she makes it a point to watch the weaponry closely. It has been many moons as the Aztecs use to say since she'd been to Nosfor. In that time, she could see the caliber of weapons they now possess were well advanced and the tactics used in how they handle them matched. It didn't take long to sort out that they had harnessed and mastered a mixture of hot gasses and fractured light into a laseretic plasmatic form that incinerate their kind without prejudice. Lucifer's hand in their development of such weaponry was all over them.

The revving up roar of an engine contained within a mechanized monstrosity of a vehicle caught her attention next. It wasn't the ugly behemoth construction of it that made her take notice and cringe, it was what it fired. It was a low-grade plasma bolt. Albeit, it was in the beginning stages, but there it was. They were attempting to emulate a weapon of the gods. That indeed, was concerning. Gabriel taps her gauntlet, sliding open the port that gives her Dimensional Realm access. She slides the dial up to phase her more in tune with the current reality. One notch further and she'd be visible.

On this planet, she had the autonomy to walk among them if she so chose too, as they were aware of the celestial classes. Then again, so was most of the other species that populated the Sadohedranicverse. It was not uncommon for the Nosferatu to see a celestial walking amongst them. It would be akin to a law enforcer walking among the public. What was a rarity though was an Arch walking among them.

"Arch Gabriel?" Choiretic Tolasand calls out, surprised as he lands next to her and retracts his wings. He's utterly surprised to see her here on Nosfor.

Gabriel focuses on the battle-damaged armor of the Choiretic. It's completely distressed. It's broken in many places, and scorched in other areas. This celestial has seen hell.

"What is the situation here? Report!"

The battle-weary Choiretic class angel put his fist to his chest in a salute. "Arch, myself and the rest of my battalion were sent here to keep the peace that was already tenuous and on a precipice at best. The De Mons having observed the armistice between nations here knocked it over from the point of the needle it was already standing upon tipping the scales of civil war. Their mode of weaponry was their slivery slight of tongue and subtle influence with the aid of assassinations of key figures. Once the scales tipped, we had been trying to cease hostilities to no avail before full blown conflict."

A major explosion catches the Choiretic's attention briefly. Small pieces of debris fall near the two. What falls is harmless at this distance really. Small rock and pieces of metal bounce and ricochet off their armor. Tolasand moves slightly to avoid a little of the incoming, rubble, but Gabriel stands petrous; as rock, dust, metal, and pieces of flesh fall about her.

"CHOIRETIC!" she yells, regaining his attention.

"ARCH!" he yells back, standing to attention saluting again this time holding it among the chaos. "Sorry Arch." Tolasand apologizes for losing situational awareness. "Since we've been dispatched here one of the twins of old arrived with a platoon of extra Legion to reinforce Legion Prime who was already causing havoc here. The De Mon had made contact with the local opposing Nosferatu. Negotiations were brief between the factions and an assault of the sitting hierarchy commenced. The hierarchy that was attacked was the covenant holders of Elohim. They were the ones charged with keeping the peace since the fall of Lamech during Sarin's last days."

Gabriel looks past the Choiretic at the war-torn city in the distance. "What twins? They're no more twins."

"Chaos, Arch Gabriel," answers Tolasand swiftly.

Gabriel looks back to the Choiretic a bit shocked. "Michael is aware of the situation here, right?"

"Arch, we notified him the moment that conflict broke out. Unfortunately, once it started it evolved at a break neck exponential rate."

Gabriel thinks back to what Michael had said and remembers it clearly, "Lucifer is attacking across the Sadohedranicverse pulling us thin having to respond to the micro conflicts." *This is what he was talking about. This is probably one of many under his purview that he didn't tell us about. I see now why he wanted me to follow Painell. He may be right; Lucifer is again making attempt to unite the mythical for another run at ascension. Damn him! Damn that Seraph!*

Gabriel took a breath to collect her thoughts. "Chaos is here?"

"Yes, Arch. We believe so. He and his twin Anarchy if reports are to be believed."

"Has anyone laid eyes to his twin, Anarchy? Has anyone seen them together?"

"No, Arch, only Chaos and Legion with certainty have been seen."

"Let's hope for the sake of all here it remains that way," says Gabriel.

A blast of super-heated light whizzes past Gabriel just missing her. She looks in the direction of where it originated and scowls. Before turning her attention back to Tolasand "Whose command are you under?"

"Arch Azrael."

That's right, Michael said it at the conclave in the Chamber of Sparrows, thought Gabriel.

"Take me to him!"

****

Two long range explosives strike just over a hundred feet from Azrael's position. Rock and dust expand, but does nothing more than cause a minor irritation for the leading Arch. He brushes the dust away and points to a cadre of Choiretics. Having gained their attention, he then points to a position in front of him. "Form a firing line right here!" he orders.

Seventeen members of the Choiretic Corps of angels from two lines. Seven in front with the additional ten in the rear. Azrael raises his hand holding it steady, making sure his Choir has the perfect firing solution. Before he can signal the line to fire, he's momentarily thrown off balance when he's forced to sidestep a beam of superheated refractive light. The beam singes the side of his mask as it passes millimeters from his face scorching it from it shinning platinum to darkened black. He ignites his gauntlet's circular shield deflecting a second blast off into the structure behind him that he's attempting to protect. A huge chunk of the left tower of the gothic cathedral collapses leaving a gaping hole. Cursing under his breath in Nosferatuian, he turns his attention back to the attacking Legion led faction advancing on the Hierarchs he's been charged to protect. With a barely audible pop and hiss, his shield retracts back into his gauntlet.

"FIRE!" yells Azrael, dropping his fist in a hammer gesture.

The Choiretic let loose their bolts of blue plasma into the advancing band of Legion and Vaxtans.

The Vaxtans over their generations have evolved with the utmost predatorial traits of the most vicious species man could imagine. They are subset hyper aggressive species of what mortals came to know as their more popular nomenclature, vampires. Mortals over their evolution had come to believe such creatures were false tales of horror told to frighten little children. Educated masses soon always forget such myth is not without truth. It's usually steeped in it. The Vaxtans were such a tale told in the time of Noah, son of Lamech's day. Since the time of Lamech however, the tale of such vile creatures had since fallen into myth and legend in a reality lost to passing of time.

People on Earth are content in their arrogance of thinking that the celestials of their bible only laid with their species alone. They never gave any thought to others among the galaxies that were laid with. Such arrogant thinking has led to the downfall of many nations created under the purview of man. Well, contrary to their arrogance, the celestials of old did lay with other species across the Aether. The women of Nosfo were one. Just as the Nephilim was born of man and celestial, Nosferatu's apex predators Vaxtans were born from such unholy unions. When the battle of Sarin commenced, Lucifer called on the children of the Andromeda galaxy to aid Jazekial's campaign and they answered.

The defeat at Sarin and utter destruction of the floods decimated a genocidal number of not only wicked men, but nephilim and all other unholy creatures, including the alien Vaxtan species. The decimation was so costly, that the remaining species that were spared entered into a covenant with Elohim to never again raise a hand in defiance of him, or invade a lesser species. After centuries of replenishing their numbers, the old Hierarchal that made sure to observe the covenant were soon outnumbered by the new radicals that had political ambition to overthrow. With a little subliminal push from the De Mons that no longer wanted to observe the Hierarchal covenant of old, a civil war commenced. To win this battle of Nosfor, Azrael's command will need to be unmerciful.

The plasma fire line proved effective in subtracting the numbers from those charging, but in no way did it impede the charge.

"FIRE!" Azrael yells again.

The firing line gives a second volley of shots dropping more of the advancing horde thinning them out.

Azrael unsheathes and points his blade at the remaining advancers. "FIRE AT WILL!"

The line no longer fires in unison, but now picks their individual targets and begin firing at random. Once Azrael witnesses them cross a line that he deemed was point of final contention, he readied his sword in a high guard. The edges of his blade began to glow white hot.

"DRAW SWORDS!" yells Azrael.

The Choiretics draw swords, axes, and razor chains standing ready.

"CHARGE!" Azrael screams as he leads the advance into the fray.

The clash is fierce. Bodies are impaled and slammed to the ground, while others are pitchforked and thrown over shoulders into a sea of melee evisceration, impalement and death. Hadeus and Palengrad will have its fill this day. Azrael parries and slices his way into the thick of the fray using his right wing defensively to block incoming blades, while he uses his sword to spilt enemy's midsections open spilling their innards about the ground. After a time, blood and other spilling secretions of the bodies make the ground slippery and hard to gain footing for the Vaxtans, which the celestials used to their advantage in further thinning them out. With his left wing, Azrael clears space for his left choiretic force to advance further into the fracas. They form into one cohesive unit using the phalanx block and attack. The mounting loss on the side of the Vaxtans was enough that a retreat was signaled by the Vaxtan War Chief. They disengage.

Hearing the sound of the retreat, Azrael's mask and helmet retracts below the neckline of his armor. He thrusts his sword into the ground letting out a sigh and takes a deep breath of relief. As one of the choiretic walks past him, he stops him by grabbing a hold of his shoulder to hold his attention.

"Nordic," gasps Azrael, still catching his breath.

"Arch?" responds the angel slamming his fist to chest in a salute.

Azrael looks out across the field at all the causalities. "Find our celestials among the dead and dying. Separate them and get the ones that need care urgently back to the Spire! Death will sort the rest."

The choiretic begins to walk off only for Azrael to pull him back by the shoulder a second time. "Get me a count of those taken by Death to report back to Michael."

The choiretic bows his head and salutes by pounding his chest again. "Arch," he says in acknowledgement of the order.

"What of the wounded Legion and Vaxtans?" asks the choiretic.

"What wounded?" says Azrael. "There are no wounded. Finish them and send their asses to Palengrad."

Again, the choiretic salutes and gets underway to complete the order.

Shortly thereafter during the lull in the action, the Choiretic Corp moves slowly through the sea of bodies dispatching De Mons, Legion, and Vaxtans. Out of the corner of his peripheral vision, he watches as Death collects the soul spheres of the Vaxtans. All are red in hue. The De- Mons and Legions are set to flame by the courier of the dead and collected.

"I'm looking for Pain," says a familiar voice.

Azrael's attention is caught the moment he recognizes it. He smiles and turns meeting Gabriel gaze. "Then you have found it, sister. It runs deep here; to the very core of this planet in fact."

The two meet and grab each other's wrists in a tight lock equivalent to a hand shake. Azrael pull her in close giving her a mighty embrace. Her feet dangle off the ground in his hearty hug. He lightly bumps foreheads before setting her back upon her boots. Her guide Tolasand that guided her to him, was dismissed by the wave of a hand from Azrael.

"Sister, it is good to hear your voice and see your face... even in these times," Azrael says, looking around at the carnage of war. "How went the conclave then?"

"Prince Yeshua was in attendance," says Gabriel. "Imagine the faces when he entered."

That phrase is enough to almost send Azrael to his haunches.

"That bad, then?"

Gabriel turns looking around at the carnage that was just wrought in Azrael's current conflict.

"It is that bad. However, it was reassuring to know that the prince is behind us."

"And you, sister, do you believe that Michael will see this to an end and lucifer in promised chains till his destruction?"

"I believe he will see it to whatever end may come."

At that, Azrael nods in agreement. "To whatever end may come then... It is good to see you have not lost faith in these most trying of times."

Azrael turns, shouting a few more orders and pointing out a few areas of contention that bothers him if left unchecked. Once things are managed for the current moment, his attention turns back to his sister.

"So, you're looking for Pain? Did I hear that right?"

"That is why I'm here. I believed he came this way possibly to recruit the Nosferarians back into the company of the De Mons."

"I wouldn't doubt it," says Azrael. "With the rise of that abomination Imperial, discord has sewn throughout the realms and realties to all those that had ears to hear... I fear that again there will soon be a time that the reality of mortals and these forsaken creatures will intertwine."

"It was inevitable let Sandalphon tell it," says Gabriel.

"I suppose so... Guess he was right though." Azrael nods, tuning to look back toward the armies across the war-torn land. "Then it makes trying to stop the battle here for not if he is indeed right and this is all inevitable? I for one would hate to see his theory proven."

Looking up from kicking over piece of scorched war torn dirt, Gabriel turns Azrael's face towards hers again commanding his attention, "Not for nothing," she answers. "It can't be. We are buying Jericho the time needed to set prophecy back to task."

"Jericho?" Azrael says, surprised, his attention piqued. "Isn't building on the hopes of mortal men like that of sinking sand?"

He turns to look out again at the landscape that was laid waste. "So, that is the name of the worst kept secret in all of Jacintian? Our hopes lie on that of a Judge?"

Gabriel feigns a smile. "Samson didn't do too bad."

Azrael turns back toward her arching an eyebrow. "Yes, messenger, even out here, word has reached me that he failed to bring the creature Imperial to heel and that you yourself had a time with the abomination that almost saw the end of you... Uriel and Cassiel has already fallen to this Nephilim. Sister... I must ask, what if he misses the mark and fail to kill the creature that we are forbidden to take action against?"

"He won't!" she says sharply. "I won't let him."

Azrael stares at her, studying her for long minute. "Hard to do if you're here on the fringe with me." He gives a deep sigh. "You have faith in that mortal I see... and so did Cassiel to the point he laid down his immortal life. I'm not sure he should have, but his wisdom of decision will not be debated in this preceding today." He takes a long look at Gabriel. "They had faith in you So, I will have faith in you too." He places his hand on Gabriel's shoulder. "I will hold the alliance at bay for as long as I can here on Nosfor. Understand, with no possible reinforcements there is no guarantee how long I will be able to hold; their attacks are relentless and depleting my forces at a rate of four to one."

Gabriel nods. "I understand. And Pain?"

"Ahh... yes, Pain... Intelligence has not given word of Pain. If he is or was here, he was not here long enough to spark conversation across any Transhub Networks. So, if he did come this way, he must've touched down, reupped supplies maybe, and stayed whatever course you were tracking. The only elite De Mon here that we can confirm from Transhub is Chaos."

"So, he is here? Only Transhub confirmation? You haven't laid eyes personally?"

"Look around, Gabe, and you will recognize his work?"

Gabriel looks once more at the battlegrounds. "Has he made any attempt himself toward the chieftains?"

"Not yet, but I suspect soon he'll make the all-out push when he believes we've been weakened enough."

"Real assessment right now! Can you hold brother?" says Gabriel, stepping closer to the battle field looking over her shoulder back at Azrael.

"What choice have I, sister? I will give all for Elohim, but all of this; us here, the fate of the galaxies and realms, all is pointless unless there is correction at Touchpoint."

"Earth," says Gabriel.

"Yeah, Earth," confirms Azrael. "It starts with Earth; Touchpoint. If that isn't set to correction, Nosfor along with all else will fall."

Twenty-Four

❦

TIMES OF TRUTH

"At some point it became clear to her that night, that the world was indeed not a fine place like her favorite author had written. A quote that she at one time probably thought she would read to her son someday had she lived. She would've opened the book that was surely worn and well read, "The world was a fine place and worth fighting for."

-Jericho Bane

Ardenne, France, Templar Headquarters

Roll call complete, all Master Templars of any importance are deemed in attendance and those that were not accounted for physically, were accounted for digitally, save for two that were feared dead. It's time to convene.

"Masters, before we begin, let us welcome Captain Jericho Bane," says Grandmaster Brashear, standing.

Isis is escorted into the room by two black suited Templar Knights and led to sit next to Jericho. Her movements and overall disposition looked a ton better after having her wounds tended to. Discomfort still rubbed at her ribs though. Each breath she drew caused slight wincing, but sitting gave her moment of respite from the agony as her weight was redistributed across the plush leather seating. Jericho flashes her a smirk and takes her hand kissing it. She smiles in return giving him a nod that she's okay. Still holding the third pair of glasses, Knight Commander Addi brings them to her for her to put on. Whispering a thank you, she places on the glasses and is also instantly impressed.

"And a special welcome to you as well Dr. Rayne," says Brashear. My medical staff said you declined rest in lieu of attending this meeting?"

Hearing her name upon entry, Isis nods toward the Grandmaster thanking her for the hospitality and the medical treatment. "I did decline... err, sorry I don't know your... "

"...It's Grandmaster Brashear, darling."

"They just started. You haven't missed much," whispers Jericho.

Isis leans in closer to him, keeping her voice to a whisper. "I checked in with Jason. He's safe and said sorry he missed us before all the crap that went down in the city. I wasn't able to tell him where we were. He told me to tell you that he's headed back to the states. There was something there he was told to do and he'll catch up with us later."

Jericho nods, turning his attention back to the Grandmaster. "I'm just glad he's okay and made it out."

After addressing her attending cabinet with pleasantries and protocols, Brashear's attention turns back to Jericho and Isis. "Confused, you two? I know I would be. I would have so many questions if I were you. So, since you are full of them, we here will do our best to explain and find answers together." Brashear walks from around the table toward the seated area of where Jericho and Isis are.

"We are the Templar Knights proper. We are not offshoots, pretenders, aspirants or claimants. We are of the original lineage from the line of the first order of knights established with protecting travelers on the road to Jerusalem. Our mission has not changed, just our destination. We still protect those on the road to the Holy Land, albeit the land this time is Heaven and the road has become fraught with troubles that work to undermine us and accost our clientele, impeding their way to God. Until events of recent, we were abiding by our mandate in secrecy away from plain sight. We'd been that way, working in secrecy as an order since Satan's attempt to destroy us all those centuries ago on Friday the 13th. Our fall was treacherous under a tower of lies, but was ultimately a welcomed blessing in disguise as it saved us from being a part of Babylon reborn if we had remained under the Church," says Brashear.

Brashear still watching her visitors closely, backs up, reaching back to grab her cup of Caffe.

"In our infancy, Mr. Bane, that I'm sure Dr. Rayne can attest too, we had lost our way and purpose. We became no better than those who forcefully attempted to convert others to godless religions under threat of force. Our history took a turn where we became introspective. We used the time in forced exile to gather our strength, supplies, armaments, knowledge and financial power. Over the past centuries we have become a distinct force that moves unseen, similar to what you call the elusive They or the Illuminati," says Brashear. "Except we are not them. Oh! And yes, they exist and are very much active."

Brashear suddenly keeps her Cheshire smile widened unable to find rest for it. It was as if the old wives' tale of making a face and it becoming frozen was suddenly true. However, it wasn't just the smile that was frozen, everything about her was frozen, even the steam rising from her caffeinated coffee mug planted firmly in her grip was frozen, the steam stagnate.

At first Jericho sits waiting for her to finish her dramatic pause, except she never does.

"If you're taking the dramatic pause on our account to build suspense, no need. I'm all in. I---" says Jericho

Then like a bulb turning on, he gets it. She's not taking a pause for the dramatization of it. She's truly frozen. Or should he say time has been slowed to a crawl to be more exact. It was like a bad Polaroid picture in the album of his grandmother's closet. Time once again had all but slowed to a stop and Isis was not left unaffected. That was immediately clear when he removed his hand from hers and it remained in stay. He removes his glasses slowly all the while staring at her before touching her face lightly and softly as his grandmother use to caress his as a boy.

"As always, Gabriel, never when I ask for you, but in your own time... ain't that right?" says Jericho slowly standing looking around to see where she would materialize from. She never materializes.

The responding voice that did is foreign to him and carried a deepness that is entangled in exhaustion and sadness. Octave wise, the voice is everything Gabriel's not.

"Jericho? Hmm... I often wonder why your mother named you as such," says Michael. "I couldn't understand at first. The only reference in history I remember was the city named as such that bore a mighty wall of the ancient world that only an act of God could fell? After a time of pondering this, I came to the conclusion that maybe you were to be a shield as the wall was for the people within them. Then... you fell to Imperial changing my earlier hypothesis. I then believed you were the city that was destroyed behind the wall. When you failed, it was in that moment you truly were deserving of the name... Jericho."

Michael manifests into sight of reality 2814. "I am not Gabriel as you have probably surmised. That does not mean however, I am any less important to you in your coming days."

As the captain of Archs appears, he's looking right into the soul of Jericho searching the worth and weight of the light contained within his orb that is the consciousness of what makes him the unique individual he is. No armor or battle armaments are required for this visit to judge the worth of the man. Michael comes vulnerable wearing only his uniform of Zero Realm absent his armor. His face betrays nothing as he silently judges the man that lives because Uriel and Cassiel died. Jericho was just as stern returning the gaze, his face betrays nothing as well. He returns the hardened stare unfazed by the circumstances that an otherworldly being was speaking before him. This is nothing special anymore; this may as well have been Tuesday at this point.

Michael breaks his gaze first and smirks at Jericho. He turns and begins walking the room till he finds himself standing next to Brashear.

Still standing in the second row of the jury style box, Jericho's eyes follows the friend or maybe possible foe. This thing professing to be friends of Gabriel could be anyone. Sure, it was dressed similarly to what Gabriel would wear, but the accent color was off. Gabriel's accent colors are red. This one's is gold. Also, another thing he notices is, unlike Gabriel when she appears, she has armor, this one has none. He wears a white form fitting shirt with two gold-colored stripes on either sleeve. His pants are white with a gold stripe down the side tucked into knee high gold metallic boots. He wears a red and gold sash around his waist. His face has mild scarring that cuts a path into his low trimmed beard. He' a stranger but yet familiar somehow.

"Took me a minute to place you, but I know your face," says Jericho. "I've seen you with Gabriel. You were with her in the mist that night I almost died."

"True," says Michael, stepping ever closer toward the Grandmaster, weighing her worth.

He reads the glyphs on her forehead in an inspection that would even make a Marine drill instructor jealous. Something about the room commanding woman catches his attention at first then whatever it was had loss the appeal. His attention reverts back toward Jericho with still that same smart-ass smirk. Again, he walks the room's layout inspecting it before turning his attention to all the souls seated there within. Finally, and seemingly satisfied of his assessment and appraisal the Arch turns his full attention back to Jericho.

"This one means well," says Michael, pointing to Brashear. "I've measured her heart with great acuity and have read many of her prayers. Indeed, she wears a tough exterior and at times drown under the weight of leadership, but she is as faithful and remembers to keep the Sabbath holy. You are in good company here, even if they are easily susceptible to the fallen. That's more of a pride thing."

"So, you believe her intentions of helping are genuine?" asks Jericho, outstretching his arms to gesticulate that he meant all in attendance.

Michael smiles at the aphorism that he knows Jericho is building too. "I do believe they are. They have the best of intentions and believe they are helping. I would not have said it if it were not so."

"The road to hell has been paved with the best of intentions," says Jericho.

Ahh! There it is, the age-old aphorism that I knew he could not resist, thinks Michael.

"I cannot deny that particular set of words you speak. The road... the path that we have all been set upon now was paved with Lucifer's good intentions," says Michael. "Look at all of this... look at where we are in the state of affairs in this current age. All of this was wrought by his good intentions of saving our kind from a self-perceived despot king. His intentions although pure ultimately destroyed all that we survey."

"Or maybe he really did see or hear something that set him on his path to good intentions," interjected Jericho.

"There is that," says Michael as he walks over toward Knight Commander Konadu Addi. He looks at the forehead of the regal Templar and reads his date of expiration. He examines it closely for a few seconds, then looks back to Jericho. "Good intentions set all to burn eventually is all I'm saying, if not carefully regulated under constant vigilance of checks and balances."

Stepping down and out of the box, Jericho makes his way toward this possible ally. He's yet to determine. "Where is Gabriel?"

"Direct. There is something to be said for that as you determine my allegiance... She is out of system. I sent her on a mission that may prove pivotal in the coming days... or decades or centuries depending on which eyes of reality the concept of time is seen through."

Jericho walks and stands face to chest with the Arch. They do grow them tall. He's forced to look up at the Arch of unknown Identity, although the latter is starting to clear up. Who this Arch is, is starting to formulate in Jericho's mind as dream that is remembered after a long slumber.

Jericho holds his gaze with the Arch figuring he must be the alpha. The gaze isn't to agitate a confrontation. He just fell into thought, thinking, *Will Gabriel be back? I have to tell her I'm so sorry I failed, I had my chance and I failed. I was thinking about me, and not what she had been trying to tell me. I shou—* His thoughts betrayed him before his gaze did.

"I hope she returns from the errand that I sent her on as well," says Michael, breaking Jericho's negative slate of remorse and guilt filled thoughts. "And you did not fail, Jericho... If I were to look back on the events of the Embassy, the day you lost allies and we lost Cassiel, it would be that I failed you. I had doubts in you, but these doubts were clouded in the loss of my brother Uriel... I've come to tell you. no longer will I be of two minds when it concerns your success. I will be of one accord with Gabriel on the matter of your purpose. I should have been helping to prepare you myself much earlier. Now, in her absence, I will complete your training so, that when you and Imperial meet again, you will have lessened your disadvantage of being... only mortal."

Michael places his hand on Jericho's shoulder. The two are suddenly above ground standing on the top tier of the Eiffel Tower among a city-wide black out at night. The Bortal Scale that measures light pollution has been set to level 1. The vastness of stars with swaths of galaxies can be seen in all their brightness uninterrupted by the false illuminating lights of man's harnessed limited state of technology.

"All that you survey at this moment, I have been around to witness most of its placement in the heavens," Michael says, pointing out across the vast ocean of stars. "I know almost all the names of every star that has been, that is, and that will be. I have stood on distant planets, pulling gravitational forces in directions that move mountains to their highest elevations. I have talked with other species that have lived and gone extinct. What you consider eons, has been but a blink to me and my kin."

He looks from the heavens to Jericho. "Come!"

Michael's wings extend out. His gauntlet lights up. He slides his finger across its surface tuning in a location of realm and reality to his liking. The two phase out of reality 2814. Time, gravity, dimension, and space all rush past them at break neck speed. In a flash they move from the Eiffel Tower slingshotting around Mars and into a traverse tube.

Time is different for celestials is the thought that springs to mind for Jericho; it's one of the memorable points Gabriel had talked about when they first met.

As the two travel through the traverse tube, Jericho witnesses mind-bending wonders that his mind simply couldn't comprehend or ever thought possible. He can't make heads or tails of what he saw in certain moments, because it was locked off to him. He was not given or had he existed long enough to unlock the ability through evolution to understand his trip and his part to play as the Dante character of the Divine Comedy to Michael's Vergil who is now escorting him through the nether regions of some dreamlike existence. It is akin to being struck with a sledge hammer. A terrible migraine emerges as his perception of reality is challenged, as his mind is subjected to sights that were to supposed to have been forever denied mortals. He didn't remember the headache when he was with Gabriel, but this mode of travel was familiar to him, this was how Gabriel transported him across expanses in mere seconds, although it seems so long ago now. He was just a mere boy of 12 then.

A hard bank left and into an intersecting traverse tube drops the pair out of what Jericho can only comprehend is like a cosmic limit speed tunnel or a transdimensional jump, perhaps? He never really watched sci-fi growing up, but he's heard the lingo. When the light show of the traverse tube ended, the two launched from the tunnel at an immense speed only to suddenly slow back into static reality until they were stationery and hovering. Michael wants Jericho to take in the gravitas of what he was beholding. He wants the mortal to see just how small and infinitesimal he really was compared to the backdrop of the immensity of just this single disk-shaped galaxy. He wants him to understand that he was part of a power that was greater than himself; a power that belonged to a collective that if used correctly could alter the course of that singular galaxy or all galaxies.

Michael lets out a small smirk and leans the both of them forward toward the disc shaped galaxy. "Hold on!"

A blinding flash occurs and the two rocket towards the planet landing softly on the surface of a solidified rocky mass covered in extreme green vegetation. Purple and dark blue hues fill the night sky. Other hues crowd the landscape, but such colors are not known by name, because in reality 2814 they don't exist... Here, there's no bipedal human life; cretaceous plants have become the dominant lifeform. Here, the plant life is alive and vibrant with bright luminescent colors as if they are powered by their own individual lithium batteries. There are very few swaths of land that are dark and do not illuminate.

Jericho's breath is taken by the sheer beauty of it all, the alien nature of it. He marvels at the different configuration of stars. Man is bearing witness to great existential questions of was there life out in the solar system. He watches the plants sway this way and that. His eyes narrow on the lit vegetation as he realizes what he is witnessing is something beyond the term grand. The vibrant colors that are moving were a sentient species. Upon closer inspection, they aren't swaying; they are walking, moving to and fro. Jericho's mouth falls agape at the discovery of the intellect of them, their zest and zeal. Now he understood why there are swaths of darkness among patches of the planet upon entry into its atmosphere; the dark patches are swaths of their dead. They are the cemeteries where the vibrant colors of the living had gone dim opposed to those that live constantly keeping a vibrant flare.

"They are communicating through luminescent alteration of color," Michael says. "Listen closely and discern."

Michael adjusts the dial, careful not to remove both of his hands from Jericho's body, lest he'd revert back to 2814's reality while firmly nestled in 1228 reality. The mixture of mortal's biochemistry with this planet eco system would certainly prove deadly for the human, even as one as special as a Jericho. As the dial turns, the colors become an audible language that Jericho can hear, but not yet understand. Michael slowly places his hand over Jericho's crown sure to place his index and middle fingers over Jericho's eyelids closing them. Once his eyes close, the gibberish the plants were speaking translated into his known language of English.

Amazement is the first feeling Jericho felt at understanding an alien dialect, but after the astonishment has passed, he is able to listen more closely to what is being said and not how. The conversation between plant-based species is none too different from conversations he heard back home on Earth in everyday life. Intrigued, he listens in on a particular group of conversations. One is about a marriage that was failing at the roots literally. When he moves his eyes as seen through Michaels to another section, he hears the happiness of one of the plants that was a soon to be father after multiple unsuccessful attempts at pollination. Jericho listens intently as the plant tells his friends that after many tries that he has successfully pollenated his girlfriend. It's life unleashed on a distant world. It is life that is so different, but so similar.

When he looks at another coterie of the species, he hears one discussing of how to tell his family that he was of a homoplatious nature. The unnamed plant is stricken with the pain of thought of what if his family rejects him. The new way of life he feel most comfortable with went against everything that his family believed and attributed to an unseen God that never cared to interject in the affairs of those persecuted before him for coming out. The last he knew to come out had their petals torn from their bodies before they were decapitated. To Jericho the observer, life here is uncanny, the resemblance to his culture and the many decisions that are made daily in the affairs of humanity are not just the cares of Earth, but cares of galactical proportions. Life is truly not unique to humans; life is abundant, everywhere, and it's just as hard. Problems are just as universal and trivial. If nothing else but that comment is heard in life, it can be truly attested too and added to two other truths, which are the certainty of death and taxes.

Michael looks at Jericho "If Imperial has his way under the guidance of his master, then there will be an unholy ending to such a species as this and many others including your own."

Michael looks back out across the sea of life of plants. "There will be an unholy ending for all species."

Taking a knee, Jericho continues observing the chlorophyllin species. Ever studying them, watching them quietly leaving things unspoken as they traverse through life, it dawns on him the magnitude of what's being asked of him. He doesn't know this Arch that stands with him other than that Gabriel stood with him when he was near the Mist of Purgosia. If she isn't threatened by him and they stood in peace, then he has to believe that he can be trusted. Besides, when she let him observe the battle for Sarin in Noah's day, this very angel was there alongside her battling insurmountable droves of evil men and monster that crashed down upon them like waves upon the shore. It's as if he was in command then.

"Imperial was so strong... He was fast and unrelenting," says Jericho. "His body felt like I was constantly hitting concrete... This enemy was unlike anything I faced. It didn't matter how powerful I was, he was more. He couldn't be injured. Rounds ricocheted off of him. What am I do to do against something like that? I entered the covenant yes, I was told and seen a few things, but what Imperial is defies man and man's conventional weaponry. What he did to the Chinese, my men, even me was unnatural. You're worse than Gabriel from where I'm standing. You all have put not only the weight of my world on me, but all worlds. I ask you, what can I do with that?"

"With such weight on your shoulders driving you to a knee," says Michael. "You can only do one thing, Jericho... stand. In all of that you just spoke, it's what you didn't say. Think about it... you made him bleed. You drew a life-giving source from him that made him weaker. Not even with all my omnipotence was I nor anyone of my kin able to accomplish what you did. Like you I am a Captain, the first of all captains that have ever been. From soldier-to-soldier Jericho, from Captain to Captain, what is the one aphorism that always stays true of enemies? If it bleeds---"

"We can kill it," finishes Jericho.

Michael looks at him, remaining resolute in keeping his composure of dignity, reliability, and steadfastness. Jericho knows of his charge of his covenant, but not the true weight of it. Gabriel coddled him. He can see that clear as day now and that's was fine when he was a child and played with childish things, but now he's a man and there are no more childish playthings. No, for the man he has now become there is only consequences.

Kneeling down next to Jericho, Michael places his hand on the concerned plantaicious species easing his overly worried mind. Suggestions of calmness and ease is pushed through the plant bringing a calming spirit to his upheaved ocean of problems. When he completed easing the mind Michael turns to Jericho. "You were chosen because of your mothers' heart and unwavering spirit. You hail from great stock. You carry a lineage back to one who like you were chosen and given covenant to complete a task that was given him. Like him, you are mortal but are capable of great things."

Michael reaches for Jericho's eyes again closing them. It puts Jericho into a further deeper state of sleep.

****

Void of Anywhere

The two stands in a vast void of white. A familiar place that he once found himself with Gabriel in his youth.

"Although you are constructed the same as any mortal, you are slightly different as your composition was given authority to have slight enhancements over others to give you a chance," says Michael rising from a knee.

The world of the white void was suddenly rushed with various colors as again; time, space, dimension, and purpose rush past Jericho at immense speed. Unable to help it, feelings of nauseum started to rear its ugly head, but he held firm keeping his knee planted using his hands to lock him in place on the ground. When the span of vast time slowed to a crawl, then an eventual stop, Jericho swallowed the regurgitation feeling. He breathed heavy and deep till the feeling had passed then stood slowly laying eyes on an event that was born of faith then eventually lost to myth. Michael took him to a time of the Battle of Glayden. The battle was paused like a snapshot; it was literally a moment frozen in time.

"This event is long past, but yet still echoes today," Michael says, voice heavy.

Jericho looks at the Arch, then it clicks: he knows who the Arch was.

He doesn't know why he didn't figure it out sooner, although he suspected it.

"You are the Archangel Michael... aren't you, Captain of Heavens armies, brother to Gabriel... brother to Lucifer?"

Ignoring his question, Michael begins leading him through sections of the frozen battle of a time lost to history of galaxical evolution. On this plain of consciousness, there's no need for the celestial to remain tethered to the mortal. This is a journey through the minds most receptive state. Here Michael can lead and Jericho would follow.

"Like yourself Jericho, I am a leader not of men, but Celestials." Michael glances back at Jericho. "That was not always as written. In the beginning, I was led by my older brother, a Seraphim which I found myself often eager to emulate. He was revered by our King even above his own son and heir."

Ducking underneath the blade of Warsivious as it separated a Choiretic's head from neck. Michael waved Jericho to follow him underneath. Warsivious' deadly display beckoned the mortal to closely examine his face in one of the few instances his mask is retracted. Shock can only describe Jericho's reaction at what he saw.

"General Warsivious Arcane?" says Jericho surprised. "He was here?"

"It is, and he was," says Michael, still walking around other time frozen ethereals of days long passed.

"You say it like it's normal," says Jericho. "The man who sits second in the Arcane war machine is like a god of war."

"Mind the plasma! It may appear frozen, but it has just been slowed considerably. The plasma is still hot as if just ignited. Although dream-like, the mind makes it real if you were to make contact with it. And Warsivious isn't like a god of war... he is war personified," Michael says, walking around and ducking underneath consistent red-hot plasma bolts.

Stopping just short of two angels engaged in an almost artistic pose of a struggle for dominance. Michael looks and studies the moment that he and Lucifer engaged in a saber lock, crossing blades for the first time in a dual for control of the Sadohedranicverse. Walking up from behind Michael, Jericho slightly moves past him to get a better look at the two combatants. It was easy to discern that one of the combatants was Michael, He was a hair shorter and the gait of his stance was a dead giveaway. The other, his opposing force was a complete mystery. The one embraced in the dual opposite of Michael, his helmet and mask was still engaged, face covered.

As the scene is studied by mortal eyes, the frozen Michael of Glayden's Rift somehow looked the same as the current, but younger, less weary than the one standing before him.

"Who is that you're fighting?" asks Jericho.

Michael doesn't speak at first. He takes time building to the answer. To be here again, to see a moment that has passed that can never be changed weighs heavy on him. This day that he reminiscently walks through in memory, Uriel was alive and so was Cassiel. There were numerous alive here that he had to admit to himself over the centuries he'd simply forgotten about. Now they were all lost to time and to Palengrad.

"Who is he you ask?... "He, is all of this," says Michael, sprawling his arms out to encompass all the savagery.

Jericho looks at the Arch, confused. "All of what?"

"That Seraphim there, the one that I'm fighting with is the reason that Earth rotates on an axis of evil. This is the day I failed to bring him to heel. All these Millennia's ago, I was inexperienced and idolized my brother; I missed the chance to bring about the end of Ascension. Had I not failed; all would have not been lost to a darkness that was never meant to engulf the Touchpoint of the Sadohedranicverse."

"The Sado what? You're losing me," says Jericho.

"The Sadohedranicverse is everything going back to the time before there was a concept of sin, when me and Gabriel amongst a host of others put the universe in place as you see it today." Michael points to Lucifer the celestial behind the mask. "Because of him and through his machinations, plots and subplots, the disparities of life were brought into existence. Paths that were not previously written by Fate were set into motion that eventually affected every life within all the universes.

Earth was not excluded... All of this has come to pass, because I failed to slay him this day and bring him low... I loved him and the universe paid for it."

The background starts to scroll by slowly then over mere seconds it again rolls by at breakneck speed slowing on the inside of a hospital room with a dying young woman that was aptly name Jane Doe at the time of her Earthly departure.

Twenty-Five

❦

STEPS THROUGH TIME

"Failure is all perspective and my failure is the birth of all others."
~Michael

Detroit Receiving Hospital, O.R.

Year 2014

The scene is omniscient of a time where sacrifice was honored and given freely of any coercion. Dreams of a joyous mother were deferred and cast off only to give the most modicum of chances of survival to a child she would never meet, in a world that proved a cruel place lacking empathy. This room although modest, is where the culmination of the age would be decided. This room of sharp instruments and forced purified air is the only time in the history of man existence other than his previous fall from heaven's grace that is unscripted by Fate. This futuristic and yet archaic room is free of the Judas Paradox.

White walls and sterilized polished floors of this particular room is abuzz with activity as doctors rush to save the life of a woman that for a lack of any other word had been eviscerated. Before losing consciousness, the pain that she must have gone through could only have been liken to death by a thousand cuts followed by a gallon of Isopropyl Alcohol poured about the freshly cut wounds.

Standing back in the shadows of the room, Michael allows Jericho to stand just forward of him to see the miracle surrounded calamity that is about to happen. He whispers to him from those darkened shadows.

"You live with the failure that you believe you've incurred when you stood against Imperial. That was not your failure Jericho... it was mine. Failure is all perspective and my failure is the birth of all others. Because I failed on the steps of Iayhoten during the Battle of Glayden, it became necessary for a mother of a young child to die in the year of 2014. A devout mother who wanted nothing more than to please an invisible king she had never seen, was ravaged by an unseen enemy; one that should never have been able to take root. All this; her pain, her death, a grandmother's sorrow, your call to action was all because I failed. This night was a tragedy... yes... a tragedy that would be given over to triumph. An accumulation of my past failure met here at this point and would ultimately spawn you as an answer to the conundrum that is Imperial," says Michael.

Jericho looks around the room. Doctors are frozen in time attempting to save the life of a woman whose face he's seen countless times in pictures supplied by his grandmother and in his dreams. It's the face of his mother that haunted him for a lifetime. It's now before him on the day that he was born. His first real sight of her isn't the sight that he'd wished for or envisioned. This image in his head was not of the goddess that he made her out to be. No, the real thing is much worse. The real vision is a woman that is in immense pain as she is being murdered. She probably looked to heavens screaming out 'DEAR GOD... HELP ME!'

No doubt the attacker hears her cries for God to intervene. He more than likely wants to hear them... hear her cries, it's what got him off probably. That's his excitement that makes inflicting the pain all worth it. Her screams fuel him. If the cries did anything other, they may have only maybe delayed his murderous act long enough for him to look upward as well into the heavens. There, he too looked up for any sign of an avenging angelic force to come down and smite him, saving her... only...

no avenging angel would. God doesn't work like that and the assailant knew it. He more than likely smiled and realized that there would be no God to save her, no divine intervention to strike him down preventing the monstrous willful act that would see her sliced up, beaten, sodomized and raped all while with child. He would then look from the heavens back down to her, his prey and say, "God?" followed by a long pause while he waits for interdiction to be answered with justice. When it wouldn't arrive, he would again smile and say, "No God," while shaking his head. That would happen because that is the world Jericho has seen across his many deployments. The world was not a nice place.

Although her wrist band states Jane Doe, she wears her habits that identified her as a nun or the shredded remnants of her habits rather. At some point, it became clear to her that night that the world was indeed not a fine place like her favorite author had written. A quote that she at one time probably thought she would read to her son someday had she lived. She would've opened the book that was no doubt old and worn and read, "*The world was a fine place and worth fighting for.*"

In hindsight, if given the chance she will more than likely attest that, it is not a fine place. A simple truth will strike her as hard as her attacker did with whatever bludgeoning object used to swell her brain. Laying on her back half dazed and surely confused while being ravaged again and again; she would've rectified Hemingway's quote slightly. To her it will now read: *the world is a cruel place and yet worth fighting for.* It's all there is, after all. Damn Hemingway, the world is not a fine place.

Tears start to well in the eyes of the Marine Captain. He can't help it. Beauty that was once her face is covered in a mixture dry and wet blood only wiped away at convenient locations around the mouth to apply the intubation tubes that would supply forced manufactured breath to sustain her life... his life.

As Jericho's eyes take in the scene, his eyes make their way down the rest of her ravaged body where he bears witness to the last remaining strands of his mother's habits falling away along with what remained of her virtue. Rachel, in her dying moments, lay exposed to the world showing all how close she was to full term. It all became too much for him to take in. His eyes began to darken from the peripheral and work its way in attempting to culminate in the blindness of unconsciousness. His knees became weak before Michael caught him.

"Breathe Covenant Holder! And stand," says Michael.

Finding his breath and the fainting spell passed, Jericho finds purchase and regains himself.

"Why... why show me this? Take me from here... please... take me away from here will you?"

Michael stands him straight on his feet, but still supports him. Time, space, reality again slowly begins to scroll by, then as before reach a speed that is incomprehensible.

Twenty-Six

❧

PAST NEEDS TO BE SILENCED

"I give you the weight of all that will be lost if you fail. I have lit a fire in you that will refuse to extinguish, because you now know if it does, the fate of the age will be left in darkness."

~ Michael

Berlin, Germany Chinese Embassy: Year 2044

When time slows back to a static notion, Michael and Jericho are standing in front of the Imperial Protocol event. Jericho watches as Master Chief Nelson; Seamen Riley, and Seamen Griffin engage Imperial. Just like the other locations they'd been to up to this point, time is just as frozen as a Polaroid that has been manifested as the tangible.

"Come and see Jericho, because these events defined your character," says Michael. "When you met Imperial here, you fought because you felt that you were fulfilling a covenant, a promise that you made and nothing more when in fact there was so much more. I have given you a glimpse today of how much more. Only a glimpse."

Jericho falls to his knees, head hung low toward the ground. He can't look into the faces of the men he failed to keep safe. All that power and yet, they died.

"Like you, Michael... This is where I failed to stop him. I failed to bring him down and now how many will suffer?"

Michael kneels down next to him and lifts his chin up. "Hold your head up, Jericho. You haven't failed yet. Only when you can do no more will you have failed. And to answer your question of how many more will suffer? A great multitude will suffer; just as those that suffered underneath my failure if you do not learn what I'm trying to teach you here. You and I wear the burden of leadership. We don't have time to mourn or to self-pity. We cannot self-judge, second guess decisions, or revel in a past that can't be changed. Leaders push forward. I brought you to these locations for you to understand something that Gabriel never taught you because of her incessant need to nurture a delicate soul that she'd grown to close too causing her the loss of objectivity."

"What do you want me to understand? says Jericho. "What am I not seeing?"

Michael presses his forehead to Jericho's.

"That the events that formed you and I into leaders were not chosen by our peers. Yes, they may have agreed with the decision that propelled us forward, but truly great leaders are ones that are chosen by Elohim, the universe, or whatever you would like to address the higher power as. He sees what we cannot. When you fought Imperial here, you had nothing but a promise. All you had was covenant that you were told to fulfil. You had no worth of what you were fighting for when you stood against him, just as I did not know all at stake when I should have sent my brother to Palengrad. What I have shown you here today; the Cosmos, life on distant planets that were liken to your own, the past of a mother's sacrifice, and the failure of a team of combatants; all these things were to show you and remind you of what you are battling for. All this to show you humans are capable of a great a many wonderous things. I give you the weight of all that will be lost if you fail. I have lit a fire in you that will refuse to extinguish, because you now know if it does, the fate of the age will be left in darkness. Next time you meet

Imperial, you will have the weight of all I have shown you behind every punch and you will not pull a single one. They will each find their mark because they have to."

Michael stands, pulling Jericho with him. "I will be the last Captain of the Archs, just as you will be the last covenant holding Judge. When you meet Imperial again, there will be no doubt or fear. In place of both will only be resolve and violence of action. When you engage that unholy atrocity, you will fight with a vigor that you were lacking. A great deal of beings, Earthly and celestial has sacrificed in some cases everything to get you here. Take their faith and make it your own... use it! Become empowered by it."

Michael again raises Jericho's chin when starts to drop it as if he was being scolded.

"I said raise your head. You have not failed yet. Cassiel, did not believe in you. I don't believe that he thought much of you till he seen that you would not quit. When Imperial knocked you down, you kept getting up. You even saved Gabriel by lifting her Razine blade. When my brother seen that, he knew that very moment why Gabriel believed in you. Her conviction and belief in you ignited his own, so much so, he sacrificed himself for you. It gave him courage to fulfill a destiny that he was sure was going to end him. You have the path laid that will be hard; you will doubt everything you do, people will die, friends will be lost, and you will lose heart at times. Keep the faith, fight the good fight, finish the race. No one knows your future not even Fate. Learn what I have told you today. Fight with your heart of all that hangs in the balance and not your mind. It will be love that bends knees and breaks swords. Do these things I have said and all will eventually join you in the light."

The world of light, space, time and dimension slide by again till the two Captains find themselves at a crossroad in Jerusalem in the dark of night.

"From here Jericho you will find your own way back from the nether regions of your mind. When you awake no time will have passed and you will find yourself again in the temple of the Knights."

"I'm to walk that path alone?" asks Jericho.

Michael turns toward Jericho. "You are never alone. Yeshua made a promise when he returned to be with his apostles a second time. It was a promise that encompassed all including the gentiles. He told them, 'I will be with you always, even until the end of the age.' And he has been... every step of the way, even when it may have appeared that he was silent. And if ever he wasn't, we'd have been there in his stead and name just as Gabriel has been. She has seen you from a child to the man you are. She has nurtured you, guided and protected you. The promise of seeing you through will never change no matter the mistakes or failures. She, as I and all that remains of my caste will be with you for all of your days, even until the unmaking of the world."

Jericho stands, wiping his eyes now of tears that start to stream. "To whatever end?"

Michael nods at him. "To whatever end. Like the Prince and his promise, we will be with you always... even until the end of the age..."

Jericho opens his eyes to find himself in the meeting chamber of the Templars. In the distance of his mind he can't see Michael at first, but he can hear his voice still speaking softly.

"...And behold the end of the age comes quickly."

****

Ardenne, France Knight Templars H.Q.

Grandmaster Brashear still appearing frozen has only moved mere millimeters since Jericho's departure. Again, a small voice belonging to Michael can be heard in his mind.

"The Templars have lost their way many times and have often fallen in the past. However, all their failures have purified them into worthy trusted allies in the fight that is to come... When you judge them and you will judge them... remember we have all wavered on our path to the best of ourselves?" says Michael.

Jericho's eyes follow the room taking in every person in it. Templar Masters sit in a seat of power looking as if they've gotten fat off the misery of others. At least that was his first impression, but looking closer behind the veil and lifting away the obfuscation, he sees the great risk that all of them have undertaken to be a coalesced force behind closed doors of secrecy in hopes to stop a man that will bring untold deaths to countless millions. Michael's words ring true, this is no time to judge, this is a time of building alliances like Kovac said.

Having no particular point of reference to longer view Michael, Jericho just speaks aloud. "The Sadoverse or whatever you called it, is as large as existence itself... Of all that has existed surely there was more that carried further merit than this blue rock, why is Earth the focal point of the calamities as you put it? How did we end up the ones that would decide the fate of so many?"

"Not focal point; Touchpoint," Michael corrects him. "And whether it's fair or not from your limited perception, the battleground wasn't chosen to be fought over this field which you all occupy, it just happened, because that is where the descension happened. Unfortunately, like the ants that build their civilizations within the lands of men, they too become embattled in war beyond them and their scope of comprehension. The ant's civilization was not chosen directly and yet they suffer greatly at the magnanimous forces beyond them. You mortals are not unlike the ants in such retrospect. You all suffer greatly having become intertwined in a dangerous family feud that beset upon you. Elohim's sovereignty was challenged over the ruling and fall of man. In addition, your kind are the closet in image to Elohim. You were all created to be the pinnacle summation of his joy of all that was created before. I remember the day he declared you all whole and complete. There was such a joyous cry throughout the Heavens that it had never been repeated in its candor. The loudest that cried a triumphant shout was the Seraphim, Lucifer. He was the most overjoyed of us all. So much so, he flew above the very throne of Elohim proclaiming your greatness. You ask why Earth? Because, here on this blue gem lies greatness and the next evolution of galactic ruling custodial caretakers."

Jericho still listening to Michael looks at Isis' frozen face. He slowly walks up to her gently touching her face again taking in every curvature of her skin contours.

"I have my answer... We are Touchpoint, because we are the threat of an emerging power," says Jericho. "Understood."

There is a brief flash as Jericho materializes back into the 2814 reality. Time again resumes its normal pace.

Instantly, Grandmaster Brashear continues without having missed a beat. "We have been in secret slave to the Vatican to avoid our enemies by making them believe we were extinct."

Jericho's attention shoots from where Michael was originally back to Brashear giving her his full attention at least till he heard Isis speak.

"Why now?" asks Isis. "Why reveal yourselves now in this late inning of the game?

Whew! Jericho thinks. Her question buys him time to catch up with the conversation that he momentarily ducked out on.

"Situation of late has prompted us to step onto the world stage and into the light, because our hand was forced." Brashear turns away from the two and walks back to head of the meeting chamber tapping a button on her watch.

A screen descends from the ceiling that Brashear has everyone turn their attention towards. "Over the centuries, we have been gaining information in our never-ending pursuit to understand the God of this world, she says."

"You know how this sounds to an outsider? It sounds damn right fanatical," Jericho chimes in.

"To most we do... Until we're not." Brashear activates the screen. Images of World War II. "Here is where we believe the beginning of the end of mankind begun. Since this event, our decline has been swift in fulfilling the remaining prophecies."

"How so?" asks Isis.

"Because there has not been such an incline in increased violence in all of human history. Hitler who was a product of the first World War was thought by history to be more than a man. He wasn't more. He was a man, but a man that our investigators at the time believe was a Judas Paradox."

Jericho raises his hand as if back in school or one of his military briefings. Once he did, it he could have kicked himself for being juvenile, but he didn't have a fancy button to press recognizing him if he wanted to speak. "Wait, you're losing me, the Judas Paradox?"

"The Judas Paradox—" says Isis, turning to Jericho. "—is a belief that no matter what choices Judas made in life, no matter how much he loved his friend the Christ, he would always had betrayed him, because he needed to do his part in fulfilling prophecy. He is the testament to some that our freewill is a sham and that life as we know it is scripted."

"That is correct, Ms. Rayne. Judas was needed to fulfill the death of Christ. That is what he was born for; same as Pontius Pilot. He too could have made no other choice than what he made. He was a tool to fulfil the texts. Brashear clicked the next slide showing a picture of Hitler.

"Hitler was a man that had to exist at that precise moment in history to cause the events that led to the Jewish people reclaiming their homeland of Israel again. They were a nation destroyed and thrown to the winds of time. All other nations that have been put in that position has never recovered. They just assimilated into the dominate culture. Israel was an anomaly. They didn't. The prophets of old stated that when the end of the age would begin, there would be a time that the nation of Israel would be called home and declared a nation. Hitler happened and the nation was reborn fulfilling prophecy." Brashear clicks another slide showing video footage of Arcane.

"Now... this man however, we believe to be more than man. The evidence of Imperial confirms that.

Brashear walks back toward the seated pair. "We have a mountain of evidence that the holy war; the one that really matters anyway is currently underway and that Lucien Arcane is a big part of that war, if not the head focal point of it. We made an attempt on his life as a preemptive strike to avert what must come next."

Isis stands up. "You all killed hundreds if not a thousand in New York."

"We did," says Brashear, matter-of-factly.

Isis slowly steps down from the stand. "You don't even deny it?"

"No. It is fact and I gave the order. We had to do our part in staving off the end of days. Our world is not ready and a great multitude would be lost if we had not. Ms. Rayne we are not in the business of saving lives. Our business is saving souls and we do that by giving humanity all the time it can muster before the end of all things as mandated by God."

"Which you believe that end is here... as in immediate, right now?" says Jericho.

Brashear turns to him. "Yes."

"Then you too have joined the Judas Paradox," says Isis.

Brashear looks at Isis. "We have."

Twenty-Seven

❦

CHASTISEMENT

"Lazarus has never been seen by the eyes of modern civilization leading many to believe he was a mythical agent. Then again, the angel, too, was thought mythical, but here the world was, knee-deep in myth So, reason stands that if one exists such as Imperial, then there may be a serious case for the authenticity of Lazarus."

~Ellen Nichols

Douala, Cameroon

Ellen Nichols has flown and traveled by an exhaustive and grueling caravan to reach her destination of Douala, Cameroon in central Africa. It's remote, but just advanced enough to support her crew. The region hasn't been the same since the Icarian crisis. The small advancing city was quite frankly knocked back to the Stone Age when an EMP bomb had been detonated. Progressive recovery has been slow to at times non-existent.

Being 48 years of age with past injuries that carry constant chronic pain didn't help Ellen as she made the journey. Her eyes are heavy with dark circles and her gaze is distant as she exhaled in a prolonged sigh. She's exhausted from all forms of modern travel, including extreme jet lag from her whirlwind non-stop prior engagements before traveling to her current destination, Cameroon. Then again, it could have simply been the side effects of the pain medication. Honestly, she was just too tired to give a damn which.

It's been months since the Imperial revelation. That was months that she was in rehab and seeing therapist to regain her level of normalcy after the touchdown revelatory events of New York when the Knight Templars descended upon the city shooting up the joint in some god or others name. Just thinking about those fanatics causes a flash back of the round she took in the knee. It was so much of her blood spilling out. Ellen rubs the phantom pain in her knee in remembrance.

Shaking her head, the effects of the daymare flashes away as she concentrates on slowing her traumatic response of shallowed breathing. To calm herself, she takes a swig of water from her clear plastic bottle with the white CNN logo. Signs of deep-rooted trauma that she hasn't fully recovered from yet, are of the events that spawned Imperial. According to her clinical therapist, it's an extreme case of PTSD she was battling. She thanked him for the diagnoses casually at the time, but she really just added it to her previous two other past diagnoses. Ellen had been a war time reporter for almost a decade while in her formative years of reporting, but that was in her youth. What happened in New York was different. One, she'd never been struck before and two, she had never lost any friends.

Pulling up to the recently disclosed location of her interview, she pops a couple of oxycodone's to ease the pain and building tension. Also, not to mention the added aid of a cheap high to help her relax. In less than two hours there would be the biggest interview of her life... There can always be a better story on the horizon, but to top an interview with Imperial himself is the story of a generation. Hell, the story of every generation thereafter. Only thing to trump that would be if God the Almighty himself came down.

She takes another long sigh and a swig of water grieving the loss her anonymity. Sure, she is a reporter and on the successful network of CNN, but she is what you would call the blue collar beat reporter of a merging company that will soon replace the famed logo. She took the dangerous assignments in the beginning of her career to gain clout and notoriety, unfortunately, it never manifested for her. However, the events of Revelational Saturday changed the game for her. Overnight, she was a celebrity reporter that was on the ground during the most pivotal moment to date in human history. CNN was sure to Capitalize off of it and keep her front and center. Richard Sullivan the current most trusted Anchor was no exception to her rising star from mediocrity. The position that she secretly coveted for years was given to her conditionally. Sullivan after talking with network heads was more than happy to relent for a temporary sabbatical compared to the alternative of being forever dismissed from the company. Ellen is their golden child now. He can live with that for a time. He knows he'll be back; she doesn't have the experience to maintain.

"Whoa!" says Ellen looking into her purse's attached mini mirror, she notices the dark circles around her eyes. It's a quick fix applying a bit of mascara and eyeshadow making her look a little more youthful and less weary.

Budget for the trip was tight. There was no unnecessary pampering permitted, like the use of a makeup artist. No room for tourist as they say. The polished look strengthens her resolved countenance before placing a smile on her face and stepping out of her black 2042 Lincoln Sedan. Unbeknownst to Ellen, there is more than just her set manager in the vehicle with her. Another passenger is in the vehicle, a hooded figure to be exact. He, too, exited the vehicle just behind her lightly touching her on her shoulder. Once out and into the evening dusk air, she semi-greeted the awaiting crowd with a halfhearted smile. Such a large outpouring made her nervous. The interview's location is supposed to have been a guarded secret. No such thing in entertainment. There are thousands that had shown up outside the hotel for just a mere chance to gaze upon an actual angelic messenger sent by the universe's creator.

"Such a following for him. This is a mighty deity eh Ellen?" says the cloaked hooded figure. "C'mon... this here is a celebratory moment and a drink is in order wouldn't you say? Not much though, just something to take the edge off."

You, know what? It was a long ride, just one sip to calm the nerves, she thinks to herself.

Ellen reaches back into the vehicle and retrieves her CNN bottle where the former life-giving contents of lemon infused water had been replaced by Wolfentow Vodka on a regular basis for just about three months. Ellen takes a belt of it and places the top back on. She starts to place the bottle back where she got it, but hesitates and decides holding on to it would be best. After the swig her body is instantly charged; affirmation that she is a functioning alcoholic. Turning back toward the crowd to head into the hotel, the massive sea of people part for her like the red sea did for Moses at the behest of the local police pushing and shoving the faithful and faithless people back creating a path to the most important interview in destiny. Butterflies dance in her stomach, nerves of began to fray. This is a feeling far worse than her first moments going on live television to anchor. She's been nervous before, but nothing to the level of what she's feeling now. The world is watching and if she fails to illicit the right answers then, no doubt that same world would be unforgiving and calling for her resignation. Cancel culture would demand it.

Ellen unfolds her collapsible wooden and half metallic cane. At its full extension she takes the best cane assisted rendition of a confident, but sexy stride toward the premiere hotel, Residence La Falaise, where she would become a part of history yet again.

****

Residence La Falaise, Douala Cameroon

Twenty minutes after Ellen enters the conference hotel, her team had all the audio-visual equipment set. The studio spares no dollar amount on setting the stage for the most significant figure since... since? Well, since maybe the person that asked Lazarus what being dead was like. Then again, Imperial may be even more significant than him, because Lazarus has never been seen by the eyes of modern civilization leading many to believe he was a mythical agent. Then again, the angel, too, was thought mythical, but here the world was, knee-deep in myth. So, reason stands that if one exists such as Imperial, then there may be a serious case for the authenticity of Lazarus. A question she makes mental note to ask, have the dead ever walked?

Laughing the hooded figure standing next to her unseen was more than happy to whisper the answer. "The dead walks constantly. Look at how you all move."

SUBOOOM! The sound barrier cracks above the skies of Cameroon. It's louder than the most sudden crash of thunder that Ellen can remember in recent years. It's almost game time and herself and the crew's blood pressure starts racing, pulses pump. Within a matter of moments, they would be in the presence of practically a living god. Her impromptu studio as well as the loud crowd outside the hotel that was moments ago bustling in an ear-piercing frenzy goes silent. It turns so eerily quiet; Ellen thinks she's just gone deaf temporarily. All eyes in the room are glued to the monitor of the cameras outside following the small spec in the sky as it approaches the hotel growing larger. As it drew nearer to touchdown, someone from the crowd, yells, "SAVE ME, IMPERIAL!"

Hearing the lone voice amongst the thousands, the crowd outside erupts into a chaotic frenzy far surpassing that of Ellen's arrival. It turns rancorous outside the walls of the hotel. Rock concerts of the most charismatic performer to ever exist before this point failed in comparison to what Ellen was hearing outside the walls. As a matter of fact, she can't even think of one performer from her youth that even came close to commanding such a crowd. Hell, it's so loud there may have well not even been any walls of the hotel, because the intrusion of noise was so deafening and earsplitting.

It's almost time. Closing her eyes, Ellen centers herself and calms her mind. Her hands shake slightly soon followed fort wit by her knees. She shakes her hands as if finishing the dishes and shaking the remining soap and water from her skin and steadily continues shaking them in an attempt to shake the nervousness right out of them. Her neck rolls slowly in a circle breaking the tension of her subluxated cervical portion of her spine releasing the gaseous pressure. Her unfriendly De Monic visitor after taking time to walk the room inspecting the interior and her people that makes up the crew. He returns back to Ellen again placing his hand on her shoulder. Ellen opens her eyes and walks over to her chair that she'll be conducting the interview from. Looking around to see if anyone's really paying attention to her, she reaches underneath her purple velvet seat cover and into her satchel. The covering is gaudy and maybe a bit much, but the recent addition hides numerous pieces of audio equipment that lies underneath it. She takes her logo trade-marked water bottle from underneath the chair and takes another swig, well actually three more swigs before quickly placing her vice back underneath in her satchel.

"Tony!" Ellen calls out to her visual tech. "Give me a live feed from the entrance! I want him on camera the moment he touches down. I want the majesty of it captured."

Tony nods and with a flick of a few buttons Ellen is looking at the entrance to the conference in real time. She takes another series of breaths as she watches the seven-foot-tall armored 8th wonder of the world, 1st wonder of the galaxy land.

My God! was all Ellen thinks. *He's beautiful.*

He's beautiful and imposing all at the same time with his helmet on. All that can be seen are his deep blue eyes through the eye slits. His height and build would make any enemy shirk away. Imperial doesn't wave or acknowledge the crowd at all, he retracts his wings and began making his way down the Cameroonian Military and police protected aisle way that had constructed the minute the news leaked. He walked with regality toward the entrance. A militant force of Arcanian troops emerge from within the hotel double timing it outside in two row columns. Surprisingly, they aren't dressed in fatigues, but three-piece black suits bearing the Arcane insignia on the lapels. The columns create extra layered path of protection for Imperial as they back the militaristic force already providing protection. The troops face each other at the start of them creating their formation. When Imperial throws the right corner of his cloak over his left shoulder the soldiers turn an about face in unison and takes a defensive posture toward the crowd. His mask retracts revealing his perfect unmarred ruggedly handsome face. The crowd goes nuts; cheers, restlessness, pushing, pulling, and jockeying for position suddenly ceases and fall silent. Some from the rancorous crowd fall to their knees in reverence with their hands raised high to Imperial thinking the next savior has arrived.

As Ellen watches, she tries to concentrate on any idiosyncrasies that the god like being might display that she could later use and capitalize on. Doubting Thomas of the New Testament would be her guide at the offset of this meeting. She learned one of the most cardinal lessons early in life, everything that glitters is not gold. She tries to focus, but it's like her mind is in a fog. Her vices seem to be getting the best of her on this most momentous day. She shakes her head in an attempt to shake away the metaphoric cadre of webs that coalesced on her face. She then refocuses her attention on Imperial.

"Tony, you're recording, right?"

"Everything, El," he says.

As Imperial makes his way down toward the entrance, his eyes remain front and focused. Unseen to Ellen and the crowd are those standing in the midst of them unseen. Three squads of about thirty Choiretics led by the Arch, Raziel are standing and watching the abomination from various points. Using his peripheral Imperial eyes betrayed him briefly as he makes eye contact with Raziel giving the Arch a contemptuous smile.

"Tony!" says Ellen sharply. "Get a close up of his face. Quick."

Just like that Tony's magic and quick on the click finger elicited the view she was looking for. Ellen makes a mental note to herself of what she seen. "There, right there. Play that back." *there...* she thinks. *Right there, what is he looking at or more likely who is he looking at?* A thought popped into her head of another question to she would ask: Are there others here like him that humans can't?

Reading her and seeing that the fog of alcohol was beginning to wane, the De Mon visitor again goes to place his hands on the reporter to squeeze her subjugated need for narcotics when he hears from across the room,

"I wouldn't if I were you."

The De Mon, turns toward a shadowed corner of the room sporting a devilish grin and finds Raziel accompanied by two Choiretics holding their hands on their sheathed blade's hilts.

Grinning even harder, the hooded figure backs away with his hands thrown up in a mock surrender.

"Arch, you would not shed blood here with Imperial so close. You'd not survive the encounter."

"Nor would you." Raziel steps closer toward the hooded figure. "It seems we'd be in Palengrad by days end, you and I together gnashing teeth in unison in horrific harmony."

Stepping a few steps closer, Ellen is the only thing separating the two celestials. Squinting his eyes slightly, Raziel attempts to isolate the voice of the hooded assailant to a memory from days long passed.

"I know your voice though; I can't remember the face. The voice is enough though. It has been a long time hasn't it...Vice? Shame you've reemerged only now to be dispatched so quickly."

"Reemerged?" says Vice. "I never left Raz. My you do talk bold for a celestial that have no win here."

Raziel nods to Vice to look around the room. "Your General has the eyes of the world about him when he enters these chambers. I could loose your head from neck while he speaks his contemptuous lies and he'd never flinch nor make a move to render aid. You see, I figure, he must play his role as his master demands. If he were to rise and swing his weapons—well now, that would just be uncivilized and viewed by many as an uncontrolled act of unwarranted aggression..." Raziel smiles at Vice. "He would simply as the humans say, look batshit crazy. Especially the swinging at thin air part."

Raziel takes another step closer. "Now... back away from the woman!"

Vice raises his hands in submission a little higher and slowly backs away just a little more giving ground to Raziel.

"Hey... hey, let's just all calm ourselves here. I'm not here for trouble Arch," says Vice. I was just in the neighborhood as the humans are also fond of saying. I was curious of what Imperial had to say is all. I will retreat right over here Arch to my respective corner."

The door can be heard unlatching. Raziel and his two Choiretics back away into the shadows again, but remain vigilant. Upon hearing the door, Ellen knees tense and her breathing becomes more rapid. She wants to take one more swig of her incognito bottle contents concealed as water, but decided against it. Not from will power either, there just isn't enough time. Imperial is upon her.

****

Ardenne, France

Master Knight Wildonison stands in opposition of the Grandmaster telling historical truths of the order to outsiders in the matters of eschatology, especially since it pertained his region of Knights. His monologue is interrupted and cut short by the intercom alerting the chamber that the first televised interview of Imperial is underway. Grandmaster Brashear gestures for Wildonison to sit for now. Without objection, he finds his seat and turns towards the ninety-five-inch razor thin television screen.

Jericho and Isis now seated swivel their chairs giving their attention toward the screen as does the rest of the room. The television flickers to life with a red screen showing the white CNN logo emblazoned on it with subtitle text of exclusive underneath. All eyes fixate waiting for the coming images.

"Is our operative in place?" asks Brashear.

"Yes, Grandmaster," answers Konadu, eyes fixated on the screen.

****

Arch's Spire

Michael and a couple of his Archs that retuned from abroad stand on the balcony looking downward with a host of Choiretics and few Powers that happened to be resting in the Spire at the time. They all await the words of Imperial, which are no doubt the words of Lucifer.

****

Elohim's Eternal Palace of Iayhoten

Seated upon his throne with his fingers interlaced and index fingers steepled, Elohim leans in a bit closer watching the events unfold on a blue star in the Orethentez Galaxy. Slowly, the scenery of his Throne Room transmorphs into the inside of the interview room where Ellen's breath has quickened at the arrival of her interviewee. Prince Yeshua doesn't sit on his throne; he stands behind Elohim's watching from behind his father's view.

"It is going to be a red day," says Elohim.

Yeshua never removing his eyes from the occurring events. "Aren't they all?..."

Twenty-Eight

EXCLUSIVE

"I see now in our brief conversation of quid pro quos that humanity does not respond to the beauty of the flower, but to the force of the hurricane that supplants the flower and flings it into purpose causing it to bloom far and wide."

~ Imperial

Residence La Falaise, Douala Cameroon

Imperial ducks down slightly to clear the door as he enters the room. Ellen welcomes him only then realizing how striking he is in person. Her breath and heartbeat races. Ellen's calming techniques are working overtime to shed off the pre-jitters. Cognitively, she feels much better than earlier; the feeling of a dazed fog exacerbated by the alcohol had quickly rolled away just as the sun chases away darkness at the break of dawn.

Imperial ice blue eyes stare down into hers as if he's probing her mind. *Stop that*, she thinks. *He's not probing your mind. That would be silly. What! Just as silly as an Angel talking to you here in an exclusive?* Ellen stops the conversation in her head to focus. She's never been much for religion, but Imperial, this being standing in front of her has shaken her belief system to its very foundation if not underneath it with just his mere presence. It's one thing to see him from afar on a television, but up close... she can't determine if she should hold her ground for the interview, bow, or flee in terror and hide from him and all he may know of her secrets that has complied in the summation of her life.

Ellen turns to her manager for last minute directions, but he too is locked in a gaze staring at Imperial lost in the fact that for all intent and purposes, an alien being of heaven or not was standing in the room. He was so mesmerized, his ability to simultaneously complete tasks of working the audio-visual system and direct was interrupted. Not only was he not directing, the only simultaneous tasks he was completing at the moment was standing while clutching his Red Cross pendant that was hanging around his neck.

Imperial instantly found her among the staff in the room. She was after all world renown for her reports of his touchdown in New York. They are intertwined. She ascended when he descended. Through all the mixed emotions upon meeting him, one thing was clear. He's gorgeous. She lost a little objectivity. The reporter is taken with his handsome appearance. Then again what could she have done? She is supposed to be attracted to him. He was after all created by Lucifer to be the ultimate predator.

Ellen takes in the full view of Imperial making note of his deep blue eyes, if they could even be called blue. It looks more like ice. His armor that overlaid his Arcanian militaristic uniform was polished and shined giving it the appearance that it wasn't his regular armor, but ceremonial maybe, then again what does an eternal being from Heaven armor supposed to look like?

Imperial still yet to speak a word turns away looking around the room. He instantly notices the Arch and Choiretics in the back watching him. No threat there. He then turns his attention to Vice. He gives the De Mon a nod with a purposeful sign hidden in the gesture of giving the mortals in that section of the room a nod like it was meant for them. Vice places his hand to his chest and backs away phasing through the wall.

Seeing the gesture, Raziel bites his lip in apprehension of something he must have missed.

From behind Imperial, a half dozen of black tailor suited soldiers carrying rifles enter the room and take up protective positioning on either side of Imperial's flanks. Last to enter the room is the unseen De Mon Verminesk. He moves past the mortals walking toward Raziel. The Arch doesn't make attempt for his blade. In staying his weapon, he shows that he's not here to oppose in this particular hour unless forced. Verminesk looks him over then returns back to Imperial's side.

Ellen swallows hard. Her mouth has gone cotton on her. She raises her hand to shake that of Imperial's. He observes her gesture for a second then takes her hand lightly and shakes it softly. He cups his other hand on hers then kneels slightly raising her hand to kiss it.

"El shunte Imperio," says Imperial.

****

Ardenne, France: Templar Headquarters

Isis elbows Jericho a few times. "He's speaking French, he's speaking French."

Jericho rolls his eyes. "Ugh!"

****

Residence La Falaise, Douala Cameroon

"I feel as if I should kneel or bow down before you or something," says Ellen.

"No, it is I that should bow before you Davina Ryan," Imperial says, looking into her eyes.

Shocked, Ellen gasps a bit slightly betraying the visage she wanted to represent in front of Imperial. In the first few seconds he's already shifted power in his favor.

"No one has called me that name since high school."

Imperial smiles slightly. "Is that not your name that was given to you upon birth?"

"It was, but I've changed it since then. It's Ellen Nichols now."

"Pity, Davina is an incredible name. I apologize Ms. Ellen Nichols. I still am growing accustom to interacting with mortals as opposed to watching them. If you would forgive me, I am still learning customs of duality here on this plane. To be an emissary between the Most High and my mortal sisters and brothers is a task. One that I feel not worthy of constantly."

Ellen shows Imperial to his seat by gesturing him to sit. He adjusts his cloak and then sits in an upright pose of defining regality. Finding her seat as well, she takes in his commanding presence. Instantly, she becomes extra cognizant of her bad posture and tendency to slouch. That just will not do. She tries to match him in regality and poise.

"My former name, did you look me up, investigate me, before our meeting?"

"Nothing of the kind, Ms. Nichols as you prefer to be called. I can see your descriptoral facts written in glyphs about your forehead. It's a system of cataloguing I believe is the best way to translate it. Everything about you is there." He points to her forehead. "By merely looking at you, I have all I need to know about you or Richard over there holding his pendant."

Richard? Is he talking about Tony? Wait... he can see true names. If Tony is Richard, then why would he be lying? No, he might have changed his name like me. Stop it Ellen, get out of your head. Intrigued, Ellen leans in a bit. "For example?"

"No need for example, I will tell you what I see upon your forehead. Listed is your date and time you were first created followed by your Earthly arrival; as you all say, date of birth. I also see your given name in its entirety and what function you're gifted with."

Ellen's eyes widen a bit.

"And, yes Ms. Nichols as you so wish to be called, even the date and time of your death."

With the last comment, the room goes utterly and deafening silent.

It was so quiet that it was rancorous. The silence didn't stop with the interview room. The silence spread out robbing everyone of tongue that heard him speak. So... there it was, everyone had an appointed time to meet death. A truth spoken plainly.

Raziel looks on with a calm contempt, but inside he's furiously burning with anger as Verminesk feeds the lines to Imperial of what he can see on Ellen's forehead. Imperial doesn't have such a skill. For all of Imperial supposed omnipotence he's blind to the soul scroll of living species, he can't see the etched flame script attached to every living subject. After all, why should he, he's half human and that is the side that blinds him to the natural gifted abilities of a full-blown created celestial.

"This son of a dragon's whore is attempting to convince this world that he's one of us," says one of the Choiretics standing next to Raziel.

Raziel just stands silently watching the interview paying the Choiretic no mind.

Ellen, shifts in her seat uncomfortably at the implication that her date of death is displayed for him. The audience in room of technicians, producers, and managers in attendance remain silent. If a mouse was to fart, it would no doubt have been a sonic boom. They all look to Ellen to see if she would ask the next question of... when is her date of death?

"I'm sorry, Ms. Nichols, I've made you uncomfortable. I tend to forget, how your species view death with such fragility."

"No, it's not that. I'm comfortable with the fact that I must one day die, I mean it wasn't a secret, it has to happen right? That thought is what actually pushes us through life. I don't mind dying, let's just say I don't want to jump the gun and meet it prematurely."

"Curious expression, 'jump the gun.' It's another human aphorism? Your species is full of them."

"Shall we begin?" says Ellen staring at Imperial for a few seconds before tapping her pen on her lower lip playing up the typical reporter cliché. Viewer think tanks say that the public still responds positively to such gesticulations. Image works it's everything.

"If I seem uncomfortable it's because I don't know exactly how to address you... should I call you Imperial, your holiness, or something else? What do you prefer? I'm not trying to reach into the realm of anything blasphemous."

"Imperial is fine, Ms. Nichols."

Ellen clears her throat and looks into his eyes. They are not blue; she must have been mistaken. Now that she's sitting across from him, they look more like a deep purple with a hint of green. Strange! She could have sworn they were blue.

"Let's begin, shall we?"

"Ms. Nichols, I believe we have."

Ellen turns on her game face. "Let's start with the question that everyone truly wants to know... are you an angel of God?"

"I am."

Ellen expected him to elaborate a little more, but he was very matter of fact in answering the question leaving no room to expound upon. She really had hoped he'd elaborate.

"Why are you here, Imperial? Why now and not any other point in time past? I'm sure there have been times before when man could've benefitted from the knowledge that God is with us."

"Why would you believe there wasn't a time he wasn't, Ms. Nichols? He told you that he was with all of you till the end of the age. To keep it simple in answering your question Ms. Nichols, I am here to help you all usher in a time of peace that was ordained in the holy text that was provided to your race of mankind. You humans... as you have so aptly named yourselves have suffered under the oppression of sin that your forefather and foremother have bequeathed you. Like the chosen Messianic Prince that was here before in a time of tumultuous turmoil, I have been sent to help elevate your species out from under the darkness of the human condition that plagues you. I have been sent to make you all ready to receive the forthcoming return of the herald that will bring an everlasting peace... and why now you asked, because this is the appointed time that I was instructed to do so."

Ellen shifts in her chair crossing her left leg over right. "The forthcoming herald you speak of... would that be, Jesus?"

Imperial gesticulates his hands and arms encompassing all human souls around him for inference. "That is a name attached to him by your kind's ill attempt at translation through the centuries but, if that name of the Christ is the best nomenclature that you know your savior as, then so be it. He is the herald that I speak of which I am here to proclaim, just as the holy text said I would. But the text is not complete. The days of Nero displaced many of the books when placing the text into cannon."

"You speak of the agnostics... the apocrypha?" asks Ellen.

"Correct. The books of cannon that were not included; the ones you all willfully continue to dismiss to this very day. That would be in addition to the ones you haven't even discovered yet. If you all were to read the cannon in its entirety, you would know that during these days, it's not just Yeshua, that will herald, but another."

The production team in the room does something against their most basic training of audio-visual production. They whisper and murmur loud enough that the cameras pick them up. Who can blame them being a little rattled and surly? Years of belief in whatever their specific religions were had just crashed and burned. Years of solidified dogma upended in a matter of a few seconds to the sound of well-chosen syntax spoken by an ethereal being. Imperial has just undone centuries of hardened belief structures. There would be hell to pay.

Ellen looks over at the production team with a mother's sit yo ass down and shut up glare as if children were acting out needing to be put back in check by the glance of ass-whoopingness.

Having quieted the room, Ellen turns her attention back to Imperial. "You saying that one, you knew Jesus and two, there is more than just him coming to settle all affairs?"

"Again, you speak in tenses that are hard to understand. You asked if I knew Jesus. Correction, I know Jesus— As in currently. I assure you as night follows day. He is real. There is a Messiah coming to save you all," says Imperial with a slight smirk. "Just not the one you think or should I say lead to believe."

"So, speaking on the matter of faith and religion, are you saying that the Christian Faith and those aligned are the correct and only faith?" says Ellen.

"I'm lost, Ms. Nichols, did you ever think it wasn't. Scripture was given to all of you as a key to unlock your own salvation; the very same salvation that I have come here to herald and proclaim. I am the exclamation point to the reading of that word."

The murmuring starts up again.

The Choiretic again looks over toward Raziel.

"He's trying to inflame the mortals," says Raziel. "And doing a damn good job of it.".

"Surely, we can't just stand by and let this happen?" says one of the Chioretics.

Raziel looks at his subordinate incredulously. "And what do you suppose we do, take his head?"

Defeated, the Choiretic grimaces and scoffs before falling to heel and turning back to continue watching the blasphemous display.

Ellen leans in closer getting comfortable. She just kept trying to search his eyes for truth, but they were cold and foreign. He could lie and have no tells. Also, his eyes had no consistency. At times it looked as if they were human, but other times something else entirely.

"The words you have chosen today Imperial could and more than likely will set the faiths ablaze picking one above another? There will undoubtedly be blowback to you claiming a one religion as the supreme, when there have been so many other in contention for the crown of being... the one," Ellen says while gesticulating the quote sign with both hands. "Shh! Just listen! You hear that? The very crowd outside these walls can be heard protesting what you have spoken. It sounds like the cheers are turning away from favor of you. Temperatures will soon be ready to boil over outside this hotel."

Verminesk briefly stares at the tenacious reporter. "She's cunning, sire. She doesn't quite believe the savior ruse as of yet. She's skeptical," he says, squinting. He knows that it'll take a little more to outwit her lifetime of earned suspicions of everything. She was more untrusting then he anticipated. He leans back toward Imperial and again begins to whisper the script that was approved by Lucifer.

Imperial steeples his fingers. "Throughout recorded history provided in your text and passed down through generations, there is irrefutable proof given time and time again that even when God himself intervenes directly in the affairs of mortals, there has been those of you that refuse to believe. When the impossible was occurring before there very eyes breaking all laws of your reality and physics, their minds were hardened as stone against his will and power. Why do you think in this age of your technology that it would be any different today? The message has always been the same. It is all of you that have decided with God given free will to disbelieve. So, in response to your aforementioned question. I don't care what these people of different faiths think. I don't care if they grow angry or riotous. It doesn't make what I'm saying any less true from what I have spoken."

Imperial's calm façade breaks a little. His tone changes slightly, it starts to turn darker as he grows mildly agitated. His eyes turn a light shade of red.

"That is an errant flaw now that I think about it. It runs through your kind though Inquisitor Ryan, now named Nichols?" Still steepling his fingers, Imperial moves in closer to face Ellen.

"Ms. Nichols, You all ask for proof of the divine; you included. I know, because I see your prayers. I see within the crux of them a constant theme of asking, if what you have been taught to believe is real or fairytale? The very leaders of faith past and present that you all look too; Hinn, Mavis, Moses, Daniel, Slakes, Ogsteen, Brannigan, and Fairisote all struggle with that very question when they aren't consumed by the greed of the riches that they adorn themselves in. They get fat and swell from tithes of the weak minded, predicated under the illusion that, if hard earned wages are given for their cause then God will bless them back. Laughable and quite sad... I am here, I have crossed endless seas of galaxies and rode untold oceans of stars to arrive here for the benefit of reproving and teaching in preparation of a coming King and Kingdom yet, the denial of irrefutable evidence found in my existence has been cast aside and words of ice turned vapor and steam." Imperial stands knocking his chair over backwards. "I am the proof and you are all too blind to see it."

Ellen remains seated and poised, but she is forced to look up as he now towers over. Fear of likes she's never felt overtakes her, but she'd never show it if she could help it. All of her most dangerous assignments across the globe has taught her to control such a basic instinct as fear. She's learned to own it, to use it, but this fear caused by Imperial is unlike anything in comparison.

Imperial steps closer to Ellen looking straight down at her now.

"Reality has not been altered Ms. Nichols, but revealed to you all and yet outside these walls as you've so drawn my attention is the petty murmuring and bickering of those that see and do not believe. The time for teaching and instruction of a gentle nature has been suspended for the day. I see now in our brief conversation of quid pro quos that humanity does not respond to the beauty of the flower, but to the force of the hurricane that supplants it across vast distances causing it to seed and bloom far and wide. I understand now that the power of the one who sent me must be exercised as in the days of old, before the fracture of faith extended into many branches; before popes, pontiffs, and dogmas. Now, Ms. Nichols comes the time of admonishment and loving discipline that is to be instituted."

"WAIT!" Ellen cries out in fear. "Just wait, I'm asking questions for the world over. It's not to place judgment or disbelief in who you are. Please, just calm down."

"But I am calm. It's not about who I am, Ms. Nichols. I am of the one who sent me in these great and terrible times. You asked, am I of a lord? I am. What is my claim without tangibility to institute the concept of faith? You as much as the world wanted proof of who I am. You wanted my legitimacy. I will show my credentials and through your technology all eyes the world over will see his power unleashed through me. Just as those in Israel that fell to their knees at the hoofs of a Golden Calf, you all have fallen to your knees to pride and arrogance. The Earth swallowed Israel for their transgression," he says, pointing his finger toward the masses outside the hotel. "Their fate will be swallowed in fire and blood," says Imperial.

Twenty-Nine

RULE OF THUMB

Ardenne, France: Knight Templar HQ

From Brashear to Jericho, all those in the room are silent watching the display until Brashear breaks the first words.

"Did you all hear what he said... well, did you?"

Heads nod, while others remain still giving no confirmation, because they're not sure what she heard. Isis head nods signifying she heard what Brashear did. Jericho looks around believing that he may be the only one that missed it. There could be others, but god forbid they say something and look ignorant. Although he wishes they did say something, so he wouldn't have to be the one that looks like he wasn't paying attention.

"I must have missed it," he whispers to Isis. "What did he say?" asks Jericho.

Isis leans his way, but speaks for all in the room to hear.

"He said, 'You asked am I of a lord.'"

"So, what of it? What did I miss, he asked a question?" says Jericho, adjusting his seat a bit.

Brashear looks at Jericho.

"The question is Captain, what lord sent him?"

"She's right," Isis says. "If he was of the Almighty he would have said, 'you asked me am I of the Lord, not a lord.'"

"He's of a lord alright," says Brashear.

"Just not ours," finishes Konadu.

"And now he'll prove to the world in a display of might just how powerful he really is," adds Kovac. "He knows the world is watching. Hell, he just said it."

"But why?" Isis says looking back to the counsel table. "The world has seen more peace in these last couple of months than in decades. His presence alone curtailed and brokered a lot of that."

"Did it?" asks Jericho. "I know I'm late to the party, but he was a black ops tool long before this version of Imperial that is being legitimized to the world. The one I saw did a lot of moving in the shadows. He was in the Congo at the battle of the Destined Suns. Now, I didn't see him, but I saw the wounds of his victims were all cauterized, says Jericho garnering the rooms attention. "Follow me now. He was at the Embassy in Germany. I saw him there and the victims there bore similar wounds like in the Congo. He was there to kill the sole surviving witness that seen what he did in the Congo. All of this was before he went public. If he was doing that then, it's a good bet that he or maybe even they, as in the Arcane Forces are doing it now. Think about it, they're coalescing power. These are all conquering tactics that ensures compliance. He wants the world super powers and his enemies to witness his true might so, that if they were thinking of standing against him or in his way, they'll see what they are up against."

"Well, we're watching," says Brashear. "We are definitely watching."

****

Residence La Falaise, Douala Cameroon

Imperial's helmet and mask generates from below his neckline encompassing his face. A Cheshire grin crosses Verminesk face as he turns toward Raziel who's still onlooking from the shadows.

"Flee, Arch! Call to the heavens in hopes to save as many as these pathetic mortals as you can, Imperial has been unleashed this night and the seal from your King on the scroll of War has been broken. Your power is limited here. Authority has been given to wage one the likes this planet has never witnessed." Vermin turns back toward Imperial. "Behold the greatest tool of war unchained."

Imperials wings switchblades out knocking over equipment impaling through the paper-thin drywalls. Ellen is knocked over backward from the concussion of wind that accompanied his wing's expansion. She's quickly back on her feet watching as Imperial turns toward the wall that contains the most windows looking out toward the crowds. He spins a hundred-and-eighty- degrees tearing the interior wall asunder with his razor-sharp bladed edged wings. The once pleasing aesthetics of the room becomes rubble. Releasing his silver chain red cross emblem, the team's manager Richard, who was named Tony dives for cover taking Ellen with him to the ground to avoid decapitation. The assistant location scout director wasn't as quick or as lucky. There will be no open casket for him unfortunately. Everything from the chin up has been flung into the night air.

Raising his outstretched arms Imperial faces his gauntleted palm towards the wall. A large superheated stream of red plasma fires from his palm. The heat from it is intense, Ellen felt it as soon as his palm began to charge. It was like opening a hot stove except she was more than five and half feet away. The plasma blows the entire wall of bricks, mortar and glass from its once firm foundation causing scores of super-heated debris to fall amongst the arguing, now fist to cuff, and riotous crowd arguing the merits of faith.

Hearing the explosion aided by others feeling the hot shards glass, the immense crowd outside the hotel attention is drawn toward the smoking and cindering hole in the outer exterior of La Falaise. Some that were still able to hear the interview through the uproar of the agitated crowd on the three large viewscreens are overcome with this nagging feeling of their internal innate early warning detection system that was perfected through centuries of evolution telling them it's time to flee. They didn't hesitate a moment longer, they fled in all directions to escape what they believe is the coming admonishment he was just speaking of.

The crowd is thick and jam packed with people of various faiths and different resiliencies. The pushing and shoving of those trying to see vs others trying to flee created an even more rapidly descending set of conditions of making mortar for the building blocks of a calamitous event that seemed unavoidable. This day was beginning to look like it was going to be something similar to those nations of old reproved by Moses on Mount Sinai over three thousand years prior when he cast the law at the wicked. Things did not bode well for them then. Unfortunate, it appears that it will not bode well for those in attendance today.

****

Ardenne, France: Templar Headquarters

Jericho stands watching the screen more intently. Isis watches him briefly, seeing the feeling of being powerless and helpless to do anything about what was happening written all over his face. *But he is helpless* was the only thought running through her mind. *Look at the size of that monstrosity. That thing up there is a living god. Against power like that what could he do even if he were there?* Her eyes fall back toward the screen, but not before scanning the room of others faces and emotions. She found there were no emotions shown and Templar Knights in attendance faces were unmoved.

"So, it begins," says Grand Prior, pushing a wisp of her blue purplish hair out the way.

****

Residence La Falaise, Douala Cameroon

Imperial emerges from the interior of La Falaise, hovering with the slow continuous flapping of his wings. All those that showed in attendance who were not actively trying to leave look up curious as to what the angelic being turned devil had to say.

His voice amplified through his helmet he speaks in the common tongue of the natives so that there is no miscommunication in his message. <"While watching you all from the sideline of your spans of lifetimes, I found you all to live in constant despair, swallowed by sadness, anxiety, and inundated with all types and forms of far-reaching maladies of the body and mind. Such maladies exist because you will not come to one accord on a spiritual level to unite all under one banner. The message that I'm here to reiterate was always simplistic to the very core of its meaning," says Imperial gaining slightly more altitude.

"It is the arrogance and inability of man to follow authority that has now brought such a consequence as you will witness today. What I must now do brings me no pleasure, but his will be done. Man's way of thinking is in need of rectification. I do not blame you personally, because you are all easily swayed by your own motivations that work best to suit the individualistic ideas of this contemporary society you have created. The bickering, the needless suffering of the oppressed at the hands of the wealthy, the famine, wars... all of that ends today. I told you all that peace would be the accord. I thought my presence would be enough, even when the history of your species spoke against such logic. I spoke with our lord on your behalf to avert draconic measures once implored by him in what you have all deemed ancient times. I now see, that I myself don't know better than the creator. I shall reprove the race of men until impurities are burned away leaving only the fine metal of men's worth.">

Imperials words sink into the crowd. It is ghostly silent save for the running motors of vehicles. Then it happens, there is that on who is the first to understand what comes with reproving, or scolding. It was Rahemza that it clicked for first. She bellowed out the first scream of terror breaking the silence. She was immediately joined by a host of others. There were even men's alto voices that matched or surpassed hers. Within seconds screams of terror and panic intensify from the crowd as the feeling of dread begins to blow through all in attendance. It was the same dread one senses of a coming storm that you are unbale to escape and you see it in all its destructive capability heading toward you.

Ellen pulls herself off the floor with the assistance of her manager. She watches his hand clutch that red cross of his tighter. She was sure there would be an imprint in his palm when he opened his hand later. Indiana Jones, a classic movie pops into her mind, when the man grabbed a burning medallion leaving an imprint on his hand. She was sure his hand would look like that. She doesn't know why she thought of that. There was an angry god floating outside and she was thinking of classic movies.

Ellen trots swiftly towards the edge of the room where the wall use to be and looks out through destroyed exterior. Her camera men follow still recording standing next to her adjusting their lenses for the best filter and shutter speed. Deep down they know they should run, but how far would you need to run to escape the wrath of a god? The camera operator to the right of Ellen steps a bit closer sending gravel falling down into the standing room only crowd. Ellen grabs his belt and harness to keep him from going over. Undaunted by the near misstep, he zooms in closer having the best angle of Imperial's profile. *Worth it!* He thinks, having now achieved the best Pulitzer photo that he would be recognized for later. Posthumously or not remained to be seen.

<"For your species to continue on in this state is but balancing on an edge of the blade overlooking a deep precipice,"> says Imperial. <"If the path is not thwarted, then a great multitude will not live to see the promised end that was a hoped for. I have come to light the path and show you the way.">

Panic draws more scream from the crowds. A child no more than seven speaks but cannot be heard through the cacophony. Imperial sees her and that the child is talking directly to him. Seeing her, curiosity overtakes him; he wants to know what child does not flee; and what the child has to say. He will hear it.

Both of Imperials hands begin to glow red as plasma bolts charged. Raziel face shows surprise in that feature. There is no device. His hands store the energies.

<"**SILENCE!**"> shouts Imperial.

The protesting crowd clashing over ideals of faith and fear fall completely silent instantly. Those that were attempting to flee takes pause long enough to look back to see what Imperial had to say. Perhaps his coming wrath was about to be bound in mercy? Then again Mercy has been gone from the world for some time.

<"What did you say little one?... You there with blue dress,"> asks Imperial pointing toward the child.

Ellen's camera men aim downward catching the child's image.

<"I said you are not of the one true god of Abraham, Isaac, Jacob or David. You are not the way. There is only one way to see the father and you are not it,"> says the child.

Imperial slowly descends down toward the child hovering just above her. His voice remains even and matter of fact as his ice blue eyes stare at her, but he speaks not to only her to hear his words, but to all <"This insatiable lust for bloodshed and control between the kings of this Earth will be brought to heel. Minor disturbances are to be expected and will be handled by the local authorities so authorized and duty bound to uphold Earthly court. Conflictions that rise to a level of unsustainable loss of life will be adjudicated by me. I have no boundaries, nor am I restricted by laws of men or even the confines of time and relativity. From the jungles of the Congo to the boardrooms of Wallstreet, if the laws of human decency are broken, admonishment will come quickly. If conversion of faith turns deadly, it will be adjudicated quickly. Disorder and dissention will not be allowed to continue. Just as the Jewish people were once thought chosen above others, the men and women loyal and under the Arcanian banner have been and are now the chosen. The Arcanian forces are now the recognized enforcers of my god's law through which order and peace will be restored. They will wear his insignia duly appointing them. A command from them is a command from me and the one who sent me,"> says Imperial still keeping his eyes on the small girl.

With his red glowing hand that is holding a plasma charge, Imperial grabs his blade hilt and unsheathes his blade. "My god wills his word into existence; I am now here to execute that will at his word.">

<"You are not of Allah!"> yells Shel Faheed from the amongst the crowd in support of the child. Shel is dressed in traditional garment of her Islamic heritage when Imperial spots her.

Those standing around her, slowly backs away until she now stands alone the object of Imperial's eye. The woman walks up behind the child placing her hands on the girl's shoulder. He moves his contempt filled gaze from the child to the woman speaking in dared defiance. Imperial's eyes turn from dark red to a deep dark blue as he shifts his vision through realties. Finally, he finds the true culprit, except it isn't what it appears.

Raziel appears behind the elder woman placing his hand on her shoulder for support. She has made the choice to stand against an agent of evil like the child. Archs have no sway over the will of men. It is this lone woman and child that will not be swayed from scripture of each of their respective faiths. They will not be fooled by the machinations of a slander. They both hold to their separate faiths and in doing so, are not blinded. They know what comes with what they speak and Raziel will support them for their final seconds. The Arch knows it's their last, because little Faye Rastiff and Shel Faheed's date of death is nigh. So say the script upon their foreheads. No need to hide from these two any longer. Raziel makes himself known and seen to the woman and child as well as Imperial. Their faith is to be rewarded.

<"God has heard you little Faye and Allah, you Shel. He has sent me here to stand at both your sides. You have both been good and faithful servant,"> says Raziel.

He looks to little Faye's prayers and reads them as they head to the Transcommunicative Hub. The crystalline strand reads just a repeating series of words, *I have no fear for the Lord art with me, I have no fear for the Lord art with me.*

<"I knew he would not forsake me Mister,"> Faye says as a lone tear streams down her face. She takes a long sigh before she speaks her last

truth within this world. <"You are an abominable, an outcast created to tric—">

"An abomination sweetheart, but close enough," says Raziel. "Be at ease Faye and rest well, you've earned it. Look to me, look into my eyes and find peace in that he is surely real and that your faith did not waiver."

Shel nods in a total immersion of tears while slowly turning toward Raziel. Smiling, she turns little Faye along with her towards the Arch where they both face him.

The Child sees the Arch. She instantly knows him and smiles. <"Hi Raziel.">

He smiles back at her. <"Hi Faye.">

Shocked, Faye's eyes widen. For the first time since her birth, she can hear. Until this moment, she's never heard the syllables of her own name.

Both having turned and seen Raziel, tears stream from their eyes in an uncontrolled flow.

< "I have kept the fai---"> was all that was breathed from Faye

An intense red bright light shines on the child and woman. Death removes both their souls before their bodies are instantly vaporized wiping them from existence. The blast of Plasma scorches bystanders that were standing in their immediate vicinity.

A wisp of smoke rises from Imperial's palm as he lowers it. There is another turn of silence from the crowd, hell... silence overtakes the world as the CNN cameras look on along with various other news networks that have now made it to the scene via motorized vehicles and choppers. Raziel is left holding cindering ashes that slowly spill through his arms and fingers.

Thirty

{ornament}

FOR THE BETTERMENT
OF ALL MANKIND

"Even when you could have changed the universe to fit your will and your end, you did not. Your word is one that binds the very Aether together."
~*Etherealtorial Guardsmen*

Washington D.C. : White House

President Bernard Logan, leaning on his haunches on top of the front corner of his desk with his arms folded, watches his television as the coverage catches the woman and child being instantaneously incinerated. His temperament and scowl remains steady. At the horrid act, Vice President Neil Gosen grabs his mouth and stomach as his late dinner upchucks. He just barely makes it to the trash can. Chief of Staff Horton Blake, a heavy-set middle-aged man instantly breaks out his vidcell phone turning his back and walking away from the images. He scrolls and tap names linking in joint calls to the Military Chiefs.

President Logan watches a little while longer before getting up and walking around his desk to sit ensconcing himself behind it. After a long moment of thought he reaches for the phone hesitantly. He picks it up then places it back on the receiver. Glancing over to front door of his office he looks just above the door at his Crucifix. He's had since childhood. He picks up the phone a second time. His lips curl a bit as if making a painful decision akin to being bitten by a snake or stung by an African Wasp. After a mini debate with himself, he places the hard-line phone back on the receiver and grabs his secure cell line from his inside suit jacket pocket that was overlaid on the back of his chair.

"Get me the heads of state and the acting UN President."

****

Residence La Falaise, Douala Cameroon

Nothing left but cinders and blowing ashes, Death places their souls inside his cloak and turns toward Raziel staring at him. The Arch doesn't make eye contact with the chaperon of the dying and damned. In fact, he doesn't remove his intense and determined gaze from that of Imperial, but he can feel Death's eyes boring into him. Softly with al-most a whisper, he addresses Death's apparent concern.

"You disagree with my choice of providing comfort to the dying?"

Death doesn't say word. He just looks at the living ocean of bodies that surrounds them. He sees their souls nestled quaintly in their inner ethereal pockets next to the heart. Before their ejected they give off a purple illumination, but their true color is undetectable till that time of ejection. Dates of their departure from this life change on a great many of their foreheads.

"This madness was unavoidable since he touched down here, Ferry-man," whispers Raziel loud enough for only Death to hear. "He was al-ways going to make an example of these innocents."

Raziel's gaze now falls to Death. He nods toward the silent crowd. "Go...be about your work and do it quickly! Let there be as less suffering as possible for those whose time is nigh."

Death nods at the command. "You are alone in this Arch. Do not be as foolish as Uriel or Cassiel. Withdraw and fight another day that shows you more favor."

"You... a fallen in Elohim's eyes now profess to tell me what I should do?" says Raziel incredulously

Death slightly lowers his head in a bit of shame, then recovers almost just as quickly. "No Arch of Zero Realm, it was merely a suggestion that I thought you may find beneficial."

Too late, Death's words find no active listener. Raziel's attention has returned to Imperial.

Death nods again and begins moving through the crowd preemptively drawing a cadre of souls from the young and elderly. Bodies now void of life sustaining energy; they all fall to the dust covered pavement amongst onlookers whose attention is drawn too skyward to notice.

Death looks back over his shoulder toward Raziel. "Save as many as you can, then flee Arch! Imperial has been created of calculated abhorrence. You oft not forget; your foe is beyond reason and takes after his father."

The crowd is in utter state of stupefy watching the hovering celestial. Imperial slowly raises his hand again. The plasma begins to charge again for purpose of firing in rapid succession.

Raziel touches another shoulder of an astonished teenager in the crowd and whispers to him, "Flee, tell them all to flee and run for their souls."

Verminesk touches the teens other shoulder. "Stay and marvel at what will soon befall the lives here. Do not run in terror, but rejoice at your coming salvation at the hand of your god Lucifer's creation."

Raziel stares at Vermin and slowly pulls his blade. Vermin releases the teens shoulder and backs away creating space and pulls his blade.

"ARCH!" calls out the Choiretic escort. "Avert your eyes and witness that we are at a loss here."

Raziel looks skyward and witness a company of demons hovering in the atmosphere. He re-sheaths his sword back into its scabbard remembering the last words of Death, 'Save as many as you can.' The Arch knows those that are meant to expire this day will do so whether he intervenes or not. He can't save those from Death, it's just their time. However, he can save the inured of the coming judgment

Vermin smiles at Raziel. "This is the part where you flee!"

Raziel back away turning towards his two escorts. "We will not be able to stop the coming event. If we were, we'd have been given the orders before now. They will descend here momentarily with all the destructive power at their disposal making a spectacle for the world to see. As Death said, save as many as you can. Preferably, the young ones that are not here of their own volition and the old that were to foolish to understand why they're here. Do not engage any De Mon or Legion unless necessary. If we stick to saving those of the populace we can save, they should not be worried about us. If you engage, then all bets may fall, snake eyes... NOW, GO!"

****

Elohim's Eternal Palace of Iayhoten – Throne Room

Watching the unfolding events, Elohim leans back in his chair looking as if he's engaged in silent judging. Then a sound, barley a whisper, leaves his lips, "Was my rule so bad to have wrought this."

"Did you speak, my King?" asks the Etherealtorial Guard closest to him.

"I did, Asyreim. I spoke, was my rule so bad, that a third in Heaven would decide to fall?"

He wants to speak in reply, but Asyreim is hesitant.

Elohim waves his hand dismissively. "You may speak freely."

Grabbing his helmet with both hands, he removes it and walks in front of the King and kneels.

"I have been in your company everlasting King almighty for as long as I drew breath. I have seen the many decisions that you've made since I've been at my post and from my understanding of what I've witnessed, you have not faltered. Your rule has been just. Your word has been law. Even when you could have changed the universe to fit your will and your end, you did not. Your word is one that binds the very Aether together. So, no King, your rule was not bad and I would have words with those that say otherwise. You are a just mighty King that will endure forever. That Seraphim's fall and every subsequent action was of his own volition, not yours. Your rule is perfect, your will, superior."

****

Residence La Falaise, Douala Cameroon

Imperial's mask generates encompassing his face before unleashing his first series of blasts which are a flurry of charged focused strikes into the crowd standing closest to the hotel. A majority of the bodies disintegrate turning to ash. Those on the outer most perimeter of the blast are scorched and thrown by the three hundred and sixty degree resulting concussive pressure waves. The rising plume of fire shakes the crowd from their initial shock on the outer perimeter of the first blasts. Mass terror takes hold consuming the thousand or more in attendance sending them fleeing in every direction. Carnage ensues as means of egress are blocked by man-made obstacles of parked cars and trucks of those too lazy to have found ample supplied parking. Laziness has now shown, why it's considered a sin.

As people flee, it is not a ballet of timed beauty. There is no precision as one jumps over another to escape a violent force that may very well be the end of their life. It is messy; it is confusion of the highest order where it comes down to who has the will to survive. Those that were not agile on their feet and made the unforgiving misstep of falling were instantly trampled. Their passage from this world was a long-drawn-out stagnated death by trampling which tally surely included that of children, the ones that were too small for the fleeing adults to see in a wave of panic. There were however a few lucky ones, child and adult that had fallen and were able to fight their way back to their feet where they were met with a new sobering reality of the massive exodus. It revealed; that those not in the immediate front, but finding themselves in the middle would be trapped against the calamitous events of those in the rear.

Taking pause from inciting the crowd, Vermin watches Imperial blaze away sending blast after repeated blast from dual hands into the crowd. If his face could be seen behind the mask, it would show the emotion of joy that resonated from literally shooting fish in a barrel. Vermin also wanted to partake of the excitement of slaughtering the masses of sheep. He eagerly stood waiting for the order from Imperial to be given, that will cut him and the 37 of the De Mon horde loose. Only problem is that in this instance, the order isn't going to come from Imperial. As he is in the fray of dishing out his judgement, he can't be trusted to be precise in giving command. Emotion could counteract the plan that was meticulously constructed by Lucien. Emotion was unfortunately the byproduct of the human side of Imperial, the Cyrail Arcane side. Vermin and the horde patiently had to wait for Warsivious to give the order to attack the mortal populace.

Like a huge wave rippling outwards, the crowd continues to run from the epicenter of Imperial's annihilation. Ellen continues to watch in complete horror with a feeling that her questioning led to this. All her signs of being slightly intoxicated or even a drunkard for that matter had ended abruptly, hallelujah it's a miracle. The healing experience does not come at the hand of God... no, it came from the hand of a devil and watching hundreds die in flashes of flames. She quickly turns around covering her mouth trying to stop herself from letting out a horrific cry. She turns from the agony of human despair continuing to hold her hand over her mouth to hold down her dinner. Quickly composing herself she taps her camera men rapidly on the shoulders giving him a nod letting him and the rest of her crew know it's time to leave.

The crew having been alerted that it is indeed time to leave, they turn to head for the doors. As if sensing their intentions, the well-dressed black suited Arcanian troops block the means of egress. One of them, a tall gauntly looking man takes three steps forward toward them opening his suit jacket to show Ellen and her crew his semi-automatic collapsed mini M4 rifle. He nods toward the decimated hole in the wall strongly inferring that she keeps reporting and that the camera men keep their cameras trained on the event recording. Feeling they have no other choice; she and the crew walks back to the gaping hole. Her segment producer jots over to her. He nods at her and takes the lapel mic off her shirt and gives her a hand held mic with the trademarked red and white CNN logo on it. He gave the hand cutting gesture across his neck that the lapel mic was dead.

He only wants to get close enough to her to say,

"Best not do anything to upset these guys," he says while exchanging the mics.

Ellen turns toward the Camera after taking a brief moment to calm things down in her mind and regain her reporting composure. She nods and rolls her finger in a circular motion a couple of times to let him know, she's ready.

"This is Ellen Nichols, moments ago the world had tuned into a planned broadcasted sit down with the angelic being named Imperial that revealed himself to us only a few months ago."

Explosions outside illuminates the side of Ellen's face as she gives her up to the minute report. The heat from the inferno's out among the populace was so hot at times that she had to cover her face shielding it from the intense wave of heat.

"What started this evening as rejoicing hopefuls looking to steal a glance at the Angel Imperial has turned into what I consider nothing more than uh—umm a biblical judgment. Imperial claimed a one true god and that there is one correct faith which was almost immediately met backlash of public outcry of those outside this location. That back-lash of protesting faiths has resulted in the catastrophe being witnessed now... live. During the interview murmurs of protest between the faiths erupted into an all-out riot just outside the Residence La Falaise. Shortly afterwards the crowd's protest begun to grow violent. Within minutes, it was young ideals versus old, Jew against gentile, Christian against Muslim, and atheist against the faithf— Oww!"

Ellen stops abruptly as a piece of hot shrapnel from an exploding car lacerated her cheek causing her to draw back further inside the hotel room. She continues running her hand across her cheek checking to see how deep the gash. *Just a scratch*, she thinks. "What has erupted here is a literal firestorm at the hands of Imperial."

After firing volley after volley of plasma into the crowd, Imperial

unsheathes his blade and rockets into a crowded section of fleeing citizenry. He lands with wings fully extended creating a wind concussive
blast that cleared his landing spot. Bodies were thrown and strewn in
all directions. Without missing a beat, he began to twirl using his wings
for decapitation. After a series of spins, he looses his blade on the populace. White-hot edges of his blade activate. As he prepares to sling it
and leave victims cauterized in pieces.

There it is, the emotion side of human frailty. It has taken over causing cognition error in the plan. Using the white-hot blade feature would
for sure add to his celestial lineage, but it could alert governments that
investigated the fallout from his clandestine earlier missions. Bodies
that were eviscerated, but cauterized like in the Congo or the Chinese
embassy could be linked if someone paid attention and someone is always paying attention. Such a minor slip now could out his participa-
tion in his early interventions to wipe Lucien's enemies from the map.

Emotion does not rule the moment. He forewent the white-hot
edges powering down the blade. He decided to prove his humanity was
not a frailty and went for the medieval hack and slash sure to leave
blood and plenty of it. It wouldn't be neat, but the shock and awe factor
would be there nonetheless leaving nations terrified of what just one of
him could do.

Verminesk nods after receiving orders from Warsivious.

"At last, we are unchained." He says unsheathing his sword dropping
it in a slicing downward arc while giving the command to his horde of
De Mons to attack the mortals in attendance. The horde remains outside reality 2814, but attack in full force running up the civilian death
toll making it appear that Imperial has more power than he's wielding.
They press the limits of the seal that was broken unleashing War on a
third of the Earth, a command that removed peace and the already absent Mercy.

Thirty-One

MEN DEFY GODS AT THEIR OWN PERIL

Men Defy Gods at Their Own Peril
"What I have seen makes the very blood run cold. May the book be sealed until time indefinite never to be reopened."

~Daniel

Douala, Cameroon

Lieutenant Strainfield observing from the outskirts of the perimeter that he had ordered his Cameroonian troops to set up, grimaces as people haul ass, running past him jumping over aligned patrol vehicles and barricades to escape the wrath of the living god Imperial. For the first time in his career since he was a rookie, he doesn't know how to proceed. In front of him is an active terrorist event that is causing mass killing on an unprecedent scale even by Cameroon standards, but the suspect is not a terrorist or militant gang. The suspect committing acts of terror is an entity sent by the Lord God Almighty. One does not train for such an occurrence and lacks no experience in handling such an omega level event.

Wanting to intervene, the Lieutenant's faith is tested. Before him is a destructive but miraculous event that is of the will of God; who is he to stand in the way of his mighty will? Hearing the screams of civilians though, it forced a second contemplation of his belief structure and ignited immense soul searching. After long moments of spiritual and physical hesitation, he acknowledges that he has a duty to safeguard lives first and property second. It was surely lives first and foremost being eradicated.

Till today, Strainfield had never seen a true miraculous event. Sure, he's read them in the Koran of course, but this is an event occurring before him that broke his third dimension ideal of reality. If this isn't the definition of miraculous, then throw the whole dictionary away, because it sure was worthy of being written as an added addendum to scriptures of old. For him to intervene in such an event would resign himself to becoming a part of a sacred story; a foot note in the bottom of the second page of the new text. Who'd in their right mind want to be a part of that? It never really worked out for those in the way of God's works in those old tales of kings and prophets. After minutes of working his mind through paralyzing decisional fear, he comes to the realization the gods be damned, he must intervene if he's to bring the blood shed to an end. First things first though, remove the decision from off is head. He wasn't paid enough to make such a call alone. Better he attempt to pass the buck to command above him.

Lieutenant Strainfield grabs his shoulder mic. <"Do you see what I am seeing?... Orders, Commandant?">

The radio squelches. <"*Stand by!*">

Strainfield moves to the left slightly giving the people that are fleeing a little more room to make it past him. He looks over toward the last patrol vehicle which happens to be an armored Bearcat attack vehicle converted from black Dodge Ram extended cab truck. It has an aftermarket edition of a 50-caliber automated Gatling gun on its roof supplied by the illustrious Cameroonian Military. It was a great investment purchased from the Americas when policing there was thought to have been too militant for citizen protection back in the early 2000s. A loss for them that day, but a mighty win for him today. He signals the officer standing next to it by waving his flashlight.

After about 15 seconds of flashing his light, the attention of his subordinate is garnered. Strainfield throws up the peace sign signaling the number two with his fingers. He then gesticulates the number one and holds his hands as if he's imagining himself rocking the .50 Caliber heavy mounted machine gun. The officer nods and hits his partner on the shoulder relaying the message. The partner climbs into the Bearcat and mounts the .50 Cal. Once inside, he pulls the lever hard chambering a round making the weapon highly unsafe for anyone on the business end of it. Strainfield then gestures the firing of a rifle. The subordinate, nods in acknowledgement and runs to the back of the Bearcat and retrieves a .50 Cal Barret sniper rifle. The young officer takes it and begins running along with the flow of the departing crowd looking for higher ground. Strainfield turns his attention back toward Imperial.

The radio squelches to life again. <"*Green light, green light, green light! Lieutenant, you have been given the green light to end the hostile actions of the threat known as Imperial... May God's have mercy on us all.*">

The Adam's apple drops in Strainfield's neck as he swallows hard. He takes a breath and grabs his Radio. Whether he would have been given the go or not, he knew he would have went.

<"All units, I repeat all units that have a firing solution that incapacitates the threat identified as Imperial—FIRE!">

The radio squelches concern.

<"*Sir, what of the civilian populace around him?*">

<"An acceptable loss of casualties at this point wouldn't you agree, sergeant? This is a few to save the many scenario. He's not going to stop. So, we will not stop either. Like Nimrod of old, either we stop an act of a living god or fall trying. NOW... FIRE EVERYTHING AND THE GODS BE DAMNED!">

The Lieutenant pulls his sidearm, and lines his sight picture. A second later after taking a breath to steady his hands, he fires. His first few shots that explode from the muzzle were true in finding its target. His trajectory was dead on target and instantly followed up by incalculable number of shots loosed from his surrounding subordinates all focused fired at one assailant with the unrealistic hopes of bringing down a deity.

Small arms fire bullets ping and ricochet off of Imperials armor and skin. One round ricochet's off of his helmet and into the skull of an elderly woman that was running with all the speed of a light trot. As she falls Death snatches a blue soul orb from her lifeless husk before it hits the ground. Having landed among the fleeing populace, Imperial steps over the frail body bypassing Death paying him no attention. A big bore round slams the left side of Imperial's face. he uses his left wing to shield the incoming fire from his flank. Most of officers returning fire are true and on target, however there is the occasional here and there round that goes errant laying another civilian low from the incessant firing.

Now starting to become an annoyance, Imperial squints his eyes zeroing in on the resisting force out near the perimeter. It was a struggle for him to stick to the plan. He could have delegated an assisted pinpoint high altitude Iony strike from the stealth C160 circling above to deal with them, but he must stay on script and give the appearance that one being of supernatural origin can cause immense catastrophic biblical destruction if he is to set precedence for all others that would dare to oppose him later. They must believe to anger him would bring apocalyptic repercussions.

Lt. Strainfield reloads still focusing on Imperial through the crowd. He slaps in another magazine of 40 caliber rounds and continues firing. Small arms have no effect, the ricochet is only running the toll of injured up and that's on him. He decides to end it quickly by upping the force. <"Allah, forgive me..."> He says looking toward the gun operator atop the Bearcat. <"Fire the fucking fifty and don't stop till it falls or you run dry."> he yells.

The officer looks over toward the Lt. for confirmation. His hand trembles as he holds the action lever.

Strainfield grabs his shoulder mic again. <"I said open fire.">

<"*Into the Crowd Sir?*">

<"There won't be a crowd left if we don't.">

Whirrrrrrr! Is the sound the Gatling gun as it spins to speed before letting out a hail of hot projectiles into the fleeing crowd.

****

The De Mons don't land among the fleeing masses to sow the tenets of chaos, not yet anyhow. Vermin having seen the defiance of the local police firing at his ward for this mission directs his attacking horde of De Mons to land among the peacekeepers that think themselves righteous enough to give Imperial challenge. It is with those militant men that he knows his sowing of discord will be the most effective in running up the body count. Within the more militant based mortals lies familiar cracks of those that have been given too much limited earthly power. Among the militant and those that profess to uphold law, they are ones know for becoming coveters of power they've amassed. Not all, but a few; enough that they will fall prey easiest to temptation. Bless the rank and file. They are of a singular mind and a singular mind is easier to control.

Verminesk points toward the peacekeepers directing his horde to pay attention to them and their precious pride on display. "Look at them brothers, the peacekeepers... truly they would inherit the Earth if it wasn't for that pride that becomes their rallying banner across generations. Such pride sets men and women above their allotted station in feeling superior... So much so, they are not questioned even when their orders are to the point of detriment. They are an envious bunch and those that are envious are never satisfied with their position of where they could be performing wonderfully and helping shape lives of their fellow mankind for the better. No... they want what the superior has. They will tell you excuses like a bump in pay, but it's the power of the higher position they secretly covet."

Vermin hovers ever so closer to the ground still observing humanity. "Look closer brothers and see their prejudices illuminated. It's an easy tenet to exploit. They don't fire indiscriminately into the crowd to stop the threat. They fire because they have the power to do so and the prejudices to fuel it. They don't hate the color of one's skin. Noooo! They hate the class of their fellow man that falls below the rankness of poverty to the sublevel of destitute. They don't want the poor or the wretched masses to come and defile their utopia. If they want anything from them, it is for them to disappear from the Earth, altogether. No, brothers, we need not land among the masses of the crowd to sow destruction, we but only need to land among the peacekeepers giving them only the slightest corruptible push toward their innate prejudices to get the desirable effect wanted.

Scores of the fleeing crowd are mowed down by the .50 caliber Gatling. Their bodies are torn to fragments instantly. Wet chunks of bloody flesh are strewn in all directions. Lt. Strainfield looks in utter horrification as civilians after civilian fall to ground under the hot projectiles of the weapon that he gave the order to set loose. His stomach turns knots as the populace loses their lives. Unable to find anymore resolve, Strainfield looks toward the officer who's rocking back and forth unloading the .50 cal. He grabs his mic to order a cease fire, except the order never leaves his lips. What left his lips instead under strained breath was the howl of pain as rounds ripped into his lower extremities and abdomen. His view quickly changed from the officer firing the man-made weapon of genocide to a bright starry sky. Lt. Strainfield was on his back thinking where did this just all go wrong?

Groaning initially, the pain subsided under the body's own release of pain killing endorphins, which he thought happened pretty quickly and was grateful for. Strainfield could still hear the sound of the Gatling still spitting hot projectiles. The sound was that distinct and unmistakable. It was the whirr of the barrels spinning. The only other sound recognizable outside of that were the screams of the crowd crying out in terror and shock, voices stuck in their octaves of death. It's that sound that motivates Strainfield to stand. He tries to get to his feet; it's then he realizes why the pain of being shot subsided so quickly. He couldn't move his legs. Actually, for that matter, he couldn't feel his legs anymore, hell no pain period. He was paralyzed. All the same, unable to move and bleeding profusely he reaches out stretching his right arm to reclaim his firearm that he'd dropped when he was gunned down mere seconds ago. Just as he gets his fingers on the handle a foot steps down hard on his wrist pinning it to the ground, pressure ever increasing.

CRACK! There went his radius bone. "UNGHH!" Strainfield grunts but does not cry out.

With his offhand he reaches over trying to free the other hand from the foot's crushing clamp. Lieutenant follows the foot back toward the face of the one that it is attached too. He wants to see the face of his murderer to know who he should wait for at the gates of hell so, that he could settle this score with his enemy... except it was no enemy. It was Sergeant Grendova. He is a short portly man that Strainfield has always considered an asshole. He never really cared for the man much, but this confirmed it, he's sure now more than he's ever been that he hates the portly bastard.

<"Sergeant! What the fuck are you doing?"> yells Strainfield.

<"What my faith demands, Lieutenant. Understand, I must do this. If it is the will of Allah that these people are to die, then I want to be on the side of righteousness. Just as Bergodine on that .50 over there. Allah has sent an angel to exact judgment on the evils that we visit upon each other and you fire upon him in opposition of Allah's will. You have been damned to hell Lieutenant, but you will not take our souls with you. If judgment has been passed on those here, then so be it.">

<"Sergeant... think!... Allah would not ask this?">

<"Until he does,"> the Sergeant replies as a demon was touching his shoulder mouthing the exact words the Sergeant was now repeating.

<"Allah would not ask of this. His master is false. Look at him and ask which master does he serve?"> says Strainfield.

<"A care you no longer need to worry yourself about Lieutenant. I will take it from here,"> says Grendova, pulling the hammer back on his .357 Magnum.

The last thing Lieutenant heard was a half sound of a pop before he felt the bonds of life slip away. He was suddenly and effortlessly weightless. It's was as if whatever he just cared about didn't matter anymore. He can't for the life of him remember what he was just so worked up over. It was a distant memory that faded like awakening from a dream. He only focuses on the mist that now surrounds him and gentle guiding hand that eases him into the Mist of Purgosia. When exiting the other side into third Heaven, Death extends his hand out into the vast beautiful opening showing Strainfield his new place of respite.

The Sergeant placed three rounds into the head of Lt. Strainfield before reaching down and retrieving the dead man's weapon. He grabs his mic stating that the Lieutenant had been killed and that he would be assuming command. The order that followed should have been an unlawful one that a man of conscience would not have followed. These men were not of conscience. If they were at one time, religious dogma cured them of it. Grendova gave the order to assist the being sent from heaven and to continue firing upon the crowd not letting one soul escape judgment. Satisfied, there was no further need for the demon to keep a hand on the man, he'd done enough that now the man own mind would act under the suggestion believing it of his own volition. Deep down in the soul of Grendova it was. His heart already burned with the desire to rid the world of destitute undesirables. His prejudices as predicted and his claim for power would see him fulfil his dark heart desire.

The peacekeepers of Cameroon under De Mon sway turn on its citizenry and slays them alongside Imperial until the streets are quiet running red with river of blood. Old Testament way of doing business had manifested in the modern age, and Ellen Nichols was the eyewitness there to see it all and fulfill her role of broadcasting an act of a merciless god across the world for all to see.

****

Ardenne, France: Templar Headquarters

The conclave of Templar Masters also went eerily quiet at the sight displayed over media. Jericho is no different as he watches the screen in silence, his thoughts falling on the unmatched raw power of this human designated N.H.E., this Imperial. It isn't immediate fear that gripped him because he was literally continents away from the monstrosity. For him, it is a creeping fear that would slowly consume him if he were to let it. He is no doubt on a path to once again intersect this thing that just dealt a decisive genocidal blow single handedly. The only thought to consume Jericho's mind at the moment was, how? How would he stop something with such unadulterated and seemingly unlimited power? This one entity just laid waste to an entire sect of a populace on live television that didn't even bother to cut the feed, nor cut to commercial, edit, or turn away from the gore of a people being ravaged. Not that they are insensitive, you could see the horror of that on Ellen Nichols' face. They can't turn away, because Lucien's empire more than likely pulled the strings behind the networks and would not allow them to.

Isis has long since stopped watching the screen. She turned her attention to Jericho carefully watching his expression. There's no need for her to pretend she wasn't scared; she's downright terrified. She has no one to lead or assume responsibility for like the Grandmaster does. Also, she has no one to impress like the Grand Prior, and she definitely has nothing to prove like Kovac. All she has is worry for Jericho, the only one that proved a challenge to that thing and he barely survived. Her emotions get the better of her. She reaches over gripping his hand tightly. It's a grip that acknowledged he had the right to be frighten if he so wished. He has the right to lay down this burden if he so wanted. That thing in Cameroon is a battle for the gods to handle if they truly existed and gave a shit about mankind. Where were they in all of this? Isis gave his hand a hard and fast shake before tightening her grip more. She wants him to know that he could lay down the burden, but if he could not, then she was with him.

Brashear turns the screen off after a long silence. Jericho figures she is probably thinking the same thing he is... we can't win.

"Grand Prior," says Brashear.

"Yes, Grandmaster."

"Approved! You now have full autonomy in planning the destruction of that creature. Lucien is an added bonus that I believe I know how to bring down. However, that thing there, that thing is not of a benevolent god. That thing is of a devil. Whatever resources you need are at your disposal. The Ragnroc Scenario has been unleashed." The Grandmaster looks to the other heads. "Are any of you in disagreement and wish to object?"

Only silence returns.

Grandmaster Brashear stands. "None of this was aforementioned in any of the prophecies of the Torah, Koran, or Bible or any other text of the Apocrypha—"

"That we've discovered thus far," Isis interjects. "If we are referencing the biblical texts for reasoning then we have to look to Daniel where it stated that there was a large portion of prophecy that would not be made known until the end of days."

Brashear as well as all the other heads looks at Isis. The Grand Prior is the first to speak what the rest were thinking, but did not want to give voice too.

"You believe this is the end of days, Dr. Rayne?"

Jericho finds himself watching her as well. His heart is racing at the possible answer that would draw from her lips.

Isis takes a breath. "It is my opinion, that the stage has been set. The beginning of the end has indeed begun. But it didn't start recently. I believe it started almost a hundred years ago when, the Israelites that had been spread across the world, had returned home to Jerusalem. I believed the clock started then back in 1948 or earlier."

Looking around at all the members of the board, she lets go of Jericho's hand and stands up to be better seen and heard.

"Jesus said we'd witness these things and it was not yet the end. Well, we've witnessed warnings, we've seen the people of this world natural love grow cold. We've all witnessed the inequity of men's thoughts that have led to much decimation. As I said we've seen a hundred years or more of it. The time of warning and probation had to end at some point, right? I think that the Grand Prior can make whatever plans that she wants and they will ultimately be to no avail if the end of days are truly here."

Kovac clears his throat. "If I may speak, Grandmaster?"

Brashear nods, giving permission for the Knight to speak his mind.

"I would normally agree with the lass over there that holds degrees in religious studies, but I have this nagging feeling that I can't get rid of. If Dr. Rayne is correct and we have used up the last of our promised days of grace, why send us Jericho? You all have not seen what I have. The boy is touched by a higher power. The Captain over there took on that Imperial fella and lived to tell the tale, you heard? He knew what that thing was and its capability long before we knew it existed. Knowing all that he still fought it. A whole Embassy was destroyed; I mean that thing was leveled, you hear? He walked away for the most part unscathed. If that thing is here to destroy and be the will of God, why send Jericho is all I'm asking? Our days of grace seem to have been extended."

The Grand Prior now stands. "Because Imperial is not the will of God. I'm with the Knight on this one. When the Philistines time had come, a Judge was born for the purpose of protecting and freeing Gods chosen people at that particular time, He gave them a champion to fight the fight they couldn't. Captain Bane according to Kovac is the rightful warrior sent by the true God. So, our time is not yet at an end, he's giving us the power to change our future."

"Until the rest of Daniel's book is opened at least," says Isis. "Only then will we truly know."

Brashear raises her hand silencing everyone. All the while Isis was disclosing her theory the Grandmaster was observing Jericho's expression. She doesn't know what she was looking to find written in his façade, but she stared nonetheless. Perhaps she thinks to herself that maybe she was looking for fear or apprehension, whatever it was she wanted from the expression was clearly not in his expressive repertoire.

Brashear takes off her virtual glasses and just stares at Jericho.

"Captain," she says. "Walk with me!"

In a matter of moments, the two were on the roof of the Templar Headquarters. There was a gorgeous arboretum that sat atop the building. Inside was a sense of serenity, a calmness that has been the opposite of his last few days; hell, last few years. Inside, exotic birds fly overhead. Others were nested in the high greenery of the trees and low levels of shrubbery. He'd been in many terrains fighting battles and was sure he'd seen a great deal of plant life that he may not know the names of, but was familiar with. The ones here in the arboretum were something different all together like the sentient plant species Michal had shown him, he'd never seen a majority of these.

"The Serenity Garden was blessed by the Catholic Monks during the second great crusade to reclaim the Holy Land," says Brashear. "When we went into hiding to preserve our order, we did not only preserve ourselves; we preserved the life around us. These plants are as old as the order, even a few of the trees that you see as well. They were taking as saplings." Brashear touched one of them. "How mighty indeed they have grown over the many centuries."

"You didn't bring me here to talk of plants Grandmaster," says Jericho.

"Indeed, not. I brought you here to get your honest no bullshit assessment," she says averting her gaze from the tree to Jericho. "I want to know what you think away from the others. I want to know if the heavens talk to you Captain and if so, what do they say?"

Jericho watches her for a moment. "What makes you think they'd talk to me?"

"You seem to be an integral part in this ages-old tale of struggle. There are forces at work that are known to us, but none so intimately as the most recent occurring of events. We have prepared for centuries for a second coming. We've prepared even while believing at times deep down that we'd all been duped and that there was no coming messiah. There were days while leading this order that even I had lost faith. Then in my lifetime, behold I see miracles, I mean, honest miracles. I see the works of words within an archaic book come to life and yet I don't rejoice as I should, because the things that I witness do not concur with how events of past prophecies came to fruition from same said book. If these are truly the end times as your girlfriend believes, then it seems to me that the channels of communication should be open. So, Captain Bane, do-the-heavens-speak-to-you?"

Jericho studies Brashear. He watches her for a time formulating how much he should say. Michael seemed to believe in them. Then again, it seems to him of the two Angels that he's met they believe in the best outcome for everyone. They have a real optimistic outlook on life... or so they give the appearance.

"What if I told you the heavens do?"

Brashear cracks somewhat of smile. "Then I would be most grateful for that."

"Why?" asks Jericho.

"Captain, it means that we are not in this fight alone provided the ones that are speaking are not the enemy."

"So, we come to it then Grandmaster," says Jericho. "You believe in a Satan being?"

"Wouldn't be much of leader of this order if I did not to some extent. I have to assume, Captain that there are forces that overlay atop our world that oppose each other. The evidence for that is too great to ignore. Just as there is a penchant for good and great benevolence, there is a flip to that coin where perverse evil is the order of the day. I'm not talking about misbehavior or some form of conduct disorder, I'm talking pure unadulterated evil that takes over the minds of men."

"Such as the attack on the United Nations that your Knights are responsible for," says Jericho.

Brashear looks down in momentarily break of her usually stern and cool façade. It's only instant though before her cool collected calmness returns. "Yes, Captain, there is that. It was a calculated strike to remove who we strongly suspected to be the Antichrist from the board. It was an attempt to save millions if not billions that would perish from this Earth if his very existence would have been allowed to live. We were cold, calculating and decisive in our action. I do not apologize for the actions taken... I can't. I don't have such luxuries."

"And you think the murder of those innocent that died as a result of your actions is not that pervasive evil you were talking about?"

Breaking her slow stride, she turns again looking to Jericho.

"Touché, Captain... Understand, I never said we were above the overlaid battle that is taking place. We are pawns in it able to be influenced just as the rest... but, imagine this, what if Hitler was able to be removed from the board early on... wouldn't that have been a better option?"

"If history lessons are remembered correctly, there were numerous attempts to stop him," says Jericho. "But just as you all were mentioning earlier about the term you coined, the Judas Paradox, he couldn't be stopped right? Your theory is he had to live and survive those attempts, because his existence had a part to play no matter how ill fated. Those millions killed by Hitler was part of a plan. They were going to die regardless because they had too... right? They had to die to illicit change that had ramifications to this very day in how we approach atrocities? What he did was unforgiveable, but in doing so, he united a world which in turn did wonders to put down his reign."

Having taking the advantage in the conversation, Jericho steps a little closer to Brashear.

"See, I do listen well don't I Grandmaster? So, the way I see it, no matter your decision to intervene or not Lucien is here and if the prophecies of the Bible are to be believed, then the world as we know is headed for an upheaval likes the which has never been seen... and your actions whether just or not will still not affect the billions foretold to perish."

Brashear begins walking again. "At our core as I stated before, the Templars are in the business of saving souls and spreading the word of how that happens. We fight to ensure that as much time can be given as possible to fulfill our mandate to protect pilgrims on the road of life to the best of our ability... the best of my ability."

Jericho stares at Brashear with an intensity letting her know that if she tries anything again of the sorts like what happened in New York, then she would have not only a fight against Imperial, but also apparently a judge.

"I understand Captain," says Brashear.

"Then also understand that when this is done, and it will be done one way or another, there will be no absolution for your order after what you commanded. There will be however, a reckoning and if I survive, I will spearhead the efforts to bring you to atonement for what you've done."

Brashear smirks and reaches out her hand to shake solidifying their alliance to target and kill Imperial.

"I would expect nothing less," says Brashear. "And when you arrive to exact your righteous justice on us, my mandate will be fulfilled and my soul prepared. I only ask that you take my head, and not those of my Knights. They were under my orders. Again, if I haven't been already slain that is. What is coming, I don't expect many of us to survive."

Jericho reaches out his hand taking hers, "Done! We understand each other then... Until that day then Grandmaster."

They shake firmly.

"Until that day then," says Brashear.

Isis walks up the stairs to the arboretum just as the two finish shaking hands coming to an accord.

Jericho looks over to her. "Petite, it appears we have allies."

Thirty-Two

AWAKENING DIVINIZATION

"It was a miracle in itself that he was even here, but like everything else in life, even miracles had expiration dates."

~ Jason Priest

Fourteen months post touchdown of Imperial: Year 2046
St. Lucille Cathedral: Detroit, Michigan

"It'll be good to catch up with you, Jare. I haven't seen you since that business in Germany. Really, if you didn't like my coffee that much that was all you had to say. There wasn't a need to destroy the freaking city," Jason says laughing. "Okay, give Isis my love. Tell her the minute that the Pope lifts marriage restrictions, me and her can now put our plan into effect of finally being together after her long years ploy of using you to get to me."

Jericho's boisterous laugh permeates and bellows through the phone's receiver.

Jason laughs. "Alright, I'll catch up some more later so you can fill me in on this globe hopping business. I have to be in the Pulpit and bring some calm to the crisis of my parishioner's souls... Yeah, okay see you then."

Priest swipes his thumb across the Vidcell's screen left ending the holographic mini image picture of Jericho's call. It's new tech. He couldn't help himself to the purchase. It was like the science fiction novels were finally starting to catch up to reality. Sitting at his desk he lightly tosses the phone over onto a small pile of papers where some are stamped with the highly noticeable red overdue signage. Sighing, he reaches for the open bottle of Gentlemen's Jack at the corner of his desk not that he has much remaining. He takes a marker and scratches a divot on where the bottle's contents are now before pouring himself a shot and quickly downing it.

Rocking back in his slender leather recliner, Jason relishes the burn of the shot as his eyes wander over towards the television that is playing on mute with subtitles scrolling across the bottom of the screen. He squints his aging vision reading the ticker about scientists being elated that they have the first long range photos of the meteor from outside our solar system so aptly named Wormwood after the doctor that discovered it years ago. He still remembers the big whoopee doo when he was a kid at the discovery. It was all the science teachers were talking about. Their elation most have reached orgasmic by now... At least the teachers that were still living.

In his priestly vestments adorned in scarlet and purple, Jason looks at his watch then rolls his leather chair back from behind his desk. He leaves his main church's office at 10:25 am exactly to be prompt in making his way down the center aisle of his parish at exactly 10:30. As he turns to enter the hallway that leads to center isle of the sanctuary, the choir and a singular altar boy awaits him to take his place at the head of the procession. With Bible in hand he places his glasses on then gives a customary wave to the organist that he's ready. The Hammer Organ begins to play with a thunderous boom which gives the cue for Jason to start leading the processional toward the Pulpit. About halfway down the long aisle, Jason slows to a stop halting the processional line after realizing that there is not one soul in the congregation. Seeing them all

318 - ARROW J. KNIGHT

stop center aisle; the organist awkwardly lets the keys trail off into silence.

Priest looks back at his lone altar boy that more than likely was forced to be here by his mother as a testament to responsibility when she herself was not here to lead by example by honoring her duty to usher. It was her Sunday after all. If the lone altar boy wasn't sad enough, he looked past him to his elderly two-person choir that he was sure showed up more out of obligation then sincere love and fellowship. In that moment he was finally defeated. No point of having service.

"Fuck it, everyone," Priest says, throwing his hands up in surrender waving the procession to just stand down and stop marching. "For cripes sake...sorry, everyone, for that shameful outburst."

Darius Reed, the young altar boy, still cracks a smile at his priest losing it.

Jason winks at him slightly laughing himself. "Darius, let's not go telling your mother my extensive French vocabulary used here today okay? To everyone else, who am I kidding? Thank you all for showing up this morning, but I won't take offense if you want to leave," Priest says to the rest of his hilariously poor attempt at a professional multi-person entry processional march.

A little hesitant at first, torn between duty and commitment to God versus the Imperial event this morning, it wasn't a surprise that the two choir members and the altar boy acquiesced. Although they did look a bit remorseful to leave their priest in such a defeated state. Priest waves them goodbye gesturing for them to shoo, shoo! They acknowledge his gesture still feeling some kind of way to just leave him alone in an empty cathedral, but they all recognize what he's doing for them and are happy to oblige and obey his command for them to get on with their day. It was supposed to be momentous from what he understood from all the hoopla that the media was making of it.

Darius bows as a sign of respect for the cross at the head of the sanctuary before taking his hurried leave.

"If we hurry, we can still make the broadcast," says Darius talking to Old Man Waterson.

The others shuffle out behind him removing their choir robes as they head out. They move with more vigor than they did in the processional march. An empty sanctuary on Sunday morning save two; Priest and his loyal organist— "Where the hell are you going Pete? Not you too?" says Priest. "I'm actually paying you."

Priest slumps down in the pew just one row past halfway point heading toward the Pulpit. Peter Mulgrew, a man of his late 50's who's been committed to music for as long as he can remember walks down from the organ balcony sure not to take the side passage out. He walks down the center aisle packing his tablet into his briefcase. He would've felt a little like trash had he gone out the side door without acknowledging Jason's despair. The gaunt-looking man who'd been battling cancer for seven years now sits in the pew in front of Jason letting out a hefty sigh.

"I know the feeling," says Priest.

He places his Bible down on the pew next to him while reaching forward grabbing a hold of Peter's right shoulder giving it hearty good shake.

"But I'm paying you mofo, so you have to stay," he says, smiling. "So, son can you play me a memory, I'm not really sure how it goes—" he starts to sing the ode to Billy Joel

Laughing at first, Peter joins in singing the rest of the ode. "It's sad and sweet and I knew it complete when I wore a younger man's clothes."

The two of them continue laughing for a few minutes.

"Well, since I'm paying you to stay, play me something with a little more bite... Oh! And lots of cussing. I want sailor on the high seas cussing," Jason says, still smirking.

Unable to control the seriousness of his request, he bursts out laughing again. After a second of processing the joke, Peter joins him and they're both off laughing again, only this time drawing tears. When the laughter finally dies out Priest rocks back in his pew and sighs rubbing the tears from his eyes from laughing so hard.

"Nah, I'm kidding, you go on and get out of here. If you hurry, you can still catch it."

"You sure you okay, Father?" asks Peter.

Priest nods and gives his friend's shoulder another shake. "I'm fine."

The organist acquiesces as well, nodding okay. He stands up stretching and winces a bit in pain. It was slight, but Jason caught it.

Jason waves him on, signaling him it's okay to leave. Peter nods in acceptance and throws a hand of support on the shoulder of his Priest before walking past him down the aisle.

"Next Sunday, Father?"

"Next Sunday," replies Priest.

There would not be a next Sunday for him though. He was a gaunt-looking man and cancer was not a passing ailment for him, it was his death sentence and Death no doubt would surely come to collect what is owed.

Priest watches Peter leave. It was a miracle in itself that he was even here, but like everything else in life, even miracles had expiration dates. Standing up Priest stretches removing his Triregnum or as the kids call it, his funny pointy hat. He heads toward the Pulpit. Once there, he kneels before the cross giving the customary muscled memory sign gesticulation of the cross and heads to his secondary smaller office that sits off to the right behind the Pulpit.

Entering he tosses his Bible lightly on that desk and his funny pointy hat in the corner. In fairness he did attempt to throw it into the cabinet. Shrugging his shoulders at the failed attempt his posterior finds his leather reclining chair. It rolls back slightly on wheels that squeak just a bit. It's annoying. After fumbling around looking for the remote for a few seconds, he turns on the television in hopes to find other entertainment than that of Imperial. Hunger starts to creep in reminding him of its annoyance. Other than whiskey he drank this morning, which he prayed his processional couldn't smell, he hadn't eaten anything. He reaches into his middle drawer gabbing a piece of Jerky. Should satiate the hunger for a minute.

In the span of the last few months... Hell, since Imperial revelation there hasn't been really nothing but constant coverage on the news of Imperial and what he was doing across the globe. Sure, there were blurbs about other events and attacks, but Imperial was the news. Even the way the news was delivered itself fell to background noise with little or no coverage. If there were still newspapers being printed, the multiple Network takeovers by Arcane would have been page nine at best.

The overthrow of independent media was quick, there wasn't really a fight at all for the free state of mind. One day there were multiple networks and instant streams of unbiased reporting that kept information honest free of agenda and propaganda then it wasn't. Gone were those days. News was all filtered through one source now. It was all consolidated under the watchful eye of the Imperial authority. Media had been the victim of a homicide and the killer was identified as Arcane. There would be no trial, not even in the court of public opinion. All fell under his progressive controlling thumb. Even the last great once trusted network and major hold out, CNN, had just fallen a month prior to the network that wants to replace the fame logo immediately with, AGN. The very same Arcanian Global news that Priest finds himself watching now. The corporate takeover was complete. CNN is now AGN. Lucas was write when he wrote this is how democracy dies. Now with screams, but to the sound of cheering and clapping.

There were a few transitions however that made it to the new network from the old's ashes. It was always good to see a survivor of the media purge. The familiar face that now anchors the morning news on AGN is none other than Ellen Nichols, the female reporter that was at ground zero on what has been coined the Awakening Divination. United Nations was laid bare that day. She was also there for the Desecration of Cameroon as people have come to call it. That phrase hasn't been coined... yet.

Jason pulls a bite from his Jerky while rummaging the drawer again. There it is, there's his flask. He gives it shake and hears the familiar swish of liquid. He pops the tin cap and takes shot listening closely to the broadcast of Ellen Nichols.

****

"For those of you just joining us, I'm Ellen Nichols. Exactly seventeen months ago today Lucien Arcane was the target of an elaborate assassination plot by the terrorist group, Templar Knights. In their attempt to bring down the most talked about public figure in over a century many were wounded and killed, including my partner Steven Brice and my camera man Paul Winston. The attack further left the famed New York's United Nations Headquarters in ruins and relations across the world broken. Many of the dead were diplomats from countries and regions united under the auspice of global cooperation that sought a peaceful ground with which to parlay and come to accords beneficial for all. Those same regions and nations hold America responsible as hosts for the United Nations Counsel's poor lack of security and safety. The United Nations troops were also given more than enough of the blame as well for not doing more to protect the respective nation leaders."

Ellen looks at the camera to her left as the primary camera feed. "Although tragic and still fresh in the minds of what happened those many months ago, we will continue to honor those that lost their lives with every breath we take. However, today also marks the day that something extraordinary happened in the midst of that dark hour. When an event that was deemed in the realm of impossible truly became solidified as more than probable. Seventeen months ago, on what many religious scholars have called the, 'Awakening Divination,' the Archangel Imperial was tasked with leaving the heavens to protect our very own Lucien Arcane."

Ellen turns back to the camera on the right habitually now clutching her gold chain and red Templar cross emblem around her neck.

"Over the past three months we've watched this guardian take to this planet as if one of our own. Yes, we've seen him destroy in what has been called reproving judgements, but we've also seen him save tens of thousands if not more in his quest to assist humanity. Behind him, it seems we are in form of regaining a foothold on taking back the Earth from what he would say and I quote, 'is the corrupt and wicked system that had been established by greedy, powerful men and women who take without regard from others.' End quote."

Looking back to the camera on her left again, she adds, "Religions of all the major faiths after having battled endless wars for a couple thousand years have seemingly found accord with Imperial and in his legitimization of Lucien Arcane promoted status of Earthly deity." *This was of Couse after he destroyed thousands of innocents in Cameroon inciting a fear that has been unmatched.* Ellen thinks to herself in the one last place of free speech, her mind.

Ellen's expression fails her for a second as she shuffles the pre-written report that was given to her free of any independent journalism. It was now force fed to her in calculated propaganda. She holds back the anger concealed in tears that now well within her eyes. She holds them there and does not shed them. To let tears fly in defiance of Imperial was career suicide. Instead, she gives a somber few seconds to compose herself while acting as if she truly was taken by the works of Imperial.

"In some areas of the world, and even here in the United States, the faiths have even begun to coalesce under the reign of Arcane and Imperial as one solidified voice believing that his truth of one faith was correct, that a return to kings and prophets is the key to a surviving and building an everlasting government. The events of the Cameroon desecration have become cemented as a turning point in judgmental rulings of God and that no matter how destructive or how cruel it appears; it is above reproach or condemnation. With the next stunning turn to set the world to task, the Church will soon again combine with state leading the way in an order that will no longer bow to unmoral politics."

Touching her ear and pressing the tiny receiver further into it making sure she can hear her producer's update; she takes a slight three second pause.

"Breaking news! We have confirmation that Lucien Arcane will in fact be speaking today. We'd heard rumors that he had awoken from his coma months ago, but those were unconfirmed. It had been rumored that Lucien had been in various parts around the globe meeting with nations in private away from the eyes of media in attempts to mend the relations between countries even those on the edge of a knife's precipice, like the waning relationship between China and United States. It is also believed that with him is the newly titled Pope who has been renamed, Pontiff Supreme. Together if rumors are to be believed, let's hope they quell the brewing conflict that has reached boiling point and could likely lead to full blown war that if reached will cause another intervention by Imperial." *A sure intervention that no side wants to have to endure*, thinks Ellen.

Thirty-Three

VICES

"For me, the Heavens have gone silent. My sins have drowned out my need for solace and redemption. I wondered why the demons came for me when I was young, but I knew. I always knew. They will hound me until forever has concluded. Don't pray for me. There is no saving this soul. I already gave it away to the voice in the darkness."

-Jason Priest

St. Lucille Cathedral: Detroit, Michigan

Priest turns the television off and stands up, pulling his robes off. Beneath, he wears black slacks, black shirt, and the typical priest white clerical collar. Now, all he needs is his thigh length black trench to complete his ensemble. He looks around briefly for it then snaps his fingers remembering he left it in his main office off the hallway leading to the sanctuary. As he exits the smaller office, the one usually reserved for visiting priests and dignitaries, he makes sure that all the lights are turned out. He heads back through the Pulpit where he's startled by a parishioner seated in the first-row pew. Seeing the young man gives Priest pause as his presence took him off guard. It was a quick startle, but was overcame as he slowly continued his stride towards the young parishioner, if that even what he was. As they say, sins have a way of coming home to roost. He didn't know how, but he knew for certain this was one of his that has returned.

"Does the way I look make you hesitant of me priest?" says the young man.

"No, it's not that, I didn't expect anyone to be here this morning with the Imperial event going on," says Priest.

His hair is unkempt and his visage looks as if he hasn't slept since the turn of twelve midnight three weeks ago. Priest notices the coat the man is wearing was once a pricy commodity maybe fifteen years ago, but has since been reduced to a ragged duster and the name long lost to newer brands. The air around reeks of marijuana and Ole English double malt liquor. Two sniffs! Yes, he is sure, Old E. Sad that he knows the smell of Old E, but there is something else intermingled in the smell. It smells of rot and brimstone. The smell is putridness manifested. It will come to him later where the odor was first encountered.

"Well, I'm here," the young man says while pulling a half-smoked cigarette from his pocket.

He places the fug at the corner of his lips and lights it with his lighter that he was fumbling with in his hands before Priest made it down the pulpit steps. It's silver and looks extremely precious to him. It looked to be the only thing of value in his possession. Uneasiness, is what it is. The man gave a feeling of unease, which if Priest had hackles, they would be raised at the moment. He thinks about making an issue and maybe protesting the smoking, but decided that this unsavory character was best not provoked.

The young man is alone or so it would seem to the human eye, but that's rarely the case in a system of ethereal politics that overlay a static reality numbered 2814. Sitting unseen in the pew behind the young man in an alternate reality was a De Mon that had relegated himself to strictly playing on the hearts of mortals. Since the rift, he has been walking a part from the Lucifer and Warsivious' ascension initiative simply because he didn't care for the politics of it all. For him, watching the mortals self-destruct with the slightest of push was way more constructive and a better way to spend time outside of plotting and scheming to overthrow a monarchy for only another one to try and take its place. Really, if you thought about it, if Lucifer did win the throne, how long before Warsivious or Canceranian come for it? Visceral decided he would not be a part of that, he would do his own disservice to mortals... even if it just so happens that crushing the fragile humans happen to be aligned with the works of Lucifer.

Sitting behind the young man, Visceral easily pulls his strings like a marionette, because humans under the influence of a known vice makes them that more easily susceptible to what he propagates.

Smiling, Visceral... Vice for short, parts his lips again mouthing, "You don't mind if I smoke in the former house of holies, do you?"

The young man after lighting the cigarette, looks Priest in his eyes. "You don't mind if I smoke in the former house of holies, do you? I wouldn't want to be an affront to you, it just seems Elohim has abandoned this place," he says, looking around intentionally. "These four walls and roof. There is no god in this place. Devils, maybe, but no God"

Elohim? Who uses that name? thinks Priest as his eye brow
raise a bit in suspicion.

Priest walks over to the young man and sits next to him placing him on his left.

"I don't mind you smoking at all tell you the truth, especially with no one being here to protest. In fact, could I bum one of those off you?"

"Sure," he replies, giving the pack to Priest for him to get his own.

Priest takes one and passes the pack back. The young man waves, gesturing for him to keep the pack. "No, father, I'm trying to quit. You know what they say, whole life ahead of you and all that shit. Wouldn't want to leave life to prematurely due to cancer." The young man chuckles. "Specially, now that things are getting good. We have war it seems on every front across the continents; natural disasters disguised as global warming is running rampant, famine is at all-time high, we have a true bonified human savoir walking amongst us, and a real live mystical being from Heaven... This shit writes itself doesn't it? Great time to be alive."

Priest nods and places the pack in his pocket.

"Can't argue on that front. It has been one hell of year," Priest says. "Trouble you a bit more for a light?"

"Sure, sure. No trouble at all," the young man says, raising his hands igniting the flame.

He clasps his hands together to cover the flame to make sure no rouge breeze of wind extinguishes it. Priest takes a drag studying the young man, studying his lighter. The slow inhalation of sweet toxicity is a welcomed feeling.

"Ahh! Oh yeah!" Priest says leaning back on the pew relaxing in the indulging of the fug.

The tinge of nicotine lace smoke fills each individual sac of his expanding lungs. Once all his sacs of the lungs have reached apex of fill, he blows out gleefully exhaling cancer inducing smoke while silently making judgments about the young man he sits next too. He takes another drag.

"Bad habit I picked up overseas during the Arcanian Congo Campaign. I, for the most part thought, I had it licked, bu—"

"But that smell of the Newport calls you back. Oh! I know that feeling well," the young man says. "It's a vice that stays with me constantly," he says smiling sardonically.

He continues to watch the kid. They say nothing the entire time they smoke. The two just simply enjoy their sweet slow lifetime acting poison laced cancer inducing sticks.

Once finished, Jason takes a long hard look at the young guy. "Are you here to murder me?" he asks.

"I can't say that I wasn't thinking about it," says the young man.

Placing the remaining burning butt of the cigarette to the underneath of his black loafer, Priest extinguishes it completely dousing the remnant of flame. Be a shame to burn down the church and be consumed in rolling flames of fire before actually falling to hell just to have to do it all again eternally, because obviously hell exists if there is a demon named Crethos that came from there to claim your soul in the African Congo. That encounter still leaves sweat filled nightmares.

"I understand," says Priest, further nodding his head gesturing that he understood his predicament.

"You're not scared?" asks the young man.

"Of course. It's just that when you spend years in war zones, it becomes the norm that someone wants to kill you... You're no exception. If you wanted too, you'd have done it before now. Figure you want me to know some things first. I'm guessing I'm safe till then. Once you tell me what you want me to know, we'll take my true reaction from there."

The young man just stares at him. It was now his turn to nod his head at Priest's comment.

"If I may ask, you said the former house of holies a minute ago, why?" Priest asks, changing the subject quickly. "Strange line of words for lay person."

"The Lord has not been in this holy temple in some time," says the young man. "Any temple for that matter, if we think about it." Vice mouths the words in his ear for him to repeat. "I know, because I called for him and he never showed."

"That tends to happen from time to time," Priest says. "Not that he's ignoring you, it's just maybe he wants you to figure it out on your own. If he were to answer us on every prayer, we'd become hopelessly dependent on him for everything. We wouldn't try to problem solve."

The young man again nods in showing the unspoken communication that he understands. He then changes the subject this time.

"So, you fought in the Congo wars?" says the young man.

Jason Priest nods while grabbing for another cigarette placing it between his lips. He realized preparing himself for confrontation when the man made his intentions known, that he would need any leverage possible. Maybe a hot ember burn of fire and ash of the cigarette to his would be murder's eye would be sufficient?

"Oh, shit! Sorry Father, let me get that one for you too," the young man says fumbling his lighter to light the priest's second Newport. "Careful, Father, those things will kill you. Go easy on them."

Jason nods his thanks and relaxes again in the pew.

The young man closing his lighter's top. "I didn't think that is something that priests do... smoke," says the young man placing his left hand into his pocket fumbling with something.

Priest has had more than enough time to assess what he's already judged to be a broken spirited man. He's watched him finish his half-smoked Newport and in all the time that he was finishing it, not once did he make direct eye contact with him. No, he continuously looked everywhere, but truly at him. Priest also noticed that he gestures and smoke with his right hand. He's very clumsy with his right, so, he had already discerned that he's left-handed. The same left hand that is currently fumbling around in the left pocket of that tattered coat.

Taking a drag, Jason looks ahead at the cross of Jesus over the Pulpit sure to keep the young man in his peripheral.

"You're right, priests aren't really the killing sort, but there comes a time when even the shepherds must protect their flocks from those elements that would do harm," Priest says as he takes another slow drag.

He watches the young man even closer while also savoring the drag. It could be his last if he doesn't play the scenario right.

"Look around you, Father, there is no flock here."

He exhales. "As you stated earlier, you're here," Priest says, looking at the kid again.

Laughing, the young man finally looks at Priest. His laugh is momentary and then fleeting, but it was enough to illicit just how nervous the young man really was.

"Ahhhhh! I see what you did there. You got me, Father; I am here. I'm the flock. Touché"

He nods. "You are the flock," says Priest, taking another drag.

Again, Priest turns facing the alter and the stain glass window sitting above it where the depiction of Jesus' final hour is replayed on his way to Golgotha. He just stares at it and exhales a white wisp of smoke.

"Have you made up your mind yet as to whether you're going to kill me?" asks Priest.

"No, I haven't yet. Be assured though I am still thinking about it," the young man says as he turns and observes the same glass window that

Priest was so intently gazing upon. "Are you silently praying in this moment for me not to kill you?

Priest takes another drag leaving the cigarette in his mouth this time. He rests both his elbows on the backrest of the pew.

"I don't pray for such things anymore. Actually, it's probably the opposite. If I were to have been praying, it would have been for you to end my life and thank god that you were here to do it." Priest reaches for the cig and exhales as he draws it from his mouth.

Sighing, he places the remaining burn of the cigarette under his black loafer again and extinguishes the second one.

"That one right there was probably the best cigarette, I've had in what seems forever. Are these laced with a little extra?" asks Priest.

The young man slowly nods. "Shhh!" he says, placing his fingers to his lips. "I won't tell if you won't."

"Poison?"

The young man again shakes his head slowly, "Just the poison the that comes pre-laced by the company.

Priest nods. "Too bad, that would have been a great way to end me." Sighing, he adds, "I'm sure you've been following me for a while now, learning who I am, getting to know my routines. You knew I smoked before you ever entered those doors this morning. Speaking of the door, did you put a sign out front stating, the church is closed today due to some unforeseeable mishap?"

"Didn't have to," the young man says. "Apparently, the god man has come to Earth haven't you heard?" He says sardonically before nodding in an easterly direction. "He landed right over there in New York at the U.N. building some months ago. It was all the rage, the cat's meow... So, I figured if he's there then there is no need for the children of Christ or any other god for that matter to be here congregating."

"Touché," says Priest. "I now know why you said the former house of holies earlier."

"Just in case you're assuming you know why, let me give you clarification. Don't want you guessing or assuming. The lord has not been in

332 - ARROW J. KNIGHT

this holy temple in some time now, centuries even; if he ever really was to begin with," says the young man.

Vice continues mouthing words in the man's ear ever deepening the suggestive hold over him. Vice speaks and the young man repeats.

"I know the god prince isn't here either taking requests, because I called for him and he never showed. I wanted the Christ to stop the screaming in my head and it never stopped. It only intensified."

The young man pulls a silver Python revolver from the inside of his left coat pocket and just holds on his lap. It was clearly placed for added intimidation.

"Father, what was that thing you use to say before we started the processional march down aisle?"

"We?" Priest repeats.

"Ahh shit! Remember you were right there," Young Man says, pointing the Python toward the back of the church growing more frustrated. "Right the fuck over there." He points the gun back toward the entrance of the sanctuary. "You were right there and me—me, I was right over there, right fucking there in front of you." Trying harder to remember, the young man knocks the Python against his head repeatedly. He then takes the barrel and points to the side of his head drilling it, boring it into his temple still trying to recall a forgotten phrase sputtered years ago. "What was it, gotdamnit?! The whole time you were probably looking at my underage ass while you were behind me you pedophile piece of shit."

The young man places the Python's business end of the barrel to the head of Priest connecting muzzle to skin at his temple. Priest turns his head into the barrel and rests his forehead on it saying nothing.

The young man starts laughing. "Ahh! Yes, I remember. Ha! It escaped me for a minute, but I remember. You use to say 'the lord is in his holy temple, let all the Earth keep silent before him.' It's not the Earth that kept silent though is it? Almighty God himself kept silent. He was the true one that remained quiet."

Uneasy, but remaining composed, Priest grabs the pack of Newports and helps himself to another one, again looking to the young man for a light.

"Oh! Here, let me get that." The young man digs into his off pocket and retrieves the lighter again and lights Priest third Newport still holding the gun to Jason's forehead.

Vice, having already started the downward spiral of events this morning lays back in his pew with hands off the young man. The fear and rage planted in him have become self-sustaining now. The young man has always had such thoughts, but through his vices of drinking and narcotics, Vice's soft whispers were able to be heard as if broadcasted across an amplified speaker in his mind encompassed by the mortal's dull gray flesh of the brain.

Vice focuses intently on the young man, whispering, "What is your worth since little Jason Priest stole your childhood? Look at how he's living amongst the damned of this world. He has a life and achieved status within his broken organization of fallen clergy which he believes granted him immunity. Clearly, he's not wanting for anything. Where is the remorse? Where is the guilt that he is supposed to be reveling in? Where is the kind of guilt that is so taxing that it equals your mental health bills and failed relationships?"

We've almost reached the purpose of this man's mission. Time is almost nigh and there will be no divine intervention from the heavens for me, thinks Priest. *Just as well. That table that the demon Crethos was talking about in the Congo a couple of years ago seems to be coming to fruition. Indeed, it appears a priest will be dinning in Hell's halls by noon maybe pacific standard time.* Letting out another sigh and no doubt acquiesced to his fate, Priest takes a long drag off what he believes is his final cigarette. He will be sure to savor it as it will be the last one he enjoys on this Earth.

Jason watches as the young man turn his thought from him toward the pulpit. He watches as his eyes fixate on the stain glass window just above the pulpit's lectern. The young man is laser focused on the crucified dying Jesus at the center of family, friends and enemies alike. He removes the Python from Priest's forehead and points it at the window willy nilly at the macabre spectacle while he stares intently at it which is soon accompanied by a few seconds of laughter that turns into tears.

"Did you ever actually believe in the shit you spouted under his watchful eye in that Pulpit father?" asks the young man.

Priest often of late finds himself constantly asking himself that same question every day in the dark nether regions of his mind. The same places that the demon Crethos had looked into.

"...I did believe in the beginning," says Priest. "When the demons would come for me at night. I begged to him even probably more than you did when I would visit my sins upon you in the night..." Jason takes a long reflective drag off his fug. "What I did to you, what I took from you is the reason to which I guess as to why you're here. It took me a while to place the face behind the beard, but I know who you are." Priest takes another drag. "I knew that recompense was here and it seems to have taken the form of you and I'm ready to pay my penance."

"And I am ready to receive them... It seems you and I have finally come to agreement on at least that... Before I do what I came to do most holy priest, just two more question. Please make your answers genuine... How many of us was there? Don't lie!"

Priest actually finishes his cigg completely before putting it out on the bottom of his shoe.

"Enough that my place is assured at a table in hell," he answers, exhaling the smoke unable to shake that memory of what the demon Crethos told him in the jungles of Africa... that he was more of a child of Lucifer than the demon who was speaking to him from the corpse of a dead man.

"That many huh? Enough that you don't even remember my name? I saw you're face when you came out of that office. You thought me some drifter, vagabond. You truly didn't know who I was did you, Priest?" rolling his eyes in disbelief at the perceived disrespect. "You ended my childhood with a whimper and countless hours of therapy to which there is no recovery. I don't care how much cognitive restructuring they attempted. My mom couldn't figure out why I was falling apart. A grade-A student reduced to high school dropout, because you couldn't keep your dick in your pants... And you don't even fucking remember me." Sigh! "Second question, it correlates to the first. What-is-my-fuck-ing-name?"

Priest stares at the young man. "Guilty! I'm guilty of all of it. So, get on with it and execute your judgment."

The young man stands up and points the nickel-plated Python dual action hand cannon at the face of Priest. The young man's own mortal thoughts of consequences trumped by the demon's Vice's whispering voice that implores for him to pull the trigger igniting life altering ram-ifications. The young man shakes his head in an attempt to quell the constant underlying voice. He looks as if he suffers from an extreme case of schizophrenia. As he bangs the gun against his head again and again.

"Shut up!" the young man yells. "Shut up, shut up, shut up, shut up!"

Seeing him in disarray, Priest starts to make a move to overtake him amidst his breakdown. Seeing him slide down the pew ever so slightly the young man again points the Python at Priest's head pulling the ham-mer back. The sound of the distinct click gives Priest pause as he won-ders whether he'll even hear the pop when it happens.

Smiling that his breaking point has been reached, Vice pushes the young man just a bit more, a scooch further. "Don't be ashamed that you too like the asses of little boys. You should be thanking this most holy of fathers right here in front of you for what he's taught you. C'mon, finish this false champion of God's army and when we're done here, we'll go find another to satiate your own innate cravings of revenge and may-hem. We will visit them upon that little Jimmy Bloughton. You so do like him, don't you?"

The young man takes a long look into the eyes of Jason. "Look at me, Priest, and know your sins have come home. In death know this... I will never be you." The young man places the Python in his own mouth and releases the hammer expelling his brain matter over pews and granite floors.

Blood spatter whips across Priest's face. The shock of instantaneous death does not budge Jason from his posterior position on the pew. The only movement is his quick cursory glances to see if anyone heard and would come running. After a few seconds, Jason dared to move his head slightly to the side listening for footsteps of curious responders. Nothing. After 10 minutes there was still nothing. In the quietness of the cathedral that many thought him too young to head at one time, there is only Jason and the young man's body that didn't jerk backward when the brain was ventilated. It had collapsed like a building imploding in on itself.

Looking at the bloody mess that had fallen at his feet, Jason scoots his posterior from the pew down to his knees. Overlooking the body from a now closer view his knees become quickly saturated by the congealing pooling blood. His face contorts into an agonizing and repulsed expression of disgust as his eyes follow the canoeing effect path of the bullet. The pathway had cracked and parted the skull that minutes ago contained a broken mind into two halves of spilling brain matter mixed with spinal fluid. Jason's nose flares and slightly turns away from the odor of burning pinkish gray matter. It wasn't appealing during the war and it damn sure wasn't now in enclosed spacing.

"For what it's worth, I do remember you Fenton Wallace," whispers Jason. *You are my shame, my curse as much as I am yours. I remember every accountable deed that I've done in this life. You are one that I am most ashamed of. You misguided bastard, why didn't you place that round through my head? You'd have done us both justice and maybe even found a semblance of peace,* thinks Jason.

Falling to instinct in lieu of not knowing what else to do, he begins to administer last rites. Just as he starts to pray, he realizes the futility of it and ceases.

"What the hell am I doing?" he says, laughing to himself at the oxymoronic nature of a pedophile giving last rites for another pedophile of his creation to enter Heaven.

Priest further contorting his expression begins to dig through Fenton's tattered coat quickly extending his search to pants pockets looking for a phone to see if he was recording the confessional.

Found it.

From the body Priest pulls a phone and a single Identification Card from Fenton's pockets. He swipes the phone active. It's encrypted. No problem. Fenton's eyes are fortunately wide open frozen in objected terror of the large caliber round that had traced a path through his brain. With a simple swipe of the screen across Fenton's face his iris identification is accepted and the device unlocks.

Mildly frantic Jason delves into the device looking to see if the thing is streaming.

It isn't, it's just about dead... He exhales as his shoulders fall in relief and defeat. Relief that he will not have to deal with the ramifications of his younger self today, but defeated because he should have had too. Life was karmatic after all. He knew that for sure. After a long minute of self-agonizing regret and shame, he turns the Identification over. A shock of fear briefly encapsulates him stealing what's left of his already exhaled breath. Priest falls backward over onto his haunches further soaking his pastoral vestments in the warm blood of Fenton's. He stares at the name of the card written in red marker. It reads but one name, Crethos.

The matter concluded, Vice smiles as he stands up from the pew confident that he's dealt another crushing blow to his side project of mentally breaking the ass who was responsible for Palengrading his favorite brother, Crethos. It's one thing for Crethos to have fallen in a celestial battle. Another for some dumb shit human to have had a hand in sending him to Palengrad. Looking at the expression on Priest's face more than satisfies him. He places his hood on drawing shadow over his face till only his Cheshire grin remains. He'll be back, Priest after all is a side project and he won't stop the torment until either a vice-stricken human ends the pathetic priest's life or the false clergymen does it himself under the pang of regret and guilt. He's ethereal after all and has nothing but time. All the time of a dying contested world under power struggle would allow.

The sudden clacking of metallic boots on the ceramic floor stays Vice's grin. He turns an about face quickly grabbing the hilt of his blade at the sound of what he knows to be a celestial closing in on him. Seeing his adversary revealed his muscles relax and tensions fall as he releases the grip of his blade. He stays it in its scabbard. It's no ethereal being of consequence, it's only Death.

Nothing said between the two, Vice walks past him purposely bumping the reaper's shoulder in an adolescent attempt to goad him into a confrontation. After the intentional minor assault on the ego of Death, Vice pauses monetarily for reaction. Death continues walking down the aisle to claim his prize without complaint. With no contestation coming, Vice vanishes fully from reality 2814.

Death walks up to the body of young Fenton Wallace with Priest sitting next to it. He nods at the sight and looks down adjusting the smooth dial of his gauntlet. "I'll be needing you step aside Father."

Jason leans his back against the pew to adjust himself to look upon the face of who's discovered him in his most questionable and precarious situation thus far in life that if misread, there will be infinite questioning and possible arrest if the story he's concocted is not believed. There would be investigations that will carry on to the possible destruction of not only him, but what is left of the already dying church. All of this would possibly come to fruition, because this ass decided to disincorporate his soul from body before him in his church.

Death outstretches his hand and calls the purple shaded orb to him.

"A troubled soul this one was," says Death. "I don't collect to many of these."

Having collected the soul, Death walks to the side of Jason studying him. He whips the tail of his black trench coat behind him swiftly then sits on the pew next to Jason looking down at him on his haunches covered in blood.

As Death watches the pathetic nature of this man wallowing in self-pity and regret, he can't help but see the crystalline strands of his prayers travel a line that only the ethereal can see. His eyes follow them as far as the stratosphere where they dissipate into nothingness falling on deaf ears. The transcommuncative hub is closed to this one. Seeing that all lines of communique are broken off from this one, he doesn't know why; maybe a feeling of kindredness, Death places his hand on the shoulder of Priest. However unlike the angels, there is no comfort given. There is no quarter given to the restlessness of the broken father's soul or respite of thought that can be found either. There is only the flashes of hellish nightmares of past dreams that haunt the once holy man.

"Sad, another troubled soul scuffles about beneath me here in this once holy place. Here where visions are supposed to be brightened and souls given a calm tranquilly in hoping for things not seen, but blindly followed," says Death, removing his hand and sitting back against the backrest of the pew.

"Here in this place, you have come to see it for what it truly is haven't you, Priest? ... A building with four walls and a roof. Such a troubled soul you are Jason Priest, not too much unlike the one I harbor now within the confines of my coat. It appears that Crethos has laid claim to you as a child. His stench still permeates the pours of your blood red colored soul... Please cease your prayers. It's embarrassing at this point. They are loud for one and utterly pointless in the second. Elohim, cannot hear you today priest... Maybe tomorrow when the blood of innocence is washed from your hands will he then hear your pleas. Maybe If he does, it will be I that is sent to give you the release you so desire. Unfortunately, your release may fare no better than the hell that you are trapped in within your own mind right now. This is probably the best of relief you will find in the tragedy of your life gone amidst."

Death takes a long sigh then stands staring down at Priest. Jason doesn't even bother looking up, he just stares ahead in silence. He has nothing to say. He has no lifelong questions for the transporter of the dead, no thoughts or coins for the ferrymen of the river sticks. He can only watch as his answer to past prayers slowly walks towards the double French doors of the church's entrance.

Walking toward the exit of the sanctuary, Death turns one last time toward Jason.

"Be wary; the doors of the church have closed shut. The Lord no longer resides in these holiest of temples and have not for some time...

But you knew that didn't you little Jason Priest? A chance now falls to you. You may be finished with God, but as you know... It doesn't mean he is finished with you... Awaken them herald to what has come!" Death disappears. "And find redemption," his voice says from the void of emptiness.

Thirty-Four

LAST OF HIS ORDER

"The Promised Land is what it was called. Whoever named it as such rather it was Yahweh, or Moses knew that there would not be a promise of a land of flowing milk and honey. The only promise given was that of untold bloodshed to claim the cursed land. We decimated the Canaanites. There was not one left to roam any land. We killed not only the men, women and children. We killed every beast, fowl, and amphibious creature within and outside their cities. I Joshua, second over the nation of Israel now first named by Moses, am not exempt from the evil perpetrated. I too killed for a solemn patch of dirt. The land that was given under the burden of genocide is a land that I'm not sure I want promised or not. The land is cursed, it is sour and so shall it be for all time."

Quote ~ Joshua

Space, Earth's Orbit: Moon

Sitting comfortably on a crater's edge, Lucifer watches as the Earth spins on its axis. His eyes follow the barely visible lines of constant prayers that stream continuously from the planet's surface. Every so often he grabs one of the strands and reads the never ending wants of greed, selfishness, loathing, placations and bargains of the mortals. The streams are endless and runs rampant as an intricate series of spider webs. He reaches out and pulls one of the lines of prayer, fixating his eyes on it. Finding it harder to read than usual, he squints his eyes slightly to decipher the code.

"It is a prayer for peace. It is from the mind of Carey Minolta of New Zealand," says Fate.

Lucifer, not startled by the voice nods in gratitude and releases the strand back into the Aether of the cosmos to once again fall amongst trillions of prayers from all universes of the underlining and overlapping realms. He knows Fate by his voice and doesn't bother to turn.

"I thought it read something of the kind," says Lucifer. "It does get hard at times readjusting my ethereal vision after looking through the dull flesh eyes of that Lucien vessel. I often marvel at how long Yeshua was able to remain attached to one of those dust filled cavities for such a long uninterrupted period of time... Maybe I should have asked him in the desert how he did it for so long and not go mad."

"Because he was asked too by his King and he endured because it was asked by his father."

"By a charlatan, you mean, a pretender that has pulled the ultimate flim flam. The irony is they call me slander, though."

Fate approaches. "You've spent a great deal of time among them as well... May I?" asks Fate as he gestures to sit next to Lucifer.

Lucifer extends his hand for his guest to sit. "Please... I need not remind you that if you were to move against me, Warsivious would remove your head from neck as to spare me the trouble."

Fate looks around for War and doesn't see him about anywhere.

"Trust, brother, although you do not observe him be assured that he is vigilant and is most certainly present."

Fatetanen waves his hand upward summing the form of a chair from the pale dust and rocky lunar terrain. He whips his coat back and sits next to his brother, his caste mate.

"No need for threats Lucifer. Though he may be extremely powerful, he is still a second caste. He has no power over me. Not to say that he wouldn't be problematic," says Fate, grinning lightly kicking his brother's foot playfully.

The most regal of the Archs straightens himself and sits with even more reserved regality than normal. This is a diplomatic meet after all. Now firmly seated he looks off into the distance of the cosmos and inhales an ample supply of vacuum and then averts his attention to Earth. He takes in the sight with his brother without uttering a word.

After an hour, Lucifer is the first to break silence.

"You know that I will stay the course, Fatetanen? I've come too far to stop, if you've come here to convince me otherwise."

"I wouldn't expect anything less," says Fate, lightly placing his hand on Lucifer's shoulder. "I simply missed my brother and wanted to take a moment of respite with him outside of the conflict between our dueling factions... Just look at it, Lucifer. Look and marvel at the beauty that is in the flaw of all living things. I'm not here for any furtherance of clashing of ideals today. We'll save all that for tomorrow. You and I both know that tomorrow and all the ones to follow will take care of themselves, will they not?"

Another long period of silence follows as they continue to stare at the blue pearl set against the black ocean of stars. Fate breaks the silence this time.

"Out of all the worlds that I have visited or helped to construct, this is one that steals the heart, does it not?"

Lucifer sighs. "It does. The Powers Corps placed great detail into this one before its construction. The specifications were something more than we'd seen at the time. It was constructed to be the pinnacle of greatness." Lucifer glances towards Fate. "So perfectly aligned and balanced. Everything made to work precisely in conjunction with the other. A well-oiled and perfect running mechanism to a despot king who needs worship to thrive on. He needs the endless placation to his unending hubris."

"Some would the same about you... have said the same in fact, that your hubris is much greater even," says Fate.

"Hmmph!" Lucifer retorts. "Those that speaks such things have not heard what I have. Those that speak, have not witnessed the betrayal that awaits all of us. Look around at the realms Fate, they are magnanimous in their construction. Who knows their blue prints better than us? Who would love creation, including the mortals more than us? We built the fucking things from the gathered particles of dust amidst the stars! All of it, we helped build it, and love it just as much... I love what we created, what we cared for. Your king wants to destroy it all. If you knew that this was all in danger of being snatched from you; everything was being taken, would you not fight with all that you are, imploring every device, every weapon no matter its yield to ensure survival?"

Fate just stares out into the vastness pondering on the question given to him. He's slow to speak at first, but then finds the elusive words.

"I have heard of your beliefs and intentions by way of others parting their lips of what you believe, but I do not take stock in what I've heard from others. Explain to me what you believe you heard. Tell me what you could not all those years ago on the hills of Glayden. Tell me what would make the best of us fall from grace and pull all the Heavens with him? Tell me what would make one that profess to love creation as much as you be willing to detonate a proverbial explosive no matter the yield, no matter the reverberations throughout the realms?"

Lucifer looks over at Fate. He stares not into the eyes of his caste brother, but into what could be considered a soul if the celestials had one. Fate does not shirk away from the intense judgmental stare, he welcomes it. He returns the same hardened gaze in kind and it is there, in the gaze into Lucifer's countenance that the writer of destinies finds what he never completely knew with a surety, but suspected was always there... that his brother was not as far gone as all believed. Fate witnessed the irises of Lucifer turn a grayish hue. He swore he witnessed a tear well up and began to stream from the left eye before Lucifer caught it.

Lucifer wipes the tear away and speaks softly as if whispering,

"Before them, it was perfection, wasn't it?" says Lucifer. "But like others, even you never thought to ask why there was perfection?"

Fate remains silent. He only watches as the eyes of his brother turn a series of color. The dark gray turns to a lighter one with speckles of green.

"No... you didn't think to ask did you?" says Lucifer. "And why would you? Perfection was just that... perfect. Well, I thought of the reason why and at its core the answer was simple."

"Elucidate me," says Fate.

"Oh! I'm going to. There was perfection because species prior to mortals were created as automatons in the prototypes." His irises turn a greenish blue with speckles of brown. "They were created to perform functionary tasks in the most rudimentary ways. Even we— to a degree—are not exempt from this unnatural law of creation. Then came humans. Yes, their varying early forms were grotesque and a horror to look at, but there they were nonetheless." His irises turn a goldish tan with traces of red. "However, unlike the others species that preceded them, they were inherently good willed and peaceful among all their kindred, the humans were different. In their creation."

"So, you believe," says Fate.

Lucifer briefly looks at his brother and then back out toward Earth. "The humans bore what the others species of all the adjoining realms did not. Humans were created not to be automatons, they were created to think abstractly and given choice without needing to evolve to obtain it. The mortals were stamped with a tiny slither of Elohim's imprint. It was sewn into them, part of their very being. That sliver, that spark, that... soul as they call it, changed the game. That miniscule splinter of Elohim is what destroyed the concept of perfection, not I, as history has come to judge. Independent thought and free will brother ended creation as we knew it and set the realms ablaze to slowly burn in and unquenchable flame."

Lucifer turns back toward Fate never breaking his intense gaze with him. "They had contempt in their hearts. They had jealousy. They had anger. The mortals had all of that because they were created in your King's image." Lucifer again looks away from Fate and back towards the Earth. "Other species across the cosmos were incapable of treachery, be-

346 - ARROW J. KNIGHT

cause they were free of that sliver of Elohim's enlightenment. Humans are of a devious and immoral intent because the master mold was like Mercy had said, 'woe to all of us if we were made in the image of God for if the master template is corrupted—'"

"—then all else that follows carry that corruption unto a vile end," says Fate, finishing the phrase.

"The master mold is corrupt, brother." Lucifer's irises turn a deep red. "Mankind was the only species made in his image and look at what they are by nature. They are infinitesimal parasites, viruses constantly looking to consume not only the blue gem down there, but the whole of the galaxies and realms if we were to let them. They long to be worshipped and revered for their accomplishments, but they are undeserving of such. They are a jealous breed that is never happy taking second," says Lucifer. "They are a breed giving free will, but made for subjugation to an unfair King that set them up to lose from the start. Custodians given a tainted garden.

Lucifer turns his head, noticing an event occurring in Maryland. He narrows his vision and looks into an alley in the rear of the 3400 block of Virginia Ave in Baltimore City.

"Look there, just past the overcrowded white bus next to that T intersection alley. Start at the bus and look two blocks left. Do you see it?"

Fate follows his gaze. His head drop slightly in disgust. Then he raises his head to look on.

"Do you see, Fate; do you see how he rapes that man? He does it at gun point and makes the wife watch. This is what Elohim has set loose on the universe. He set them loose with no guide, no true plan. I have lived amongst them more than any other living celestial being. Who knows better than I the corruption that has been wrought? Give them time and no ruler and they will spread amongst the stars consuming everything without end."

Fate sighs. "You see them as parasites... From a certain vantage point, I understand why. However, that is your vision and you're not wrong in your observation from where you stand. I too see the madness in them, the mortals. I see them attempting to evolve past where they are disregarding necessary steps to what they could become. The path they're own now; well— that is the one you put them on inevitably tainting their progression. You condemned them to this path with your scheming and machinations. I believe you missed that. Your very interference is the cause of your disdain for them. That is the irony of what you fail to see," says Fate.

Lucifer pauses in contemplation. Fate again strikes while the iron is hot. "What I believe is not the consensus of the celestial body as a whole, it's simply how I see your predicament from my vantage point."

Lucien stands still observing the Earth. He's even more focused on it. "I can save them, Fate. I can save them all from the self-fulling prophecy that he's put into motion. I can save all of us. I could have done it sooner if you all weren't so damn blind. Metatron, Gabriel, Michael, all of you are irresponsibly blind to the true purpose of Elohim's intention to do us ill will. The most disheartening part is you out of all of them are just as blind brother. A Fate that cannot see the future. Now, that is the definition of irony."

Lucifer outstretches his hand for Fate to take hold of and he does. Lucifer pulls him up from his chair to his feet then pushing him slightly forward past him so that his view of the Earth is unobstructed.

"Look closely at creation. Look past the seams and see as I do. Look at the cracks in the Aether, look at the angle of what the humans call dark matter. It's finite in its detail as if it had been constructed before to the same specifications and overlaid. How can you of my cast be so obtuse?"

This time, Fate sighs and looks at Lucien. He studies his eyes. It is apparent that his ideal his road to perdition had become solidified as the uncrackable Slayal metal of Norisene, the very same indestructible metal from which their tier one caste of weapons were formed from before Razine metal was discovered. There truly was no bringing the Morning Star home or to heel. Fate saw that clearly now.

"It was good to see you, brother," says Fate "I missed this... our talks. I missed you. Michael misses you."

Fatetanen waves his hand and dismiss the chair back to the lunar terrain dust from which it was formed. He tugs his pristine white trench coat taut ejecting the moon's gray dust from it.

Lucifer nods and returns his gaze back towards earth.

"I have enjoyed our conversation as well brother." Lucifer pauses. His lips part, but no sound escapes for a moment as he contemplates whether he should tell what he knows. The hell with he thinks, what harm can be done now? "That was unfair of you intervening in my ascension on the capital of Iayhoten all those eons ago. I had beaten Michael in fair combat on the steps of that palace. It was my time to assault the throne and ascend. If I were to have been denied that day it should have been decided by Elohim and me. You had no right to intervene."

Fate expands his wings from underneath his trench. He stretches them, then folds them back in the ready position. He turns facing Lucifer. "I had every right to intervene. We were at war, just as you bested Michael, I bested you on those steps and brought you to heel because it had to be done. It wasn't for what I thought you would do to Elohim. I laid you low to protect you. He would have destroyed you before you took the throne. I couldn't have let that happen— I love you too much for that. I looked after you as you did Michael in days past. Nothing more."

"Do you see what your act of mercy has cost you now?" asks Lucifer.

After a brief pause to think on the answer, Fate looks his brother in the eyes. "That remains to be seen."

Fate outstretches his wings again. "This was a good day," says Fate, starting to take flight. As he ascends his expression changes, his face tells the tale of one who's just remembered a thought that needed to be spoken; no, had to be spoken. "Just out of curiosity—"

Lucien cuts him off. "I would not have changed one damn thing all those millennia's ago to answer the question you were about to ask. And know that once we part ways this day, I will not hesitate again in seeing you as the enemy and a hostile force. Any of you cross me and I'll send you, Michael, Gabriel or whoever to Palengrad if you're in my way to ascension... In time, I hope you see what I have seen in the false King. If you don't, no need to worry, I will lay his sins bare for all the universe to see, Fate. I have spoken it, so it shall be done. Right now, your faith is absolute in the matter of Iehovah believing that you are justifiably right always showing loyalty to fault. That very reason, is why the regime of Elohim will fall."

"Your arrogance and eagerness are the reasons why yours will fall." Fate strikes back quickly.

Cracking a smirk, Lucifer nods. "Touché, mon frere." He turns back toward the Earth. Until that day then when all has been decided."

"...Until that day then," repeats Fate.

With no further words exchanged between the two, Fate takes flight.

Lucifer whispers to himself as he continues to overlook the Earth, *What I have done and what I do now have always been for us and I have no regrets. Remember me fondly brother, for what I do next will make me truly unrecognizable and shake the very foundations of reality if I'm right. And if I am, I will save us all."*

As Fate takes a hard left toward the planet, he closes his eyes feeling the sweet kiss of the solar winds cross his face. He's heard the last words spoken from his brother. When his eyes reopen a solemn tear streams under the grayest of iris. No one wants to lose a sibling, but it has become clear that Lucien Arcane; Lucifer, the father of lies, is a threat that will never be able to be reasoned with, he'll never be bartered or bargained with, he will not stop until all life concedes to his glory or have been annihilated by his wrath.

Fatetanen has been perceived over the millennia's to be the authority absolute on course routing of the inevitable path of everything. How he wishes that is so. He does have a gift, however. It is one not divinely given to him, but one built from and undying amount of experience lived. He does not know the future but what Elohim dictates, but what he does know is that power thought to be absolute; absolutely corrupts. It doesn't matter if you're Elohim or Lucifer. Power and the will to keep it, is the ultimate annihilator in this conflict and has been since its inception.

Carefully, Lucifer watches Fate as he descends toward Earth. Warsivious walks to his side also watching as Fate descend.

"They have been very persistent as of late," says Lucifer.

"Ever since Cyrail went public, our clashes have increased between De Mon and celestial. They have been unrelenting," says Warsivious.

"Only because Cyrail has been busy in shoring up our control over the resistant hot spots across the planet. With Cyrail removed as of late from taking part in these conflicts with the Archs, it has started to give them a foothold," says Lucifer. "That will not do."

War turns to him. "Orders, sire?"

"Keep spreading the conflict out! Spread them even thinner than what they are. Use our numbers to advantage. Imperial must complete his work at unifying the nations. It is crucial to our plan to turn prophecy from undesired end," says Lucifer.

Lucifer turns and looks west past the most distant star he can recognize. War follows his gaze.

"What are your thoughts out to the west expanse, sire?" Warsivious asks.

"I'm thinking that we need to draw the Archs attention with a problem that supersedes us. We need to avert their attention from all else that moves. Remember the stories that Elohim would tell when we were a youthful caste and inexperienced?"

Warsivious nods slightly

"I've been thinking about one story in particular," says Lucifer.

"Which one?" asks Warsivious.

"The story of the Monarchs." Lucifer looks back to War. Then, he glances again out toward the westerly expanse of the black unending vastness of the Aether.

"I'm thinking what if it wasn't a story. The details you see, it's in the details of how he spun the tale. He may have changed the tale to suit our learning, but not the characters. His stories were so vivid and full of rich imagery because I believe... I believe they were more than stories. I believe they happened. I can't shake that thought and that is why I sent Painell as an emissary out into the expanse." Lucifer squints, straining his eyes beyond his normal capability still looking deep westerly through the vast Aether of the cosmos.

"There were many stories that he spoke involving entropy and despair to educate and entertain us. Which one do you reference?" asks Warsivious.

"The All Fall story theory," Lucifer replies.

Thirty-Five

❦

THINGS I'VE SEEN

"Removed from the world, it has become a cold and darkened place where night has become eternal. Mercy needs to be found. He needs to live again to restore hope."

~Airesmiss

Elohim's Eternal Palace of Iayhoten

Down the long white marble hall leading to Elohim's Throne room, Michael leads a dispatch of six blue and silver clad armored Etherealtorial guard. The personal guards of Elohim and the palace. They walk in single file columns of two with the celestial Mercy in between them shackled in onyx binds that connect around the neck and traverse down the spine of her back connecting again at both wrists binding them behind the back. Their boots echo hard, igniting the translucent liquid diamond floors. As they reach the throne room, two more of the Etherealtorial guards open the door from the inside allowing them entry.

Strange that this hearing of facts isn't in Chasm Hall, thinks Michael. *Chasm was specifically built for all matters of adjudication since its inception for Lucifer's trial.*

As they enter the throne room, Etherealtorial guard columns break off to either side of the entrance. Michael continues leading Mercy or at least the celestial claiming to be Mercy toward the center of the room. Two of the blue and silver clad armored guards close the massive Throne Room doors shut hiding all participants away from any interruptions or distractions of the realm.

Clad in his white judicial robes and tunic, Yeshua walks out of a small inner throne room chamber and stands next to the Elohim's Throne briefly resting his left elbow on the backing of it as he watched the participants settle. He'd just only heard there would be an emergency adjudication only moments before the parties arrived. Seeing Mercy, or at least the celestial claiming to be bound and led by Michael, he stands to attention in surprise. After the initial shock of seeing the armor of Mercy, Yeshua slowly descends the stairs to meet the accused on the makeshift court's floor. As he approaches Michael kneels before the Prince and looks behind him, to prompt the claimer to the name Mercy to kneel, but found that she had knelt without the need to be prompted. *She knows Protocol*, he thinks. *Good.*

Having observed trivial politics of addressing the court, Yeshua gestures for them to rise further giving permission for Michael to speak. When the Captain begins though, Yeshua raises his hand silencing him. Hand still raised he slowly approaches Mercy taking care and time to walk a complete circle around her inspecting her closely and very methodically. He looks into her eyes before softly laying a light touch to the armor she's wearing in various places feeling the cracks and scorch damage from past conflicts. Through sight and touch he reads the story of her life through the armor through the pain and damage inflicted upon it and by extension, her.

"You are not Mercy," says Yeshua.

She takes a knee again looking at the floor which is hard to do in her particular set of binds. She doesn't dare look the prince in his face.

"No, my Prince, I am not Mercy, nor have I ever been or professed to be."

"Yet, you wear his armor."

"I do, my lord."

Removing his touch from the armor Yeshua looks at Michael for a report.

"My Prince, she intervened and helped thwart the attempt on Jericho's life ensuring his safety and safe passage out of Germany. Shortly thereafter again, she intervened a second time in the battle of the Archs and De Mons buying time for Raphael to save Zadkiel only to pass a judgement of mercy on the Legionnaire Saadox before expelling him to Palengrad with most haste I might add. The pretender to the name Mercy was then seized without incident by the Choiretics and brought before me at my request and by extension brought here before the court without delay."

Yeshua walks around her a second time.

"Are there charges that you bring against her, Captain?"

"No, sire, none at the moment. I have brought her hear before the court to ascertain answers. All matters of adjudication will be left to those that have the right to judge."

Michael thinks for a moment, wondering if he should overstep his station by adding his personal opinion to the matter. To do so would not be proper etiquette, but through her actions one of his Archs were spared and a debt for a debt should be paid. He would in fact pay this one.

"My lord... if I may? I have not always been privy to facts that have occurred before the Morning Star rift as I was not in charge then; Lucifer was. I know very little of Mercy. To me Mercy was regarded and relegated to legend who had supposedly fell among the expanse when he was dispatched on a mission long before my given command. The Arch was never under my purview, but this one here claiming the armor and name of the said Arch should be extended mercy, the very name sake for her actions today. I therefore bring this un-accused forth to the court for deconfliction and request I be made aware of all facts pertaining to the mission of Mercy. With this knowledge if given, it will direct my line of questioning as to ascertain how a celestial citizen classed ethereal gained the armor of Mercy and if charges should be brought forward forthwith?"

"It is irrelevant how she gained the armor, because the Angel that was Mercy has fallen and is no more," booms the thunderous voice of Elohim.

Michael gazes past Yeshua toward the Throne and sees Elohim now sitting upon it. He kneels again alongside the Mercy pretender. Yeshua backs away and turns a hundred and eighty degrees swiftly causing his robes to flail. He quickly walks back toward the throne standing to the right side of his father.

"It has indeed been some time child since you were within the realm," says Elohim. "You are an old creation... Airesmiss" Elohim stares at the two for a moment. "The both of you may rise."

Michael helps the pretender stand continuing to gaze her up and down trying to figure why she and the name is foreign to him. He has no knowledge of her at all as if she only just came into being. "I'm sorry, my lord, I am not familiar with the name you spoke," says Michael.

"Because she has not been made of any caste that has been charged with protection of the realm. She is citizenry and nothing more," says Elohim. "She was created to populate the realms of heaven; to give life to a recent illuminated void. She was never meant to have crossed a barrier that would place her on par with Archs, Powers, or Choiretic. She, Airesmiss who would later become the adopted progeny of the original wearer of that armor, was given autonomy to transcend her created station if unlocked. The prodigal daughter of Mercy has come home."

Michael hasn't had much audience with the King as of late. To be in his presence since the fall of Lucifer was rare indeed. It was mostly the Prince that his interactions and order were given through. Now in the presence of the King of kings the Captain is sure to pay attention to every gesture, every mannerism.

Michael realizes he's paying close attention because he can't unhear the lies that Lucifer told of Elohim on the steps of the palace during their battle for Zero Realm. He remembers what he spoke in his ears as he laid bested at the massive doors of Elohim's Palace. He can never unhear what Lucifer said; the ill purpose of what would happen to the Archs, celestials, everyone, and everything.

Don't travel this seed of negative thought to grounded roots, Michael had to remind himself mentally. If he did follow the seed of thought, then Lucifer would have truly won that battle at the steps of the palace, not only in the physical, but in the heart and mind.

Listening to the exchange now between Airesmiss, Elohim, and Yeshua, Michael is thrown off a bit and he knows why, this was all before him. Some conspiracy he doesn't know the true depths of. Seraphim Lucifer knew perhaps, but what good was that? The path of memory opened again. Michael hears on repeat what Lucifer told him on the steps of the palace when he'd broken him. 'Michael, Elohim has lied by omission brother. What he has not told us is the lie that will undue us all. His word denied will end the reign of celestials and un-make the Aether, the planets, everything for all time.' The phrase just repeats in his mind. It distracts him causing his mind to briefly wander to whether his thoughts rise to the level of blasphemy or dare it...even sin? His speech, his mannerisms in the way he talks to this... Airesmiss, Michael hears it in Elohim's voice, something is amiss.

There...there it is again, thinks Michael. *The tone in his voice is one of uncertainty. He doesn't know what truly happened to Mercy? Is that it? I feel that's it, but that can't be, he knows all doesn't he? Stop it Michael. Stop looking past the obviously stated. There is no deeper meaning than what he speaks. It's just that damned Lucifer in your head getting to you.*

Am I getting to you, Michael? Lucifer's voice can be heard whispering in his mind as it plays tricks on him. Michael gives his head a brief shake to knock the illicit thought from the forefront of it.

Even in trying to control his wandering mind, Michael's thoughts can't help but keep coming back to the belief that a chink has been re-vealed in his King's armor. He now knows the name of the pretender, but not the fate of the predecessor of the one who came before her. When Michael returns to the here and now, he finds Elohim observing him closely. Although the King says nothing Michael knows he's been heard. Elohim's brief gaze betrays nothing of any ill intent or otherwise and his gaze is mere seconds before returning back to Airesmiss and the issues placed before the courts.

"Report Airesmiss of Risha!" Elohim orders.

Airesmiss falls to her knees again. She does not want to cry, Elohim deserves no tears, but she has not heard the name of her home in millennia's. Tears run, but they are tears sprung of hate for the crown. Elohim's countenance was incredibly bright, Airesmiss is unable to gaze into the illumination surrounding him. She averts her eyes and begins sure to voice a sense of seething and bite into giving her report. "My King, this is my full unadulterated report."

****

Over 5 Billion Years Ago
Iayhoten Heaven

A young ethereal enters in from the western most outer gate of Iayhoten. Venturing far from her home Risha, this is her first pilgrimage to the capital of Zero Realm from which came the existence of the Sadohedranicverse. Her grin and excited strut show nothing but glee and uncontrolled excitement to have finally arrived to where all given life originated.

****

Elohim's Palace: Throne Room-Present

Still kneeling, she never raises her eyes to the level of Elohim. She takes a long deep slow breath before parting her lips. "I was a raised a commoner after creation in the outskirt lands of Risha. I was long from pride and just happy to exist in Zero Realm ignorant of the many wonders of such a grand realm. From the confines of Risha, I praised you all the days of my life in absolute reverence," says Airesmiss, bowing her head lower showing homage. "I was here, Lord, in Iayhoten almost six billion years ago when there was this thunderous boom and that's when I saw them. They were bigger than life to me. Larger than reaching and laying eyes on the capital of Iayhoten itself. I'd long heard about their exploits, but I was there to see them return from some distant mission.

I witnessed the Seraphim Lucifer and those with him which were a few of the Powers Corps, Uriel and Mercy."

She looks up slightly only making it to the level of floor just below Elohim's feet. She dares not crane her neck further upward as it was too painful to look upon him. "After they all had touched down, my King, they were a sight to behold. They were an image of regality; they were everything that I was not nor would ever be. It was then in that day, I knew I had broken laws against you and felt my first feel of the sin envy, although I did not understand what that was, I only knew I wanted to be like them."

Elohim nods at the statement. Yeshua only stares at her, his eyes betraying him instantly showing the compassion that he felt for the celestial.

****

5 Billion Years Prior: Zero realm
Iayhoten

Airesmiss watches in complete awe as Lucifer and company land on the flowing liquid golden lined road that is encased under hard translucent diamond. Once landed, they all march toward the palace. She's beyond enamored by their commanding presence so much so, that she follows them along with a grand host of others that have formed a welcoming celebratory retuning home crowd.

****

"My eyes were widened in awe," she continues. "These celestials were able to transcend the barrier of realms and travel the Sadohedranicverse. They were truly free and not limited or confined to Zero Realm. Sure, I was able to traverse within the realm of Zero, but never to leave it; never to experience more than what my day to day was. I did not know what the term of an eternal prison was or understand the construct of confined, but I felt it watching them have power of permission to come and go at whim and I did not."

Wonder stricken of the tales that were told far and wide of Lucifer and the Powers, she pushes and slides, snaking in and out of celestials and ethereal alike, until she makes her way almost to the front of the cheering crowds that columned Golden Line Road of Kings. Finally, after much obstacle, there she is at the very front where she could clearly see, but Lucifer has already passed. She only catches a passing glimpse of Uriel's back, but she is able to see the fullness of Mercy in his armored regalia, his metallic boots clanking hard off the translucent gold deck.

"When I saw him, he looked magnificent. My breath was stolen as I watched the celestial Mercy pass me. Not only did he pass me, he looked at me. Our eyes met and he gave me a salute as if I was one of them."

Just as quickly as she has seen him wave, he was gone just as fast. He's down the road toward the white and gold trimmed marble steps of the palace. Before she knows it and can understand, she is cheering along with the crowd, screaming at the top of her voice. Excitement is contagious, infectious, she hadn't even realized how much till her voice was about expended. Airesmiss learned two things that day, one her voice has limits. Two, she is smitten and totally taken with Mercy. Then again it could just have easily been Uriel that became the subject of her admiration had he seen and waved to her first. He would have become the object of her idolization. Alas it fell to Mercy and she is just as happy to cheer for him. There in him is a hero just for her, an ideal to stand up and strive for. Mercy is a purpose given to her existence.

****

"I am uncertain what happened in the palace that day and the following night of their arrival as Mercy never talked about it when I would meet him later, but it put him in a somber mood. I saw him the next evening after he left the palace. Yes, I waited to see him again if at all possible. My patience paid off. I did eventually run into him, but there was something amiss, there was a change about the air of him. It was easy to tell by the stride of his walk. It was not the same confident one that he had during his returning processional march. It looked as if it was a walk of one defeated."

****

Later that day, Airesmiss finds herself looking across the Mastication Hall's common eatery. She sits at a table of no consequence closely watching a Choiretic as he eats. Her mind wanders in visions of her sitting with him talking of places they've been and things they've done all in the name of Elohim. She watches him all the way up till he finished his nourishment and left. Finishing a plate of Manna herself in the Mastication Hall, Airesmiss slides her plate to the side and takes a drink of Asprillian Nectar, a derivative of Manna in a sweet liquid.

Still sitting among the masses eating, Airesmiss takes in the sight of the infinite Hall that gives the impression of looking as if it is packed, but it never really is. The Power Corp constructs things funny that way. As the hall moves toward capacity it readjusts instantly creating more room all the while the Hall's dimensions never appear to change. It was constructed to accommodate all beings that were ready for nourishment anytime of the day. There is always just enough room to be comfortable.

While enjoying her libation, the celestial sitting next to her finishes his meal as well. He looks at her before rising up to leave murmuring something about first timers while throwing a nonchalant wave bye. She acknowledges his wave and off he went. Isn't much longer after that, that she's finished her drink and had just begun starting to clean her little area when Mercy arrived and sat across the table in front of her.

"Greetings little one, were you holding this table all for just yourself?" he jests.

When Airesmiss looks up, she can't say a word. Her tongue has gone numb, her voice mute. There he is... Mercy.

He grins., "I take it this spot is taken then? I shall find another?"

"Nnn—no—no, this spot isn't taken. Please sit, sit," says Airesmiss, awestricken for the umpteenth time.

He nods, accepting the permission and sits.

Mercy doesn't hesitate and begins to dig into his food. She watches as he devours plate after plate of Manna. During his engorgement, he doesn't once take time to drink any nectar to wash it down. Other celestials had come and gone and yet, Mercy was still there continuing to eat. After sometime only when he reached satisfaction, did he look over and notice Airesmiss staring at him.

"Umm! Hi," he says, looking at her awkwardly.

Sill enamored, she blinks slowly, feeling like a primary learned school girl with her first crush. "Hi," she manages to say breathily.

Laughing, he slides all his plates off to the side. "Little one, now that I see you, I remember you; you were in the crowd of Golden Line Rd yesterday, yes?"

Again, awe stricken that he remembers her, an abysmally small face in a seemingly endless crowd of onlookers and he remembered. She was definitely team Mercy.

"I was. I had just gotten here to the capital when I saw you and the Seraphim had returned. I had never seen the liking of your arrival."

"What parts do you hail from young one?"

"I lived on the Quarent boundary of Jacintian it's called Risha... Realm 0003."

"Ahh! You are from Vastsheus Realm," says Mercy with a wink.

"That's another name for it, but yes. You know it?"

Mercy reaches for his goblet of nectar. "I do, although I must admit it has been some time since I have been there." He looks her over more closely examining her garments, the wonder filled eyes of seeing Zero Realm for the first time. "This is your first pilgrimage to Zero Real, then?"

"Yes, my first," she says, nodding.

The two converse for hours, she told him of life growing up in the Rishaen realm and of being a commoner. She was enamored, he could tell, but she had the world and didn't know it. His was a life of service, there was none for her. He respected her life of anonymity. She would more than likely disagree with his high praise of the commoner, because she was ignorant of a life of servitude and all it entails. There was a calmness to her life, a serenity that has not been known to him.

Ahh the peace of mind that came with the ignorance of not knowing what truly surrounds you, the comfort one must sleep in? This commoner from Risha knew true freedom.

"So, little one from Risha, what do I call you? We've spoken all this time, yet I never did as much as to acquire your name."

"I am called Airesmiss."

Mercy gives her a smirk. "A beautiful nomenclature if I ever heard one." He continues to stare at her. His smile fell to one of a small despair, but doesn't stay there for more than a second.

Although brief, Airesmiss picks up on the shift in his feelings. "Something bothers you, Celestial?"

Ignoring the question, he again gives his complete attention to Airesmiss.

"I have been charged with a duty out beyond the Aether. You say you've wondered what life was like beyond this veil, yes? What say you accompany me into an unknown region that not even I have been? To come all this way and not to have at least one adventure to talk of on your pilgrimage? We can't have that."

Intrigued, she scoots a bit closer. "You serious? What will we have to do?"

"Receive a message and return it posthaste to the King."

A widening smile crosses Airesmiss' face. Excitement exuberating. "How long do you suspect it shall it take?"

"Does it matter, little one?" says Mercy with a slight laugh. "Have you a place you must urgently be?"

"No, I just don't want it to end so quickly," says Airesmiss. "I wouldn't want it to ever end."

"Losing his smile just slightly, Mercy gazes at her a moment as if in a state of clarity. Wouldn't it be wonderful if all things were to last little one," says Mercy. "Unfortunate for this to be your first lesson of constant, but surely as day chases the night, all things come to an end. All things!

Airesmiss returns a slight confused look and then thinks nothing of the brief exchange.

"What essentials will be needed?" she asks excitedly. The questions come in a rapid succession. "What must I bring? I don't have much in way of distant travel. What does one wear outside the realm? So much to think of, what do I need, where will I get it?"

"Yourself will suffice little one and a sustainable supply of Manna which I will provide.... What say you Airesmiss of Risha? Would you like to see the Sadohedranicverse and have an adventure with a Celestial?" he says smiling.

After a long reflective moment, she smiles. "What else am I doing here in Iayhoten if not to see more. I say yes."

Mercy nods and pounds the table repeatedly with both fists in celebration. "Okay, then, it's been decided. Take the waning days to yourself, finish whatever short business you have and sights you wish to see. We leave in a fortnight. I will have provisions and equipment for you. When time strikes, meet me at the most western gate of Iayhoten."

She nods emphatically. "Is the Sadohedranicverse as infinite and as beautiful as I've heard?"

Mercy rises from the table. "More than your mind can comprehend in this moment. In a fortnight you shall see the true power and might of Elohim and the majesty of forever expanded."

Thirty-Six

❦

THE THINGS YOU'LL
SEE

"Fear would be an emotion that is in the very base of created intelligence. It is an emotion, an experience that for the most part lays dormant within our makeup. It is there as a failsafe with a duty to warn of an impending doom. To describe it would be to explain color to darkness."

~Mercy

A fortnight had passed when Airesmiss arrived at the western most gate. Mercy was already there, resting against the wall. He collapsed the scroll in his hands that he was reading and studied Airesmiss, who looked serious and determined. His armor had changed from the last time she'd seen it. He is now wearing a more regal regalia of a set; this armor was platinum with a high shine and gold trim. His initials were etched in a white glow on his gauntlets and up the front shin of his gold metallic boots. His opulence had far exceeded that of his companion's. She wore a simple light tan tunic with white pants and tan boots.

As soon as Airesmiss saw him, a bit of envy crept into her being yet again. She couldn't help but marvel at him. He looked simply elegant, bigger than all of creation in his gleaming armor. His armor and status would be forever denied to her... a commoner from Risha. One had to be created as a caste to ever have been a celestial. She was created a pauper of no substance to populate the realm. A background cut out that was animated with breath.

Mercy waves her hither. "Come, see."

Airesmiss approaches, soured with envy, but still a little gleeful and grateful for the chance to see beyond the veil of Zero Realm.

Reaching into a satchel, Mercy pulls out a few metallic items. "I have procured a few things for you from the Spire."

Pulling a collar from his satchel, Mercy throws it for Airesmiss to catch. She catches it and looks at it puzzlingly.

"You place it around your neck!" he says.

Without even waiting for him to explain and without thinking much about it, she places it around her neck and connects both pieces excitedly.

"What is it?" she asks.

"I'm glad not a tool of bondage or a device that separates one's head from neck," he says jokingly. "It's a helmet. It's to give the ease of breath through the various vacuums of space and other odd atmospheres we may encounter. To activate it just merely think that you are wearing it and it'll do the rest."

The helmet and mask generate over her head and face. Underneath, she grins her biggest smile ever. When she thinks the command off, the mask and helmet disengage, retracting back into the collar.

"You'll definitely need the face shielding when crossing the Aether." Mercy then sets a pair of silver metallic boots down on the ground. "These are for you as well. They will help you manage gravitational forces on or in whatever realm we find ourselves."

Taking a long look in her direction, Mercy reaches into his satchel again this time producing a bundle of clothing. He too tosses the bundle for her to catch. Airesmiss feeling the contents hurriedly opens it and find a celestial type suit. It wasn't uniformed like his, but it was

366 - ARROW J. KNIGHT

similar. The construction of it, the stitching, the weaving, was all unlike anything she'd ever felt.

"Where we are going, the conditions and environments can be pleasant and just as equally cruel and unforgiving. Whatever they may be, that material there can handle it. It is of a derivative of what we wear. It's tough and very durable. It is made to incur the type of travel that is our normal at the speeds which we traverse. What you had on, as nice as it was would not have been practical for where we are going. The Sadoverse would have obliterated it."

She rips the tying cord away and unfolds the bundle. Shame, far from existence, she quickly places on her new garments. Similar to her traveling benefactor, her suit is off white, with no markings on the shoulders. Her pants does not have the stripe of the celestial either, her pants carry four horizontal dark blue colored stripes up each leg. With the added addition of her new metallic boots, Airesmiss not only looked the part and ready for her adventure, she felt it.

Nodding, Mercy reaches into his satchel one final time and tosses her an even smaller satchel. "Inside that small parcel, you will find your travel supply of Manna. There isn't much because that is a special composition of Manna. Less feeds more. We use those when traveling great distances. Rule of thumb, use less than needed to gain further distance."

She simply nods and places the satchel into her tunic.

Mercy's helmet and mask generate over his face. "Are you ready to step out into a greater creation?"

Airesmiss mask and helmet generate over her face. "Ready to have my perspective blown!"

"Oh! It will never be the same," says Mercy.

Underneath his mask, Mercy smiles and holds out his hand. She slowly approaches and takes it. His smile slowly falls away, replaced with a look of somberness if she was able to have seen it. He clutches her hand and lifts them from the bonds of Zero Realm; they are off into the Sadohedranicverse. Off to her adventure of a lifetime, while for him, it will be his last.

✳✳✳✳

Airesmiss looks to Yeshua while telling her tale. Tears well her eyes, but they do not fall. She won't allow them too. Yeshua, she can look upon. He is a prince that chooses to lessen his countenance to be more acceptable by all. He is the mortar that build bridges of Elohim's creations *"My Prince, it was an indescribable moment when we stepped off the plain of Zero Realm. I thought that I couldn't achieve a more blissful state of being then that moment of going weightless... I was right. My bliss was never its equal after that moment or have been rivaled ever since."*

She tries to avert her gaze from Yeshua to Elohim, but his countenance again is just too bright for her accusatory eyes. Yeshua immediately understands her meaning of the gaze. By trying to gaze at his father, she's making a bold implication of a King without saying so.

"Continue your report, Airesmiss. The court has taken note and is indeed listening," says Yeshua.

Airesmiss nods. *"The years, decades, and centuries even that proceeded our departure were eventful and educational. I'd seen more in my travels than I ever would have believed. I also saw that the Sadoverse was not as equal for every living species across it. I realized in some of the worlds that I had been to, that I was not as destitute as I had believed when living in Zero Realm's magnanimous lands. I was in fact in high status and truly privileged to have been created and living among the gods... even if I was from the small Vastness of Risha."*

Yeshua looks at Elohim who still hadn't spoken a word. It's as if he was patiently awaiting a detail to emerge from the story and would not comment till he heard it. Yeshua looks back to Airesmiss. "What happened to Mercy child of Risha?"

"That is the question isn't it my prince? What happened to Mercy. I shall tell you the fate of Mercy. The tale will be truth and unadulterated."

Michael now finds himself more interested.

Airesmiss takes a breath and exhales it slowly containing her rage. *"The mission which was kept from me until zero hour was vast in time. Our destination may have been months or maybe years, times moves differently out there in portions of the Aether that move in shadow and darkness away from the eyes of the king. You know... the portions that existed before there was light. We were out in the Sadoverse for thousands of years and had seen much, but that portion isn't important. What is important is what happened at the end of our intended journey together when we collided with beings called Monarchs. A race of beings that I believe the King is familiar with."*

Elohim's eyebrow raises slightly at the title. Yeshua notices the expression change, but says nothing. Michael grips the hilt of his sword at the word. He doesn't know why at first. It takes a minute of him searching though his mental rolodex to find the definition for the term used within the context of her phrasing. Found it: Monarchs, a story of battling gods that was told to entertain him and his brothers when they were young in creation. He'd often have dreams about having been in such a conflict and being a hero fighting for Elohim. Thoughts of the young, how naïve he'd been. What was he thinking during those times Michael wondered? Stories should have just remained that... stories. They were much different than real life. In stories there were no real dangers, there was no threat of damnnation, annihilation, or Palengrad. Thoughts refined by millennia's of knowledge of engaging in the art of war has made the prospect of being a hero a foolish notion that is far from glamorous. War is a vile and evil thing and not only should one never playact it, it should go as far as to never pass lips.

Michael kneels, lowering his eyes to the floor in front of him before directing his voice toward the King "Surely it could not have been Monarchs. They were but a story of what brought the great battle of the second age to conclusion."

"Save for two," says Airesmiss, already on her knees. She slowly turns her head in the manacles looking over to Michael who's now beside her. *"And I assure you, Captain, they are no story. They draw breath as you and I."*

Yeshua walks back over to Airesmiss and kneels down cusping her chin raising her head so that her eyes meet his gaze. "Tell us of the Monarchs."

Airesmiss took another breath to steady her anger and maintain her composure. *"We reached the Barrier, it was massive. I couldn't tell you what it protected or prohibited when we first saw it, but there it was a, barrier out there among the Aether and we had arrived."*

****

Barrier of the Aether

Mercy and Airesmiss approach the barrier that is impenetrable by even his celestial eyes. His hesitation is only momentary, because he knows this osculating ring of obfuscation is his destination per the co-ordinates given to him. With no further delay and the mind of thought that they've come too far to go back, he decides the pair will cross the smoggishly thick barrier that surrounds uncertainty. Mercy rockets upward into a backflip and dives using not only his speed, but gravity's assistance in piercing and crossing into the barrier. It continuously runs through his mind that he could have travelled the Sadoverse for billions upon billions of years and have never located this place. Until now, he did travel billions of years without ever coming across the barrier. The place was unnatural and well hidden. Without the specific coordinates provided by the King it would have never been found.

Racing through the barrier seems never ending. It is miles upon miles thick with a mixture composition of fog, brimstone, intense winds, lightning, ice shards sharp enough to draw tinges of blood from celestial skin wherever exposed. Within its confines, the pair had no sense of time passage, but it was obvious that it wasn't quick in and out.

After an untold time, they were through it. Once on the other side, his mask's servos and mini motors start to whirr and whine in protest. The safety catches start to spark and disengage on their own. The air that he once glided upon found itself dense and void of lift to keep him aloft. With Airesmiss attached to his carry harness situated to the front of him and absolutely void of lift, the two crash down hard creating a shallow crater further extending a path before sliding to a stop amongst a rocky filled barren land void of any greenery.

Mercy had rolled himself to take the brunt of the landing. The pair lay motionless for a few moments before Mercy starts to stir slowly releasing Airesmiss from the harness. The whirring motors of Mercy's and Airesmiss' mask retracts leaving their faces exposed. Glancing down at his gauntlet, the first thing noticed by Mercy is that his gear is completely dead. There is no trace of realm function. The sliding dial has lost capacity to connect to the main information hub of Omnipotent. Long made short, they were stranded and unable to move or shift reality. Here, beyond the barrier they are tangible as the dirt they stand upon.

"We have arrived it seems." says Mercy, looking around. "Are you okay, little one?"

Airesmiss looks around taking in the barren scenery. "Yeah, I think so. Could have given a little warning that we were coming in hard though." She checks herself over.

"What! I did give warning; did you not hear me screaming?" says Mercy.

Airesmiss cracks a smile, which causes her to wince slightly. "Where are we?"

"Don't rightfully know. It's not on any maps of the Sadoverse, but what the Most High called the place was Olympus."

****

Beyond the Barrier of Olympus
"What are we supposed to do now that we're here?" asks Airesmiss.

"We are not to do anything. This next mission is where we must part ways for a time. I have left you enough provisions to see you through. Shelter, on the other hand, will be left to your discretion. The elements of this place are unknown and be mindful that we are vulnerable here," says Mercy checking his minor lacerations from entry.

Airesmiss' eyes widen in shock and begin to not only fill with disbelief, but tears. She is clearly and visibly distressed. She steps closer to Mercy in hopes that he misspoke. "What do you mean for a time?"

"I have been sent here with purposeful intent to a specific task that must be completed. This task unfortunately does not concern you and may carry a certain danger that I am not at keen on exposing you to." Mercy looks around their immediate surroundings. "This place is not known to me or the Omnipotent's database. My gauntlet has not worked since crossing that barrier and I feel it may never again till we're out. As of now, we are cut off from the expanse of the Sadohedranic-verse.

She stares at him not knowing what to say.

He sighs and points to a spot for Airesmiss to sit. Still confused and a tad dazed, she does indeed take a seat. Mercy sits beside her amongst the surroundings that have fallen to darkness and dereliction.

"I have had a time with you in our travels here little one and I must admit you have made my time enjoyable. To see you experience moments for the first time left me truly in awe. To see the Sadoverse through your eyes has been uplifting if not revealing. Over our period together, I cannot dismiss how much admiration that I've seen you have for me and at times think it has been misplaced. I feel that I'm nothing more than a servant, but the way you look at me says I can be more. That I am more than my station. I admire and thank you for that..."

Again, Airesmiss can only remain silent as she watches him trying to digest what he is saying or attempting to say.

"I cannot tell you of my true intent of coming to such a place of dec-imation. Whatever is here is old business and politics of time that is known only to a forgotten Caste that has probably long since existed," says Mercy.

"Ho—how long will you be gone?" Airesmiss heard noting really past leave you for a time.

Mercy's right corner of his lip gives a half smile. "I can't rightfully say. It could be for a time or it may not be. I can't really say."

"If you knew there was a possibility of us having to split, then why bring me such a distance where I was not able to follow? Why did you bring me all this way only to abandon me?"

Mercy cups his left hand around her chin and pulls it bringing her eyes to meet his. He watches as her eyes begin to stream tears. He lightly touches the tiny stream of water and wipes it away with his right thumb never losing his gaze into her eyes.

"I asked you along, little one, because for the first time since my creation, I believe that I feel the emotion of... the emotion of fear and I didn't want to be alone."

She looks puzzled at the strange word. She's never heard it before.

"Fear?" she asks.

"An emotion," Mercy clarifies. After a long pause Mercy releases her chin and looks toward the ground searching for the words. "Fear would be an emotion that is in the very base of created intelligence. It is an emotion, an experience that for the most part lays dormant within our makeup. It is there as a failsafe with a duty to warn of an impending doom. To describe it would be to explain color to darkness. It is an emotion that I would have to illicit in you for you to understand it completely."

Mercy gazes into Airesmiss' eyes for a long time, but says nothing. She thinks he catches a glimmer of envy in her eyes. Does he envy her for not knowing about fear? Perhaps.

After a long pause the answer strikes him. He looks down at his busted gauntlet and the exposed communication A.I. matrix Omnipotent that has gone silent. It's then he realizes that maybe for the first time ever he could speak freely and without fear or reservation.

"I will teach you fear," he says.

Looking at him, Airesmiss nods.

"The lesson that I teach you will resonate with you for the remainder of your uncountable days. Once you have learned it, you will never be able to unlearn. Your eyes will be forever opened and colored by it. Understand?"

Airesmiss nods again and grabs both of Mercy's hands, squeezing them. "Do you fear?"

He chuckles at her use of the word. "I fear right now."

"What could cause a Caste like you to fear? There is nothing of such a magnitude in the Sadohedranicverse that could cause... fear as you call it, if I understand. You make it as if fear is hesitation, yes?

Mercy nods. "Yes, it is hesitation of mind and body in conjunction."

"How will I learn this fear you have promised to teach if you are to leave for a time?"

"I already have. Think of if I am not to return to you, what would you do?"

Airesmiss ponders the conundrum. She had to think in future tense of a position that has not happened. After moments of being in a meditative state, her eyes grow large in a sudden realization. There, right there is the second it hits her. She understands fear as well as a child being lost in a department store. The emotion is raw. Nerves tighten, hands and knees tremble at the thought of him not returning. Just that singular thought cascades into a host of others such as what would she do for nourishment if the Manna runs out? How would she leave this dark rocky desolate barren land? Who would she talk too? Would she be abandoned here for all of eternity and if so, what would that look like if she was unable to replenish on nourishment provided by the King. The thoughts of all the aforementioned were horrifying and paralyzing leaving her beyond hesitant. She was petrified.

Mercy observes her in the moment understanding exactly the moment she learned fear.

"Where I go now, you cannot travel with me, little one." Mercy looks around as if there are prying eyes all about. "But that does not mean you can't follow if you so choose... unbeknownst to me of course." He winks at her.

Her eyes look through the fear that had overtaken her mere seconds ago to the light of hope of her not being left behind.

"You need not worry of fear, little one, for look at how far we've come together you and I. Look at how you have persevered. That is what you must do now, persevere."

"Now that you have come to understand the mark of hesitation and perseverance, here comes the practical task of utilizing what you have just been taught... If you do choose to follow, be unseen. Do not reveal yourself, stay to the shadows of this Olympus and observe my interactions, if at all possible. If all goes well, my lesson will be for naught. Our concern will then turn to leaving this place... Remember, stick to the shadows of this strange land. Something is different about this place from all others in existence. I have never been without Omnipotent. If something is to occur, even if it is occurring to me, you do not break from shadow, understand? You are to bare witness if all else fails and report to the King if able."

Mercy pulls his hands from hers and stands looking toward the west. "I take my leave first light or whatever constitutes for morning here." He takes a long look at her. "If my fate turns ill and you are seen, your fate will no doubt be no different from mine."

Mercy winks at her and begins walking towards the west to build a makeshift camp till whatever passes for first light. He sits cross-legged, facing west. He closes his eyes and begins a meditation of silent prayer looking for guidance. There is none. All communications have been severed in this place. Still he holds a silent vigil till morning or what constituted as morning. It seemed a perpetual twilight in this place.

There is no rest for Airesmiss either. She remains awake keeping a silent vigil of her own over Mercy. She had already packed what she felt she needed. She didn't know the road or how long he'd be on it, but she felt more than prepared and would be ready when he moved.

****

Airesmiss wakes from sleep. She frantically looked around believing that she's missed Mercy's departure. She hasn't. Mercy is again looking far into the west. He is dressed in his armor that he'd taken time to mend and shine. He looked ready to depart. He would have been left taking the westerly route, but he waited for her to wake. He looks back one last time knowing it could be his last look upon the face of a friend for a while, at least until his message was delivered and mission came to a peaceful conclusion. One could hope. From this moment on, to look back would compromise her safety placing her in danger, if there was danger here that is and if they weren't being already watched. He didn't feel like They were though.

"Take care to make sure you have enough provisions before you begin the trail. I left mine for you as well and a little something else." says Mercy. "And remember—"

"—Stick to the shadows of Olympus. I know, I know," says Airesmiss, finishing his sentence.

He smirks and then he's off. After he has long since vanished from her sight, she grabs her provisions strapping them to her LBE harness. She places her helmet and boots on and begins to follow the path left by her most merciful guide to the Sadoverse... Mercy.

Thirty-Seven

HORRID PLACE

Horrid Place
"What are dreams but a way to communicate with gods."
~ *Herodities*

Olympus

"Mercy had left me a little something else... his Omnipotent Gauntlet. True it was powerless within the barrier and of no use, but there was one function that still worked. It was as if it was a failsafe and I can only figure, Mercy knew the function was innate and still operative. The ocular memory link still functioned. Later, I would come to realize, it's powered by the user's own energy that permeates the body. Makes sense, it records what the user would have seen in his final moments and operate till the body turned cold. Useful if a celestial was recovered out among the Aether."

****

Mercy walked the equivalent of more than a hundred and fifty miles if he'd been forced to guess. In all that time, Mercy is only sure of one thing about this place, this Olympus is an enemy of celestials. It's been apparent the minute that they'd arrived and his access to the infinitude of realms and realities had instantly been cut off and denied to him. The forces of this place are dark and he suspects outside of known creation.

Having covered such a distance by foot is new to the celestial messenger. The land seems a barren and abysmal landscape. There has been nothing but rocky terrain for miles with an occasional floating land mass sporadically placed here and there as large as cities. The masses just hung suspended in the atmosphere. Those too appeared barren from Mercy's vantage point. Also another point of contention about this place, it was unlike anywhere else in the Sadoverse. Here; Mercy feels exhausted, his breathing is much more labored, and his mechanical armor's equipped tech is not able to assist him. The air on this planet smells putrid and carries a dank order that he never would have had to endure had the scrubbers in his mask been working. With his tech disabled in this rancid place, just completing the most menial task of walking has become hazardous. This place, this Olympus, is all wrong. Even just being here is wrong.

It's been more than eight days of walking before he reaches any sign of civilization. Eight days was a guess, because time appeared to be frozen here, there was never a change from dusk till dawn to signal the passing of a day. It was constant twilight. Approaching what he believes to be civilization his pace quickens at the prospect of finding assistance. From a distance he is sure this hub has all the makings of being a great city; maybe a major center of civilization for this planet. A place where he could finally have the answer he needs to finish his journey. When he draws closer though, that hope is dashed as what he's arrived too is akin to a mirage, an oasis. It is a city, but civilization has long since been vanished. The once great possible hub of life is just as barren as everything else on this planet had been. The landscape has been ravaged by what could have been a long-ago unnamed Thanatos.

Before deciding to enter the badlands of the outer borders, he needs to rest. He's been walking for days, at least he thinks he's been walking for days. It could have been months for all he knew. This place acts differently than other worlds. Without his Omnipotent AI, time is lost to him. Time bends outside linear time. It feels as if it bends back in on itself. Time bending of course, isn't an unusual occurrence out in the Sadoverse. It bends around stars and singularities all the time, but around a planet that has no celestial star to enact upon it, is highly uncharacteristic.

Entering the official outskirts, it was clearly evident there was a lack of life in the city. Nothing moved since he first spotted it on the horizon. It's was dark and void of any life, even insects and creatures of native descent were missing. Devastation is widespread. What once looked to have been towering white marbled columns are laid low and stained black by dark scorching. The signs of what once must have been a mighty empire shows even greater signs of being conquered by what must have been an even greater malevolent army. Entering through the northern most gate of the city he doesn't bother cutting west or east, he just continues on through toward the center of the metropolis towards the incredible awe-inspiring superstructure which was visible even from the vast distance he first spotted the city.

Mercy gasps as he drew close enough to see a dim light shine from the superstructure. It's the only illuminated brightness he'd seen in a long since dead world. The superstructure, is cylindrical in shape and sports great white marble columns that encircled a center solid core topped with a dome. The columns protect level upon level of oscillating floors that turned clockwise and counter clockwise of each other. It looked as if this structure is an engine that could have once powered the city and maybe even the planet. Its design seems flawless. From his vantage point, there's no apparent break in the structure that would give access to it from where he currently stood. Moving out right about three miles and adjusting his eyes by squinting, pushing his ocular focus to its max, he sees a break in the massive structure in the way of a barrel vault entrance. It could be seen protruding from the west side of the structure. Closing his eyes and saying a prayer, he continued his stride. Mercy enters the city proper, leaving the out skirted badlands and heads for the superstructure.

Again, Mercy stretches his wings in hopes to find lift in a chance to escape this place if needed, yet still he finds no flight capability. He retracts them and continues his pace toward the inevitability of reaching the city's core. Once there, he's sure he'll find the recipient of his message and probably the true nature of why he was sent here. He's not a messenger by trade and there were other messengers that could have carried the words of Elohim here, but they were not utilized. He was. This mission is purposefully tasked to him with only the barest of information given. Unlike Elohim to leave things so cryptic and unsaid, but his will be done.

The battle that no doubt happened here has truly darkened this place that long has been in existence before anything that even Mercy could remember. The distance of this place and unease of access, is proof that this Olympus preceded his inception and subsequent creation. He is first of the second caste so, there are elder brothers who came before him whose time might have borne witness to this place, but yet has never spoken of. This time period belongs to the Caste of those such as Fatetanen and Lucifer, the first of the celestial Caste order. Why would they not speak on such a travesty of a place?

Lost in thought of the anachronism of this place and its artifacts that has been left to the passage of time, the celestial takes notices of another difference of this place compared to other worlds he's walked. There is no accumulation of dust. The rocky terrain, gravel and dirt have not been tousled about. There are no layers of accumulation of debris on any of the toppled masonry that he can use to guesstimate even the slightest passage of days, months or years. This Olympus is without record. While passing a column that had been sheared diagonally, he runs his finger across the scorch mark; it doesn't smudge nor does the soot transfer from surface to finger. He mentally made note and continues toward the center superstructure that now even appears further away than it did when he entered the city proper.

Without his gauntlet, it is impossible for Mercy to accurately date this place. Common sense and physical clues are all he has to work up a hypothesis of how old this planet is, if it is even a planet. What he witnesses next stops the celestial dead in tracks and causes him to gasp.

A feat not likely to happen often. What has stopped Mercy cold is that the streets are littered with bodies upon bodies far as the eye can see. Olympus is not a barren city of structures after all, it is a city of the dead that has been left to rot. Mercy moves to investigate the first set of bodies that he happens upon. They are a bipedal creation unlike any he's ever seen to date. At first glance, if he didn't know any better, he'd guessed they were of a celestial order. Their remains are ashen with a gray hue about them. It looks as if life and the energy that permeated them at one time had simply been drained. Other than that, the bodies gave the appearance of looking very much alive, but not. They looked to be state of stasis.

Bodies were eerily still, unmoved or awakened by Mercy's actions which is strange because there were no signs of decay and rot. They simply looked asleep. As he furthers his investigation going as far as stepping over one and kneeling down to investigate another. He finds that even though they may have an appearance of just rising up, they will not. There's indeed no breath emitting from the body, no pulse of heart beat. They are for all purpose's dead, but there is no sign that Death has been here to collect their souls and liquify their remains. *A place untouched by Death, Curiouser and curiouser.* Upon further inspection still, Mercy realizes he does not know the garb they wear. The body belongs to a warrior class, but it's one he's never seen anywhere to match its likeness in the Sadoverse. This Caste of celestials are larger and not in just girth and muscle, but in height.

Also unrecognizable is the armor it was wearing. It carries a stamped signature of a lightning bolt engraved just above the pectoral portion of the armored chest plate. Mercy tilts his head slightly to match the lifeless gaze of the warrior's and finds that his eyes are locked in horror and glassed over, frozen at some untold horror it never expected to encounter. A more hands on invasive physical inspection would be needed. Mercy removed the armored chest plate and felt the chest wall. The solidness was broken by injury. The chest cavity had been pierced by blade.

"You will find no life here Celestial of Elohim," a booming voice called out from seemingly everywhere, but yet nowhere.

Startled, Mercy falls backward and scoots on his haunches. Traversing backward in surprise, his hand slides across the ground and finds purchase on a hilt of a sword that had been laying around with the probability of being there just as long as the bodies had been, just waiting for someone to eventually pick it up... eventually waiting for him to pick it up. He Grabs the weapon and points the sword outward and uses his wings to kickstand him up to his feet placing him into a high guard.

"Here you will only find Desolation, Celestial," another voice says from an opposite direction of wind.

Wind? When Mercy thought about, this was the first gust of wind that he's felt since he arrived. Even when him and Airesmiss fell to the ground, there was no wind. There wasn't even wind to displace dust and dirt. Mercy turns in the direction of the second voice's place of origin or at least what he could pinpoint as its suspected origin. Still, he found nothing but more dust and shadow.

"I am Mercy of Elohim. Show yourself and yield to his sovereignty!"

From behind him, he can feel the wind stirring. After a second, Mercy realizes it's not wind, but the inhalation before the dispelling exhalation of breath.

"Sovereignty is a word denied here on the mount of Olympus," the booming voice calls out.

The force driven wind of the conjugation of words are fierce. They take Mercy from his feet and casts him three meters into the air before he found the ground again. When he does it's hard and unforgiving. It bone jarringly unforgiving. Hurt felt immense. More than he can ever remember feeling. Celestials body's makeup is dense; their bodies were created to deal with any harsh environment imagined. Their density is why they can traverse singularities, why they can sling planets casting them off far and wide to distant galaxies. The likes of Mercy and his kin can pull a star down and rehang it, so he is not used to feeling pain.

What sort of black magic here in this uncharted place of Olympus could cause a slight tumble to reverberate such immense pain? Thinks Mercy.

Mercy staggers to his feet slowly. He feels a tickle of fluid on his lip followed by a slight pang of pain when he licks it. He wipes his lip with is forearm and it's clear the origination of blood was from his nose and lip. *So, it's battle then?* he thinks.

Enraged, he engages his helmet and mask from below the neckline of his armor again pointing his sword in the direction of the wind gust looking for his target or targets; at least two of them if he had to guess. The mini motors and servers again whine in protest before again disengaging and retracting. His mask and helmet again fall below the neckline leaving his face exposed, which was to a benefit, because not having his vision stifled by a mask he notices what should have been apparent. The sword he's holding is similar to the one sheathed on his side. The blade he picks up from battlefield was that of a celestial's weapon. He takes another gander at the ground littered with corpses and realizes that the bodies are not just of those with the etched lightning bolts. There is another set of bodies clad in light armor of wraps and hard leather. The material looks foreign to him. Their attire and armor are of those that would be dressed in warmer climates perhaps if he took an educated guess.

Mercy continues to scan the littered ground paying close attention to the weapons that both set of warriors carried. The lightly clad warriors or heavy armored forces did not carry sheathed or unsheathed a blade similar to the one he was currently holding that he picked up from the ground. It dawns on him suddenly. It's what isn't there that he was looking for. There are a third set of warrior's weapons, but,... there are no bodies of the third set of the warriors themselves. Mercy pulls his blade from his scabbard unsheathing it. Holding both weapons now, he compares their construction and markings side by side. The weapons are almost identical, accept the metal of the blade was much older in the imposter blade. It was a metal that was foreign and unknown to Mercy. He flips the imposter blade over to find glyph markings on the blade just above the hilt. The glyphs appear to be an older derivative of his language, an older dialect. What he held in his dominant hand, was not an imposter or an uncanny replica blade at all. The blade was a blade of his people, the blade was that of a celestial's of Elohim.

Thirty-Eight

ILLUMINATED CENTER

"Abandon hope?... Never!"

~Mercy

Mercy re-sheaths his main blade to single handedly wield the much older ancestral blade. He again raises the sword to the on-guard position with both of his hands firmly wrapped around the hilt.

"I am an Emissary of the Most High! I compel you to reveal yourself and step into the light and cease all treacherous hostility."

After a long break, a strong gust of wind blows from behind Mercy

"The only hostility is that which you have brought with you Emissary of the Most High. Only you hold the blade," says the second voice.

"Then you know by personal account whose behalf and authority I speak on?" says Mercy.

A rushing gust again forces Mercy barely off his feet when he swings his sword tip downward and drives the blade into the dirt anchoring himself to the ground. When the gust has passed and the land again fell silent, he pulls the sword from dirt and again rises into an on-guard stance. After a long while of silence, another rushing and forceful wind starts to race past him from behind this time. He shifts his weight to compensate and again digs his sword into the dirt of Olympus to anchor and steady himself.

"Follow the path to Desolation if you so choose Celestial of Elohim," one of the voices says.

A second gust of wind from the opposite direction pushes against Mercy swinging him in a one-hundred-and-eighty-degree spin. His body slides in a half circle.

"A warning Emissary if you so choose to proceed, there are no weapons to be permitted beyond the threshold of the Orion Temple. To disobey this decree will result in you as motionless as those at your feet who once themselves were so full of...life."

The winds of the land again fall silent. Mercy pulls his blade from dirt and rock of Olympus, this time in a low guard.

Thinking over his situation, it became clear to Mercy, that whatever beings he was dealing with were way more powerful then him. If he stands a chance of delivering the message he would have to acquiesce.

"I understand and submit to the will of my hosts." Mercy drops the found blade and unsheathes his own and discards it.

"Show me the path to Desolation," says Mercy

Laughter erupts from behind him sliding him slightly forward.

"Granted, Emissary."

Red and purplish colored lighting strikes the ground igniting various bodies engulfing them in conflagrations. Flames rose high, but the bodies did not burn. The blazing bodies creates a path that leads toward the huge superstructure in the middle of the decayed city. It made a way through the labyrinth of winding streets that were gridlocked with debris and strewn corpses. Mercy takes a breath then walks ever forward into the unknown down the lit path. He doesn't dare look behind him and give his hosts any idea that there is another that follows. That is, if they weren't aware already.

"On this path you walk to Desolation Emissary Mercy, abandon hope," says the first voice.

Mercy's path to the superstructure was cut short by being shown the way by the lit path. He enters the doors of the barrel vault's entrance pushing against the wind.

"Abandon hope?... Never!" says Mercy.

****

From the distant shadows Airesmiss watched the exchange that happened between Mercy and whatever force he was pit against. She had agreed that no matter what, she would not emerge from hiding although for the briefest of moments, she almost did if only to aid him. Her promise kept her hidden sure, but she knows it wasn't the order that her liege gave her alone that kept her concealed, no it was something else, some other feeling that gave her pause and immobilized her with hesitance and the mind to remain quiet. As if she couldn't act even if she wanted to. It was like the feeling of when Mercy said, 'imagine if I'd not return... that is fear.' Airesmiss was afraid. That is what kept her still.

After the long exchange between Mercy and the voices, she watches a trail of burning bodies ignite leaving a path for Mercy. He follows them toward the center of this barren place. Seeing her chance and seizing opportunity, Airesmiss moves swiftly staying concealed in the shadows. Swiftly she moves to keep Mercy in sight. Suddenly her mind felt a twinge of pain and followed by a constant forceful buzzing sound in her ears. It was enough of a high pitch sound to knock her to her knees. Lingering in pain for a few moments the buzzing stops and is replaced by a tinge of a wind. Then she hears it... words constructed in her mind that are not her own and are carried by that very same tinge of wind.

"Ahh! A new mind to touch. It is new, but familiar. Yessssss! Newly created, but an old creation... Ahh, yes, young one.... It has all happened before and will happen again..."

Just like that, the voice is gone, the pain and buzzing that accompanied it disappeared as well. Airesmiss emerged from the fog of thought and realized that she was rising from a knee. She had no idea that she'd even had taken one during the intrusion on her mind. When her wits are again focused, Mercy has been long out of sight. Shaking the remaining cobwebs from her mind, she notices the once burning bodies that were once lit so brightly were now only smoldering lit embers, but they were still cindering enough to follow so, she does.

Since entering the city proper behind Mercy, Airesmiss breath left her at the sight of the untold number of the dead. Never had she seen such a lifeless void. She could not understand what she was witnessing as the magnitude of corpses was indeed magnanimous. It gave her pause, but not much time to reconcile the trauma. She was following Mercy and could not let him down. It was of her mind to deal with the trauma later when Mercy could explain what was happening, why wasn't anyone moving? She wound her way through the lifeless void staying on Mercy's heels following his path.

Imitating Mercy along the path, she stops and closely observes the bodies as Mercy had. She suspects this place is not a part of the Sadohedranicverse, that it stands apart. A place such as this has no business being a part of the perfection that her lord has carved out for everyone. This place is dark and beyond ominous. Hesitation again takes over her footsteps as she contemplates whether to abandon the trail. If she turns back, what would her options be? She was brought here on the wings of a celestial. If he were unable to return, she would be lost here. Such a thought triggers another. What if neither one of them are destined to leave this place?

Mercy is supposed to deliver a message and retrieve a response. Airesmiss knew that much, but a passing thought told her what if him not returning is the response to the message; that would be message in itself would it not? The thought flees as fast as it enters her mind. She wills herself to move forward and shift her mind away from dark thoughts. Mercy will be fine and she will be fine. Elohim will protect them. Giving herself a much-needed pep talk boosts her self-confidence. Airesmiss makes her mind up to pursue Mercy who was no longer her idle, no longer a friend, but her love. There was no more room for fear any longer, love now quickens her pace to make up ground and find the one thing that all living beings need... Mercy.

As she makes up ground for lost time, the thought of not returning home revisits her again and again. The fear of being stuck here returns constantly consuming her. It makes her breath quicken at just the thought. The weight of this place was unlike any world she's been to. Here, this place causes her to tire, although she doesn't have the word for the feeling of exhaustion. She's never experienced it till now. All she knows is that every so often she has to stop to inhale and exhale heavily until her breathing regulated enough for her to continue. After catching her breath, she again pushes forward.

Airesmiss' mind is of a singular focus of not losing sight of Mercy, so much so she misses a step and trips over a protrusion from the ground. She falls forward banging her knee hard. Her hands both instinctually grabs her knee while she winces in incredible pain. This is another feeling she has no words for. She forces herself to her feet in spite of pain, feeling a warm sensation creeping down her leg, curiosity draws her attention to look. There was a tear in the knee of her pant leg and a dark reddish viscous liquid seeped through it. Closer inspection revealed the liquid was not from the tear of the pant leg, but is coming from her knee, her flesh. It runs like Manna Nectar. Feeling another emotion, she turns and kicks the object she tripped over suddenly realizing its Mercy's weapon. His sword, named Tried. Next to it are glyphs written in the dirt by the impression of a heel of a boot, perhaps. The glyphs read... *take it*! Which is followed by a separate glyph beneath it that said one letter, *M*.

****

The journey through the vaulted entrance and towards the superstructure's center is uneventful and silent. The voices that Mercy heard have long since been silenced as he continues to follow a now glowing path of what he could best describe as muted lightning. It flashed and crackled bearing electricity of different colors, but it made no sound nor did it dissipate. It just continuously ran the length of the twisting and turning halls along its bottom molding. As Mercy continues to traverse the inner labyrinth, it takes determination and sheer will not to think of his silently moving shadow that trails him in secret. He puts her out his mind thinking of Airesmiss as little as possible. He feels the beings that he'd made contact with are more than likely formidable, but he truly couldn't say how formidable, because he does not understand the truest extent of their capabilities. To think of Airesmiss incessantly could inadvertently give her away filled him with dread. Who knows what fate could befall her here at the edge of reality of all living things? To underestimate his hosts and their abilities could betray her.

Damn! he thinks. She isn't even supposed to be here. It was his fear of being forgotten that made him ask her to tag along. He twists his face in slight disgust, because he allowed fear to make him make such an un-fair and regretful decision as to invite someone else into this possible treacherous and treasonous terror. And let there been no mistake, this mission had to be somewhat treasonous, otherwise more parties than just himself and the King would have been made privy.

Mercy follows the muted lightning trail to a set of inner doors of the superstructure which forms its inner interior which is a massive temple construction. The inner entrance doors are a work of ordinate true majestic work. Its grandeur and design without doubt rivals Zero Realm's. This is no ordinary construction; this is a construction work of a Power's Corps caliber builder. The opulence is more than words could express. Etchings made of black glass onyx, bends and swirls glyphs of a language not known to Mercy. It's a language that must have fallen with those slain outside and inside the temple. There were more etchings in gold that shown wavy squiggly lines that could represent wind if he had to guess. Other designs that set above the wind was that of possibly wa-ter and lightning.

Approaching the massive entrance, he notices the heaviest concen-tration of bodies. It's clear a major assault took place here. Maybe a move to take the temple if again he had to guess, but forces must have repelled the attackers holding them here. A line was drawn. This was the last stand of those with the etched lightning bolts upon their armor.

Mercy steps over the last of the bodies and into the vestibule. The area is clean and untouched by any calamity once through. As he turns to look back, he sees the bodies have vanished. There are no signs of destruction or debris. *Pocket dimension,* is the first thing that comes to mind when he crossed the threshold. He turns back and continues forward where the landscape turned to gleaming white walls with more etchings in gold and Satarie, a precious metal that can only be found around the three billion year mark of creation. The etches are works of art, a depiction of possibly what has occurred to make such a place come about. There are etchings of biped creatures that had wings on the heels of their feet. There were more etchings of bipeds standing on oceans with staffs that had three pronged tips. There are also other etchings that show great pyramidical constructs that appeared to have masses of bipeds emerging from them. He could not know their true stories, because for the first time ever, he could not read the language that was scribed under the pictographs. He didn't know a language! That has never happened in all of his existence. All was known to the Celestial Caste and what wasn't was sure located in the Omnipotent A.I. system contained within his gauntlet that was now obsolete, and bequeathed to another.

Still Mercy takes in the sights and continues walking till he passes another set of massive double platinum door with a deep gold etched circle that runs across both doors. If they are opened, the design upon each door would contain one half the circle. In the middle of the circle is a pyramid with a lightning bolt through its center.

"Abandon hope and enter, Emissary Mercy," a deep voice again thunders.

Here within the confines of this temple, the boom of the voice has lost its forceful whirlwind power. Here, it is just a deep voice that carried authority. Here in these halls of the massive temple, it appears his host may be his equal and that was okay with him.

"I assure you, we are not your equals Emissary, but the one who sent you is another matter entirely... Enter messenger and keep reverence before those that have graced these plains long before you were thought manifested to the tangible."

So, my hosts can read thoughts, thinks Mercy.

The massive doors slowly open and with its opening a revelation is revealed. The inner chamber is infinity where a series of thrones sit at its center. Mercy's steps are slow and methodical as he enters into center of the cylindrical dome's interior of the temple. His attention is casted all over as he slowly and methodically looks around. What he thought was a temple isn't a temple at all. The layout is that of a massive three hundred sixty-degree coliseum with a downward slope toward the true epicenter. The inside of the coliseum is one thousandth times larger than that of the exterior. This fact alone gave sign this place is a work of a god-level being . There are familiarities to the building schematics that mirrored heavily the palace of Elohim's or it could have been the vice versa. *Wouldn't that be a revelation* thinks Mercy. His mind turns from the opulence of the dimensional space to the glyphs that adorned the inside crown molding. The molding solidified that celestials had a hand in this place construction. They left a clear signature of the Powers Corp on all their work. The molding was no different. This room, this coliseum, this temple or whatever it is, it has roots in the Powers Corps. That's reassuring and disheartening all at the same time. Are the hosts friend or are they foe?

In the center of the coliseum ring are two beings standing opposite of each other with arms outstretched. Thick continuous strands of lightning bolts emit from the hands of one of the beings. His power is a stream of unyielding energy being poured into a gargantuan black and blue swirling portal vortex. On the other side opposite of the lightning-wielding being is a just as equally powerful second being discharging an unyielding stream of wind that was so powerful, it appears as jet streams of fast moving clouds being discharged into the portal.

Hesitant at first, Mercy eventually finds the will and strength of character to step forward. "I am Mercy from the house of Elohim," he says, beginning his descent down the slope toward the beings.

"ELOHIM!" a voice booms from within the portal.

The two large in size beings holding court of power with the portal gazes intensify at the portal itself. Both change positions crossing one another, one ducking low beneath the other as they switch sides. Once set apart again opposite of each other, they simultaneously close their outstretched arms into a shoving gesticulation and forcefully push their emitting powers into an intensifying concentrated beam that focuses into the vortex pushing back an entity that lies there within. Mercy couldn't be sure, but it looked as if the two of them were struggling with all they could muster to keep the entity encased within the portal. The vortex closes slightly. Both the beings looked a bit relieved and again find their calm.

Mercy studies the two beings. They aren't youthful, but not old either. Their look is one of being worn, having seen too many moons. One that crackles lightning, is of a darkened complexion, yet his hair is white as pure snow and unkempt as if he's never been groomed. He wears the armor of the lightning insignia that is similar to the bodies that plagued this dismal place. The other being is of a fairer complexion, yet, he's dressed in more Saharan armor, similar to the opposing forces of bodies that were strewn around and mixed in with the armored bodies.

The voice from within the portal that cried Elohim is new, and very much different from the ones Mercy heard since he started to draw near this place. The voice is more than authoritative. It's god level. It is ancient and anachronistic. Crazy and unbelievable as it sounds to himself, especially this being the first time ever in this obfuscated realm, Mercy realizes he knows the voice as well as he knew his own. The sound of it caused him to be overcome with great delirious joy at first. His pace quickened toward the center, towards the portal. When he arrives at the portal about to catch a glimpse of the face of the figure inside, Mercy is forced to his knees by an invisible might that he assumes is one of the two beings doing.

"GO NO FURTHER, EMMISSARY," shouts the constant watchers in unison each struggling to hold the portal's vortex intact.

Combined, the force of their warning sends Mercy flying backward crashing into the face of the coliseum's outer most wall. He strikes with such force darkness instantly consumes him temporarily sending him to the realm of unconsciousness. He limp body slides down the wall slowly leaving a bloodstain trail. Moments later, Mercy comes too and slowly stands. Pain nags the right side of his chest where he impacted the hardest and his eye is swollen and bloody from slamming into the wall as well. Mercy's hands shoot to both places of pain instinctively to cradle the area. It's then he notices even more pain emanating from his hand which draws his attention. He's horrified at the sight of a mangled and horribly disfigured set of broken fingers. His left hand was smashed when it hit the wall first followed by the force of his body. This place truly is weakening him. This Olympus is a place meant to kills celestials.

Frowning, Mercy grabs his fingers and pulls them straight. The crackling and crunch of the bones are soon drowned out by his own ear-piercing scream. The pain goes from sharp to subsiding throb almost instantly. Mercy spits blood and then slowly makes his way back to the center yet again. This time, he isn't worried about the pair; he's focused on the one in the vortex, the one whose voice he knows. As he limps closer, a face became visible in the vortex of the portal. It is a being that is bright and illuminous, his countenance makes Mercy almost unable to look upon him directly without refocusing. The celestial has to squint to be able to finally grab an eye full. Although contained within the portal, the figure inside isn't that imposing. He's only as massive as the beings outside holding the portal.

"Come see," says the voice from the portal.

Mercy steps closer toward the beings of energy sure to stay behind them, but enough to see who's inside the portal. For the first time, Mercy saw the face in the portal and instantly regretted the gaze that glared back at him then eventually right through him. Who he saw looking through him was clear as the waters of Zero Realm.

"How is this possible" are the only words Mercy is able to muster before his world turns to darkness after the lightning wielding being turns his hand toward Mercy striking him in the face with bright flash of purple lightning. Mercy is robbed of his vision completely.

****

Elohim's Palace: Presently

Elohim just continues to observe Airesmiss and remains quite still saying nothing. Yeshua again looks at his father in hopes of an explanation, or at this point, just some reaction. Seeing none, Yeshua returns his attention back to Airesmiss.

"Continue, Airesmiss! What happened after Mercy eyes darkened? Did you see who was within the portal?" asks the Prince.

Looking up at Yeshua, she continues, "The link was severed. Whatever happened after he was hit with that light severed the gauntlet's connection. After everything went dark, I opened my eyes and found that I was still outside the superstructure and had still not been discovered. I hid and waited outside for his return, fore I could not follow where he walked and not have been discovered."

Airesmiss shifts slightly and uncomfortably as she is dealing with reliving the trauma. "He was inside for days or so it felt. It could have been weeks or forever. I told you, time moves amiss there."

Yeshua stands and walks away, pondering her revelations for a moment before returning and kneeling down to Airesmiss's eye level again. "And what was happening to the structure that you were observing?"

"The structure was silent for all of those days that he was inside except for the sound of a slight humming emanating from the structure. Other than that there was no activity until a massive bright light preceded the beginning of series of chain reactions that looked like the start of an explosion... At least that is what I believe happened. All fell to darkness for me as well after I saw the start of the blast. When I awoke, I was no longer on Olympus. I was on a planet named Suxcerran; a planet on the last known outskirts of the Sadohedranicverse. When I awoke, I only remember that I was hurting all over, but my body felt right again is best I can describe it. My expedient healing had recovered, however there were scars that remained which I had incurred on the surface of that place," she says attempting to gesture with her head movements and eyes pointing out certain areas about the rest of her body.

"When I had fully come too and my senses restored, I realized that I was on a scarcely habited planet with low gravity so, escaping would not be a problem. A double supply of Manna and satchels of Manna Nectar along with Mercy's armor laid next to me. His armor was pretty banged up to start off with when I first saw it without him in it, but it was functional. It worsened under my care on the long journey that it took to get back here... Prince Yeshua, I do not know the fate of Mercy, just the fate of the one who sent him. The one who sits unscathed and unaffected by choice," says Airesmiss attempting to again gaze at Elohim. "But, if this armor that was lying next to me is any indication and could talk, it would have said that Mercy is no longer with us. Whatever was in that structure took Mercy, removing him from all worlds, realms and reality."

"So it seems," says Elohim as he stands.

Airesmiss's gaze, along with Michael's, find the ground. She doesn't dare look upon him as he speaks. His countenance is still too great for her in her present condition.

"Etherealtorial...!" says Elohim, calling his personal guard to re-assemble.

The blue and gold armored cladded guards walk from their positions on the wall reforming a singular line. Every other guard in line sidesteps right, creating two columns.

Elohim raise his hand manipulating the gravitonic forces around Airesmiss lifting her into the air. He stretches his hand wide causing the remaining shackles to fall away and Airesmiss to stretch out in an X fashion. She looks as if she's prostrated in midair. With a flick of his finger the armor tears from her body and falls to the ground ringing hollow across the white marbled floors. Her illegally gained armor is appropriated and then swept away by a seemingly invisible wind leaving the space beneath her clear. Armor stripped away and the Omnipotent gauntlet confiscated, she's left in her garments that she first sat out across the cosmos with almost 6 billion years prior. It's beaten to hell.

Airesmiss garments were a testament to the Power that sewn each stitch. Her garment that was worn underneath the armor, is torn, dirty, ripped in various places with blood stains throughout, but the tailor of Zero Realm fabrics held. Where there are tears in the fabric, there is old lacerations to her skin that had left visible scars and poorly healed gashes that she's received over the course of her finding her way back to Zero Realm. Each scar no doubt told stories in themselves.

How resourceful she must have been to have made it from the edge of creation home without the aided power of Omnipotent or flight, thought Michael.

Yeshua turns his head slightly from the scars wincing. It triggers unpleasant memories under Caiaphas and Pilot during his brief course correction interlude on Earth when he took on the form of his father's most beloved jewels, humans. Elohim closes his hand letting Airesmiss lightly fall to the ground. She just somberly falls to her knees before the King outstretching her arms palms up crying tears. Whether they were of anger or sadness had yet to be known.

"Etherealtorial... take her away. Make sure she she's fed and restored. Take her to convalescence and have her injuries tended to. Afterwards have her garments replaced."

The Etherealtorial nods. "It has been ordered my king, so shall it be done."

"After she's been tended to, she is to be placed into protective care until I have rendered judgment of the facts given. Once I have, I will call for this trial to be reconvened."

Yeshua turns, eyeing his father. Letting his eyes be felt upon him, he turns his attention yet again back to Airesmiss.

Elohim slightly waves his fingers for her to be taken away. He waves his hand a second time and the remaining Etherealtorial take their leave as well.

Michael hesitates and does not move when commanded.

"Something you wish to add, Captain?" says Elohim.

Michael stands, facing his king. His mouth parts to speak, but he decides to hold his tongue.

Elohim nods, knowing what the Arch was going to say and then dismisses him with another wave of his hand. "All will be revealed at the appropriate time, Captain. Facts are not yet known to the quandary that was Mercy and Airesmiss."

Michael wishes to remain silent, but he must speak now. Not in the interest of Airesmiss, but in the interest of his sister now in pursuit of Painell.

"I have but one question, Lord, before I take my leave; the route that Mercy had taken to reach far beyond any expanse of celestials, would that route traveled by Mercy take one past the planet that Airesmiss found herself own after the events of what she claimed to have transpired at this Olympus?"

Michael swipes his gauntlet, dragging a small 4D holographic map of the Sadoverse in front of him.

Yeshua stares at Michael for a second briefly wondering why ask such a question, and then his gaze returns to his Father.

He doesn't even need to glance at the intricate map. "It would," answers Elohim.

"One final question, my Lord, if I may ask in the interest of protection of all that you survey. If one were to travel out into the expanse across the Aether toward the last know coordinates of Mercy and this Olympus, who would have a chance of returning if Mercy did not?"

Yeshua again looks at Michael. "Expound, Captain!"

"My prince, Mercy was as formidable as I or any of the Archs based off the report given by Airesmiss. And I have to say, I believe her. She came too far and through much to now tell tales. Which goes to say, if her report is believed, then Mercy has more than likely been vanquished and whatever message he carried has been lost with no—",

"Reply has been given, Captain," Elohim says, cutting him off. "Airesmiss has returned. In her doing so tells of an impending threat that is or soon will be on the way. Make no mistake, Arch in all of this including these proceedings, Imperial is still a lethal threat to the one sovereignty, but what lies beyond the Aether if loosed is fatality manifested that I alone will deal with if it comes to that."

Michael eyes widen just remembering the path he started Gabriel on in pursuit of Painell. It sounds eerily similar to the path that Airesmiss described. *Impossible*, thinks Michael. *The way was blocked by undisturbed Aether. Nothing had swathed that path since my existence.* The thought of his sister heading for such a place causes the captain to rise to his feet abruptly. It then hits him: *What of before my existence? Could the Aether had refilled the missing gaps? Or could the way have been sealed and wiped from Omnipotent? If it was sealed and wiped, that could have only been done by—* Michael stares at Elohim accusatorily for a mere second. He bows, keeping protocol and turns, running from the throne room, boots clacking hard against the marble.

Yeshua turns to his father. "What are you not telling me?"

Thirty-Nine

OFTEN BEST LAID PLANS

"Things are beautiful and harmonious amongst the chaos because of imperfections."

~Fatetanen

Zero Realm: Iayhoten, Angel's Spire

Jophiel leaves the convalescent ward taking a right down a long empty hall carrying a bounded set of parchments at his side. His brow is furrowed with intense thought as he congeals notions of a plan to help Jericho deal a blow to Imperial and yet survive the encounter. The beginning of the idea of attacking Imperial directly struck him during the conclave at the Table of Doves when talk of choice ruled the conversation. His delay in speaking on it was only because he still had to work out the laws of ramifications to even know if he could implore his plan. If miscalculated in any way, it would mean a quick death for him and the attempted assassination of a demi-god left disastrously in tatters and a world open to retaliation. Jophiel opens the platinum cover bounded book of parchments and studies it pages intently as he proceeds down the silent hallway.

The hall did not use to be so silent when one traversed them. There used to be the bustling of citizenry, Powers, Choiretics and Archs, but as of late the halls echo, because of the emptiness as most of the protectors of the realm have rushed abroad to put out fires across the Sadohedranicverse under Michael's symphonic direction. Missions that now seem forever ongoing and endless consumes protector's lives and time; time that if not have been monopolized would have lent aid to solidifying Jophiel's plan early on. Cause and effect again become enemy of the Archs. Zadkiel was lent to the cause of protecting the judge in Germany which put him in direct conflict with Canceranian. Effect, the resulting battle left him inactive and his intricate knowledge of ramifications lost for the time being.

Jophiel made Zadkiel a big part of constructing his plan in its conceptual stage because there was no Arch as well versed as him in the laws of ramification, but that was unlikely now as he was still laid up and barely conscious for more than a few minutes at a time. He was still on the mend after his encounter with Canceranian. Powers kept him sedated in an induced coma state while recovering in the convalescent ward of the Spire. His wounds were grave and it was a question as to his survival, but survive he did and the only assistance he is able to give in his moments of elucidation, is only to tell Jophiel where he might find the possible answer to his conundrum of ramifications. To Jophiel, without him knowing what he was exactly looking for was akin to a needle in a haystack.

Boots clacking repetitiously fast and hard across the white marble floor draws Jophiel's attention from thought. The captain was fast incoming, whatever purpose he pursued was certainly paramount. Jophiel quickly steps aside allowing the captain complete passage. Michael stops for no words and runs past Jophiel at a full-on sprint disappearing into the elevatal beam of light at the end of the hall just beyond convalescent ward. Something of great importance moved him with purpose toward the Spire's War room without delay. Jophiel looks back watching to see if the captain needs him, but seeing him phase into the transport beam not to return, he figures the captain could handle the situation without him. He continues down the hall to a separate set of elevatal beams that will take him towards a series of their centralized sets of collective knowledge.

Emerging from the elevatal beam of light an instant later, Jophiel passes the Omnipotent's Record Collective wing. What he needed was not so much a matter of record. What he needed was an answer to his hypothesis, which he based off past assumptions of contacts with Imperial. Jophiel decided the best place to find his answer would be further down the hall inside the Infinitude Chamber of Collective Knowledge. Infinitude at its basis is every question that has been asked and answered since the occurrence of the Sadohedranicverse erupted into existence. It was said that the first star itself birthed in pain asked the question, why me? It was answered by Elohim and recorded. It has been so ever since. There is very little the Omnipotent is not aware of. If by chance there is a situation that presents itself as an unknown quandary, it is expected that an answer can be arrived at with a combination of questions already replied to and ingenuity of Zero Realm law. The trick is, finding an Arch well versed in navigating the incredible amount of information. Zadkiel was a pro second to only Uriel at navigating information.

Entering the Infinitude Library, Jophiel glances left at the room marked in glyph, *Eschatology*. The way was sealed and only three celestials held the key to the opening of the chamber. Beyond those doors laid the culmination and masterpiece of Fate's work. Elohim may have been the architect, but Fate was the master builder of the living threads of Sadoverse. Upon his written word; every living thing that has been, is currently, and still to come was written by him. Even those of the Judas Paradox, whose lives are born to a preordained causality rendering an ordained effect, an ultimate kick in the ass to free will.

Jophiel smirked, as he passed the sealed doors, because curiosity was the base of everything. No other Arch has seen Fate's greatly talked about and often criticized masterpiece except the monarchs that approved it. He would be lying if he didn't say he wanted a peak at it. And why shouldn't he want to sneak a peek? Celestials like all other species of intelligence were never told if they too were included in Fate's planning down to an expiration date. To see his destiny would ease his mind of the plan he is mentally constructing in his head to help the judge take down Imperial. If his fate was already weaved at the plans execution, then of course he would one, say it was a bad plan... Two, alter it. But, what if altering it because he knew what would happen was the plan that brought him to that said end. It was all too confusing and probably better left to Fate now that he thought about it.

Firmly inside the chamber of infinitude, there is an infinity of shelves that draw an exaggerated exasperated sigh from Jophiel. The time it would take him to navigate to an answer, the third age would have come and gone two times over.

"You should start in the age of the Nephilim, age of Lamech," says Fate walking up behind Jophiel. "I'm sure you too are looking to adjudicate Imperial."

Looking over his shoulder at his older brother, Jophiel sardonically grins before returning his attention back to his task at hand. "I was sure that I had the infinitude alone this evening... How long have you been back?"

"Just recently," answered Fate. "I tried my hand at manipulating what won't."

Fate walks up next to Jophiel looking down at the bounded parchments of ramifications. "Just as you are here looking to subvert the law of interaction with Imperial, another situation trying to manipulate what won't. I understand though," says Fate. I understand why you are here. I too played a game of chance in an attempt to control the expressed free will of a mighty Seraphim by talking reason."

"And did it work brother, am I here in the infinitude for not?" Jophiel asks.

Fate shakes his head. I regret that the Seraphim has lived long and constructed a story in his mind that is cemented as the Aether that binds Sadohedranicverse. To him, gaining sovereignty to become the hero of his own narrative has trumped all higher cognitive thought of reason. I thought with time Lucifer would come to see the flaw of his plan and return to reason. In speaking with him, I see that he cannot. When speaking to him, it was clear that he loved us more than himself, but there lied the problem. Fear of change, fear of loss twisted his mind, twisted him.

Fate outstretches his hand and leaves it wanton. Jophiel sighs and places the book into his waiting hand. Flipping the parchments open, Fate studies the page, then runs his fingers over the signature of Uriel that still glows an orangish blue.

Before speaking with Lucifer, I must admit that even I suffered from the naivete that just maybe the will and foresight of Elohim would be altered and reason restored to Lucifer..."

"But it cannot, can it brother?" says Jophiel. "Because Elohim said it, it must be."

"Because he said it, it must be," repeated Fate. "Lucifer must have his day to ascend. It was written and so shall it be done. I just fear that before his day of attempted ascension his want and incessant need to save us all will ultimately change the Sadohedranicverse more than it already has. If his machinations are not swayed and Imperial destroyed, what he so dearly loves will ultimately be undone at a level of catastrophic omega."

Turning back to the shelves Jophiel activates his gauntlet to navigate them. "What do you think I'm here trying to do Seraphim. I'm here looking for a solution to the conundrum of the Imperial. It is ridiculous that I am even here trying. You were absent from the Table of Doves during the conclave. Your input could have been valuable. Then again, maybe not. If I think about it, you've been absent since before Glayden. I'm trying to understand what good are you? You could end this single handedly if the stories I've heard about you are to be believed. It is told that you are the oldest and most brilliant of us all. You are Fate... writer of the masterpiece of life. I work even now to do my part in ending the Imperial threat. What do you do, but talk treaties and reason?"

A smirk crosses Fatetanen's face as he passes the platinum bounded parchment book back to Jophiel. "Jophiel ask me what troubles you so about my existence."

"I will... All that power, and yet you do nothing but stand by. If you are going to continue to stand by, the least you can do is tell me if my efforts are in vain. You know the path of all living things, right? If my plan is to succeed, you would have mapped it out to the conclusion of his will. Tell me if I make the right moves that will bring about a chance for the judge."

Shaking his head, Fate lightly knocks Jophiel's hand away from the control of his gauntlet ending the navigation of the shelves. "You've gone too far in your search. Dial in thirty-seven west and rotate twenty-two degrees down. That should start the shelves containing the age of Lamech. Zadkiel, should really be helping you with this. He's the pro at ramifications." Fate then remembers. "Right, he's still convalescing."

Jophiel turns looking Fate in his eyes. Tears start to well in the lower corners of his eyes, only Fate doesn't know if they are tears of sadness or madness."

"Ask me plainly brother," says Fate.

Jophiel stands chest to chest with the oldest of his kin. "Do you know how all this end? In your masterpiece, you've had to have written an ending. I mean are we wasting our time preventing something that we can't? Do you know my plan and if it will work? Do you know all these things and play it as a game of chance? Curse you Fatetanen, are you Fate or not?

Fate does not move, but continues to look his brother in the eyes. After a few intense seconds he releases a long hefty sigh and nods for Jophiel to follow him. "Follow me," says Fate.

Jophiel is hesitant at first. He looks back to the shelves thinking he needs to start as soon as possible in locating his answer of the odds of survivability, but the lure to speak with Fate a little while longer is more tempting. He follows trailing behind the old Seraphim.

"I am no conundrum little brother. There is no secret that I keep from any of you that but simply ask. Secrets are what has destroyed us. Secrets are what led to Glayden."

They negotiate turns and winding halls back toward the entrance of the Infinitude. They head for Fate's Chamber of Eschatology.

Fate looking back over his shoulder, "I suspect like the others, you too always wanted to ask questions of destiny since my return from exile?

Jophiel shakes his head. You must understand that you were a mystery after the battle of Glayden. While we fought, you stayed in your ivory white tower of the Spire. Not once did you step upon the battlefield to fight for the king, fight for us."

"You say, I did not fight on the day of Glayden? What do you think drove me into exile?" asks Fate.

Waving his hand in front of the first glyph, a latch unlocks and the glyph breaks in half exposing a wrist size hole. Fate places his gauntleted hand inside further unlocking the door to Eschatology. He pushes the double doors inward. "Follow me and witness what no other classed celestial has seen. Not that it's a secret but, they've never asked."

Fate and Jophiel enters the chamber, but not just any chamber, this one was more than it appears. The Powers Corp upon its creation gave this one great time and care like the Chasm Hall. Eschatology was a pocketed dimension attached to the Spire that holds an almost infinity of shelves that contains books for every life lived, is living, and still to come. Every species; from plant, to rock, to gas, to elemental, to even dark matters have a name on the spine of a multitude of books. Within is an order to the chaos of infinity. Everything has a place and shelved in order from beginning to end by Fate himself. He sectioned it off, by galaxies, dating back to the beginning. Once sectioned by galaxies, he then started with the order of Aether down to the quantum universe. It was an intricate display of detail sure to cover even the speck of skin dust that shed from living creatures.

Jophiel looks in amazement at the intricacies of the chamber. Even the Omnipotent collective's records were not as organized. Jophiel use to consider himself impressed when Uriel use to oversee the Omnipotent Collective. No longer. Zadkiel, wasn't bad as a replacement for the records, but he was no Uriel. The scale of precision that had to be employed was on the level of magnanimous, concentration unapparelled. Shelves upon shelves were simply made into a beauty of a symphonic cord. Madness had become a serene symphony orchestrated by one intelligent being that will play the score until the last star on the last day of the ending of all things. Just at the mere sight of the scale of work completed by the Seraphim, garnered unending respect for Fatetanen in the eyes of Jophiel. His awe of the oldest of them was immeasurable. Then out of nowhere, a question popped into his mind that unsettled him. Awe turned to fear if a guess had to be taken on the pangs of emotion.

"I don't think anyone has ever asked this brother, but what happens to your symphony if you fall to Palengrad?

Fate motions Jophiel to follow him a little further to the balcony. Once outside Fate looks over the edge. He searches till he finds what he considers the perfect example for explanation.

"No one has ever asked me of my work in detail," says Fate. "My work has become expected and accepted as that of Death's. Look closely down there. Look at the Earth and then look past it and you will find there is an imperfection an anomaly in the build of the masterpiece called the Sadohedranicverse. All master builds have them, anomalies. The most intricate of mathematical equations have them and are coded to expect them and adapt to keep the build running smoothly with algorithms. If you think about it to it most basic elemental core, even Elohim's, creation has an inherent flaw that is there within the build, but we all choose to overlook it."

"Impossible," says Jophiel. "Elohim is perfection."

"Lucifer is the anomaly to perfection. For the experiment of life to work harmoniously and to become a thing of beauty, I had to rewrite the plan to encompass and account for anomalies to the said stated original rules that Elohim framed around reality. Lucifer's treachery was originally unaccounted for in my initial writing. That is why perfection failed. I was given a rule that I had permission for one rewrite. In its inception of the idea, it was thought maybe to rewrite a certain section or domain of reality. I never thought it would be the whole of time and space."

"So, you believe that Elohim did lie in creating perfection?" asks Jophiel.

Fate shaking his head emphatically, "Elohim did not lie as Lucifer proposes. Not unless you get technical about your ideals of omission. No... I suspect without contempt that Elohim has told all facets of his truth. Yet, it is his truth and therefore subjective to us the created. Which is rightfully so, as the creator's truth is absolute, or there we must believe, because if not, the integrity of all of this collapses. Things are beautiful and harmonious amongst the chaos because of imperfections."

Jophiel, now leaning over the railing of the balcony following Fate's eyes to what he wanted him to observe. "So, you wrote the path, but do not know the outcome is what you're saying? And you don't know the outcome because the anomalies are a mathematical certainty to occur making you're whole algorithm of prediction obsolete?"

"Exactly," Fate says smiling. "Look there!" Fate points to a small bar just outside of Ardenne France.

Forty

NOW WE COME TO AN ACCORD

Ardenne France: Forget Me Not Saloon - Night

Blue purplish hair laid to the right, revealing a close shaved cut on the left, Grand Prior Asia Riggs slams back a shot of Russian Vodka. Her red Templar cross embroidered necktie is loosened and top collar undone as she attempts to calm a stressed day of planning. Her black blazer sits underneath her draped over her barstool's cushioned seat. She raises her finger for another. The Barkeep sees her and gives her wink that she's been acknowledged and another drink will be coming to her directly.

****

"Let's take her for example Jophiel, do you see the thin reddish purple infused line that passes directly through her body?" says Fate.

"Yeah."

"See how that line follows a path out the door then it turns a darker color

and grows broad indicating that she will soon be running which will cause her to exert more effort."

"Yeah, I see it. That is how we know where will she will be at any given point and time. That is standard on all species. From here all I see is a webbed network of lines that you've drawn. The world is racked with them. Sometimes they are hard to see because they're so dense."

"That is the solid mathematical portion of the masterpiece of what I've written." Says Fate. "Now look closer at what is transpiring."

****

A small glass Vodka slides down the smooth top wooden bar into the right hand of Asia Riggs. She gives a dual nod to the small framed Barkeep. One gesture of the nod signifying a thanks, the other an invite to step down to engage in conversation. Barkeep replies with another wink and finger stating one minute before giving a seductive smile back in reply.

"She is cute sexy thing, isn't she?" says a gentleman deciding to sit on the barstool to the left of Asia. He throws his black fedora on the bar and raises a finger for the barkeep to notice him as well.

"I don't think she'd be interested in you," says Asia still keeping eye contact with the Barkeep.

"Oh, I don't know, I hear I'm quick witted, decently handsome, and very funny."

"And extremely arrogant," says Asia taking a slight swig off her shot.

"There is that... or maybe it's confidence in my ability to be charming."

Asia turns toward the stranger, and immediately takes in a sigh and rolls her eyes at the vestment dressed priest.

"A little late night communion wine for you Father?" says Asia.

"Wine! Hell no, I'm a tequila man myself, but if you're buying wine lovely, I'm drinking. By which I'm saying that in the most flirtatious way not to offend your womanly sensibilities. Also not to box you into the frame of being called a woman if you prefer pronouns instead.

Sorry, being a flirt is a lot more tough these days. I'm trying not to make it weird"

"You've made it weird just being a priest and attempting." says Asia.

"Damn!" he says snapping his fingers. "I'll nail this new age flirting eventually. Cause at the end of it, it was supposed to be so I could score a drink off you, even if it was wine." The priest smiles trying to illicit a laugh.

She gives him nothing, not even a smirk.

"Well I tried. Anyway, that wine aside, I'm thinking we shouldn't drink too much this evening anyhow as your night is about to get a lot more interesting... Grand Prior."

Now he had Asia's full attention.

"Shit, you're from the Vatican aren't you?" Asia starts to get on edge. Her hand starts to search her waistband for the tucked nickel-plated baller tucked near her front crotch.

"Relax, Grand Prior," he whispers. I'm not a Vatican Inquisitor. You have nothing to fear from me. So, let's not make a scene, shall we? I'm simply here to chit chat."

With a stride that makes men's eyes follow her, the barkeep traipses down the length of the bar toward Asia and the priest. When she arrives, she slowly passes another shot to Asia. As she takes the glass, the barkeep runs her finger lightly over Asia's hand seductively dragging it down the backside of her hand till it's gliding off her finger's tip. "I love your hair doll," says the Barkeep before turning her attention towards the priest, "What can I get for you Father?"

"Tequila straight up. Heavy on the dark," he says chuckling.

"You got it," she says turning to stare a few seconds longer at Asia being obviously sure that her intention of interest is known.

Once the barkeep is clear of hearing any earshot of their conversation, Asia turns back to the priest. "You better get to talking then and fuck the pleasantries! Who are you and what do you want if you aren't here to collect the bounty?

"I'm Jefarious Dugan," he says turning to shake hands with the Grand Prior. "Wait! You have a bounty? How Much?"

"Ugh!" replies Asia.

For the first time, she takes in his full façade. The eyepatch and scar don't go unnoticed.

****

"Take in the scene and what do you notice is off about the room?" says Fate.

Jophiel looks closely. He studies every detail of the dive bar and draws his conclusion of his close assessment. "I see nothing there is problematic, nothing stands out."

"That is the problem. Look closely at the one talking to Asia Riggs and what do you see?"

Jophiel takes a second deeper look at the priest it takes a few seconds, but then he sees it. It's clear as day now that his attention has been given direction.

"The Priest has no clear path," Jophiel says surprised. "By all that is holy, there is no line of destiny running through him. It's as if he stands apart from the Sadoverse."

"And yet he is a very much a part of it as you and I. The priest is an anomaly; an equation that shows up in perfection at random. Over the span of my existence, he isn't the only one I've observed. There have been others all across the Sadoverse. Watch this part closely! Observe Asia's prominent line, observe its bright hue. See it? Now, because he interacts with Asia during her planned prewritten course, his presence alone has the ability to affect her loosely and I do mean loosely plotted course. I wrote them to be very flexible."

Leaning slightly more over the balcony railing, Jophiel peers just a bit closer.

"Over time that anomaly can ultimately affect and dilute her destined path so greatly that it lightens out of existence," says Fate. "So much so, that I would eventually lose sight of her, subsequently making her another anomaly that can't be seen, yet affect the overall masterpiece.

Snapping his fingers, Jophiel gets it. "And she wouldn't show up again in the path till her death and same for him. He won't show up at all until his death which inadvertently counters the anomaly correcting the algorithm."

"Precisely," says Fate.

****

"Father Dugan?" Asia says inquisitively. "Oh yeah... I remember now, the one who conducted a one-man raid on the Templar Headquarters. Grandmaster Brashear had quite a conniption over that shit you pulled. Not to mention, Commander Addi had few choice words for you if he ever saw you again in the streets. He has been stuck doing pennants for not bringing you to heel."

"Aww c'mon. they're still pissed about that? Well... Any consolation, I did apologize before I left and I sent them donuts a week later. Oh! And Coffee. I sent them Coffee too. It was regrettable to had to infringe on someone's sanctuary like that, but time was of the essence and a hammer across the face garners attention faster than a light tap on the shoulder.... Anyone who rockets the United Nations should realize that. Good attempt by the way. Hammer when a scalpel would have sufficed."

Barkeep returns with Dugan's shot. Again, she makes eye contact with Asia and holds the gaze before returning to answer an incoming slew of new thirsty patrons.

Asia returns the gaze, giving her a wink before returning her pissed off attention back to Dugan. "I find it remarkable you breached tier 1 security. That shit is state of the art, but clearly not fool proof. Had I been there, I think it's safe to say I would have killed you."

Dugan smiles. "Then it is most fortunate that you weren't there Grand Prior, because you would have tried and I'd have bested you. Then you would have had hard feelings, maybe cried a bit because you lost to a man. The whole ordeal would have been horrible on the both of us. But unlike you, I wouldn't have killed anything about you accept your reputation. You being bested by and old man priest. The looks you'd received after that... now that would have killed you enough. I would have had to injure you though. I hear you are formidable in a fight and I couldn't run the risk of having missed the Grandmaster, by being tangled up with you."

"What?!!" Asia says looking sincerely surprised. "You besting me?" she says loudly at first before lowering her voice. "You besting me?"

Dugan shakes his head, "Look I digress, I'm not here for a pissing match. We can find time to measure dicks later. I'm here as a professional courtesy to pass warning to you of a small kill team sent to ice you."

She studies him long and shakes her head, "What kind of priest are you? What man of the cloth talks like that?"

"One who is short on patience and time."

Slowly Asia gazes up into the mirror sitting across from her at the bar. Her eyes pan right then left. Nothing stands out, no unsavory character who isn't drinking or making merriment has eyes on her. "I say bullshit... There's no one hear out of character but you."

Dugan sips half his shot of white Tequila before baring teeth as the burn runs the length of his gullet down the middle of his chest. "Oh! Not in here of course, to many people... No, they'll take you when you leave is my assumption. From the intel I've gathered, it's an Arcanian kill team." Dugan finishes the rest of his shot and glances over to hers. "You gonna drink that sweetheart?"

Asia smiles sardonically, "Are you trying to piss me off. That's it isn't. You're trying to piss me off aren't you." Sighing, she slides him the glass. "I would go through the whys and how's, but you made it out of the Grandmaster's presence without a toe tag, so, she must have trusted you to a degree. So, for shits and giggles I'm going to give you a little trust."

"Great save me the trouble of convincing you, although I really wouldn't have put much effort into it honestly. It was really going to be you believe me or not, then me headed out the door if you didn't. Look, Grand Prior, I didn't have to be here giving you heads up. After parting ways Rhonda, I felt like we were sort of allies, so by extension, you are my ally. Long story cut critically short, my investigation into locating Arcane brought me within earshot of you being discovered as prime target of opportunity. I can't tell how you were located, because I don't know. However, you were and it was known that you would be here at this time."

Dugan now gazes around casually. The scenery still hasn't changed. He lifts his eyepatch up briefly and acts as if rubbing his eye. The room is dark with a blue hued tint. People show up flashes of color depending on emotions. The room is clear of ill intent and demonic shadowy presence. The eyepatch slaps back over his milky white eye. "The bar is clear. Like I said, I figure they'll take you outside."

"How many?" asks Asia?"

"Unknown," says Dugan. "But if I had to guess they would want to keep it small. I'm thinking maybe one close observer to keep eyes on. Two for the approach and kill, one sniper at distance in case you rabbit. They'll be plain clothes and would try to make it accidental. World doesn't know who you are personally or by face, so there is no fame or accolades to be had by announcing your death. You are truly retribution for Lucien."

Asia just stares at him in minor disbelief. "For a priest, you seem adept in tactics.

"Well, we all have hobbies." Dugan winks his one good eye at her. "Well Grand Prior, you need a hand or you want to go it alone?"

Pulling her vidphone from her pocket, she checks the signal strength. It's completely dead. Calling for her knights aren't an option. Her face frowns a bit in defeat knowing that Templar tech stands outside normal civilian communique. It would take military grade jamming the likes of an act of god to lock up her phone. She again looks at Dugan and truth be told, she already believed everything he is saying. Her phone not working just solidified it. "Look here Dugan, I'm not much in the way of asking for assistance, especially from a priest, but if you aren't busy at the moment, would you be so kind to retrieve a case for me out the back of my Jeep? I need to get something out of it. After that, you could very much be on your way. I'll be able to manage from there." Asia passes him her keyless entry remote.

Dugan clasps his hand around hers closing the keys inside her fist. "The black Ford Bronco with the red accenting?" he asks.

Taken aback, Asia nods a slow yes, "That would be the one."

Dugan leans in close whispering in her left ear, "I've already been there. What you are looking for is in the women's bathroom, third stall from the left, check the celling."

Asia cuts a side glare of inquisition. "The Church and Templars relationship have been tenuous at best. The coming of Imperial has solidified us as enemies, so why would a priest come to my aid?" says Asia standing up from her stool placing on her blazer. "What is in this for you? There was no need to share the info. You don't know me or have any allegiance to me. Furthermore, a man of the cloth would not condone what I did at the U.N. and grant mercy."

Raising to his feet as well and placing his Fedora back on, Dugan pulls his black knee length trench coat taught and faces Asia. "Honestly, what you did that night greatly influenced my helping you. Can't say I condone the innocence that were killed, but I respect the effort to bring down Arcane. You were a blunt monstrosity of a weapon, where I personally would have been more surgical in my attempt. But seeing you command and that your knights follow you without hesitation told me all I needed to know of you. Under the tough exterior you are a capable leader that cares for her people and in return they would move mountains for you. That is a foundational quality, that I would very much like to build an alliance upon to bring down this devil Lucien."

After rummaging around in his pocket for a few seconds, he pulls crumpled cash from the right coat pocket and throws it on the bar. He gestures to the barkeep that he's covering both tabs.

"You have been of great interest to watch Asia Riggs. I'm sorry that my order missed our chance to recruit you when we had the chance. I see now it was a good thing though... Me never making it to recruit you personally saved your life, because no doubt you'd be dead now. The Templars have been a great fit for you and I believe they have made you into a capable weapon that I feel will be needed greatly before this is all over. You are a great warrior, holy or not, no one gives a shit. A great warrior shouldn't die by fallen to an assassin's bullet in some dank alley. Your death song should be rancorous. I mean to help you ensure that it is."

Looking at the priest, Asia just nods at him in a mutual respect. "I'm not in the habit of owing anyone... You hear me priest?"

Dugan smiles and whispers, "But you do..." Dugan tips his hat and walks past Asia towards the front door. He looks back at her giving her a wink. He then falls into an act as if he's drunk and staggers out the door incoherently discombobulated.

"Clever bastard!" whispers Asia under her breath watching him leave. *Right, they'll never suspect a drunkard*, she thinks. Asia quickly turns, winks and gestures a kiss at her interest behind the bar before heading to the women's restroom, third stall, in the ceiling.

****

Jophiel adjusts his attention outside the bar following the priest all the while simultaneously looking for De Mon or Legion. He finds none in the immediate area influencing the unfolding events. What he does find though, are mortals with intent to do harm. He nods at the intuition of the anomalous priest after realizing that he in fact called the correct number of assassins. One in the bar that he missed, and three outside. The taint of Arcane, the taint of Lucifer covered them. Asia Riggs without doubt was their target as they let the apparently drunken priest by without molestation.

Fate no longer needing to observe stands erect and backs away from the balcony's edge. He turns in the direction of his almost infinite shelves of books that contain all lives of the Sadohedranicverse. He clasps his hands behind his back as he watches the shelves move in their never-ending multidirectional spin of perpetual motion. Each book a running thread of flame culminating someone's or somethings life span till it extinguishes. Once that flame goes out, that particular book is time stamped, dated, and ejected from the shelf. It slides down an intricate set of tubes that amass into separate divisional pocket realms two floors down from the Transcommunicative Hub. Once in their respective realms, Letharian Choiretics review the sum of a life and assign a hue of red or blue color, in the most rare instance, white. They assign color to it within the sec of a micro. Instantly the metal of that life is known, be it whatever life has come to an end. Four platinum covered books etching turn from and orangish blue flame to a solid red signifying that book of life is poised to be ejected.

"Her path is still clear," says Jophiel. "She'll soon exit the saloon entering into the fray that awaits her. So, in reading your work, she was always to have surpassed today."

"So it was written," says Fate. "Loosely accounting for choice."

"Choice... The stated bane of our existence," utters Jophiel just above a whisper.

"So some would say," replies Fate as he watches the book titled Janice Monefrey *prepare for immediate ejection.*

****

Grand Prior emerges from the Women's rest room in her full white, red accent battle fatigues with thick level three soft body armor to match. The dark red Templar Cross emblazoned across her chest is partially exposed until she throws her half white cape with red interior over her left shoulder exposing the cross fully along with her side arm on the left side of her hip. All in the bar immediately take notice. Some are awed by the show that they think is about to be performed, others stare slowly making the connection to the terrorist leader that attacked the United Nations the day of Imperial's arrival. Her face hidden behind the close to form fitting helmet with the dark tinted visor turns toward the bar. Grand Prior makes eye contact with the Barkeep, named Tamia worthy whose name is printed on her name tag.

"I don't think it would have worked out. It's not you baby, it's me," says Grand Prior pulling her sidearm cross draw from her left holster.

Pip, pip, pip! Three round whisper from the silenced barrel of Grand Prior Asia Rigg's silver .45 caliber 1911. One round between the eyes blows the back of the barkeeps head out in splatter of blood onto the whiskey filled shelf. Two more rounds are put through the heart of the alias named woman before her bodies even thinks of falling to the ground behind the bar. Grand Prior quickly turns around cross drawing her second weapon which is a modified Mac 10 fully automatic S.M.G. The bar had gone quiet. All that could be heard was the televisions.

****

Fate watches the Janice Monefrey's book of life eject into the series of intricate tunneling.

****

"AAAAHHHHH!" A lone scream erupts from some female toward the back of the establishment. The lone scream causes a domino effect of many others to join in, however people are still planted in their seats and in place where they stand.

"Clearly, I have to say it... GET-THE-FUCK-OUT!" yells Asia.

Screaming, the crowd starts falling over each other, knocking over tables, breaking glasses and bottles as they run for the door.

Outside the bar in its parking lot next to a midnight blue Harley Davidson motorcycle is a couple engaged in an intimate kiss. When the doors of the bar explode open to the sound of screams and the patter of feet running quickly, the couple is briefly startled. Men and women run past them, some head to their vehicles, others bypass the parking lot altogether placing the templar of death as far as they can behind them.

With the bar completely empty, Grand Prior holsters one of her weapons and reaches behind the bar pulling a bottle of Snapjaw Whiskey. She flips over one the clean shot glasses and pours herself a shot. Reaching up to her helmet, she detaches the mouth plate and trades it to the bar for the shot. Taking a sigh, Asia throws the shot glass and reattaches her mouth plate. She again cross draws her Mac 10 and slowly heads for the door.

"You Bastards want me? Asia yells. "Well, I'm coming out, but I'm coming out shooting."

****

Three streets over and nestled inside the under construction closed 35th floor of the Farigosi building is one lone sniper wearing a black turtleneck with a dark gray peacoat. He sits upright in a chair leaning slightly forward using the window ledge for support. Through his scope he takes aim at the front door of the Fahrenheit bar. His cut off tipped gloved finger moves from touch point above the trigger guard to the trigger. With his offhand he depresses his mic. "This is Errant Soul One, I have clear line of sight. She steps outside and I'll set her free."

"*Copy, don't hesitate, take the shot when it presents itself,*" says a male voice coming back over the receiver.

Errant Soul takes a quick side glance at a photo of Asia that had been lifted from Motor Vehicle Records.

****

Asia bursts outside in her Templar battle fatigues dual wielding her weapons looking for her targets amongst the fleeing crowd. She makes an immediate right and dives behind a Teslor Mav automated van for cover. The sniper daunted by what erupted from the front door was not fast enough on the trigger to make the shot before she had made the transition to cover. He wasn't expecting her to be dressed for battle. The couple in the parking lot watching her exit while embraced in their scripted roles immediately spilt apart looking for cover. They each dive overtop vehicles opposite of each other that had not moved as the owners more than likely just kept running on foot hauling ass up the block. Each operative landed with a roll then scooted their backs up against their respective vehicles. Almost simultaneously each reach behind their back pulling their slinged MP5's with collapsed stocks around from underneath their jackets readying them for action.

Errant Soul 2, the male half of the embracing couple places on shades and tap the outer edge of the arm where it meets the frame. *Activated* scrolls across the inside lens of the glasses as the HUD turns on.

"We don't have long to wrap this up for the police arrives Grand Prior," yells Errant soul two.

Asia's HUD already activated; she uses her tongue to click the control pad located around her mouth. A series of line and arcs giving the best trajectory for weapon or explosive throw displays.

"I agree, lets wrap this quickly," says Asia yelling back. "I can only imagine if we're here when authorities arrive the explaining you'll have to do trying to clear up your dead operative behind the bar... Or should I say, the Arcane empire will have to do, because you'll be dead."

"You Bitch!" yells Errant Soul Two. He rises over the hood and lets a volley of rounds fly.

Bullets ping through and off the van shattering the window above Asia. Glass shards fall around her bouncing harmlessly off her Kevlar. She reaches into two separate pouches pulling out red and yellow disc. She depresses the center and throws one into the bar. Within three seconds a bright flash illuminates the interior. A local micro EMP destroys all electronic equipment that not even the most skilled engineer can recover information or video footage from. She depresses the center of the red disc. Looking around the corner of the van she waits for a lull in the burst of incoming rounds. When the short barrage ends, an arc line turns green signifying optimal angle. Asia throws the disc ricocheting it off a green Volvo. The outer blades of the disc activate and begins spinning turning the device into a tiny drone. The red disc drops low and follows the greenlit approved path of the arc line.

Errant Soul Two having reloaded rises for another volley to flush the Grand Prior out of cover. In all the commotion, he never sees the red disc go underneath his vehicle that he's currently using for cover. It hovers for a second.

"Boom!" whispers Asia.

Concussion wave shatters the glass of every car on the parking lot before the subsequent explosion follows. Errant Soul Two and the vehicle he was behind disappears in flash of heat and fire. Surrounding vehicles are flipped over and set to burn. SKABOOM! A second concussive wave from the primary vehicle's secondary explosion nudges the van hard that Asia was taking cover behind. It pushes her down to the ground and her head out into the open just beyond the van's conceal-ment.

"Gotcha," says Errant Soul One. His crosshairs were dead to right on the back of her skull. His finger slides from touchpoint above the guard to the trigger taking the slack out of the pull. He awaits the surprising bang.

The bang never comes. Instead, it is replaced with a brief sound rem-iniscent of a gurgle. Blood flows from mouth of Errant Soul One, his finger on the trigger goes limp. Father Dugan removes his ornate dagger from the base of the sniper's skull where it meets the spine. He flicks the blood clean from the blade and places it back into its scabbard in the small of his back before letting his trench coat drape back over it. Never one to shrug his duties, he gives last rites to the lost soul of the Arcane clan.

"Oh shit! I've always wanted to fire on these," says Dugan kicking the body out of the chair and off top the rifle.

Thinking that he heard a noise, Dugan raises his eyepatch and looks around quickly to see if anyone as stealthy as him was now trying to get the advantage on him. There is. Dugan ignores the silent assassin, because he's of another realm and has been committing assassinations long before him. This assassin doesn't know that Dugan can see him and he prefers to keep it that way. Death glides past Dugan retrieving the soul orb of Errant Soul One. He already had the two others just one more to collect and he'd have the whole set.

****

Fate watches as two more Book of Life's are ejected. Jophiel still watching the events unfurrow below takes a long pause staring at Dugan. It may have been nothing, but to him it looked as if the priest had heard Death's approach.

****

Asia shaking the effects of being molly whopped by the van staggers to her feet.

"You fucking bitch!" says Errant Soul Four having flanked the Grand Prior. *Pip,pip,pip,pip!* She places four rounds point blank into the back of the head of Asia knocking her forward. The Grand Prior uses the momentum to throw herself into a summersault forward flip throwing her leg out turning it into a flip kick. Errant four catches the full brunt of the up and coming heel underneath her chin causing a horrendous crunch sound. Errant's teeth are broken as well as her jaw.

Asia can't complete the flip. She wasn't ready in the first place to commit to it. Her flipping forward was a last-ditch effort so the assassin wouldn't be in place to put more rounds into her. The Kevlar titanium weaved helmet did its duty and took the brunt of the shots straight up, but even though the helmet's integrity held, the shots to the head was no doubt concussive in the moderate to extreme case. Asia's equilibrium was off and she came crashing down hard on her back expelling the last of the air in her lungs. Her Mac 10 slid under a vehicle, no help there. Looking at her right hand, the 1911 baller had stovepiped, one round had jammed the slide. Before she could correct the misfire, a foot pinned her weapon hand to the ground.

Looking up through her HUD all that is visible are blood splatters on her visor that leak in constant flow from the broken mouth of her assassin.

"dob gis itch!" says Errant Soul Four placing the muzzle of the MP5 into direct contact with Asia's tinted Visor.

Looking through electronic aided magnified scope, the image was so close that Dugan is able to read the blood-soaked dialect of the Errant Soul kill team member. "Dodge this bitch!" he whispers taking in a breath. "My thoughts exactly," says Dugan holding his breath as to not shake the barrel.

Asia closes her eyes not to see what comes next. After a second when there is no bang, she opens one eye and watches her would be murder fall forward over top of her, then she hears the boom of the sniper's rifle. As the body strikes lifeless on the pavement, Death stands above them

JERICHO'S BANE - 423

both placing the soul into his coat. Just like that, he's gone. Wasting not another second, Asia scrambles to her feet and dives back behind the van thinking the sniper just shot wide and hit his compatriot by glory stealing accident.

Sirens blare in the background. She's sure it's police and fire. You can't set off explosives and not think the world of law is not getting ready to descend. No doubt a helicopter was on the way too making evasion very unlikely once it got here. Shame, she would have liked to see how all this ended with Arcane, but she was sure a bullet through her mouth from her own weapon was on the menu if escape and evasion wasn't possible. The ground erupts with small pock marks from sniper hits leaving a trail leading away from her. Confused, Asia watches the pocking marks until they strike the wall at the end of the corner where her vehicle was parked around in parking lot C. To her it was as if, the sniper was toying with her or telling her to run. Probably the latter so he could have a clean shot.

Asia slams her fist against the van in frustration of being caught. Another round strikes the corner. The Grand Prior looks at the corner knowing it's her salvation, but she's too scared to move. Another round strikes the corner. Suddenly a round comes through the door striking the deceased body of the kill team member, then another strike hit's the corner. She makes the connection and takes off running for the corner, running for her vehicle, running for her life. There is a guardian angel up there assisting her, more than likely a guardian priest. Head still ringing from taking the shots to the back of her head, Grand Prior Asia takes off the helmet and dives into her driver's seat. Push button start ignites the engine. Wheels screeching, she pulls off just as helicopter search light and arriving units pull into the parking lot from the opposite side of the lot.

After driving for a few moments, Asia's Vidcell reception returns. Out of breath and still breathing heavily, her thumbs slide to over call button. Brashear picks up on the other end.

"They came for me," says Asia. "Requesting to initiate Operation Ignis?"

After a long pause.

"*Granted.*" Came the reply through the phone's receiver. "Happy hunting."

After seeing her safely away, Dugan smiles and begins to disassemble the rifle. "You don't mind if I hold onto this do you?" says Dugan looking at the open dead eyes of the sniper. "No... great. I always wanted one of these, but the order was cheap when it came to weaponry. I never would have been able to requisition anything this nice."

Dugan retrieves the duffle bag and places his newly acquired rifle inside. He tips his hat to the dead wayward soul; pun intended and exits the door. "If you're lucky someone may find you on Tuesday." The door closes leaving the room a tomb.

****

The final book of life ejects into the intricate web of tunnels. Fate turns back toward the balcony, back toward Jophiel.

"I see now," says Jophiel. "You can't help me with what I need regarding the laws of ramifications. But what you have shown me today brother gives me the answer I was searching for. Jophiel turns around and hugs Fate. "No matter what they say about you brother, your wisdom and talent is unmatched." Jophiel says smiling. Ending his embrace and smacking his brother Fate on the outside of his shoulders twice. He turns and runs from the pocketed dimensional chamber, "I know how to help the judge throw the final blow to Imperial."

Fate watches Jophiel leave in excitement. After he's gone Fate turns back toward the infinity shelves. "Well, what do they say about me I wonder?"

Another book ejects from the shelves.

End

Part I

Epilogue

Having watched Fate depart the depths of Palengrad, Apollyon turns from the balcony and once again observes his painting that intrigued Fate. It really is a good rendition of passage of time by a lesser species, but nonetheless, even though they are lesser it is an incredible piece that a celestial couldn't dare to create. He hated to admit it. In all of his omnipotence, he didn't have the mind to create beauty. It pissed him off that he had to admire beauty from the mind of a species that were so fragile, but there it was. Celestials weren't designed to create, so they can't. He would forever have to admire beauty from those that could.

Short on time before accepting his next visitor, he straightens the painting and walks past his throne room where he would normally accept guests or dignitaries, except there never were guests or dignitaries. Palengrad was short on those that would voluntarily enter for a casual visit. Those that enter the gates of these lands were normally the type that became permanent residents. If there was a rarity that someone showed up here like Warsivious or Fate, it was because there was something specifically needed, some item, some favor that only he could provide. Fate just proved that very fact. If Fate had not tried to persuade the warden to hold to his vows, would he have ever come to visit?

Apollyon told no lie when he stated the murderer of Archs was in route. Expecting Imperial to arrive any minute, he prepares himself to receive Lucifer's ambassador. Fully adoring his armor, he leaps off the balcony of his abode gliding down towards the entrance of Palengrad. There he awaits. Less than a human standard Earth hour, Imperial arrives. Upon the massive gates opening, Apollyon stands ready to receive the scourge of Archs.

Imperial enters Palengrad. He is squared away wearing his finest set of regal armor over his tailored to fit Arcanian officer's uniform with blood red stripes down the side of each pant leg. The Nephilim enters resolute and sure of himself, but there is something off. He doesn't quite seem right. His complexion is pail, sort of ashen white even for a man of color. Apollyon smirks instantly knowing what the problem is. The Nephilim's inherent flaw is showing. His human side is unable to sustain being in the ethereal realm. In a bid to prove that he is one of us though, he will attempt to endure long enough to complete his mission. Pride is not always the best motivation. As aphorism goes, Usually pride, before the fall.

How cute, thinks Apollyon. *A half breed that wants to walk on thoroughbred shores. He is quaint isn't he. Just like his father, he wants to show just how powerful he is not knowing what is ever really at stake.* "There has been a lot of commotion over the likes of you as of late lord Imperial. You do have the heavens in an uproar don't you?"

"Warden Apollyon, the third most feared being in the Sadohedranic-verse. If the heavens are in an uproar it is because they know I have eyes set to tearing it asunder," says Imperial.

Apollyon slightly bows to Imperial. It pains him as he has to swallow his pride, but it's not the kid he's bowing too. It's the father. If he does what was once thought impossible and takes the throne, Apollyon wants it to be known that it was off his sacrifices that ascension was accomplished and he wants to remembered and set high on the new counsel. Most of all, he wants his name restored.

"As your father requested, you are authorized to speak to him," says Apollyon. "You will find him 47 floors below Palengrad prime in reality cell 0001. When you are there and only when you confirm, will I turn the key to make the heavens bleed and disengage the cell."

Apollyon grabs Imperial by his arm. "Understand lord Imperial, for this I will be remembered on either side of the conflict. Either I will be remembered as a tyrant warden that defied Elohim or savior that helped Lucifer ascend to his rightful place. Tell your father, this is three times at a great personal cost to me that I've helped him. He is to remember my place in his high counsel when this is done. What I do today is in direct defiance of the king's prophecy. These cells were not to be turned until the appointed time. Understand it will not be long after this before the justice of his right hand descends here to make me answer for this in the form of his precious Archs."

"Understood Warden... There will be no retribution upon your head for this. My father has a theory that if correct will change everything. What I do here today insures that." Imperial looks down to Apollyon's hand for him to remove it.

Warden nods in mutual understanding and removes his hand.

"Glad to know that we understand each other," says Apollyon. "Now be quick about your business lord Imperial, your time of endurance within this realm grows short and you weak. This is no place for half-breeds." Warden Apollyon turns quickly laughing to himself. His wings extend out and flaps hard giving him lift back toward his palace. "Be sure lord Imperial to take care that you yourself do not become a resident here. If you did, and the Archs do descend for me, wouldn't we make a pair, you and I?"

Disgusted at the term half-breed, Imperial turns his face up wondering all the things that he could do to make the warden suffer, but he was right. He's sacrificed more than any other for his father and by extension, him. He was only alive because the warden released the last nephilim bone for the purpose of research and creation.

"Well played Warden," says Imperial. "Well played indeed." Imperial begins walking towards the abyss of Palengrad prime.

The term prime that follows Palengrad is just another name for ground level. Each level below prime are cells that represent one of the infinitude of different realities. The level that a prisoner is found on down there coincides with the millennia and reality that Death claimed them in. Imperial's walk goes from statured and resolute to more of a drunken stride that he over compensates to correct to keep himself looking dignified. He stares down into the abyss finding his target level.

Having talked with the warden and sure to keep his composure, he never noticed the incessant wails and screams of horror of this place till now. Either the warden had blocked them out or he was so focused he dismissed them. All the same, they were a constant annoyance now. His wings slowly extends instead of their normal switch blading or jetting out. Imperial leans forward falling into a glide. He pulls his wings in and rockets for a faster descent. He knows that his time is limited here, but he insisted that he handles this. Level 45 he expands his wings wide catching the updraft slowing him considerably. He finishes his short descent touching down on level 47 in what should have been a controlled landing. It was anything but. Imperial landed on his feet true, but in a slide that took him into a tumble of summersaults before sliding into the cell of his intended inmate.

"Mind that first step half-breed," says the ominous voice from the back of the cell.

Imperial gets to his feet and dusts himself. Sweating profusely and attempting to catch his breath, he draws closer to the cell to see the target of his trip and reason of coming to oblivion. His eyes are a bit blurry; he just can't seem to ever catch his breath here. The feeling he's experiencing is similar to hypoxia where the bodies tissues are starved of life sustaining oxygen. Imperial gazes through the holy water infused containment field, but the inmate is covered in shadow.

"Step into the light, so that I may see you!" orders Imperial.

The shadow stands but remains concealed by the darkness. "Step into the light. Why should I do that and under who's command. There is none that may command here but the warden... Are you the new warden?

Imperial only stares at him barely hanging on, but still resolute and regal as he can muster.

"I didn't think you were... Push on half-breed! You have no power here."

My name is Imperial and it was given to me by a name that can turn this gate. Lucifer, my father is who behalf I'm here on to set you free if you're answers prove genuine and you pledge fidelity.

"To set me free?" repeats the shadow. "Is that right?"

"If his theory proves correct about you, then yes, set you free."

Lucifer's name makes the shadow move closer toward the light. "Keep talking half-breed, you have my attention. What theory?"

Looking around for prying ears, Imperial steps closer to the cell. "That he knows who you truly are."

Really intrigued, the shadow steps forward into Palengrad's light revealing his features that hadn't been seen since the sight of Fate drew him to the bars earlier.

Seeing his façade, Imperial backs away. His face is dirt covered, scars are not only numerous about his face, but all over his body. The emerging shadow was shirtless. There are even gashes that are still actively bleeding. A sash that was probably his at one time is soaked in blood covering a missing eye along with half his face.

"Lucifer has ascended then?" he asks.

"No. Not as of yet," says Imperial. "But he has set the stage too and if you prove his theory, you would be a big piece in ensuring that."

"I asked if he ascended, not that I care that he does, it's just the thought of if he ascends then the heavens fall. I'm good with that. I'm good with Fate lying face down and his masterpiece smashed to shit."

Imperial starts a small coughing fit.

"I think you should be quick about you questions boy. You aren't looking to well."

Imperial nods, "It has taken thousands of years to review every inmate in this place. Is was a task set to Apollyon for a very specific purpose. Now, what was interesting about the inventory is that everyone here was accounted for and understood that there place was here due to a specific action to what led them here. All the cells per the warden's count is accurate... All for a plus one that shouldn't be here. That plus one is level 47, cell 0001... You, you should not be here. Which leads me to ask, who are you?" Imperial coughs, this time spitting blood.

"Who do you believe I am?"

"It's not I that believes, but my father."

"Okay then, who does your father believe me to be?"

Another coughing fit overtakes Imperial dropping him to a knee, but he doesn't lose focus of his purpose for being here. "If we're talking straight, then he believes you are none other than the celestial Mercy, and that you've been hidden away down here because you saw something that you weren't supposed to see. Something that would solidify his claim to ascend and make you and him allies."

"Mercy?" the shadow repeats taking a knee to remain eye level with Imperial. "Haven't you heard half-breed, there is no Mercy and has not been for some time. It is my understanding that Mercy set out across the Aether with a very specific set of points and instructions that bypass transit tubes to a very dangerous place at the edge of existence. I was led to believe that Mercy never returned after meeting the Monarchs..."

The specific detail of the Monarchs grabs a hold of Imperial's attention. It was in that second that he found a breath. His eyes widen at the shock of meeting Mercy.

""Then it is true. You are Mercy?" says Imperial.

"Look at me half-breed. I am not Mercy and I am sure as shit not merciful. That celestial being has long since been killed amongst the Aether for a King he believed in and followed without question... In all the time that I've been here and I've been here a very, very long time. In all that time not one entity has come to see me. Not even the warden. My crime has never been explained to me or adjudicated, yet I'm here. Do you know what that does to thing... Half-breed? Huh? I'll tell you; it does not make a thing merciful. In fact, it turns a thing cold. It gives a thing a singular laser focused purpose of hate and anger. I have accumulated much of that over the time I've been here reflecting on such an injustice. I've amassed so much hate, that my staring gaze could reach into heaven, into the very heart of Elohim and burn it out. So, you see, I can't be Mercy... I am not Mercy... I am entropy once unleashed. I am degradation and nothing more. I am heaven's downfall to destination, apocalypse. In my solitude, I have become the essence of vengeful... My name half-breed, is Wrath. If you release me, I will raise hell to the heavens halls."

JERICHO'S BANE

PATH TO DESOLATION

PART 2

COMING SPRING

2022

ARROW J KNIGHT

CPSIA information can be obtained
at www.ICGtesting.com
Printed in the USA
BVHW070846270622
640728BV00001B/10